BUT THE LADY HAD A GUN...

Teddy shadowed me as I followed Jorge back to the car at the edge of the dark lot. Suddenly, blindingly, a parked car pulled on bright halogen headlights. Jorge flung one hand over his eyes, jerked open the back door, and brusquely motioned me inside.

But Teddy stood with his arms straight up, obscuring whoever was behind him, somebody who'd leaped out of the other car. When I twisted to see what Jorge thought of this, he had a pistol pointed at me.

Nobody said a word. I figured it for a standoff until I heard a *phut* and saw blood spurt from the hole in Jorge's face. He wore no expression at all as he collapsed, but I had to give him credit. He didn't let loose of the pistol.

I took in all this while diving out of the glaring headlights. I heard a second muffled *phut!* Teddy fell gasping at the shooter's feet.

"Cheney. Get in the truck. We don't have much time."

I ran for the truck. Rita Madrid had just killed two men, one of whom had been set to shoot me. As an ally, she'd do very nicely.

Bantam books by R. D. Brown

HAZZARD
VILLA HEAD

VILLA HEAD

R. D. Brown

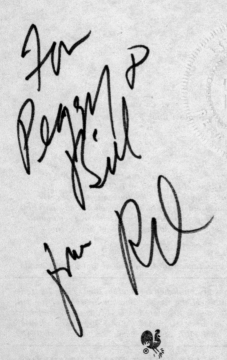

BANTAM BOOKS
TORONTO • NEW YORK • LONDON • SYDNEY • AUCKLAND

VILLA HEAD
A Bantam Book / November 1987

ISBN 0-553-26662-4

Published simultaneously in the United States and Canada

Bantam Books are published by Bantam Books, Inc. Its trademark, consisting of the words "Bantam Books" and the por-
trayal of a rooster, is Registered in U.S. Patent and Trademark
Office and in other countries. Marca Registrada. Bantam
Books, Inc., 666 Fifth Avenue, New York, New York 10103.

PRINTED IN THE UNITED STATES OF AMERICA

KR   0987654321

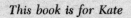

This book is for Kate

Acknowledgments

Sr. Victor Diaz, Spanish language and culture expert.

Dr. Herbert C. Taylor, Jr., for anthropological research and other assistance.

Dr. Guillermo Bultmann, a guide in the wilderness of the Sierra Madres.

PART ONE

One

Anything can happen in the Dallas/Fort Worth air terminal. Today they were having semifinals in the Only Autho-
rized International Texas Chili Cookoff. A Hare Krishna
hustler with a shaved head and saffron palms pinned a rose on
my lapel and took my pocket change. Then a contestant
offered a sample of Road Meat Chili that I had no trouble
refusing. Out of kindness, I accepted a volcanic jalapeño
tostada.

My eyes were still watering when my pager bleeped. I
glanced at the number glowing on my wrist and headed for a
phone. It was an in-terminal call, which meant my caller was
watching me. Since I was standing in front of a bank of fifty
telephones, most of them in use, that knowledge didn't help
much.

I chose the closest phone and punched in. A voice I
recognized as the one on the first instruction tape came on,
still confident and calm, telling me how to apply a Kick Me
sign to myself.

"Mr. Hazzard, go to the overseas departure satellite and
take the first men's room on the left after the security barrier.
Use the stall marked Out of Order. Lock the door. Put the
bag between your feet with the Stetson on top of it. When
you're told to push the money out, do it."

A warm avalanche of adrenaline washed over me. They
hadn't made many mistakes so far, but this was one. They
knew my name.

It was a pretty good plan. I'd guessed right that the
action wouldn't be in the concourse. The switch would take
place in the International Arrival and Departure satellite,
which was only sporadically busy. They wanted to know I

3

wasn't armed, wasn't being followed, and hadn't hidden a transmitter in the bond bundle. Having me go through the metal detector satisfied all three requirements. We'd meet in a restroom where I'd be alone and unarmed. Then they'd shoot me dead, take the money, and live happily till the money ran out. What I didn't know was how they expected to get a weapon through the metal detectors. Well, time would reveal all, and if uncertainty is hard to take, security work isn't right for you.

I was the only customer at the overseas departure gate, more of their good planning. They were playing it smart, but I had, too. As soon as I'd listened to the ransom message that morning, I'd asked the terminal to do a complete sweep of the overseas departure area and reschedule all their security people so even a bee coming in would have to check its stinger.

After the fluoroscope of my flight bag—a gift from Texas Air—the security monitor, a dynamite lady with a corn-row hairdo, had a question. "You always carry that much paper with you?"

"I'm a compulsive reader," I said and marched off, swinging the bag they'd told my client to stuff with four million in bearer bonds. A myopic observer would think I hadn't a care in the world.

The furnishings in the men's room were air-terminal universal—formica and brush-finished stainless steel, with tan ceramic tiles on the floor and up the walls. The air stank of pine. But this room offered a surprise. The out-of-order booth was occupied. A pair of size twelve lizard boots sprawled below the panel of the door.

Something about their stillness told me the man inside was either sleeping or dead.

I opened the door and found my second guess was right. A two-hundred-pound hunk with wide shoulders, a great tan, and lots of curly black hair was slumped against the back of the booth. Both eyes were closed, but a third eye in the middle of his forehead had gushed out a sticky stream of blackberry jelly that had coursed down his tanned face and stained the open collar of his sport shirt. The thieves had fallen out early.

After dipping into his wallet to discover a driver's license that said my corpse had once been Brock Turner, I pulled him upright on the throne and stuffed the flight bag between his boots. I took off my Stetson and put it on top of the bag.

One of the secrets of coming out the other end of an extortion exchange you're not supposed to survive is to use all available resources. Turner was one. Another was the photo of Mercedes Stackler her distraught husband had given me. I taped it to the door of the john above the Out-of-Order sign. Then I stepped into the next booth and closed the door.

I've done a fair number of money drops. Sometimes it's messy. Sometimes it's just a matter of depositing a bag of cash and leaving, because neither party, often a government or an international corporation, wants any problems.

But this time was different. Garrett Hardesty, president of the Liberty Forever Banking Company of South Texas, hadn't wasted much time that morning reminding me the six-figure retainer the bank had given me carried a couple of responsibilities with it. One, I was not supposed to turn loose of any money. Two, if at all possible, I was to retrieve the young woman who was being held hostage. Three—and this was the one Hardesty most enjoyed delivering—I was to bend every effort to bring the malefactors to justice.

Normally, that's all part of the job. This time, however, there were a few extra problems. I knew the principals, Chip and Mercedes Stackler. As pawns in this scam, they were hard to take seriously. Chip had inherited a bundle of oil leases with his teething ring. He played at poker and banking. Mercedes was a spectacular blonde. The night I'd met her at the Cameron Country Club's Christmas dance, she filled to perfection a red silk sheath, held up only by her own delicious self. She asked me to dance, but once on the floor, her tanned, strong body made a more explicit offer. She danced close, as if we'd been very good friends since kindergarten.

Mercedes opened proceedings by saying her husband had lost a leg in Vietnam. I said dancing with her was an experience that required no excuse. She cleared up my thinking fast in a husky whisper.

"I have a perfect excuse. I want you."

I took one look at her empty twenty-year-old face and decided she wanted some excitement in her placid, over privileged life. Apparently, that meant having a fling with someone she thought made a living by snatching raw meat out of the jaws of tigers.

I said she'd have to bring me a note from her husband, but she continued her wordless persuasion, moving in closer until the music stopped. Three more bars and she might have recruited me. Even as I handed her back to Stackler, a thin, handsome blond with rimless aviator spectacles, she had me reflecting he wasn't right for her.

Since then, I'd played poker and golf with Chip, but I hadn't seen or even thought about Mercedes. Until the kidnapping.

Garrett Hardesty, in his big office at the Liberty Forever Bank, had laid it out for me. Mercedes had disappeared two days ago. The ransom call had arrived that morning. The Stacklers were both rich enough to pay almost any ransom, but the bank was picking up the tab. Chip was a bank officer, and one of his fringe benefits was being insured against extortion. Chip's ransoming Mercedes was ironic, Hardesty said, because he'd heard husband and wife weren't getting along too well these days. Still, Chip was a gentleman. And a Texan. And a bank officer.

That wasn't much background, but it was all I had to go on when I heard the outer door of the men's room whoosh open. Boot heels tapped rapidly across the tiled floor. Very soon I'd learn if I had a future in industrial security.

No point in waiting, so I spoke right up, my head in the vee of the tiled wall and the steel booth divider. With all this tile, my voice echoed in every direction. Not much of an edge, but an edge.

"If you shoot, you'll regret it the rest of your short life. Drop the pistol!"

The next sounds were *whut! whut! whut!* followed by tiles smashing and metal shrieking. Slugs ricocheted wildly around inside the next booth. Then somebody began to cry.

I jerked open the door and stepped out cautiously. The slugs that had almost snapped the door off its hinges had been aimed at the photograph of Mercedes. It was now in tatters, like her life.

Mercedes herself stood looking at me, those devastating green eyes glassy with tears. "That's Brock!" she whimpered. "He's dead!"

I'd been expecting a man, and Mercedes was dressed as

one—jeans, boots, a checkered shirt, and a suede jacket.
With her hair tucked under the Stetson, she could have been
her husband's younger brother. The Walther P-38 with a
silencer attachment looked enormous in her hand, a toy
heavier than anything she'd ever lifted.

"Mercedes," I explained, "if you shoot through a door
and someone is behind it, the odds are they'll become dead."

She leaned against my chest and sobbed into my lapel,
doing a pretty good broken heart. "Cheney! I'm so glad
you're here."

That was a surprise, but we crisis managers never let the
public see us drop a stitch. I offered a handkerchief.

"My dear, you're in bad trouble if you don't do as I say."

"I didn't want to kill anybody!"

I took the ugly German pistol from her slack grasp. After
I dropped the clip and cleared the chamber, I stuck it under
my belt and shouldered aside the ruined door to get the flight
bag. She seemed fascinated by the scars the ricocheting
bullets had dug in the metal.

To take her mind off the very unpretty sight of the late
Brock Turner, I explained the ballistics to her. "Lead slugs
have great stopping power, but at initial velocities, they tend
to fragment on contact with hard surfaces and then lose
energy as shrapnel. Whoever put our large friend there
expected you to shoot through the door and think you killed
him. He was dead when I found him. See that hole in his
forehead? That killed him hours before you arrived."

Genuine tears finally started to trickle down those lovely
hollow cheeks. She wasn't crying for what could have happened
to me, or even for dead Brock, whoever he'd been. She was
crying for herself—which made a kind of sense. Even weepy,
she was gorgeous, but time was running short and someone
might wonder about the shooting.

"Getting killed is pretty drastic, and for myself, I don't
go along with it. I don't think you should either."

She stopped crying, but her chest still heaved with dry
sobs. The tears were real, and so was her chest, but I decided
she had the emotional depth of a coat of paint, which meant
she was ready to listen.

"Mercedes, if you had managed to kill me and walk out
of here with that flight bag, you'd be dead yourself in half an
hour."

"Chip did this," she said.

This scam had more wrinkles than an elephant's behind. "Tell me what you did. We don't have much time."

Once she started, she might have been telling the kindly old family doctor where it hurt.

"Chip stopped paying attention to me last year after he went to Mexico on business for the bank. When he came back, he was different. All he could talk about was the fabulous amounts of money that could be made down there with the right contacts. He swore he was going to move heaven and earth to free up some capital to buy Mexican real estate."

"Did he approach his family's trustees about it?"

"No, he said he didn't want to alert the old buzzards to the opportunity. That's why he asked me to make the investment."

"Did you?"

"Of course not. I don't know anything about investments. He didn't want to talk to my trustees, either. I thought he'd forgotten about it until this business with Brock came up."

I glanced around the room. I had Mercedes, and Brock was dead. I was supposed to think that was the end of it, but I didn't. I eased Mercedes toward the door. Someone sent her in here. If it was Chip, he'd already be nervous. I didn't want him to panic—just yet. The clock on the video monitor advised that the next incoming overseas flight was on time for a seven o'clock arrival.

Mercedes mourned for Brock by spilling out the information she thought I'd need to mop up this mess. I wondered if she kept talking to avoid thinking of her lover sprawled dead in the men's room or if she simply wanted to clear herself and dump all the guilt on someone else. Like she'd probably done all her life.

"I'd been having this thing with Brock Turner. He's the recreation therapist at my club. He was so beautiful.

"When Chip found out, he tried to buy Brock off, but Brock told him his feelings for me couldn't be bought off with money. So Chip came up with this plan. He and Brock would pretend to kidnap me and make the bank pay four million dollars, which we'd split, fifty-fifty."

Since she was no longer crying, I adjusted her Stetson to

shadow her eyes and pushed open the door, nodding gravely
as I urged her along. There was nobody for a city block in
either direction. If there had been a witness, I'd have taped
the out-of-order sign on the door and marched away with
Mercedes on my arm. I like to have alternate plans.

"It was a neat plan, Cheney. It wouldn't be a crime
because Chip would use bonds from his own trust fund to pay
back the bank. He'd end up with two million in discretionary
money, a four million casualty loss, and his chance to invest in
Mexican land. Nobody would be hurt. Brock would pick up
the bonds and we'd go to Mexico. There wouldn't be any
hassle about a divorce or property settlement or anything
because no laws would be broken. Brock could invest the
money and triple it in a month. Then I'd get an uncontested
Mexican divorce and we'd go our separate ways."

Maybe that story took in Mercedes, but I didn't buy it.
Extortion's a crime whether successful or not.

"I'm still wondering why you came in here to kill me,
Mercedes."

"Oh, Cheney, I'm so sorry. This whole thing was all just
make-believe till an hour ago. Then Chip met us in the
parking lot. We needed him to smuggle the pistol past the
metal detectors in his artificial leg. It wasn't to shoot anybody,
just to scare you with if you tried to stop us. We went
through the detector and sat in the coffee bar to wait for you.
Then Chip suggested that he and Brock set things up in the
bathroom. All I had to do was to buzz your pager at six
o'clock, play the instruction tape when you phoned, and then
go in there. Brock didn't want to do it that way, but Chip said
he'd turn him in to the parole office if we both didn't do
exactly what he said."

She stopped to stare up into my eyes. Mercedes Stackler
was a beautiful, healthy animal who gave off the kind of
sexual radar that alerted every male within miles. I could see
why Brock said he preferred her to two million in bonds,
though I wondered if he meant it.

"When Chip came back, he said I could still go off with
Brock, but I had to shoot through the door to get the money
because that way I'd be an accomplice, too. That would
insure Brock and I would go to Mexico and never come back.
If I refused, there'd be a messy divorce with pictures of
Brock and me in the papers and Brock would go to jail and I

might too. I think Chip was mean, putting that picture of me on the door to remind me why I had to shoot. And he killed poor Brock."

Her tears had dried. I took back my handkerchief. I'm a sucker for a helpless act.

"Mercedes, you're in bad trouble, but since you didn't kill me or Brock, I'm going to get you out of it."

"Did Daddy send you? You don't have to tell me Brock spent time in prison. He told me that as soon as I met him. It was a political offense of some sort in El Paso. He says in jail he took up meditation." Her beautiful face crumpled. "It made him a different person. Sweet, gentle, sensitive. And Chip killed him!"

Eliseo Varga, my in with the cops and one of my closest friends, had told me all about Brock Turner, but he hadn't mentioned meditation. According to Varga, Turner had been in prison for car theft and aggravated assault, which are not usually thought of as political offenses, though they may be in El Paso. I wondered why Mercedes still believed in the tooth fairy. Then I figured that so far in her life, no matter what happened to her, someone always picked up the pieces. Maybe it would work that way again.

She looked up at me through eyes flashing with tears. "I just can't believe that Chip could turn so *mean*. I just don't have good luck with men."

"Men," I agreed, "are a mixed lot. You did what he told you, and I'll deliver the bonds. What kind of car is Chip in?"

"A Mercedes," she said, answering a foolish question.

We marched off together, a couple of cowpersons stomping across the echoing canyons of the terminal to the ranges of parking lots outside. There's a lot of money in Texas, and Texans spend a large portion of it on transportation. The vast lots were parked thick with Jensons, Daimlers, Ferraries, Aston Martins, Alfa Romeos, and every other marque of distinction in automotive history. The orange-colored riot lights made all the jewel finishes sparkle, but the brilliant colors had been leached out into pastels.

The *concourse d'élégance* was beginning to get boring about the time my boots began pinching badly, so I was glad to see the red car. Chip sat behind the wheel, staring through the windshield at the afterglow of the sunset. Judging from the litter of half-smoked cigarettes outside the driver's window, Chip was suffering some too.

I had to speak to get his attention. "Good news, Chip," I said. "I got your wife back, and I have the ransom too. And here's your gun. Let's talk a deal."

I hate guns and I try to get rid of them quickly. They're a heavy symbol of power, but they're basically only as reliable as the people who carry them, which is exactly why I handed the gun through the open window of the car.

He took it, and sure enough, pointed it at me. Even though he used it to motion for the flight bag, I could see he was panicked. Nothing in his cozy life had prepared him for a Murder One charge.

I made a great show of reluctance as I pushed the bag through the window into his lap. That was when he pulled the trigger.

The click the empty gun made seemed to knock the stuffing out of him. He lost the pistol onto the floor between his feet and sat gaping at the palmful of bullets I'd extracted from the clip.

I tossed them over my shoulder and put my hands on the window ledge to inspect him. He sat stiffly behind the wheel, a dental patient expecting bad news.

Now he was ready to negotiate. Mercedes watched this transaction with the same interest she would have shown if I'd been showing the new Calvin Klein fall line.

"Chip, you stuck out like a beestung thumb from the start. The kidnapers knew too much about banking procedures. You used your artificial leg to smuggle the gun past the metal detector. Having your wife collect the loot was a nice touch. Hardesty told me that as a loan officer you were very good at limiting risks. Somewhere along the way, you decided to dump both Brock *and* Mercedes. I never thought there was more than a thirty percent chance this was Brock Turner's gig. From all accounts, he couldn't balance a checkbook."

Mercedes let out a squeak, which we both ignored. Chip stared at the bag on the seat beside him. I pushed on. "Using Brock on the tape was clever. Once you did that, you could blackmail him into anything because he'd become part of a federal jurisdiction crime. But now you're wearing the whole daisy chain—murder, conspiracy to attempt felony murder, embezzlement, and kidnaping. And Mercedes probably has a good shot at divorce. I'd say your relationship is irretrievably broken down."

Chip licked his lips. He looked a little green. "Is this newsprint or bonds, Mr. Hazzard?"

"Bonds, of course," I said. "Right after I talked to you, I told Hardesty what I figured. On my advice he decided to accept your offer. You sign these papers authorizing the Texas Liberty Forever Bank to transfer four million in bonds from your trust account and there'll be no prosecution by the bank."

He kept switching his gaze from Mercedes to the papers in my hand, but he didn't say anything.

"This other instrument is your resignation. As of now, you're unemployed, but you get the bonds and you get away. Fair enough? Maybe you can talk your wife into leaving with you—now that you've shown her how much she means to you. With this money, you can travel first class and do what you intended all the time, move the bonds down to Panama for a quick killing in the money laundry down there."

He thought it over for a half second and grabbed for the papers. Mercedes kept a tight grip on my arm. When he'd signed and handed them back, she sighed once and squeezed my biceps.

"Chip, you have two choices," I explained. "You can catch the midnight Aero Mexicano flight for Acapulco or you can cut out on your own. That way, no one will know where you went."

Chip gave me an enigmatic look before he squealed out of the lot. Which route he took didn't matter because I had police at all the parking exits and the ticket counters, but some things don't work out.

I watched in disbelief as he accelerated through the inept roadblock put up at the lot exit by the Dallas county deputies. He smashed the wooden sawhorse barrier into splinters and was gone, leaving the deputies flatfooted and openmouthed. I'd warned them earlier in the afternoon that someone would be coming out of the lot fast, but they hadn't believed me. Now the Texas taxpayers would spend a bundle in overtime as the dragnet went up for Chip.

With his money, his missing leg, and his veteran status, Chip could have had a great career in Texas politics, but that was over now. He'd lost his job and his wife and he'd murdered gullible Brock Turner. Given his head start, I estimated he had a sixty-forty chance to escape, but things like that are hard to figure in Texas.

Two

Later that evening Daisy and I ate the supper I'd postponed to rescue Mercedes. Daisy chose Alfredo's Beach Bakehouse in Port Isabel. It doesn't look like much, a shack built from parts of hurricane-damaged houses on what's left of a ferry dock still jutting out into Laguna Madre, but appearances are deceiving.

The interior is economical—cedar picnic tables with pads of butcher's paper for tablecloths and truly lethal folding chairs from a bankrupt funeral home. The only redeeming grace comes from the fresh catches of flounder, shrimp, drum, and sea bass done up *cordon bleu* by Alfredo himself. The fish are served, of course, on jailhouse china.

At midnight, the Bakehouse had the additional advantage of no customers. I'd brought along a bottle of Gewurtztraminer and the small box I hoped might alter Daisy's firmly established view that I was not marriage material, but something told me this was not the occasion to explore such a complicated topic. Maybe it was her insistence that we meet at the restaurant instead of letting me pick her up.

In the past, Daisy had found my work stories amusing. She participated by second-guessing my methods, so tonight I set out to enlighten her about the Stackler family's fun and games. I was well into the account of my fancy footwork when I noticed she was doing a great job of containing both her admiration and her usual complaint that I run too close to the wind. She picked at her flounder *en papel* silently, waiting for me to finish.

Since it wasn't going over too well, I unfolded my triumph only briefly. After all, I'd won cards, spades, and the old maid from people who had intended to leave me dead, and I'd done it alone with no gunplay, one of my foibles.

Daisy's face was impassive. "Chip Stackler resigns from the bank and leaves with millions of dollars in bonds he can use across the border to triple his money inside a month. Brock Turner is as dead as an honest citizen. Don't we count bad guys?"

Daisy is a lawyer and we occasionally disagree about legal processes. This was such an occasion, but I still had the uncomfortable feeling something else was on her mind.

"We're in Texas, counselor. Chip broke through the roadblock I'd set up at the airport, not me. Besides, do you know anybody in this state with Chip's kind of money who was ever slowed down for capital murder? I had no real evidence. And when Chip signed that receipt for four million from his trust account, he took delivery on a flight bag stuffed with neatly folded pages of the San Antonio *Express News*."

Daisy didn't smile. "I don't like to play gotcha, Cheney, but Chief Varga also happens to be a friend of mine. He wanted me to tell you that Wilson E.—Chip—Stackler died two hours ago when his car exploded and burned on Interstate 30 between Dallas and Fort Worth. So, who killed Chip? Or doesn't Vigilante Hazzard care?"

"Chip killed Brock and he was so eager to get away he didn't check the bonds. But Brock was also playing it two ways: Chip hired him to kill Mercedes, but Brock decided to wire Chip's car and keep both Mercedes and the money. Brock was convicted of car theft in El Paso. That means he could jump-start a car and probably also wire a bomb. So, even after Chip killed him, Brock got his revenge. They deserved each other, those two."

"Which means neither of them deserved the fair Mercedes?"

"One or the other was scheduled to shoot me into an untidy mess. I can't get too worked up about them."

Across the table, the distance between us could be measured in inches, but we seemed to be conversing from different time zones.

"As I see it, Daisy, Mercedes was the clear agate two playground types were quarreling over. Don't you?"

"Not any longer. Where is she now?"

"I put her on the late flight to California."

Daisy pinged the edge of her glass with her fingernail. Before the tiny bell died away, she had a comment ready.

"I'll bet she asked you to go with her."

I've never decided—either Daisy went into criminal law because she's so quick, or dealing with criminals and prosecutors has trained her mind to work at laser speed. That's why I never keep anything from her.

"As I was about to tell you, Mercedes did just that. I told her I was booked with the siren of South Texas."

If she was flattered, her expression didn't show it. "So you let her fly right out of this jurisdiction?"

"Why not? This was a cold-blooded operation from the first. Chip's marriage was simply a way of pooling two fortunes. Brock had stolen a possession of Chip's, so he planned a Texas-style divorce. No alimony, no lawyers' fees, no property division. Mercedes wasn't terribly discreet. Hardesty as much as said Chip's career at the bank was stalled as long as they stayed married. I think Chip offered Brock a fifty-fifty split of the bonds if he'd kidnap Mercedes and kill her. With Mercedes dead, Chip would be a widower with both his reputation and his fortune intact. And he'd add his wife's money to his own, no strings attached."

"If that's so, why didn't he leave it that way?"

"He should have, but Chip decided to take a cheap shot at killing Brock. That way he'd get the whole four million. In addition to the tax advantage, he would come into possession of an unsupervised chunk of cash out of his trust fund that he could convert into big multiples in the drugs-guns-money triangle in Panama. Bankers love that kind of vigorish from their money."

Daisy said nothing. I went on, checking my logic for holes. "Chip didn't need money, but he wanted it. I hear that's how fortunes are made. Anyway, he probably figured he'd get Mercedes aboard his private plane after he got Brock out of the way and drop her out in the Gulf. The police would think she was killed by the same unnamed kidnapper's partner who killed Brock. If I hadn't torn up his dollhouse, Chip might have swung it."

Daisy examined me. I knew that look. The prosecution was about to open its case. "Try this instead. Chip was dead when Mercedes decided to end the marriage."

"That little girl has gone through life doing what men tell

her to. She's not stupid, but she has never had to take the
initiative."

Daisy stuck out her lower lip in a way that till now I'd
always found charming. "Cheney, any woman in this world
can bend you around her little finger simply by looking
wistful."

"You're saying Mercedes and Chip were a couple of
overprivileged rich kids who jointly worked out a sick fantasy
that got out of hand? That Mercedes is as guilty as Chip?"

Daisy flicked her goblet again. She'd been scoring points
in a game I hadn't known we were playing.

"You're not usually so slow, Cheney. She's *much* guiltier.
Tell me again about the pistol and the metal detector."

Dammit! Daisy thought she had proved Mercedes guilty
just by putting her together with the pistol inside the metal
detector. I had a flash that changed my mind. The Walther
P-38 has a little pin sticking out of the back of the receiver to
indicate when a shell is in the chamber. If it had been Chip's
gun, he'd have known it was empty, and he wouldn't have
tried to shoot me.

Since it wasn't his gun, the most economical explanation
was that Mercedes had staged the whole thing.

Although Alfredo doesn't have air-conditioning and no
air was moving, I felt a cool breeze. I'd dropped more than
one stitch. Instinct alone kept me arguing the point while
searching out alternate explanations. "Why would Mercedes
kill Brock? She loved him. She was going to leave her
husband for him."

"Does that mean she loved you when she was climbing
all over you at that dance last winter?"

Out in the kitchen, Alfredo was singing Radames' aria to
Aïda, one more chap who got between two women. Daisy
continued to look at me. Finally, I couldn't put it off any
longer. The pieces came together in a different pattern. Same
elements, new perspective. Chip Stackler had been at the
end of his tether when I confronted him in that airport
parking lot. All those half-smoked cigarettes. He had no
stomach for violence. He'd been waiting for Mercedes and
Brock out there ever since he'd taken the gun past the metal
detector for them. When he saw me, he knew the plan had
crashed. He knew Mercedes had fed him to the sharks.

He'd gotten into this to prove to his wife what a big man

he could be. Obviously, he planned to grab his share of the
money and fly to Mexico. Maybe he thought his wife would
come along. Well, at least I didn't have a monopoly on being
a fool where women were concerned.

The bottle of Gewurztztraminer was still half full, but I
didn't want any more of it.

Daisy was thinking about the gun. "Mercedes *told* you
she killed Brock, but you didn't believe her. While Chip
waited in the car, she took Brock into that men's room and
cold-bloodedly murdered him. Then you had to prove to her
with ballistics that she didn't do it."

I hadn't wondered at the time why Mercedes was dressed
in men's clothing because Texas women count on your knowing they're females no matter what they wear. Now I saw that
she, not Brock, had always been scheduled to pick up the
money. Brock was dead as soon as she chose him. She had
intended to kill him from the first. As a nice extra touch, she
probably had Brock wire Chip's car. All the other players in
her greedy little plan came up dead. It was Mercedes, not
Chip, who had wanted the Texas-style divorce.

I surrendered. "OK. She did it. But it still seems beyond
her abilities."

Daisy's voice was chilly. "You haven't been listening to
what you told me. You described several different women, but
they were all Mercedes. First, she was a tramp trying to pick
you up at the dance. Then she was the pampered rich girl
who needs help crossing the street. Next she played the
sensitive flower who is devastated at having to shoot an
unarmed man in a men's room. Finally, she was the innocent
victim who leaves the scene sobbing after all her problems
are solved. By you. Of course, she'll probably get Chip's
entire estate. As you said, that's how fortunes are made."

I tried my napkin as a suitable white flag, but Daisy
hadn't exhausted the topic. "She played the traditional male
stereotypes of women—dizzy blonde, spoiled rich girl, and
helpless wife. And you were blinded. She took advantage of
you, Cheney. You were being auditioned for the Brock part at
the club dance last winter. She said she was looking for
somebody who could do something besides spend money."

I sorted through possible retorts, but I knew Daisy was
right. My response did me no credit, but I'm conditioned to

argue. "You're talking to a man with a dozen credit cards. What's that mean?"

"You *made* your money. Chip didn't. Rightly or wrongly, you're convinced from experience that you can handle anything. Poor dumb Chip didn't have that assurance. Mercedes knew it was his Achilles heel. I'll bet that's how she got him onto this merry-go-round.

"She told him she'd leave him unless he could prove he was more than his money. She egged him into that scheme with Brock until he was in over his head. Otherwise he wouldn't have tried to shoot you with an empty gun or settle for a bag of newspaper clippings."

I opened my mouth, but Daisy didn't yield the right of way for even a second. "But she did manage to get you involved at the end. So why isn't she under arrest? Is it because she made you do exactly what she wanted?"

I thought it over a long time, maybe a nanosecond. "I can't prove a thing. All the witnesses are dead."

"*You* were a witness and you're not dead. Is it that you can't prove her guilt? Or that you can't accept it?"

She pushed her plate away and put down her fork with a clatter. "Cheney, this is our last date. If you can't understand Mercedes, you'll never understand me."

I finally understood why Daisy had been so distant this evening. I had a million arguments, but I didn't know which one to choose. Coming up with the wrong answer to someone else's problem isn't supposed to end a relationship.

When I looked across the table, Daisy's eyes were brimming. Those unshed tears meant a lot to me, more than I could put into words. But she was in no mood to listen to anything I might say.

Alfredo brought the coffee, so we chatted with him awhile, careful not to look at each other. Alfredo was telling an anecdote about the precocity of his fifth granddaughter. I gazed past Daisy out into the parking lot, watching a Zimmer limousine, a stretched version, draw up. Four people got out, a woman in a dark flowing costume accompanied by three men. The men caught my attention because they spread out to follow the woman as if they were guards escorting royalty for a night on the town.

When she stood in the doorway, her eyes flickering over the improvised furnishings, I expected her to turn and leave.

Surprisingly, she didn't. It was after closing time, but Alfredo waddled up, offering her the hospitality of his modest establishment. He was actually bowing and scraping, an action I'd read about but never seen before.

I couldn't see her face, but Alfredo got a lot of nourishment out of her presence, because he looked beatified. He led her across the dining room toward the alcove where we were sitting, looking like a newly dubbed knight setting forth on the Crusades. It was quite an entourage—Alfredo, the woman, and her three male courtiers—except that her people looked like thugs.

As she came toward us, I began to understand Alfredo's excitement. She was wearing a billowing loose coat over a low-cut black dress. To my half-tutored eye, it looked like Paris fashion. Nothing from this country offers that mixture of convention and daring. The contrast of creamy skin with dark flowing hair set off all sorts of masculine fireworks—as it was supposed to do.

If her costume snatched at my attention, her tigerish walk held it. Certainly the deep slits in her slim skirt outlined a magnificent figure, but it was the deliberate stride of her long legs that made all sorts of frivolous ideas sizzle.

Closer now, I could see she didn't offer any conventional sort of feminine beauty. As a matter of fact, she didn't *offer* anything. She simply looked at the bounteous world and the world gave itself to her, unstintingly.

Alfredo was going to tow her right past our table. I turned to tell Daisy that the Gulf offered interesting sights at all hours, but she was on her feet, her purse clutched in her hand. Her face was pale.

I got to my feet. Daisy and I had a lot more to say, even if my only appropriate speech was to say goodbye.

But this was my night for surprises. "Cheney," Daisy said, "I want to introduce you to Rita Madrid. She wants to speak to you on business. If you're lucky, she might tell you your fortune."

Maybe I'd been misinterpreting Daisy's signals all evening. This was shaping up like a practical joke.

Rita Madrid put out her hand to take mine. Her fingers were warm and strong, and I qualified for a good hit from a perfume that suggested all sorts of things. When she spoke, her voice was what I think the poets in the nineteenth century called divinely low.

"Please accept my thanks, Daisy," she said. "You're welcome to stay while Mr. Hazzard and I discuss our business."

But Daisy left without another word. I spent an eternity in the next few seconds wondering how all this had come about, but even as I watched Daisy walk across the parking lot, I knew she was leaving my life. She never raises her voice, but her no is no. I'd phone her in the morning, but I didn't have much hope. Somehow, somewhere, I'd made a definitively wrong move—once again.

I turned back to the table. Rita was talking softly about champagne to a completely captivated Alfredo. I examined her troops. They looked rented. One, short and rail thin, wore a black denim cowboy outfit. The largest of the three was well over six feet and looked solid. The last man was older, round but strong, a foreman for some dangerous and highly paid work.

The foreman shook a switchblade out of his sleeve, popped the blade, and proceeded to examine his cuticles while the others kept their eyes on me.

"Call me Teddy Ristra," he said. "A *ristra* in Spanish is a string of chilis or onions or garlics—anything to spice up the life. I'm a freelance troublemaker of many years' standing. I've heard a good deal about you up and down the Valley, Mr. Hazzard. I've heard that to underestimate you is to ask for fatal consequences. For that reason I suggest you sit down so my friends here can relax."

I wasn't much interested in his opinion or his implied threat. With Daisy gone, I had no reason to stay. Rita Madrid was beautiful and obviously rich, but I wanted to talk to Daisy. I took out my wallet and signaled to Alfredo.

Teddy spoke softly. "It's been taken care of, Mr. Hazzard. Please sit down."

His two helpers looked positively hopeful. I don't get into bar fights, but Daisy's lecture tonight had punched a gaping hole in my ego, and I was in no mood to cooperate with anybody. As a matter of fact—but before I could do anything foolish, Rita spoke again.

"Please do me the favor of letting me consult your palm, Mr. Hazzard. I may be able to help you with your problem."

Her smoky voice didn't calm me, but it gave me the

idiotic idea that Daisy had hired some kind of counselor to make my behavior more acceptable. I sat down.

Alfredo snapped a small linen napkin onto the space between our coffee cups. The cowboy stood to one side, a fence post with his arms folded. The big man followed Alfredo back to the kitchen. Seated where Daisy had been only moments before, Rita rapped on the table. I put my right hand forward onto the linen square, but she shook her head.

"Your left hand, please," she said in that thrilling tone. When I extended my hand, she almost embraced it in both of hers. I was aware of her scent, delicate, elusively lingering on the edge of recognition—piñon smoke, patchouli?

It was, to say the least, an odd situation. Minutes before, I'd been on the verge of asking Daisy to marry me. Now Daisy had walked away, leaving me to this strange woman who seemed to think we were instant intimates. I wondered what business could be so important as to smash into our private lives this way. What kind of a friend appears at a breakup to offer a reading of the rejected lover's palm?

A Rita Madrid friend does just that. She pressed my hand flat on the napkin. She wasn't looking at my palm so much as feeling it, testing the arches of my fingers, palping the knuckles, and prodding the pads of muscle below my thumbs.

"How do you know Daisy?"

"She and I have the same godmother." Although she looking indelibly foreign, her diction was stage perfect, totally without accent.

My past, she informed me, had involved travel, study, warfare. I had become disenchanted with the use of force, but I had no idea of what should take its place. I had not valued myself appropriately, and therefore I found it difficult to establish permanent relationships.

That stung, but it wasn't anything she couldn't have been told by Daisy. She went on, doubtless giving me good advice. I had a blind spot where women were concerned. My present mode of life was not permanent. I was currently rudderless, but my future could move in many profitable directions.

She said all this very calmly. She might have been an accountant rehearsing me for a year-end audit just prior to an IRS visit.

"Have I identified your past and your present?"

I nodded unenthusiastically. "Everybody I know believes the world sells them short. We all think we undervalue ourselves. And anybody's future can move in many directions. I've heard that at PTA festivals done by ladies who live down the street."

She nodded. "You were in combat and there was an occasion that made you consider pacifism as a personal choice. It involved a bridge and the death of many men. Do your ladies at the PTA tell you such things?"

She had my attention. Not even Daisy knew about that episode.

"You read that in my palm?"

She didn't answer. "Now I will tell your future, as much as you wish to know."

She had perfect teeth, and her breath was spiced with something both sweet and astringent. Her beautiful hands were armed with nails carefully filed and sharp, colored the deep red of arterial blood. I nodded to get this over with. Vaguely I was still responding to Daisy's having driven off, out of my life.

"Your lifeline is strong and it shows that many times in the past you have been in great peril. The period you are now entering is even more dangerous. You run the risk of working great injustice, but the best you can accomplish will be to avoid that. If you achieve that small success, you will be successful in many things thereafter."

My suspicion grew that Daisy had arranged this charade. Clearly, Rita would talk of the future till I drew my hand away.

"You will father one child, with whom you will have a complex relationship. You will find your life interesting, but ultimately not satisfying."

I don't believe in fate or discernible patterns in the future, though I'd already memorized every negative thing she had said. "Will I be just?" I challenged.

Her face shifted expression so markedly she looked like a different person and I took my first objective look at this seer. She was younger than I had thought. Her imperious carriage put her beyond calculations of age, but for a reason I couldn't explain, I suddenly wanted to please her.

"You will always be just, though not always wise about your own interests."

"Then I have nothing important to worry about," I said.

Her expression was grave. I'd made a bad joke on a serious topic. "You are not a trusting person, Mr. Hazzard. That is your chief fault."

"I trust everyone," I told her, thinking of Daisy's words.

"To trust everyone is to trust no one."

She dropped my hand and turned away. Accompanied by Alfredo, who carried a tray holding two tall stemmed glasses, the big man presented a bottle of champagne with a label I didn't recognize, a Zero Brut vintage from Spain.

Had Rita Madrid given Daisy some occult bit of information about my future that had turned her off? I didn't think Daisy believed in such nonsense. What other connection could there be between these two women? What kind of relationship shares a godmother?

Teddy Ristra stood beside the table like a maître d' watching the preparations for the opening of the bottle. He caught my eye. "The ancient Macedonians debated everything once drunk and once sober. You've passed the first test. Let us see what happens now."

"Let's see what happens before we open the champagne," I said. "I've had enough wine and surprises already tonight."

I'd addressed Ristra, but Rita was the one who answered. "I am a very important client for you, Mr. Hazzard."

"Not yet, you're not," I said, still feeling put upon because Daisy had vanished herself like a magician's assistant. "Tell me exactly why you think I can help you."

"Tarahumara Shipping is one of my several enterprises. The company factors produce in the Mexican states of Chihuahua and Sonora and trucks it across the border. If you've spent any time in Arizona, New Mexico, Colorado, or West Texas, you've eaten tomatoes, peppers, squash, and stone fruit my firm has brought into the United States. This is an important enterprise for North Mexico, and now someone has been trying to disrupt the service."

She nodded at Ristra, who opened the champagne.

"The company has been in business since 1945," she went on quietly. "My bonded shipments have never been questioned. Then, last week, over fifty percent of my shipments were impounded. On no occasion were drugs found. In each instance, the cargo was ruined because the elapsed time spelled the difference between ripe and rotten. When my local manager complained, he was told it was a matter of probable cause and part of the cost of doing business."

The champagne was superb. With no sugar to mask the grape taste, it was like breathing perfume. I put my glass down. "Good. Is this for sale?"

"Everything in this world is for sale. I'll have a case sent to your house."

"Thank you, but I wasn't hinting. That random check technique is one Customs uses now and again. It's part of their public image—unreasonable. I don't think I can do anything about that."

"I don't expect you to. What I want from you is to do something about Mario Darque."

"Afraid I don't know him."

"I do. Mario is my brother-in-law. He thinks of me only as a member of his extended family, one he would like very much to seduce. If he had to deal with me as a business competitor, it would make for—difficulties. That's why I want you to handle him."

"How does he connect with your Customs problem?"

"He phoned my company manager in Juarez from El Paso last week to say he could make the Customs service stop harassing the company. He wasn't offering legal assistance because he said it would take much money. He promised to call next week in person."

"Is he from off the street or does he have assets?"

"Mario is an international lawyer, which is to say he practices on both sides of the Rio Grande. Most of his business has been to represent people arrested by your drug police. He has set up a company in El Paso called Double-check. The Better Business Bureau says it has been in business six months and as yet there is no negative information filed on it. I do not want Mario Darque acting as a parasite on my business."

All this in a calm tone. She knew what she was doing.

"I usually don't operate that far upriver," I told her. "But I'll mention your problem to some friends of mine in El Paso. This has all the signs of being a classic shill, using Customs to shake you down."

"That may be, but Mario Darque is a substantial lawyer and businessman. I understand you're used to handling people like him."

Her closing words reminded me unpleasantly of Mercedes Stackler, but Rita's context was business. I glanced at my watch. It was long after midnight and I'd had a lively few hours. On the other hand, she had offered a case of excellent champagne.

"Here's my card, Ms. Madrid. I'll put someone on it tomorrow morning and he'll get in touch with you."

"I want *you*, Mr. Hazzard. Not someone. It is you who have the reputation of solving problems without bloodshed."

Teddy had poured her some champagne, but she hadn't picked it up.

"Only when I'm lucky do I solve problems without noise, Ms. Madrid. I thought the only agricultural products Customs worried about were marijuana, cocaine, and heroin."

She finally took up her glass and watched me over the rim. "Mr. Hazzard, three-quarters of the winter vegetables in the United States come from Mexico. Surely you can see how useful it would be for Reliant to establish itself as a presence in an industry of that size?"

"When you put it that way, I'm very much interested," I told her. "I'll catch a plane to El Paso tomorrow."

She smiled. "I deal in cash in such matters."

"I report all cash transactions," I said.

"I know you do. That is one of the many reasons I want you. But you won't start on this tomorrow."

"Why not? No use dawdling."

"First you'll be seeing Arthur Chess. But that doesn't matter, I expect a fair share of your effort."

There was no way I'd ask her who Arthur Chess was. "Did you read that in my palm?"

"Arthur Chess has been observing you for some time. Now that I've hired you, Arthur certainly will. He probably has someone watching you this minute. Don't you think so, Teddy?"

Teddy Ristra smiled like a resident Buddha.

"Yes, Doña Rita. I consider it most likely."

I broke in. "How do you know?"

He gave me a sweet smile. "He hired me to do it. I

thought I could protect Doña Rita at the same time. A man must live, you know."

Rita took a sip of her champagne. "You see, like Teddy, I know many things, Mr. Hazzard." Her voice was impassive.

"Is this Chess connected with the Customs shill?"

"Not that I know of. Teddy—the money and a personal services contract for Mr. Hazzard."

Teddy accepted a briefcase from the big fellow who had brought the champagne. He extracted three stacks of hundred-dollar bills and copies of a two-page document that had my name and the new day's date on it.

"Cash transactions usually spell dope," I said.

"Texans always use cash," Rita replied. She took another taste of the champagne. "Teddy, make sure Mr. Hazzard gets two cases of this. It *is* good."

After I skimmed and signed the contract, I asked again what Rita's relationship with Daisy was.

She answered blandly, "As I said, Daisy and I share a godmother. When she has problems, she thinks of me as a resourceful sister."

"Why did she arrange to have me meet you tonight?"

"People who share a godparent can call on each other at any time."

"Which of you arranged this meeting?"

She took another sip of the excellent champagne. "You might say it was mutual. Let me ask you a question. What do you consider your relationship with Daisy to be?"

I pushed down my anger at Daisy for discussing our relationship with anyone. "I intended to ask her to marry me tonight."

Rita raised an eyebrow. "You see?"

If that was an explanation, it went past me. I watched her guards, who looked back at me with a tough neutrality. We men don't always stick together. "She didn't know that!"

Rita shook her head, patient with a dullard. "What woman does not know when a man is considering marriage? But even so, you went off on an adventure today that could have cost you your life. Now do you see?"

Finally, I saw. A lot of explanations came to mind. Rita nodded before I could say something foolish.

"You thought the Stacklers were no serious threat? Perhaps your new assignment will offer a larger challenge."

Rita and her retinue departed. I had one more cup of coffee with Alfredo and drove home alone. There I poured myself a stiff brandy, then threw it into the sink. If rich clients were going to be fighting for my services, I was going to have quite a bit of work for the foreseeable future. Maybe it would take my mind off the greatest missed opportunity of my life.

Three

When I discovered my original partner in the Brownsville Reliant Industrial Security franchise was trying to dissolve the partnership by killing me, I bought her out. To remove the unpleasant memory, I asked Olimpia to redecorate the office. I'd forgotten that most Texans like brighter colors than I do. Even on overcast days, the office looks like a beach in August, but this morning my perfect secretary was full of smiles that would have illuminated a coal mine.

"Cheney! Good news! The very best!"

"I can handle it," I said, cranking up a smile no match for hers.

That didn't matter, Olimpia was eager to share her news. "I met my friend at aerobics class last night. She mailed the Kiowa Products contract yesterday. You know what that will do for this quarter's billings?"

I was still brooding about Daisy. "Make the IRS happy. And us. That's really great, Olimpia. Lunch is on me today. Where's Esteban?"

Esteban Orosio had first joined the agency when he drove me around while I recovered from a shooting scrape, but his Marine tenacity and his innumerable relations—cousins, uncles, brothers and sisters—all over the Rio Grande Valley immediately made him next to indispensable. Right now, he's an investigator, but soon he's going to be running a branch office in El Paso. Esteban is Olimpia's brother-in-law. With those two, I can handle about five times the business I could otherwise. Someday, I'll clone them.

"He's at the Mercantile. They bought the expanded coverage, so he's making the final study. Shall we go out to Alfredo's, all three of us?"

I thought of Daisy learning that I was visiting the scene of our last date with my beautiful secretary the very next day, but I agreed Alfredo's would be great. Daisy would know it was only business. She's always fair-minded.

"Anything else?"

Olimpia barely repressed another smile. "Mr. Werkshul's secretary phoned to schedule an overseas call at nine. Otherwise, your calendar is clear till noon."

These days, Fred Werkshul has more money than he can count. He runs Reliant's home office via satellite from an island he owns in the Caribbean, but at heart he's still the hustler who started out twenty years ago with a pay phone. Since I own very profitable shares in the company as well as my franchise, I tend to respect his views.

"Did Ramon say what Fred had in mind?"

Olimpia pursed her lips in a way that surely devastated her countless suitors. "He didn't say anything, but I sensed only positive vibrations. Perhaps he wishes to congratulate you on your work last night."

I let that topic pass without comment. Among her other talents, Olimpia is a magnet for news. Some of it people tell her because they like to be rewarded with one of her smiles, but I've known her to pick up what people are thinking even over the telephone. Sometimes I suspect she's part witch. When I suggested that once, she became grave. Witchcraft in the Rio Grande Valley is nothing to joke about.

"*No* other vibrations? Not a one?"

"You are not happy this morning, Cheney. I think you should drink your coffee and make ready for Mr. Werkshul's call. I bet it is opportunity. A big one."

I filled my coffee cup and went in to sit at my desk and examine the visual ambiguities of Georgia O'Keeffe's view of a cliffside near Taos, New Mexico. It had been my contribution to the redecorated office to replace a mural of an assassinated general and I enjoyed it a lot. Olimpia was right. No use inflicting my mood on anyone else.

When isolation didn't work, I turned on the Spanish language station in Matamoros. At least I could practice my Spanish. The news reported continuing disquiet in the state

of Chihuahua, especially in Juarez, where the opposition
party's candidate who had "officially" lost last year's election
was refusing to go down quietly. Though the program didn't
say that, I worked it out from the smarmy tone of the
announcer, who quoted the governor of Chihuahua as calling
for "a resolution of unimportant differences so *todo el mundo*
could go forward into the fabulous adventure of Mexico's
future."

Then came a flash. The minister of the interior, a man
touted as a hot possibility to be the next president of Mexico,
had been shot outside his office as he stepped from his
limousine. The police had no leads on the killers.

I was still thinking about that when my phone buzzed
and Fred Werkshul came on the line, hearty and noisy as
ever. If I ignored the echoing pauses between the snatches of
our radio-transmitted conversation, it was a good connection
for an overseas call.

"Cheney, old son! I wanted to congratulate my favorite
franchise holder. Garrett Hardesty tells me you've been
showing initiative and saving him a bundle. Speaking of jobs
well done, Marvella Lassiter dropped over for lunch last
week. Beautiful woman! She sends her best and hopes for no
hard feelings. She says she's going into cattle ranching in
Colombia, but I wonder. Anyway, glad your desk is clear
because I have a dream simple assignment for you—travel,
adventure, and opportunity—as they say, first cabin all the
way."

Fred's been doing a W. C. Fields imitation so long he's
no longer aware of it, and he always goes into the con man
routine whenever discussing a job that will make money for
him and trouble for me. To get an idea of what he's really
talking about, I reverse his adjectives. "Simple" means dangerous and "dreams" tend to become nightmares. Since our
medical plan was written in Hong Kong, "first cabin" covers
hospital bills for any injuries sustained on the job at ten
percent of the customary and usual charges.

"What is it, Fred, supplying personal security for some
Middle Eastern dingbat to visit Disney World?"

After a growling laugh intended to reassure me, Fred
went into his pitch. "Cheney, this is a choice assignment. An
old friend of mine needs some help. Since it's a delicate
matter, I immediately thought of you."

"Delicate" lives just across the street from "illegal." "Tailored for me" means no one else would touch it with long tongs. Sooner or later Fred always thinks of me.

"This time, you're the only person I've talked to, Cheney. Chess wants you. If you don't take the assignment, he might go to Wackenhut."

Invoking Wackenhut, a highly respectable security firm we're trying to surpass in billings, was Fred's cute way of letting me know we had to win this one for Reliant. What got me interested, though, was Chess, the name Rita Madrid had mentioned the night before. This was getting complicated, but I owe Fred a lot, so I gave in—gradually.

"Where'd he get my name?"

"A manufacturer in the Border Industrial Program, a man called Gutierrez. He claims you saved his whole family from death, destruction, and disgrace."

"Is Chess a slow pay?"

Now that I was in camp, Fred enthusiastically started the orientation.

"Slow pay? Cheney, Arthur Chess *invented* money. The IRS estimates his personal share of Amerexco is in excess of two billion dollars. This morning, the company has a book value larger than ninety percent of the countries in the United Nations."

"Why don't I know about him?"

"He's about five years older than God. He started out as a master mechanic in El Paso, but he made a tidy bundle smuggling guns in the 1911-1915 Mexican Revolution. Chess moved the bulk of his operations to Mexico twenty-five years ago after a face-off with the IRS."

"Are you telling me your client Chess is a gangster?"

"Whatever gave you that idea? *I* have trouble with the IRS. In the Revolution he might have been a little hotheaded, but he was on the right side when those fools in Washington didn't know their arse from a legitimate tax deduction. During the Thirties, he even headed missions for President Cardenas and Franklin Roosevelt. They were both his personal friends. Now he's into oil, electronics, land, cattle, airlines, you name it. He has an unshakable reputation for integrity. In Mexico, that tells you something."

"You have any idea what he wants?"

I listened to the oceanic sounds while Fred carpentered

his answer. He isn't above a con job when necessary, but he
doesn't lie about the clients to his own people.

"He wouldn't say, but Chess never tells all he knows,
either. In Mexico they call him Arturo Ajedrez—Arthur the
Chessmaster. He's made money for people who work with
him, and even his enemies can't deny he's straight. He's the
biggest client Reliant's ever had. This is your personal big
time."

"I'm impressed. Who puts me in touch with him?"

Fred chortled. "I do, of course. There ought to be
somebody pushing smiles on that knockout secretary of yours
right now. Give her my regards and tell her to phone me if
she wants an understanding boss."

"She has one already," I said, but I was talking to a
sidereal emptiness.

I hung up and strolled out into the reception area. Sure
enough, a man with a Reliant briefcase was speaking machine-
gun Spanish to Olimpia. Fred has always been able to predict
my responses better than I would like. Lately, too many
people have shown that talent.

I'd turned off Route 77 at the sign saying Ranch Headquarters half an hour ago, and though there was a lot of it,
the real estate looked pretty hard-scrabble to be the setting
for a billionaire's kingdom. Under the empty sky, a chaparral
jungle was the only attraction. Maybe Chess was a connoisseur of thorny plants. Or just eccentric. As the odometer
ticked off miles, I decided if I ever became a billionaire, I
would not be eccentric.

For a while, to keep from brooding about Daisy, I
identified all the plants I saw. Mesquite, paddle cactus,
razor-edged swamp grasses, creosote bushes, knot grass, salt
cedar, and Texas ebony had woven themselves into an impene-
trable thicket on both sides of a scraped road of rock-hard
caliche mud.

This was obviously the only road in, so I was pretty sure
Chess wasn't going to consult me about estate security.
Anyway, he didn't have to worry about being surprised by
unwanted guests. The house-high plume of yellow dust sift-
ing down behind me would signal my arrival a long way off.

Whoever had laid out the entrance was a thinker. Just

before a pair of penitentiary gates there came a dip in the road deep enough to require downshifting. The gate itself stood at an angle to the drive. Nobody would bull through here, even with a light tank. Since I had no such ideas, I parked in the middle of the road and got out.

Immediately, I regretted it. The humid heat of a South Texas noon began converting my suit into damp laundry. The only sound was the Freddy Fender *salsa* playing on my CD. I reached in to turn it off and walked over to the stone column displaying a bronze plaque of warnings and instructions. I wasn't alone, because a spot between my shoulder blades began to tingle.

Since I was playing on somebody else's home court, I pressed the voice button and spoke into the grill. "My name is Cheney Hazzard. Mr. Chess wants to see me."

A quiet voice promptly answered through a high fidelity system. I'd be attended to within two minutes, it said. I put the time to good use by inspecting the electrified woven fence that stretched from the gates toward both horizons. Inside, there was parkland or maybe a golf course complete with lawns, live oaks, cedars. Among the artificial hillocks, clumps of topiary shrubs grew. You had to look carefully to see the video scanners tucked into the trees. Trespassers would be made unwelcome early and often. Apparently the price of Chess's success was the need to keep a constant eye out for intruders—or maybe he just liked gadgets.

A squeal of brakes announced the arrival of a car that hadn't made a sound coming right up to the other side of the pipe-bar gate. The driver, a darkly tanned anglo in a light business suit, picked up a microphone and stared at his dashboard.

"Mr. Hazzard, I'd admire to see your driver's license."

I've entered maximum security prisons with less fuss than this. I pulled out my license and held it beside my face. The likeness was good, though I thought it made me look deeply dishonest—a little like a commodity futures salesman— but it satisfied the guard.

"Sir, when I open the gate, please get in this car as quickly as you can."

I looked at my Mercedes. After converting my lease to a purchase, I was not thrilled about leaving it unattended.

"Nobody's going to touch it, Mr. Hazzard. We have twenty-four-hour guards on this gate."

He waved an arm and two men in jungle fatigues materialized at either end of the drivearound. They both held Armalite rifles. I took his advice and stopped worrying. They had good security here, but they shouldn't have stared at me. Keeping your eyes constantly on a target is a bad idea. I suppose it's programed into us from the time we were snacks for carnivores, because being stared at sounds a warning deep down in the brain core. Beautiful women have told me they live with it, a buzz that never lets up when they're around groups of men.

The guard's car looked like an outsized golfcart with a fiberglass sedan body. When the gate slid sideways, I climbed in and glanced around. Some kind of experimental vehicle, I decided, not battery powered. There was a video screen mounted in the dash and the engine hummed steadily but quietly. There was no exhaust smell.

"Shut the door! Now!" There was no mistaking the urgency in the driver's command.

Bigger than a timber wolf, the fierce head and gaping jaws of a professionally angry dog filled the window as he hurtled through the air, obscuring the sun. One hundred and fifty pounds of muscle slammed the door shut and rocked the car on its springs. The brute hadn't made a sound while running, but now each bark sounded like a tree trunk splintering. Two more of the killers bore down on us as the driver put the car in reverse.

The lead dog kept jumping at the window while I held the door shut. At each leap, his claws left scratches on the plastic window. His jaws were open, and I had a cheap thrill when I momentarily mistook a line of slaver for a crack in the plastic.

After the driver finally got us turned around and up to speed, the others fell behind, but the lead dog kept snapping at the rear tires till we crossed a wide cattle guard, where a second electric fence stretched off in another ring.

The driver let out his breath in a hiss and reached for a pack of cigarettes on the dash. He didn't much care for the dogs either.

"I like your car," I said.

He didn't answer, but offered me a cigarette to show it

was duty and not hard feelings that kept him silent. I told him no thanks and inspected the greenery that looked oddly unearthly in this arid wilderness.

Away from the gate, specimen trees, elaborately barbered groupings of shrubs, and landscaped vistas of ornamentals stretched off in all directions. It wasn't a golf course, though it was bigger than the Cameron Country Club. The amount of money this landscaping represented was hard to conceive. The water bill alone would have exhausted the budget of a small county. If Fred was right that most of Chess's property was outside Texas, I made a mental note to visit his headquarters sometime.

Noticing my interest, the driver gave me another cent and a half of conversation. "This is an experimental farm. We use desalted sea water. Nice, isn't it?"

I agreed it was nice. We drove through a citrus grove and started up an incline. I could now make out the house, dug into the reverse slope of the ridge.

At first glance it wasn't impressive—a wide, low, two-story of adobe and slate that seemed to grow out of the ground without disturbing the expanse of gray-green sage that ran off to the west like a dream of Eden, an Eden with an airstrip cut through the middle. The house offered views in every direction and there were no windows on the first floor. Despite its domestic appearance, the place was a fort.

We pulled to a stop in the middle of a stone-flagged courtyard which had video scans at each corner. The driver pointed his finger at the central door and uncocked his thumb like a hammer falling. I climbed out. As I walked up to a steel door painted to resemble wood, it swung ponderously open at the precise second I'd extended my hand to knock.

A tiny man stood in the interior darkness, an hispano wearing a checked vest and a deep black formal coat. Incongruously, he had on a pair of mirror-lensed sunglasses. When he nodded his head and stepped back, I decided he was the butler and gave him my name.

I stepped into a darkened foyer the size of a hotel lobby. The massive front door swung shut behind us with the solid *thunk!* of a safe closing.

The butler looked me thoroughly up and down. He might have been measuring me for a suit. *"Con permiso, señor,"* he said, in a voice like a rusty hinge, with that little nod that wasn't quite a bow. He turned to lead the way toward a pair of double doors at the other end of the room. This floor was stone too, but the surface was polished to a mirror brightness. Each of the formal alcoves that bordered the entrance hall contained a fortune in art.

Like a good tourist, I took advantage of the opportunity. Each alcove had as its centerpiece a painting or a piece of sculpture. All of the work came from South or Central America, and I even recognized some of the artists. Maybe the rich are like us, but billionaires cut in at a level considerably beyond that.

The tour ended when we approached the massive double doors. They swung open while we were two yards off. Inside a room illuminated by a single overhead spotlight, a tall, white-haired man stood facing me. Like the butler, he wore sunglasses. He held a sheaf of papers in his hand and waved them at me impatiently as I walked through the doorway.

Instantly, my eyes filled with a white light of a sun's intensity. I was stunned and blinded and disoriented. Two men snatched my arms while someone—the butler?—searched me for weapons.

I'd spent three months on crutches last year, and I still hadn't got my strength back, but I managed to yank the man on my right off his stance. That didn't help much because the other fellow jerked my left arm up painfully behind my back, sending jabs of electric pain up my arm as he applied pressure. The butler finished his search in silence, then stepped away.

Flare-ups of spot blindness still obscured the room and the people in it. The men holding my arms released me with one last warning twist and moved back into the shadows.

"Excellent! That light bomb is supposed to disorient subjects for five seconds, but you responded immediately. Glad to make your acquaintance, Mr. Hazzard. I'm Arthur Chess," said my white-haired host, dropping the dark glasses onto his desk. "Please pardon the zeal of my companions, but their attitude has something to do with the length of time I've been kept alive, so I hate to discourage them. I trust you're not hurt."

My eyes still teared uncontrollably, but my vision was clearing. With his white hair and eyebrows on a face as dark

and wrinkled as an old glove, Chess looked like a Santa head
made by a child out of a walnut shell and cotton.

Somewhere in his past, this Santa had experienced some
hard times. His nose had been broken. The bridge was now
level with his cheek bones, which made his wide-spaced dark
eyes look deceptively ingenuous. Since he hadn't had it fixed,
it was a souvenir of a simpler life. I estimated his age at
eighty.

Chess threw himself into his throne chair with none of
the caution of an old man. Massaging my throbbing shoulder,
I sat down in the inquisition seat. The desk which separated
us was carved of some dark wood, eight feet long, four feet
wide, and polished like a grand piano. It seemed to be one
piece. Across its wide expanse, Chess regarded me with a
humorous look that didn't bother to hide the keen assessment
behind it.

"Do you smoke cigars, Mr. Hazzard?"

He lifted the lid of a heavy box and took one out. It was
a dark panatela, probably from Cuba, but I shook my head. I
was still cranky about the light bomb and the search. The
little butler stalked up. When he bit off one end of the cigar,
Chess reached up to light it for him. With his second puff,
the butler blew a pungent cloud of blue smoke at Chess and
then pivoted to face me. The two old men stared at me like a
pair of raccoons in a tree.

Chess sighed. "I haven't been able to smoke for years.
You're wasting your life if you don't indulge in good cigars,
good liquor, and the company of the fair sex whenever you
can. They spice up your memories later on."

"On the other hand," I told him, "my life doesn't oblige
me routinely to search business associates for weapons."

Chess nodded. "Under different circumstances, I could
subscribe to that view. Fred mentioned you'd probably be
difficult because of the recent change in your domestic arrangements. But he also said you can't resist a challenge."

The network of gossip and speculation that is a part of
the border culture may be invisible, but it's damnably effective. I wasn't surprised that Chess knew all about me and I
knew nothing of him. After all, I'm a newcomer to Texas—
I've been here only two years.

"Mr. Hazzard, Fred said you could go anywhere and

puzzle out anything. To carry out this assignment you'll have to do exactly that."

Clients don't appreciate what they don't have to ask for. "Mr. Chess, we're having a misunderstanding. At Fred Werkshul's request, I came here to see you. I haven't agreed to anything yet. I don't need this job. My Reliant franchise is turning away work. Roughing me up doesn't dispose me to want to work for you and neither does the fact you have to live in an armed camp."

Chess regarded me with amusement and gave me a smile that made him everybody's uncle.

"If you won't have a cigar, may I offer you some coffee, Mr. Hazzard? Security is not simply a hobby with me. Our measures are in part to protect the art collection, which is, I'm told, unique. More importantly, I have critical work to do. My companions protect me for the sake of our shared goals."

His use of "companions" and "goals" snagged my interest, but that still didn't make the assignment legal. "What exactly is the job?" I asked.

"I want you to trace an object that is valuable beyond imagining. It has been lost for over half a century. Men have died for it and will die again."

He turned to the butler, who put down the cigar immediately. "Umberto, I can see our guest needs convincing. Let's bring it out."

Umberto about-faced to march past the guards at the door. They came to attention as he passed. The little man may have dressed like a butler, but they treated him like a prime minister.

Chess certainly knew how to build suspense. The old man studied the blue-gray ribbon climbing the air above the cigar but said nothing. As one of the guards shifted his weight, his boot heel squeaked on the gleaming parquet floor. This must have been what court life was like in the middle ages, a lot of standing around waiting for inconsequential things to happen.

Umberto's clicking heels announced his return long before he arrived. This time, the guards accompanied him across the room as he reverently set down on the vast desk a gilded ornamental box inset with crystal windows.

I thought it might be a reliquary. When Umberto

murmured *"Con permiso"* to the box, I was sure. With elaborate care, he lifted the ornate top and the sides fell away to reveal a purple silk *pouf* on which rested a mummified skull. It had the round facial planes of an Olmec head, but the furzy cap of reddish hair declared this was no sculpture. Chess sat back with a reverential sigh.

A crater pitted the left temple, and the back of the skull had been shattered and then pieced together. It hadn't been the work of anthropologists because the piecing material was hammered gold. True believers had wired two large stones, greenish serpentine flecked with red, into the empty eye sockets. Like a recruiting poster, the gemmed eyes tracked in all directions at once. Between the parched lips, large blocky teeth clamped the jaw into an eternal smile.

Chess's eyes were on me.

"The Revolution that broke Mexico free of Spain's tyranny in 1811 was begun by Miguel Hidalgo y Costilla. He was executed in Chihuahua on July 23 of that same year. This is not Hidalgo. His head is lost beyond recovering. A century later, however, the Revolution broke out again, this time led by Pancho Villa against the tyranny of the perpetual president Porfirio Diaz. Some people say this is Villa's head."

I stared at the grisly lump that contrasted so bizarrely with its regal surroundings. I had a lot of objections, but I started with the obvious one. "Villa!" I said. "He was some kind of border bandit. A clown."

Umberto's hand moved back and forth three times. The slaps didn't hurt because he wasn't strong anymore, but his signet ring caught my upper lip and blood came welling out, warm and salty in my mouth.

I ignored the cavalry pistol at full cock inches from my nose and looked past him at Chess. Chess was talking rapidly and earnestly in Spanish, but the pistol didn't budge. *"Tenemos que disculpar sus faltas,"* Chess said, his face grave, his voice hoarse with tension.

"Lo que ha hecho no tiene disculpa," Umberto rasped.

Chess turned to me and switched to English. "I told him we must excuse you. You are merely vastly ignorant. I would suggest an immediate apology."

The diameter of the .45 got bigger every second, but mostly I was vexed at my stupid response to Villa's name. I had broken every rule of courtesy in a region in which courtesy is enormously important.

"Please accept my apology, Señor Umberto. All I know about Villa is what I've seen in a late-night movie."

Umberto slid the pistol under his tailcoat as fast as it had appeared and offered me a handkerchief. As I pressed it against my lip, he turned to Chess and his lips writhed in a wry smile.

Chess stood up to plunge his hands into his pants pockets as if everything had turned out right. "Fred said you didn't have any false macho."

I went over my mistakes. Examining the head, I hadn't listened too closely to Chess, and I should have been paying attention to the guards. They'd been statues, celebrants at a ceremony with full power to bless and regenerate. Loyalty can be bought, but this was uncannily like reverence. For them, the mutilated skull held enormous power. Chess continued to look at it as he went on.

"Like Hidalgo, Villa was assassinated and his head was cut off after he was dead. Until now, it's been considered lost forever. Well, Mr. Hazzard, I have spent upwards of five hundred thousand dollars and half a century looking, and maybe I've found it. I want you to prove one of two things: —that this is Villa's head, or that it isn't."

This was a business meeting, despite the trappings of glamour and death. "Mr. Chess, my Spanish is adequate but not at professional levels. And as you have just seen, I don't know much about Mexican history."

Chess looked both dour and mocking. "Hire an interpreter. You can read a book, but you'll learn all the Mexican history you need by talking to the people you'll encounter on your search."

He came around the desk to sit down beside me. He was wearing a blue serge suit with a vest that made him look like a railway conductor. He examined me as frankly as I had stared at him. Then he crossed his legs to reveal lace-up, over-the-ankle shoes. He'd stopped paying attention to changes in men's fashions about 1928.

"1926," he said. "That was the year his grave was broken open by... somebody. His head's been missing ever since. I was in New York then, putting Amerexco together, so there was nothing I could do at the time. Finding this particular head took over fifty years. Now I must be sure it's Villa. That's your job. If you can prove it, Reliant will have the security contract for all my companies in the United States."

"If I don't?"

"The same. Your time is worth money and if you don't do it, nobody can. You see, Mr. Hazzard, I do business with two kinds of people. I hire people who want to keep me happy—suppliers, art experts, and the like. I buy them with money. Folks I treat as companions don't give a damn about my feelings because they want to do a given job just as much as I do. I think you're the second kind. And you wouldn't mind giving me bad news."

He was right about that. "What makes this job so important? Relics don't have the power they once did."

Chess got comfortable by sliding down in his chair and stretching his long spidery legs to rest on the big desk.

"Mr. Hazzard, fully half the population of Mexico today have not completed the elementary grades. Thirty percent are completely illiterate. Symbols have enormous power in our politics, and Villa's head has a mystical value that you, as an educated man, can't even begin to conceive. My doctor has become a real scold about my not living forever. For my last act I want to put Villa's head where it can never be used to destroy the values he and I spent our lives creating and protecting."

His blue eyes were chips of glacial ice under cotton-white eyebrows. "Land. Freedom. Education. For thousands of people, Villa *is* the unfinished Revolution. And whoever has his head inherits his Revolution. It could be used by anyone for any purpose."

"He was a man. Now he's dead."

Chess had a number of manners that he put on and took off like hats—old shoe, engineer, statesman. Now he became the old codger who has seen and done everything.

"Of course, Villa's dead," he told me. "But Mexico is full of ghosts. The spirits of the ancients, mortals and pre-Columbian gods alike, are reborn generation after generation until their goals are achieved. Villa, as any *curandera* will tell you, was either a witch or a god reborn. I should admit, I pretty much believe it myself."

I've become immune to all kinds of ideology. Belief can make decent people do terrible things. I've done them.

"I'll take the job, but that doesn't mean I have to believe anything."

My response was a signal. Umberto and Chess looked at each other for a fraction of a moment. Then Umberto barked a command. The guards left and closed the doors behind them. Umberto turned to open a panel in the wall behind us. Out of the concealed compartment he took a beautiful saddle leather briefcase which he placed on the vast table in front of us.

"This is a little misdirection," Chess said. "You came here without a briefcase, but you're leaving with this one. You'll find in it everything ever printed about Villa after his death. It's just an educational convenience for you, but this briefcase is going to be like a beacon, so be ready for people to home in on it. Be careful, Mr. Hazzard. Do not underestimate the power of the head or the skill of my enemies. People know how close I was to Villa and they expect me to do something about his memory now that I'm getting up in years. You take this job and a lot of people will be watching you—all the time. Not all of them will be pleasant."

Umberto stepped closer and searched in his vest pocket to bring out a small object strung on a necklace. Before he gave it to Chess, he let the chain, thread thin, run out to reveal a little medal half the size of a dime swinging at the end of it.

Chess looked at the tiny amulet a long moment. "This is the most precious item we're giving you. I'd like you to wear it around your neck. People will think it's religious and won't trifle with it. In the long run, you'll find it useful."

I took the medallion, a time-worn piece that seemed to have been passed from hand to hand for centuries. I could almost make out a word—*cisco* or *coatl*—the lettering was both contorted and worn down. The figure seemed to be a horseman in a forest. I didn't think it was a Saint Francis medal. There was a date, but I couldn't make it out.

When I started to put it in my pocket, Umberto grunted, so I did as Chess had suggested, loosened my tie and hung it around my neck to drop inside my shirt. Only then did Umberto push the beautiful briefcase across the table.

Chess watched me inspect the case, a honey-colored leather that had been polished so the sheen seemed inches deep. "No use giving you advice, but I envy you the fascinating people you'll be meeting—some of the richest and the poorest people on earth."

That brought a pair of haunting dark eyes to mind. "Is Rita Madrid one of your fascinating people? She seemed to know we'd be meeting today."

Chess grinned like a star boarder being told there was apple pie with cheese on top for dessert.

"Rita Madrid. Isn't she something? You'll probably have to deal with them all. Rita, Mario Darque, Teddy Ristra, Jesuita Contreras . . . Jesuita and I came close to getting married once. She is the only one who never lies. Darque is a businessman, which often makes him—impetuous. Teddy— but you'll have to figure out Teddy for yourself. I've never been able to. They're all convinced they're right. You'll have a lively time sorting them out."

Given an introduction to that kind of opposition, I started preparations for an uncertain future.

"Do you think of any of these people as allies? I'd appreciate some help if I'm to go into Mexico."

Chess thought about it for a while, but his answer was hardly helpful. "There's an enormous amount of idealism in Mexican politics to offset the corruption. Remember the power icons had in the twelfth century to set thousands off on Crusades about which they knew nothing. I think you'll just have to get used to a situation in which you won't have quite the control of events you're used to here in the States. Alliances in Mexican politics can change fast."

And that was the end of the briefing. Umberto summoned the guards. And then we all drank to the Villa Project in an amber tequila. It was smoother than sixty-year-old brandy, and we toasted to gunpowder, excitement, and the majesty of death.

Four

The dogs ignored us as we drove past them on our way out to the gate. There were six of them and they lolled in a

casual group, yawning and displaying their tongues while the
alpha male alone stood up to watch us leave. This time, while
I waited outside my sunbaked car for the air-conditioning to
make the interior bearable, I spotted the guards in their
blinds. Chess's security was good but not perfect. It's as
important to watch outgoing traffic as it is to monitor people
coming in. If this deal worked out, I'd be telling Chess the
dogs should accompany visitors both ways and the guards
should have alternate sentry positions.

I hadn't done much sleeping the night before, so I
decided to drive home and have an early supper instead of
returning to the office. Then the traffic going south reminded
me that today was the first day of spring break, when college
students from all over the Midwest overrun the Island's
beaches with thousands of motor trikes, hang gliders, five-
foot surfboards and—to lubricate it all—a billion sixpacks.

Even as I turned onto the highway toward Brownsville, a
covey of them zipped past honking, flirting with each other at
sixty plus mph and generally making me glad I wasn't that
young anymore. The cars were routinely of recent vintage,
not the junkers we had available for such adventures in the
bad old days.

As I inserted myself carefully into the traffic, I saw the
passengers in the cars were sex-sorted—all females in one
car, males in another. Since midnight last night, I'd been
contemplating the difficulties of relationships between the
sexes, so I was ready to generalize. If you go on holiday to
Padre or Florida or Southern California with a bunch of men,
you spend the whole time looking for women. Women in
groups have the same problem. If you go alone, people think
you're weird, but if you go with a date, it's also a no-win
situation because you're tied to the person you brought.

I was considering the problems of the next generation as
well as those of a young couple ahead of me on a Honda. She
was in the buddy seat pounding on his back to underline
some point of disagreement. I was wondering how that would
end when somebody smacked into my rear bumper.

My first thought called it an accident, some hotdog
pinched off in the speed lane, but my mirror showed only a
ladybug in an attack mode. A primer-gray VW with black
tinted glass all around was getting ready to bash my rear
bumper again. The Mercedes was built like a tank, so that

didn't worry me, but I don't like dicing when it's not a roadrace.

They backed off and started another run up on me.

I give the opposition only one shot, so I went into passing gear and let the engine wind up. In seconds the speedometer was topping a hundred. I expected to see the car become small in the mirror, but that didn't happen. The little VW must have had a Porsche mill in back because it stayed pretty well with me. I could make out two people in the front seats. The license was from the Mexican state of Tamaulipas, just across the border. These weren't college kids.

Texas is a big empty place with thirty-two thousand miles of highways impossible to patrol with much frequency. That means when someone stops being a good citizen, you're usually on your own.

I had more horsepower and a longer wheelbase than the bug. Though they could go fast, I could go faster, keep it up longer, and do a thing or two they couldn't. Still, what they were doing was dangerous. If they hit me with enough velocity, they could bump me off the road. All it would take was a panicky reaction that twirked my steering wheel even a notch and I'd be exploring the narrow shoulders and the drainage ditches. But this was no time to pull over and deliver a safe-driving lecture.

I kept up my speed but pulled on my lights, seeing if they'd think I was braking. They fell back cautiously, so I stood on the accelerator and watched the tachometer climb toward the red zone. That held them off for a while, but slowly they narrowed the interval again. It was no contest, but I was rapidly coming up on a glut of those college students ahead.

Just then, something else discouraged me. Along Texas highways where fatal accidents have occurred they erect memorial crosses. We were passing a platoon of them. I eased off a little on the gas and picked up my cellular phone to call the office.

Esteban answered immediately because he knows I don't use the private line for social engagements.

"Yes, Cheney?"

"A classic gray VW bug with a souped-up engine is sounding me on Highway 77 north of Raymondville. I'm going to take the next exit and lose them in the back roads. The license plate is Tamaulipas AO-376. See what you can find out about who owns it. No hurry because I intend to discourage them. Anyway, I won't be back to the office today."

"Will do. Want help?"

Just as I reassured him I could handle it, the Raymondville exit came up. I hung up and took the exit at the last possible second, long after the painted lines said I should. The VW driver was good. He swung after me, taking out only one barrier post. A front fender crumpled but he kept traction all the way around the tight exit curve. He was seriously intent on staying with me. Chess hadn't been melodramatic when he said the briefcase would be a beacon. That meant there'd been observers out there in the chaparral around Chess's estate. As he'd predicted, they'd seen me emerge with a briefcase and wanted to discover its contents. I was glad only he and Umberto had been present when I took the little medallion. Chess and Umberto knew what they were doing. It was time for me to show I did too.

Once off the freeway, I turned left on the frontage road toward Rio Hondo exit. I was entering a maze of farm-to-market roads where the chances were the roads would be empty. Since they'd started this, I didn't feel bad about taking the necessary measures.

I kept up my speed on the narrow two lane road designed for Model Ts till I drove through Los Coyotes, a village with a general store and one gas pump. At this time of the year, everyone was out in the citrus orchards.

I slowed down to ninety and let them come on. If there was a big enough difference in our speeds, they could do me some damage. The driver saw his chance. He accelerated, and in response I let my speed ease off another mile or two. When the bug filled my rearview mirror, I started a count-down. He was within an inch of me when I tapped the brakes.

Then he was gone, rolling end over end into the right-hand ditch, metal crunching. I braked to a stop. After two rolls, the VW was on its roof, tilted into the ditch. As I watched, one of the men kicked out the driver's side window and slid out onto the ground. I hit the accelerator. He stared me out of sight, not even offering to help his seatmate, who seemed to be still hung up in his seat harness.

I felt good, so I punched up the CD player and drove home accompanied by Vivaldi, truly a cheery companion.

Last year, as soon as I'd realized the Rio Grande Valley was an area where I could feel comfortable, I'd bought a three-bedroom ranchhouse in a distress sale. It was right on the Laguna Madre and had a pier for my sailboat, which made it fine for me. The widow who owned it hated Texas. She was from Milwaukee and part of the purchase price was to hear her story. Her husband had worked all his life to achieve the place and then died the night they moved in. She wanted to go to Florida because it was set up for retired people—shuffleboard, bridge, and lots of widowers.

The house was nothing out of the ordinary for South Texas, though to a former Bostonian like me, the adobe walls and tile roof built around an inner courtyard made it exotic. The only reminders of the frostbelt and big city living were the widow's elaborate set of security devices.

I snapped on the air conditioner and checked the house to be sure it was empty. My friends in the VW had made me cautious. Then I pulled a frozen steak out of the freezer and looked to see if the salad greens were viable. They were, and so were the snap beans. I didn't have to go out for dinner.

After I checked the moorings on the boat, I sat on the patio to have a beer and watch the water change colors as the sun went down. When it was the blue dark that comes after twilight on the coast, I broiled the steak over a pecanwood fire in the barbecue and had another beer.

Supper over, I went through the briefcase Chess had given me. A lot of information had been packed in a small space. There were Xeroxes of newspaper clippings, articles by political scientists, and several books.

I started with a picture book of the Revolution. It was edited by José Vasconcelos, subsequently a minister of education in the 1930s. He gave the dates of the Revolution as 1910 to 1920 and the casualties at ten million. It took no time to see Villa's war was as bloody as any other in this century. Pages of grainy photographs showed corpses stacked like firewood and hung on trees in a mockery of Christmas ornaments. One figure appeared often—a man with a large head and the torso of a bull. Even in the primitive photographs, his charisma communicated itself. Villa's companions regarded him with an awe which groupies reserve for rock stars these days.

I puzzled for a while over a smudgy copy of a news photo showing Villa standing in front of a firing squad. Although he was only a blurred figure, he looked to be in charge of the proceedings. The caption explained everything. In 1912, Villa had been sentenced to death on a trumped-up charge by a general in Mexico City. He was saved from execution at the last moment only by a direct order of President Madero, who never forgot Villa had saved his life by storming Juarez in 1911.

In several pictures I could make out a young Chess, smiling under a heavy mustache. His nose wasn't broken yet.

Finally, I came to a bookmark. Villa hung over the wheel of a touring car whose rusted body was stippled with bullet holes. Vultures hung in the air above. The caption proudly stated that even at the moment death surprised him, he'd managed to draw his pistol. I sighed. Villa had started collecting his miracles early.

On the facing page was a group picture taken at Villa's funeral. Again, I picked out Chess. This time his nose was broken and he was clean-shaven. He looked like a businessman who'd suffered a serious reverse. That was that—war books don't engage my attention too long. I guess it's because I'm a pacifist by hindsight. I sat in the silence and contemplated my assignment. It wasn't my country or my war. I've become a great believer in letting countries make their own political mistakes. I couldn't even keep the woman I loved. The head of a dead man carried no promise for me. If the Mexicans wanted to use their gruesome relic as a political football, let them do it without me.

I poured myself a brandy and did what I should have done first, scanned a popular biography of Villa. Time to see if I agreed with Chess that Villa's legend could still change Mexican history.

The paradoxes began immediately. Villa was born in 1877 to a family of peons. His real name had been Doroteo Aranga. At the age of thirteen, he killed an *hacendado* for raping his sister. He escaped to the Sierra Madre mountains where he took the name of Pancho Villa and became a famous outlaw. Myths sprang up about him, and songs were sung about his exploits. In 1910, he joined Madero and expanded his raids into a formal war against the oppressive government of Porfirio Diaz.

Villa's victories were based on his brilliant use of his cavalry, the *Dorados*, called the golden ones because of their khaki uniforms. As governor general of Chihuahua, he fed the populace, reopened the schools, and broke up the great estates. The lesson Chihuahua learned under his generous regime has never been forgotten.

He did it all without the usual helps—he didn't drink or swear, and he couldn't read or write. When Villa retired from battle in 1917 at Parral, he began to study, though there wasn't much time for books. He was assassinated in 1923 by a rifleman named Barraza, who bragged he had killed Villa as one would kill a wild beast. The thirty thousand mourners at Villa's funeral did not share that view. The peasants and dreamers in Mexico grieved. For them, Villa had offered Mexico her first taste of freedom.

Dead, Villa continued to cause problems. In 1926, someone dug up Villa's grave. The corpse was recovered—but the head was gone. Despite the best efforts of the military forces in the state of Chihuahua, the head was never found. The biography ended with an incredible picture of Villa's grave. The hole in the ground gaped open. The coffin had been pulled upright, and thrusting through the broken lid, the huge, headless torso of Villa emerged. The last words in the text were *Not the End*. The optimism of the writer made me smile.

Villa's story was written in primary colors, but my assignment concerned what happened to him after his death. I opened the folder labeled *1926*. It was stuffed with Xeroxes of clippings from newspapers all over the world.

I spent an hour at it. When I finished, I had three leads. The most interesting possibility had to be the man who'd been immediately suspected of cutting off Villa's head. Emile Holmdahl was an American ex-Marine and one of Villa's Dorados. Because he had the reputation of being capable of anything, he was indicted for grave robbing by a coroner's jury, but the judge found him innocent because he swore on his mother's grave that Pancho Villa was the greatest cavalryman who'd ever mounted a horse. Holmdahl had taken the correct line to persuade an impressionable Chihuahua court, but I was a little more skeptical. I'd check him out first.

I also jotted down the name of a Mexican scholar, Epifanio Valadez. Valadez had interviewed all sorts of people who had known Villa intimately and published his research back in 1951. Since he'd done the interviewing, there was no point in my duplicating it. The flap copy on his pamphlet identified him as a graduate student at USC, so he was probably still alive.

The kinkiest item had to be a clipping from the Chicago *Daily Tribune*. Dated 1926, it quoted an unnamed source at the University of Chicago as saying he expected the head to arrive "directly." According to the source, the head was interesting because Villa was "obviously a pathological case." I'll match an academic researcher for ruthlessness against any maniac in history. I added the Chicago lead to my short list.

That brought me to a stop. Villa was a saint, an animal, a lunatic, or a far-seeing statesman, depending on your perspective. What I needed was an objective opinion. I decided Eliseo Varga could help.

He was manning the phones at police headquarters himself. "Chief Varga. How can I help you?" His voice was a little weary.

Spring break is big business for South Padre Island and lots of botheration for the Island's nine-man police force. After putting in a day shift, Varga was still there.

"I know this is a bad time, Eliseo, but I'd like to share a longneck with you and talk about a new case."

"This is a good time. I'm leaving in about ten minutes. These kids are all right, just young, and they're getting older every day."

"See you at your place and I'll bring the booze," I said. "Let your assistants carry the load for a change."

"Believe it or not, I'm going to do that, Cheney. I could handle a beer. And I want to hear about Chip Stackler."

I didn't wince because I was thinking about something else. As I picked up my keys, I suddenly understood what had been itching me about that photo of the dead Villa in his car. No time like the present to let the client know I give good value. I dialed the number Chess had said was his twenty-four-hour message center.

Although it was past ten, Chess came on the line within ninety seconds. That octogenarian didn't spend much time sleeping. "You've discovered something already."

It wasn't a question. He was a sharp old fellow. "Mr. Chess, do you have confidence in this briefing material?"

"Umberto and I and several others with knowledge of the circumstances can vouch for all of it. What's the bad news?"

"I've been studying the pictures, and from Villa's position and the holes in the car door, I can see he was hit once in the right temple. The left side of his head is gone from the ear back. Your head has it exactly backwards. The right side of that skull is damaged. Your specimen is false. I can't trace the provenience of something that doesn't exist."

I wondered if Chess was sitting there in his big, dark study, staring at the phony relic. I waited to hear surprise in his voice. Instead, I heard unruffled amusement. He'd be smiling, looking the image of honor with his silvery hair and his leathery old mug with its broken nose.

"Mr. Hazzard—may I call you Cheney? You're absolutely right. That head is as phony as a politician's handshake. I have my reasons for keeping it here, but I can assure you that Villa's head—the *real* head—exists."

While I had him on the line, I decided to try a shortcut. "Chicago. That clipping suggests some academic at the University was behind digging up Villa's grave. Is there anything to it?"

Chess took his time answering. "I asked a friend on the faculty, Micah Wellington, to make that statement. I wanted to obscure the trail so whoever really had the head wouldn't be caught by the military. The head never left Mexico. I'll swear to that."

I didn't say anything and he went on. "I got out of the habit of lying so long ago I can't do it anymore, Mr. Hazzard. Now that you've proved you're the man for the job, go find the real one. Lives are at stake."

Varga lit a cigarro. The brief flare of the match lit the deep-set eyes that make a routine stop for a traffic violation an episode of high romance for most of the women in Cameron County.

"Villa was the greatest general the western hemisphere has ever seen. He was the last man to launch an infantry attack on the continental United States. When Wilson sent

Black Jack Pershing to punish him in 1916, they discovered Villa was everywhere in general and no place in particular. He could vanish into the landscape." He scowled at me speculatively, as if I were a distant relative of Pershing's.

Varga and I got off on the wrong foot when I first arrived down here two years ago. Then he saved my life once, and I paid him back in ways that he appreciated. I'm a reserve in the Island police force, but that's friendship, not duty.

Our real connection is that he and I once loved the same woman, my late wife, Sherry. Since we loved her at different times, the memory makes for only an occasional difficulty— for him, not for me. When he met Sherry, my feelings for her had dwindled down to an interested pity. On any topic except my dead wife, Eliseo Varga is eminently sane and a fountain of information.

Narrowing his eyes against the smoke, he went on. "That's if you listened to my grandfather."

"And you, Eliseo? What do you think?"

"My father," he continued imperturbably, "believed Villa was a monster. He said anyone can get a reputation as a great warrior if he has luck in battle and demands total obedience. Villa made smoking a marijuana cigarette a shooting offense in his army. That shows a Caligula in the making. Fortunately the forces of law and order killed him in good time."

"Any proof of that?" On the history of Mexico, Varga was my oracle, but I make a living looking gift horses in the mouth.

"Of course not," Varga said and put his empty down. We were sitting on the deck of his condo, watching the break kids stage a regatta on the Laguna Madre. It was pitch dark and there wasn't much wind, but with flashlights illuminating the sails of the catamarans and the help of a lot of beer, they seemed to be having a grand time. So far the only reason nobody had drowned was the knee-deep water.

Personally, I could have done without the thundering rock and country and punk music from dozens of portable blasters, all tuned to different stations, but Varga was pleased that noise was the only problem. If the uproar stopped at midnight, he was willing to accept decibels as a necessary ingredient for youthful fun. I'd have been less accommodating, but then I didn't have to keep the peace.

"Neither of them needed a speck of proof. Villa gave them enough arguing material for their whole lives."

I lifted another Carta Blanca out of the cooler between our feet and passed it over. "And you're tired of the subject? Sorry, I thought you might be my best source."

"Thanks. I *am* your best source. If it concerns Villa, I know it. I'll even give you a rule of thumb. If it's improbable, Villa did it. He made the first military use of aircraft in the western hemisphere. On the other hand, his theory of law enforcement said all crimes were capital crimes. There were no minor offenses. His firing squads worked overtime. More?"

"Who was wrong, your father or your grandfather?"

"Neither," he said, then stared out into the noisy darkness where a kid had driven a motorized trike into the water. I sat quietly. He'd tell me when he was ready.

"They were both right. Doing anything in this world means making mistakes. Villa was an ignorant man who did both terrible and wonderful things because he was unconfused by society's conventions. But I think he's probably now in purgatory, not in hell."

Sometimes it startles me that Varga is a practicing Catholic, but other times I reflect it's a wonder all cops aren't as deep into religion, given the people they meet in their line of work.

"Do you know anything about Arthur Chess?"

He sat up. "Arthur Chess made my grandfather the loan that started the family business. You should talk to Chess about Villa."

"I have," I said and enjoyed Varga's low whistle. Varga's very good at cloaking his feelings, but I could tell he was impressed. "He believes Villa was a great man."

Varga recovered from his surprise rapidly. "Now I see why you wanted to talk to me. Arthur Chess attracts lightning. If he wants you to work for him, there may be... difficulties. What does he want?"

I gave him the details. Varga's gaze never left my face. His beeper went off once, but he ignored it. When I mentioned the souped-up VW, he jutted out his jaw. "Chess is one of the few left from those times. I've seen his philanthropy at first hand and I appreciate it, but he has made many enemies, too. Like Villa, he has done both very good and very bad things. Like all of us."

He looked away for a moment and I knew he was thinking about my dead wife. She'd had the same effect on both of us, making all our other values seem secondary. In my case, I got over it, but for him, it was permanent.

"Be careful, Cheney. I have a lot invested in our friendship. Villa's legend carries enough power to bring down the government of Mexico. You are an anglo, so you cannot imagine how quickly folk beliefs can turn politics into rivers of blood."

He refused another beer, saying he wanted to make a last check on the office at midnight. He climbed into the rental cruiser with the wingnuts on the flashbar while I got aboard the fruits of private enterprise and we drove off in different directions.

It had been pleasant. We'd taken forty-five minutes out of the day to sit idly on a deck and drink four beers between us. For some reason I couldn't quite explain, I felt nourished, which was strange because I hadn't learned much. Eliseo was a friend. If I stepped into deep jam, he'd be on my side without a lot of questions. I counted on Eliseo Varga, and it felt good to know he counted on me.

The next morning, I used the office computer to visit the super-confidential files at Reliant's national headquarters. I struck out almost immediately. Social Security records aren't supposed to be public, but they're available to anyone who takes the time to access them by computer. It was the work of about three minutes to discover that Emile Holmdahl, the Marine who'd been accused of mutilating Villa's corpse, had died at ninety-six, in San Diego, California, in 1985.

I was planning out the rest of my campaign when my door flew open.

My office is soundproofed so clients don't have to worry about confidentiality. That also means a Charro Days parade could march through the foyer and I wouldn't hear it.

A large angry man I'd never seen before stood glaring at me from the doorway as if I'd misbehaved with his wife and daughter both. Behind him, Olimpia was waving her arms in impotent fury, agitated because she hadn't been able to keep him out by sheer force of character.

Even when I got to my feet, the man still looked huge.

From his bulk and the perfect teeth that gleamed in a hard
face, I guessed he was a retired pro footballer who now made
his living pushing past secretaries. He definitely wasn't sell-
ing raffle tickets for the Star of the Sea Parish Bazaar.

"I'll take care of this, Olimpia."

She vanished behind the closing door without a peep,
but I could feel her disapproval of my visitor. He was in, but
he still didn't look very happy. He put his big back to the
door, letting me see I wouldn't get through it if he took a
notion to keep me inside. He wore an anonymous blue suit
with a white shirt and a mortician's tie, black and gray
stripes. Since he also had on the regulation black IBM
oxfords, I was pretty sure he was FBI. Only the CIA issues
tassle loafers.

What puzzled me was what he wanted. None of my
clients were doing government work, and as of last week my
estimated income tax was paid six months in advance. When
he stalked ponderously across the room, he kept his eyes
locked on mine so I wouldn't vanish if he blinked.

When he spoke it was in a command voice. "Cheney
Hazzard?"

"That's my name."

Close up, he offered a lot of contrasts. At first glance he
was a blond, but his hair was so threaded with grey it looked
dirty. His apparent tan was the result of hundreds of broken
capillaries, so he seemed simultaneously young and old,
healthy and decrepit. The one thing that hadn't changed was
the arrogance that had been in good working order a long
time, maybe since he'd made the final cut for the Chicago
Bears. He surveyed the room and decided to hell with
buying it.

"I want to talk to you about Luis Montoya."

I refused to react. "Luis is dead. He died a long time
ago."

"Then you won't mind talking about him." His was the
calculated obtuseness of a professional interrogator.

"Only if I know who's asking." I had a lot of doubts about
a man who dressed like an undertaker, reeked of whiskey,
and wanted information about long-dead soldiers.

With the ease of reflex, he produced a plastic ID wallet.
I took my time inspecting it. Rasmussen, Donald G. Six-four;
two thirty-five; blue eyes; blond hair; 7-1-26. He fit the ID,

though he looked younger in the picture. I double-checked his birthdate before I let him start his questioning.

"It's taken me a long time to find you. Now I'd appreciate some cooperation."

"I haven't been hiding." I wondered which wall he'd be coming off.

"You left Boston two years ago," he said in a voice that warned his temper was close to the flash point. It was just an interrogation technique, but I didn't like it.

"You mind telling me exactly what you want from me, Mr. Rasmussen? Luis Montoya was killed in action overseas in 1971. It was fully described in the morning report at the time. What questions can you still have about it?"

"Montoya was a lot more than just a soldier in your outfit."

"Nobody on that patrol was just a soldier," I told him.

Rasmussen recited a piece he knew by heart. "Luis Montoya was a federal fugitive, a Mexican national who was a founding member of the Tomorrow group of Weatherman. Eighteen years ago, he set off a bomb on a Big Ten campus. Twenty innocent people died. I've been on his case a long time."

"Luis is dead," I repeated stubbornly.

Rasmussen stuffed his ID back in his jacket pocket and glared. "Montoya found the perfect hiding place. The bastard hid in the military, shipped off to Nam. According to the Pentagon, he's listed as missing in action, presumed dead, on a patrol led by First Lieutenant Cheney Hazzard."

Prickly heat started up in the small of my back. All this seemed like a nightmare from a past I'd thought was in dead storage. "This is quite a while after the event," I said.

Rasmussen let his impatience show. "Murder has no statute of limitations." He lifted his lip to show me his perfect teeth. "Especially since Montoya interfered with the civil rights of the people who died."

There's a certain kind of federal officer who disapproves of the concept of civil rights. They see a heavy irony when they can invoke it for their own purposes. I'd about decided to pick up the phone when Rasmussen spoke again. This time he sounded more reasonable.

"On the authority of your statement I'll be able to close the case and declare Montoya dead. I want you to tell me

everything you know about it right now. Otherwise, you'll be
questioned in Corpus Christi. I don't want that and neither
do you. This business you're in now is very sensitive."

I had no argument about that. Any suspicion I was in
trouble with the federals and, with dizzying rapidity, my
Reliant franchise would become extremely unprofitable.

"Please sit down, Mr. Rasmussen." I looked at my free-
standing institutional-size aquarium, using my motionless
angelfish as a concentration point to let my mind slide back
fifteen years. "I killed Luis, but it wasn't murder. He died in
an explosion. I'd need official clearance before I could tell you
where, but it was an ambush and bridge takeout in a country
where the opposition was using third-class routes for resupply.
Just before dawn, when we were about to blow the bridge
and make our rendezvous, a supply detachment came along."

Rasmussen sat down in the client chair but continued to
look holes in my face. All his emotional force was focused on
me, which was odd even for a case that had cost him his
objectivity. I filed that away and went on.

"It was at least a company, too many for us to cut down,
so I waited for the midpoint of the column to get on the
bridge. Luis saw what I was going to do. He threw down his
piece and ran onto the trail to warn them. He made it to the
bridge just as I set off the charges."

A million times since, always alone, always late at night
I've watched that blinding blast—and I'd have thought just
the telling of it would take an hour or so. It didn't.

"The river at the bottom of the ravine carried away a
number of the bodies—it was a fall of over a hundred meters
into a shallow stream. But at least fifty were still on the
bridge. Everyone on that bridge died."

Rasmussen stopped watching me. Now he was suspiciously
examining my aquarium. Unperturbed, my two angelfish
stared back at him. He turned back to me and lifted his lips
away from his teeth again.

"What about some supporting witnesses, Hazzard?"

"The patrol saw it."

"You killed more than just Montoya."

The angelfish floated peacefully in the clear water, their
great translucent fans barely moving. They might have been
in a cavern a world away.

"You think I don't know that!" I said, louder than I

intended. I got hold of myself. "It was a command decision, and I made it. They were the enemy. Military necessity, we called it then. You probably still do."

Rasmussen's ruddy face fell into unhappy folds. He spoke like a hanging judge. "I didn't mean the wogs. Those other witnesses are dead. You're the only one left."

"So, take the word of the only witness."

"Why *are* you the only witness?"

I stepped around the table and Rasmussen immediately hefted his bulk to his feet. He was treating me with caution, and I couldn't understand why.

"I wasn't. I went on leave to Japan, but most of the patrol chose Hawaii. Their plane went down in the Pacific, but other people are still available."

"You call him Luis. Did you usually call men in your command by their first names?"

"We were the only ones in the outfit who'd gone to college. The rest were kids fresh off the farm or out of the ghetto. We read newspapers, we talked politics. I'd been an engineer and he was a political scientist, so we had a lot to talk about. He believed we were a repressive tool of the capitalist economy. By the time I was considering agreeing with him, he was dead and I was home. Luis was a federal fugitive? He died trying to stop the death of over fifty men."

Rasmussen continued to ignore what I'd said. "There were all kinds of tie-ins between the radical student movement and our enemies. It's possible the other witnesses were killed to protect you."

You see it all the time. Paranoid politics produces paranoid behavior, or maybe it's the other way round. Rasmussen pulled the corners of his mouth down. "Come on, fella. You know what I'm building. There's only your unsupported word you're not Luis Montoya."

Until I moved down to the border, I never thought about it much, but I have brown eyes and dark hair, and I'm no more than average height. With a tan, I can pass for Mexican. Of course, in the Valley, a Spanish-surnamed resident can be redheaded, but people from elsewhere don't know that. Like a typical outsider, Rasmussen had fastened on my appearance. I shrugged. "I don't have to prove I'm not Montoya. You have to prove I am. I have a passport and a birth certificate. Since I own property in this town, run a business and have a bank account, you'd have a real problem trying to prove I'm an illegal alien."

"You're coming with me, Montoya!"

Once it would have been interesting to play along, but I've learned it's wiser to keep the police from making mistakes instead of trying to correct them later. I picked up the phone and Rasmussen's face turned to stone. I dialed Daisy's business number. When it rang, I heard her voice and experienced the usual heart thump. But it was just a message tape, and she was using her courtroom voice.

"This is Daisy Pruitt. I've decided to take a leave from the practice of law. I advise you to seek other counsel. If you need your legal records, you can get them from the firm of Hathaway and Vaca, whose offices are at 37 East Saint Francis Street. Their phone number is—"

I started talking. "Daisy, I have a fellow here named Rasmussen who claims to be an active FBI man. He's here with some cock-and-bull fairy tale that I'm not Cheney Hazzard. Could you drop over to straighten him out? Thanks. I'll wait for you."

Rasmussen's face showed nothing, but he was studying the honey-colored briefcase Chess had given me. He took a step toward my desk and then sat down in the client chair again. Now maybe he'd bring up the real subject of his call.

But before he did that, I wanted to get a few things straight. "You're not FBI. You're retired, Mr. Rasmussen. You and I both know you've broken a lot of rules. Maybe Luis killed someone important to you a long time ago, but that's over. Maybe I'm the only witness left, but I'm telling you— Luis Montoya died fifteen years ago."

That was when Esteban Orosio jerked open the door from the outer office.

"You!" he shouted at the back of Rasmussen's thick neck, his voice ringing like a drill sergeant's on Monday morning. "Up! Out! Now!"

"Mr. Rasmussen was just leaving," I said.

Rasmussen cranked around slowly to take in the forty-five Esteban was holding in one hand. In the other, he held an oily cloth. Everything was set up for an unfortunate gun-cleaning accident and Rasmussen knew it.

He sighed, then turned back to me. Minus his anger, he looked old.

"True. I found out what I came for."

"Who sent you? Tell me and I won't take this up with the Bureau."

"Take it up with anybody you want, Hazzard. My client is confidential." He got up and glared at Esteban. "I'm leaving now. Get out of my way."

His words were challenging, but he didn't move until Esteban checked with me. Even after I nodded, Rasmussen was smart enough to wait till Esteban stepped inside to free up the doorway.

Rasmussen had left the outer office before Esteban tucked the pistol into his belt. "I should have known better, Cheney, but Olimpia thought you might need help. He doesn't look like *migra* to me, and even if he is, it doesn't matter. Olimpia and I were born here."

"Thanks for the help. He isn't the Immigration, or INS, as they're calling themselves these days. What he looks like is the FBI, but he's not that either because street agents retire at sixty. I think he may have something to do with one of my new clients."

The question was which one.

Five

Rasmussen's visit bothered me. He could never prove I was Luis Montoya, but his accusation brought up two topics I didn't much care to think about. The death of Luis was the first. The other was my childhood. I grew up in an orphanage, and my name comes from two towns picked at random from a road atlas. Since nothing can be done about the past, calling an ignorance of your parentage a wound doesn't help much. A long time ago I made a policy decision not to think about it.

I wondered if Rasmussen was on his own or representing somebody else. Both Chess and Rita Madrid had done background checks on me, so they knew police interrogations wouldn't disturb me. That suggested Rasmussen might be an agent for someone who knew very little about me, like the types in the VW. Trying to put it all out of my mind, I dug into the paperwork that accumulates in our office like crab grass. Olimpia takes care of most of it, but she's convinced it all has to have my signature—or, in an emergency, a reasonable facsimile. It took half an hour to reach the bottom of it. When I finally had a clean desktop, I picked up the signed correspondence and walked out to find Olimpia on the phone. From her quiet but firm tone, I knew she was closing yet another deal.

"Mr. Hazzard is a very reasonable person, but I'm sure I couldn't make him agree to that. Perhaps you should reconsider your position. No one else can provide our services at our price. Once you discover that, you'll understand what a bargain we offer. Oh? A great deal of thought has gone into setting our prices. Fine. You just sign the contracts and we'll get back to you. Goodbye." She hung up, saw me, and smiled.

"What couldn't the reasonable Mr. Hazzard agree to?"

"Metrix Engineering. They have a professional negotiator for all contracts. He wanted what he called a routine ten percent discount on our fee schedule. I had to explain things to him. Cheney, we need more personnel or this franchise will make new records in turning business away."

"You're right. I want to set up a time when I can talk to you and Esteban about it."

Olimpia's knack for working out unstated messages functioned perfectly. She said Esteban was in Matamoros but would return within the hour and we'd all be free till lunch. She turned back to her word processor, knowing full well the meeting would be good news.

I had another cup of coffee and phoned Daisy at home. All I got was another recording, this one from the phone company saying the number I had called was no longer in service.

I knew I could find her. Only a professional can disappear without a trace, but when I found her, she'd explain that of all the people she knew, I was the only one she didn't want to see. It took a while to accept that, but when I did, the coffee was gone.

I fed the fish and gave some serious thought to what I'd been putting off. The franchise needed more personnel, but

the kind of people I wanted to hire wouldn't be reading want
ads or listing themselves with an employment agency.

When Esteban got back from Matamoros, he had news.
"It cost me twenty, but the car that chased you yesterday is
titled to Nepente International, a holding company doing
business down in Ciudad Victoria. I don't know what they're
doing with a race-tuned VW. The clerk of records says
Nepente's a money corporation connected with a Panama
bank. Not people to mess with."

I wondered which of my clients had aroused the interest
of an international money-laundering operation. I filed it
away. "Thanks. Information like that is worth whatever it
costs. Give Olimpia a voucher for it. New clients often arrive
with troubles they haven't told us about. That's what makes
them clients."

After Esteban had started working for me, I explained
that his general military stance and Marine crewcut made
him look like a cop. He let his hair grow and cultivated a
more easygoing manner, but the Marine is still there under
the Zapata mustache and the flashing eyes. His next question
showed it.

"But what would those people have to do with you? Or is
it our new clients?"

"Beats me, but I don't believe in coincidences."

"You mentioned yesterday that Mario Darque was troubling Ms. Madrid. I hear once he starts on you, he stays at it
till it's ended."

Olimpia pursed her lips into a perfect Cupid's bow,
which means she doesn't like what she's hearing. I changed
the subject.

"We'll have to teach him some new rigs. Esteban, I want
you to go to El Paso as soon as you can get free, like this
evening."

"If you're going, why do you want me along? We can't
leave Olimpia alone."

Esteban believes the Reliant name means we have to be
able to respond at any time to any emergency with a squad of
reinforcements.

"I want you there, but I don't want us to arrive together.
I'll get in touch with you tomorrow afternoon. Spend the
morning playing a guy who buys drinks for off-duty Customs
officers. Say you're on the hiring list to get into Customs, or

maybe the Border Patrol, whatever feels right. Take a room in the La Quinta Inn by the International Bridge. I'll call you there when I get in. There's no cure for leaving the office understaffed. But since we'll be out of touch, tag up with Olimpia every four hours during the day and I'll check with her every time I can."

Esteban shows a lot of ingenuity when he goes off on his own. He's had only good luck on these fact-finding missions, but I'm always nervous about someone doing the kind of thing I think of as my work.

Olimpia still wasn't satisfied. "Cheney, that's not good enough. The agency doesn't have any give at all for emergencies."

"Do either of you have any suggestions about expanding?"

"You know all sorts of people in security work. You can pick and choose whoever you want."

People down here never realize how different Texas is from the rest of the world. If they know the world isn't like Texas, they think it could be if people worked at it.

"I don't want to bring strangers down here. It's taken me quite a while to get used to South Texas."

"You didn't do too badly when you hired us," Olimpia replied. "If it's local people you want, we know some."

Before I could agree, she was building on the idea. "Of course, you'd have to make the final decision, but I know a man on the Harlingen force who would be perfect. He has a degree in police science and he was in the MPs. He's very good, but there is one thing."

She glanced at Esteban, who nodded. I felt tired. I didn't expect them to think I had a problem about hiring ethnics. As women tend to do, she surprised me.

"He's an anglo, Frank Atwood. He's from Corpus Christi."

Olimpia is breathtakingly lovely, so I try not to look at her too often. When I do, I keep the conversation objective by discussing only business. She's such a great administrator this trade-off makes sense even when I'm lonely. I went back to work.

"Set up an appointment with Atwood. In the meantime, Olimpia, I'm promoting you to office manager. You already negotiate the final contracts, so you may as well sign them. Also, hire a receptionist. And let's knock out a wall to expand into the next suite. We'll need more room."

I think Olimpia knows how fond I am of her, so she too is all business. "I'll have Daisy write up the arrangements for the signature controls."

"No," I said, wondering if there was any easy way to break the news that Daisy wasn't our legal officer any more. "I'll write a note and have Ruth Wimley over at Hurlton-Dade notarize it."

"I'll run the papers over to Daisy. It won't take any time at all. I like to have these changes entered in our administrative code," Olimpia said firmly. She's within a term of graduating with a degree in management, so she's pretty strict about some things.

"Daisy isn't our lawyer anymore."

No one said anything, so I went on. "She's taking a sabbatical from the practice of law. We'll be hiring a new firm. A notarized statement will solve it for the bank."

Olimpia looked stricken.

"I think she's leaving town," I said. I went back into my office, closed the door, and stayed there through lunch. Everything reminded me it was over for Daisy and me. Olimpia wisely put no calls through.

When I finally decided I'd done enough brooding for one day, the travel agency had delivered my tickets to El Paso. I was flying there because that's where Varga had traced Epifanio Valadez for me. Valadez had been taken into a hostel run by the Oblate Sisters, an order dedicated to good works for the handicapped. I had a hunch that Valadez, as a scholar who'd interviewed a lot of *Villistas*, could supply me valuable shortcuts in tracing the head. Then, I'd take a look at Mario Darque and settle Rita Madrid's little problem with cross-border shipping.

I was doing all this in a rush, but I wanted to get away to strange surroundings. Call it macadamia therapy, but once on board a plane, maybe I'd think about something besides Daisy.

But there's always a glitch. When I got down to my car, the Mercedes wouldn't start. Not a whine from the starter motor, not even a click. Short of pulling on coveralls and breaking out an ignition kit, I was without a car. I called the dealer in Harlingen and started walking toward the *Cinco de Mayo* Car Rental on Elizabeth Street.

Since dawn, storm clouds had been building up out in

the Gulf, and now the first scattered drops of rain started to fall. Knowing I was about to get drenched, I took the shortcut through the bonded warehouse district.

As I turned into the alley, I came upon three men examining a squashed bug. It was the old split windshield model. After it had been rolled, an amateur had pounded out the dents with a ball peen hammer. It didn't matter, because I'd already recognized the Tamaulipas license plate. The rowdies from Route 77 were interested in a replay.

The surprises didn't stop there. When the three men turned around, I saw the leader of Rita Madrid's cortege from the other night had found new followers.

Teddy Ristra tossed up something metallic and shiny and caught it. "Very important part, I'm told, even in an expensive car. Perhaps I can provide you with transportation."

Teddy smiled. The other two moved to each side to establish the classic triangle. The little guy wore a bandage across his nose. Seatbelt not tight enough? The big one was new. The little man shook out a switchblade, but his counterpart simply showed me his open hands. The idea was I'd be so scared of one of them I'd forget the other. I'm no judo master, but I do have good reflexes, and since I was slow to get my growth in high school, I had to learn a few moves. I made a couple immediately.

I spun around smashing Chess's briefcase into the little man's face. Blood spurted. The switchblade flew out of his hands as he stumbled onto his knees, grunting and clutching at his once more painful nose. With a crash, the sky opened, and the rain really began to come down. I ran at the big man. When I was four feet off, I launched a field goal kick to put my foot into the middle of his wide paunch. After that, I kept right on running. By the time my other foot met his neck, he was on the wet cement, his head in the gutter. I jumped over him and turned around.

Teddy hadn't wasted any time. Raindrops glinted on the chromium pistol in his hand. A thirty-two is not necessarily lethal but it can make a painful hole. He took a bead on my navel. Rain slicked his black hair. His patient smile suggested he expected me to be sensible. I shrugged to show cooperation.

"*Vamanos!*" he said sharply to his fellows, who stumbled reluctantly to their feet. Neither looked too happy, but I wasn't either. Two kidnapings in a week. Crime was picking up in the Rio Grande Valley.

"This is Felicio and José, Mr. Hazzard. Now, the *portapapeles, por favor,*" Ristra said.

I was dealing with a professional. Despite the downpour, he kept me in focus and at a distance all the time. I remembered Rasmussen's longing look at the briefcase. As Chess had suggested, his enemies had shown themselves.

"*No, gracias,*" I said and felt proud of myself, but then I ran out of Spanish. I can speak Spanish if I don't have to compose complicated ideas at the same time I'm planning strategy.

His friends were looking around to see how much notice had been taken of our little gavotte. The rain had emptied the alley and would keep it that way. Teddy kept his eye on the main objective—me. "The briefcase," he repeated.

"You're going to kill me for a briefcase?"

He shook his head. "No. I will wound you painfully, but I *will* get the briefcase. Then, at my leisure, I will stuff your painwracked body into the car. *Venga!*"

It was all I had for a weapon, and I wasn't going to give it up easily. When we were the only players, I'd had a chance—small—but a chance. Now the other two were up and functioning and he had that pistol. Time to do what I was told. I put the briefcase down between us and stepped back a foot. The rain was really coming down now. Drenched and seemingly defeated, I turned to walk back into the garage surrounded by my new friends.

The big fellow lifted the hood of the Mercedes while Felicio got behind the wheel. Mutely, Teddy ushered me into the back and took the passenger seat. He used a lockpick and had the briefcase open in the time it took the driver to get the car started. The big man crawled in back, standing on my foot as he climbed over me, paying me back for the football kick I'd given him. He sat heavily on the leather seat, pulled out a damp handkerchief, and blew his nose noisily.

Without more fuss, we drove out of the garage. No one offered conversation and the large one showed me a leather-covered blackjack to quench any initiative on my part.

On a weekday, downtown Brownsville close to the International Bridge is an oriental bazaar. I was sitting in the back seat of my own car, creeping along thoroughly familiar, wet, narrow, traffic-jammed streets at four miles an hour, but I might just as well have been inside a paddy wagon. All the interior doors were locked from the driver's seat, as were the windows. If I tried a sudden move, the blackjack could break an arm or leg quicker than a rattler could strike. As if to tempt me, we inched by the central police station. From being acceptable just minutes before, things had gotten pretty bleak.

"How's business at Nepente International?" I asked, just to make conversation.

Teddy looked up from the briefcase. "They declared an additional dividend this year. Where were you going?"

"Away. Business. I could still make it if you people wouldn't mind letting me off at the Harlingen airport. I'd be very grateful."

Teddy doled out another smile. "You do not seem to understand, Mr. Hazzard. You are coming with us."

Then he turned back to continue sorting through the briefcase. Since I'd mastered the materials in it, I'd leave it behind with no regrets—given an opportunity.

I couldn't do anything in all this traffic. If we got out on the open highway, that would be another question. Since I was being kidnaped, I could take extreme measures that might total the car, but the insurance would cover it. First we had to get out of this downtown gridlock.

The driver turned on the defroster to clear up the fogging windshield. The rain was sweeping the pedestrians from the sidewalks, but the traffic moved forward gingerly, each car leaving a wake in the flooding cross streets.

We came up to the intersection of Elizabeth and the Pan American Boulevard, where a five-way light regulated the constant traffic from and to Mexico. Just ahead, on the traffic island below the stoplight, stood a young woman, wearing orange dayglo shorts and an *Express News* T-shirt. Both were molded by the downpour to her impressive figure.

She was trying to sell papers, but since the frigid rain was slicing down in torrents, no driver was going to roll down a window to buy a soggy collection of day-old news. She kept smiling determinedly, though her curly black hair hung in dripping ringlets. Cold rain was raising goosebumps on her Hollywood starlet legs.

She looked oddly familiar.

The light changed again and we painstakingly advanced three car lengths. Up close, the newspaper seller had a perky, gamine face, with enormous eyes and sweet lips. She reminded me vaguely of Rita Madrid. In less uncertain circumstances, I certainly would have stopped to appreciate the tea-colored skin and magnificent body. Undaunted she waved the paper at my driver.

When he pointedly ignored her, she leaned over swiftly and plastered the soggy paper over the windshield.

He lowered the window six inches and spat *"Puta!"*

Before he could raise it again, she thrust a folded paper inside the window, jamming it right against his head.

I thought that was a nice response to his calling her a whore, but I was mistaken.

"Open up and get out," she commanded in crisp English, and I knew who she was.

Teddy looked up from the briefcase with a truly startled expression. Then he sighed. "Everybody out," he said, taking the case off his knees and setting it on the seat beside him. "Felicio, unlock us."

Felicio's quick cooperation didn't surprise me. After all, the woman had a pistol wrapped in the newspaper stuck in his ear. Teddy made the sensible decision. He was a professional. He could always get me again. But I'd thought he and Rita were allies.

Felicio ran down all the windows, unlocked the doors, and slid across the front seat to follow Teddy and the big man out into the rain. I was about to get out and make for the supermarket across the way when Rita said, "Not you, Cheney."

She dropped her bag of sopping papers on the island, slid behind the wheel and, ignoring the horns of the other irate drivers, expertly piloted us out into the flooded intersection where five lines of traffic competed. Then they were all scurrying to get out of our way as we blared through the scramble of dodgem cars.

"Climb up in the front," she said, making the invitation sound like what happened next would be fun. "I'd suggest you move fast. They'll be after us in a minute."

"Would you run up the windows, Rita?" I said. "This rain will ruin the upholstery."

She had time to smile before she slammed on the brakes to skid around a tortilla truck that had nosed unexpectedly out of an alley. Through the rear window, I kept an eye out for Teddy and his people, but I saw nothing through the roostertail of our wake, though I heard a lot of horns honk comments on Rita's bravura performance. She wasn't going to win any safe driving awards, but I didn't complain. Very shortly we were exceeding the speed limit on an arterial leading to the freeway.

Rita smiled briefly as we zipped through a yellow light and blasted onto the freeway. "Cheney," she said, "let's say I'm here to take care of you. You weren't doing very well. Teddy wanted both you and the briefcase."

"Strange," I said, wondering if Rasmussen had been the source of the fortuneteller's knowledge of my past she had exhibited two nights ago. I had the curious feeling I'd come in during the second reel of an action adventure. Chess had predicted I'd be meeting interesting people. Certainly, Rita fit the description. "By the way, thanks."

"It was nothing. I promised Daisy I'd take good care of you," she said, and then concentrated on her driving, which was a good idea, since we were travelling at 80 mph on a rainslicked highway.

"Is this another kidnaping or will you let me off at the Harlingen exit? Hold it! I'll let *you* off. This is my car."

"True," she said as she deftly put us ahead of a Sunday driver in a Corvette who was doing only seventy-five.

I tried something else. "Where are you taking me?"

Her smile flickered in the half-light. "Somewhere safe. Buckle up."

We were in the early going-home traffic that was filling the freeway in the direction of Harlingen and McAllen. She hit me again with a glance from her incredible eyes. "Teddy and I have political differences, and more often than not, we're on opposite sides. I rented his services in Port Isabel because I thought you might not want to listen to me. At the moment he's working for Darque. He's probably been instructed to kill you, so we'd better lose him."

I buckled up and took another look at Rita. For such a small woman, she had plenty of personal force—and the rare ability to juggle complicated situations. Although we were leading a string of traffic in the fast lane that resembled the closing minutes of the twenty-four hours of Le Mans, she still had time to keep glancing at me, catching my eye and giving every sign of wanting to become friends.

It was an interesting prospect. Once her hair was no longer being rained on, the curls sprang up and made her look quite different from the distant dark lady I'd met the night before last.

I quit my pleasant reconnaissance when I glimpsed the familiar, beat-up Volkswagen filling my side mirror. Their chassis wasn't much, but the Porsche engine was still giving great service.

"I think Teddy is on us already, but if you don't slow down, you're going to pick up a Texas Ranger."

To prove I was right about something, a cruiser in the slow lane lit up its dome lights. It was a long way back, but it would catch up in no time at all.

The rain suddenly redoubled and the visibility shut down, but Rita didn't relax her foot on the accelerator, though she did pull on the headlights. She changed lanes almost absently to cut off a Ferrari.

"Don't worry about the police. Teddy doesn't want you arrested any more than I do."

The rain and the cruiser's warning lights were slowing down the spooked traffic ahead of us. An Audi didn't respond soon enough and Rita took the median shoulder to get around it. The Volkswagen was only four cars behind us now. The Ranger simplified things by adding his siren to the light show, and very quickly it was down to our car, Teddy's and the Ranger.

The Volkswagen blinked its headlights and slowed down. Just then an old clunker, a heavy blue sedan, shifted into the high-speed lane behind us. But the fast company was too much for it because after a moment it slowed down and flipped on its hazard lights. Since the Ranger's siren had emptied the high-speed lane, the other lanes were suddenly jammed solid. The old clunker was now a cork in the neck of a bottle.

Even at max speed the wiper couldn't keep the windshield clear, but Rita didn't slow. I studied her profile and contemplated the solid line of cars we were passing.

"You're a good driver, but you can slow down now. I think that cop will have trouble coming after us. What are you going to do when he gets on the radio?"

After another glance in the rearview mirror, she smiled again, though she didn't ease up on the accelerator. The indicator stayed at ninety. "You have a lot of questions, Cheney."

"It doesn't matter because you don't answer them. What was that ambush back there all about? It can't have been just the briefcase."

"Darque will do anything to thwart Chess. They hate each other like poison. The Darque family was almost ruined by the Revolution, and Darque can't forget Chess was Villa's right-hand man."

"He doesn't have very good help—he came at me twice with no success."

"If Teddy wanted to kill you, you'd be dead," she said simply, leaving me to draw my own conclusions.

"Teddy doesn't show a lot of allegiance. He's worked for you and now for this fellow Darque. Does he ever work for Arthur Chess?"

"There's bad blood between Teddy and Arthur. They've never agreed on anything."

I looked at my watch. Three o'clock and my flight for Chihuahua left at four-fifteen. I tried what I hoped would be an inspired guess. "Do you know a man named Rasmussen?"

Rita reached out to pat my knee. Pretty hands. No wedding ring.

"Don't you feel flattered by all this interest?"

Her answer irritated me more than I would have thought possible, so I didn't say anything. Maybe I was angry. What connection did she have with Daisy? I wondered if she'd been conning me from the start.

Rita accelerated once more. "We're taking the next exit and then we'll see. We have to dispose of this car because every deputy between here and El Paso is going to be looking for it. Police don't like it when you make them look bad."

She'd saved me from a mess, but only at the cost of making me an object of police interest.

"You have a plan?"

She smiled. I'd finally asked the right question. "We're going to a safe apartment where we can get out of these wet things and change cars. I'm taking you where Teddy can't get at you."

Before I could think that through, she swerved in front of a thundering tractor rig loaded with scrap iron and at the last possible instant made the exit. Slewing through the arcing rain, we debouched twenty seconds later from the frontage road onto a local street.

At a stoplight she decided to honor for purposes of her own, I opened the door and stepped out. I slammed the door without saying goodbye and headed toward a telephone booth.

I gave her credit—she was fast to react, driving off as if my exit had been part of our plan. As I began to dial the office, I saw the battered VW gunning after her as she turned onto a boulevard.

Olimpia answered the phone, so I didn't waste time on preliminaries. "I need some quick assistance if I'm going to catch my flight. Send Esteban to the Marathon station at the first exit in Harlingen. You may hear some strange stories about me, Olimpia. Don't believe everything you hear."

Olimpia takes everything in stride. "Are you just going to stand around in that gas station?"

"No, I'll be in the Rancho Palacio across the street having a cup of coffee. The people in the VW came back."

"Esteban is leaving right now," she said and hung up.

He arrived twenty-five minutes later, and I made my flight with time enough to buy a magazine before I boarded. Both Chess and Rita spoke of Darque as bad news, but I hadn't had much of a problem with his hired help. I hoped it would stay that way.

Six

I was studying the sunset hurtling at us as we made our approach to El Paso. The western sky was clotted with bruise-dark clouds, but parts of the city were key-lit by golden light piercing the ranged peaks of the Organ Mountains. The redhaired stewardess who'd been so friendly earlier sank into the empty seat beside me and belted up. Then she frowned at the clouds that were stacked up like cathedrals.

"Terrific sunset," I said.

"I'm an ecology freak," she told me. "I feel deeply ambivalent about it. Put your seat back all the way up. That great sunset results from pollution by the tin smelter across the river in Juarez. They're not interested in the environment in Mexico. Do you know a good hotel? I'm stalled here for twenty-two hours with nothing to do."

I'd heard the Holiday Inn had a good restaurant and the best disco in town, so I passed that information along, but she had more questions. "Are you being met?"

"I hope not," I told her, and went back to my plans for pumping Epifanio Valadez the next morning and stopping Darque's clock in the afternoon. I had thought working these two cases in tandem would take my mind off Daisy, but as we eased to a stop on the runway I knew she'd be on my mind for a long time to come.

On the shuttle into town, Villa peddled tequila on billboards. The big face startled me every time our headlights caught it. The smile wasn't quite right, but the eyes were very good—ironic, dangerous, amused—evidence of every contradictory legend about him and of the persistent way his myth haunted Mexico. By now, I knew most of his legends—his audacity and savagery in battle, the childhood poverty and ignorance that could have destroyed him but didn't, and his uncommonly good sense, which protected him from treachery in every battle except the last.

The shuttle's first stop was at the Hilton, so I plucked up my garment bag and registered. I had dinner, a drink, and an early night with a message saying "No Calls."

I awoke, ravenous. Breakfast was delivered along with the message to call my office.

Olimpia was cheery, but sounded harried. "Thank goodness you called. The Cameron County grand jury has issued an indictment against you for the murder of that man Rasmussen!"

"Any details?"

"The police in Brownsville got a call saying to check your Mercedes in the Amigoland parking lot. Rasmussen was in the trunk, dead from a gunshot wound, close up. What are you going to do?"

I came alert with a start. Rasmussen was bad news, but not bad enough to be shot. He was dead because he'd talked to me. The last I'd seen of it, Rita had been driving the Mercedes. But she'd planned to dump it because of her antics on the freeway.

That left Teddy and his boys. They'd killed Rasmussen and stuffed him in the trunk before I came down to the car park. He must have been in the trunk the whole time they were driving me around.

Then I caught myself. On what basis besides her great body had I decided Rita wasn't implicated?

It was time to think and not feel. Daisy was right—I was a fool where women were concerned. But even after I worked it through again, Rita still came up clean. No one in their right mind hijacks an automobile with a corpse in the trunk.

I couldn't shake the feeling, though, that Rasmussen had given Rita the information about Luis Montoya.

"I'm coming back," I said.

Even though she tried, Olimpia couldn't keep the relief out of her voice. "Please do. I know we can get this straightened out."

"But I'm not coming back just yet, Olimpia. I have some business to take care of. You may issue a denial for me, but you don't know where I am, though you expect to hear from me soon. Ask Varga what he thinks of all this. Has Esteban left yet?"

"I will. Esteban took the late flight to El Paso last night and doesn't know about any of this."

"When he checks in, say our plans remain as made. I'll get in touch with him this afternoon. Everything will work out because we all know I didn't kill anybody."

I hung up, but I wasn't as hungry for breakfast as I had been. Being the subject of an All Points Bulletin has a way of killing the appetite. Every rookie policeman and cop buff in Texas—and there are a good many—would be on the lookout for me. The best plan was to polish off my business in El Paso as quickly as possible and then return to Brownsville and see how this can had been tied to my tail.

To avoid any undue interaction with the record-keeping public, I rode a bus out to the hostel of the Oblate Sisters. The order specialized in the care of the permanently disabled, and their hostel was just outside the center of El Paso, in the direction of Fort Bliss, one of the oldest military installations in the country.

The neighborhood outside the older parts of the fort dated from the nineteenth century. The bark of the gigantic cottonwoods was fissured inches deep, and the roots of the trees had heaved the brick adobe sidewalks into enormous ground swells. Each of the McKinley era houses occupied a full half acre. Behind the shrub hedges and large lawns, people seemed to be living peaceful lives. I wondered if Daisy had found a life like this.

The convent wall was high and the grillwork gate substantial. Despite the serenity of the neighborhood, the Sisters clearly wanted a barrier between them and the world. The brilliant morning light etched the ancient adobe in random patterns. The showy blossoms of the hibiscus filled the air with a heavy scent. It was oddly silent.

Until I rang the bell set into the adobe gate pillar, there was no sign of life within. After a decent interval, a Sister with a teenager's face behind old-fashioned steel-rimmed glasses came to the gate, miraculously managing to look cool in a heavy navy blue wool habit. She told me that Brother Epifanio would see me shortly in the *galería*. As she led me inside she said it was nice that fellow scholars had begun coming to see him again. In the past, for such a famous writer, he had not received many visitors. Now, within a week, here was a second researcher wishing to consult him.

To my knowledge, Valadez was not famous, but perhaps, in this retreat from the noise of the world, he seemed so. I wondered who'd been here before me. I put out a hook.

"It must be one of my colleagues from the University also studying the Revolution."

The Sister was ready to accept that. She nodded and smiled, pleased that the outside world had recognized the brilliance of the man her convent sheltered. "She was a great lady, so beautiful and so *simpatico*. An anglo, but she spoke perfect Spanish. Margarita was her name. Brother Epifanio was most pleased by her visit."

"*Margarita*" is the Spanish name for Daisy. Maybe I was clutching at straws, but the name stopped me short at the head of a flight of stone steps. The Sister waited till I caught up with her.

If an investigator named Daisy was interviewing Valadez, maybe she wasn't out of my life after all.

The Sister led me down into a gallery. The arcade floor was the same drab red tile seen everywhere in northern Mexico, but the adobe walls were painted a glistening white. At ten in the morning in the spring, the temperature outside must have been in the nineties, but the walls and roof of the gallery overlooking the garden had been built to create a natural downdraft so the echoing court offered a constant light breeze.

While I waited for Epifanio Valadez, I leaned against the wall and inspected the sundrenched garden through the row of Roman arches. It was a lavish bouquet, designed to delight the eye and ear, packed with flower masses of fierce tropical colors and surprising scents. The avocado trees that masked the towering walls were alive with the songs of birds, flashing red, blue, and gold as they darted down to the marble fountain whose delicate sounds filled the lush silence.

The garden was a symbol of a perfect world, in which the jays, raucously insisting on their rights to the fountain, were only counterpoint.

I was absorbing the ways in which the garden symbolized Eden when I heard the whisper of the rubber tires of a wheelchair. The Sister brought Valadez into the *galería*. Smiling but wordless, she left us.

The figure before me held himself tensely in his wheelchair. Dark glasses covered his thin face. Despite the heat, a crimson blanket lay across his knees. Before I could speak, he began. His voice was soft, tempered by years of illness and pain.

"It is noisy out here, is it not? The cries of the birds help me imagine the rest. Please, Mr. Hazzard, do me the honor of describing what you see."

Even if he hadn't asked for a description, I'd have known the man was blind. Although he cocked his head in my direction, his eyes were focused not on my face but on a point halfway up my chest.

I humored his request. "I see what look to be wild canaries, some parrots, a couple of green jays causing a lot of fuss, and a flock of bluebirds taking turns drinking and bathing in the pool. The flowers I recognize are hibiscus, marigolds, daisies, and hollyhocks, but there are many more."

He nodded approvingly. "The birds first, that means you are a man of action. What can I do for you, sir?"

I'd been thinking of him as a younger man because the articles Chess had given me always referred to Valadez as a student, but this man was in his fifties and looked much older. He reminded me of pictures I'd seen of André Gide—a crewcut so short his head seemed shaved, a face of astonishing intensity. Like Gide, he wore a beret and round black-lensed glasses. His face fell naturally into long wrinkles that could have come from frowning or smiling, and he was shaved so close his pallid skin was chapped.

Although he spoke slowly, Valadez struck me as a personality compressed like a spring, ready to uncoil violently at any second if his steely discipline snapped. Despite his attempt to project ease, leaning against the crimson pillows of the chair, he didn't look particularly happy. An embittered witness usually talks a lot.

I gave him the story I'd worked up the night before. I was a Ph.D. in history with a grant from a private foundation to see how far I could trace the Villa head, which, as I was sure he knew, had been missing since 1926.

Valadez grimaced ironically. "In 1926. Was it that long ago? Like all the others, you have a fool's errand, sir. After Villa's grave was broken into, the army quickly put a band of steel around the state of Chihuahua. It would have been death for anyone caught carrying the head. Death always rode at Villa's side. Whoever stole the head knew that and probably disposed of it long before a cry could be raised. And even if it were found now, sixty years later, how could you prove it Villa's? No one will admit to knowing the circumstances of the taking of that fierce head. Too many people want Villa erased from history."

Valadez held a sound view of history. Anything you think about long enough becomes impossible. I watched his hands, which fluttered oddly as he talked, at first motionless, and then abruptly flying from his lap like startled birds.

I was about to ask him about Daisy's visit when he spoke again. "Why are you looking for something that cannot be found?"

I did my best to sound like a professional academic. "It's a job, Señor Valadez. If I can't trace it, perhaps I can demonstrate that no one can."

He gave me a sweet smile. "All of us, male and female alike, use the lady Historia for our own purposes. I think she does not like it much, because despite our best efforts, we change very few things in this world. I once had such thoughts, to be an *historiadero* and do with her what I wished. I went seeking a graduate degree in the United States because I thought I would be made *jefe* of my little school. When my studies were done, I chose a topic in oral history, which was what we called 'hot' at the time. Quite by accident, I chose Villa, and it changed my life."

This sounded like one more of those long recitals of Villa as supernatural of the kind I'd read, so I settled myself on a stone bench beside his chair to listen to a boring saint's tale.

"It was Villa's political, social, and economic ideas—the *contents* of his head, not the head—that I wanted." He fell silent. The sunlight carved his face, which had become savagely bleak.

"Every research task drags up associated material," I prodded, but he chose to ignore me. If he'd opened up to Daisy, he might not do the same to me. Just when I thought he'd never speak again, he started up.

"I interviewed many tiresome old people in that year— his followers, his wives, locals. You can't imagine how they idolized him. It was enjoyable at first, being that close to history, and I made voluminous notes. But when I showed them to my supervising professor, he laughed at me. He denied the validity of my approach.

"You are a man of culture and enlightenment, Mr. Hazzard. May I make a request? If I am to know you, may I explore your face with my hands?"

I walked over to him and bent down. He ran amazingly soft fingers over my face and head. Keeping one hand on my chin, he ran the other gently down my neck and over my shoulder.

"*Hombre!*" he said. His hands fell back into his lap as I stepped away. When I didn't say anything, he went on. "I mean no disparagement, Señor. Gibbon once wrote that the *historiador* is a harmless drudge. You seem not like that."

I cleared my throat, feeling that some necessary ritual was being enacted. He touched his dark glasses tensely and started speaking again, his tone subtly altered.

"Originally, I was concerned to discover what the locals

knew of Villa's political ideas beyond the slogans associated with him. Apparently, that was too much."

He stopped again for so long I wondered if I had been dismissed.

"Everything is for the best. I discovered what I should have known, that history and the works of God never end."

He touched his glasses again like an obeisance. "The Lord God in His infinite mercy touched my eyes so that I might see Him in all his glory."

"How did that happen?" I asked, expecting some symbolic non-answer. He surprised me.

"In 1954, I spent three months, using Parral as my center of operations. I went up into the hills as far as San Francisco del Oro, and down to Chihuahua City. I met all the people still alive who knew Villa personally, his wives and his women as well as his *dorados*. It was all useless, of course. Neither he nor they were likely to exchange political and economic ideas with each other. But I did meet a retired banker, and a cousin of General Felipe Angeles, Villa's artillery officer. They offered more than all the rest."

I must have made a doubting sound of some sort because Valadez beat me to the objection I had been forming.

"The cousin of Angeles was a Marxist. The banker was not. Both of them agreed on a number of ideas they'd heard Villa express when he was the military *gobernador* of Sonora and Chihuahua. Also, importantly, the cousin of Angeles was able to put me on the track of some interviews Villa had given foreign journalists, among them, John Reed himself."

He stopped again. I had the odd sensation that he could see me, though I knew he was blind. "It is seldom I talk to anyone except the Sisters or my confessor, and even he has only a baccalaureate. I do not want to go on too long."

"I've come quite a way to speak to you," I assured him. "You were going to correct the picture of Villa as a simple peon who knew nothing of politics or economics?"

He smiled at his touchingly innocent younger self. "That was my intention. That was also when I discovered—" here he touched his sunglasses again—"that on some topics people do not want their ideas changed."

He bent to massage his forehead as if it pained him, but when he lifted his hand from his face, it was to display his usual disciplined smile.

"I always forget that the history part of my life is behind me. It is of no concern. If Villa is to have his story told, another will tell it. Perhaps you. If his head is your interest, I don't think I can be of help, sir."

"You were trained at a major institution. I'm sure you went to the area with more information than I have. Maybe you can explain why the accounts of his assassination speak of half a dozen men emptying repeating rifles at him, but only one, Salas Barraza, is called the assassin."

He turned his head toward the garden.

"You hear that? The desert finches have returned early this year. Usually they spend all the winter months in Ecuador."

I listened to some unremarkable chirps and peeps. I was sorry Valadez was blind and defeated, but he had something I needed. "I had thought, Señor Valadez, as one historian to another, you might help me. Apparently, I was mistaken."

The serene smile faded. "To research any aspect of Villa is to play with dynamite, Señor. I did so and for it was blown up."

"You think Villa took your eyes?"

He flinched, as if I had struck him. "You are right to chasten me. I am guilty of my customary sin, second-guessing God. If you are to discover Villa's head, you will do so, and for that you will pay your own price. And you, Señor, cannot, in all your sophistication, conceive how high that price might be."

He raised his voice as if I'd left and in my place were an audience of the faithful, but I knew he was berating himself. "God does not need my help. We are all His servants, from an ignorant *bruto* to the most sophisticated scholar or politician or businessman. I warn you, *historiador*."

His hands moved suddenly to jerk the dark glasses off his face. I thought I was prepared, but I felt an empathy like a kick in the solar plexis. His eyelids were sunken, looking like ancient wounds. He raised his maimed head to the light, challenging me.

A lizard appeared on the wall, its tiny claws finding purchase even on the smoothed adobe. It was a brilliant green, with a head the size of a walnut and a tail long enough to be a whiplash. It looked at me with tiny red eyes like the monitor lights on a video camera.

Finally, I found something to say. "We must all pay for our experience. My regrets for your price," I told Valadez.

My response was acceptable. He put the glasses back on and nodded gravely.

"Sitting here, in this cloister, I can tell you that the pain, while fearsome, was brief. At the moment, it seemed eternal. Yes. I talked to the members of what was called the firing squad, those few who were left. They had been hired by Barraza, they said. Barraza told them his motive in murdering Villa was to revenge his family honor, but he never told them where he got the money to pay them. After Villa was dead, Barraza spent a brief time in jail—months—then joined the army and retired a general. Some things are obvious, no? But I do not know who the paymaster was. Villa had many enemies. It could have been anyone."

"The same person who had you blinded?"

His smile was a blessing. "Who knows? I know only the instrument, a giant as strong as a tree. He had enormous forearms, like the comic, Popeye. I was a toy in his hands, as you would be."

Although his words were mild, sweat was pearling all over his head, starting in his crewcut and running down his starved temples, along his cheeks, almost like tears. His hands were still now, balled into rocks in his lap.

"You must know, Señor, that when my dissertation was refused, I had it printed at my own expense. I made a trifling sum from it. Fame did not come to me with its publication. One day, as I returned from school—I taught in the *Colegio Iturbide*—an old man was sitting in the living room of my apartment. When I asked how he had got in, he told me the door had been open. I wasn't frightened because he was respectable, white hair and an ancient but expensive suit of black that reminded me of my own father. He said he was a businessman whose hobby was history. He had read my book and wanted to buy my extra copies to give the work a wider audience."

"It happens like that sometimes," I said.

Valadez took a handkerchief from his robe and scrubbed his face and head. "In many ways I was a fool. I had these ambitions to leave the provincial college and make the name of Epifanio Valadez famous throughout the world. But I was not an idiot. This man spoke Spanish perfectly, but he made the mistake of offering me the list price for each volume, and no bookseller does that, nor does a businessman, not even a hobbyist."

He cocked his head to listen to the desert finches again. He must have heard something in their sound that I didn't. "In this country, too few people have too much money. I refused his offer. He was quite amiable about it, saying I was turning down a great piece of luck."

"Did he give you his name?"

"Oh, yes. Arthur Chess, he said his name was, but everyone in northern Mexico knows that Chess is a billionaire several times over and he would never have wasted his time with a schoolteacher. Three weeks later, it happened. That was long enough so that even if I saw a connection—you notice how I still use the verbs of sight, *see* a connection?—I could prove nothing. And who was I to prove it to?"

His face lost its customary half-smile. I wondered what could come next.

"Once I had an important vice. It took me places a respectable teacher at a college for men should never go. I was on my way to a regular appointment with a young man who was my friend. In front of his apartment building stood this giant of a man. He laughed as I went in, but I made nothing of it. My friend was not there. When I came out a few minutes later, the giant was waiting, still laughing."

Valadez' sightless eyes were fixed on the past. "As I came out the door, he dragged me bodily around the corner into an alleyway. I thrust my wallet at him because I knew I had no chance with the brute, but he laughed and threw it away. When he knocked me down and sat on my chest, it was like a horse rolling on me.

"He was sweating heavily and on his chest I could see a blue and red tattoo of the Holy Ghost. It was a dove, descending in flames. That was the last thing I ever saw, because he took out a screwdriver and gouged out first one and then my other eye. He was laughing, enjoying my reactions. He kept his forearm across my throat so that when I screamed, no sound emerged.

"That dove was the last thing I saw, but I see it always now," he concluded tranquilly.

"The police?" I asked.

He smiled again. "I was a homosexual whose jealous

friend had gone too far. It happens. But even if that had not been so, who was concerned about the elimination of one whose book might cause trouble? The last thing the giant said, the only thing he said, in a voice like an animal who has been taught to talk, was 'I might come again, niño.' And that is why I have given my days and nights to the constant glorification of Christ the King. He entered that beast to show me my unworthy life. It was finally a small price to pay."

One of the Sisters came in. I had other things to ask him, but I could see Valadez wasn't interested in telling me more about Villa.

"Brother Epifanio? Father Francisco is ready now."

Valadez wheeled his chair away and then spun it back around to face me. "No copies of that book are for sale anywhere."

"There are copies in private collections. I read one, which is how I found you," I said.

He didn't seem to notice my interruption. "My notes were destroyed. It was all for nothing. I have such paltry sins these days—patting your face, for instance—but it is necessary. Suerte, historiador," he said as he spun the chair around again for the Sister.

I thought that was it, but he raised his hand to stop her. "There was one line of inquiry I had no chance to pursue—a young man, handsome as a Greek god, formerly an undertaker's apprentice in Parral, Anselmo Vigil. You should talk to him, if he's still alive. If the Lord wishes you to succeed, the information will be somehow available. Adios."

I thanked his retreating chair, and after one last look at the flowers and the flocks of birds squabbling for water at the fountain, I found my own way out. Only on the street did I remember I hadn't asked him about Daisy's visit.

My talk with Valadez had taken away my appetite for lunch. Women can always confuse me, but Chess, it seemed, had conned me in a way that men seldom do. Still, I had work to do for Rita Madrid. Then I remembered again the APB out on me. We fairly law-abiding types have trouble remembering when we're the object of a police search. With that in mind, I didn't call a taxi or arrange to hire a car. Instead, I spent half an hour on a corner waiting for a metro bus to take me to the city library. Criminals never ride buses and seldom consult a library. That was my firm conviction, one I hoped was shared by the El Paso police.

The assignment I'd given Esteban would take most of the day, so I waited in the library until closing time, then phoned his hotel from a pay phone. He sounded nervous when we finally connected.

"Cheney, instead of meeting here, why don't we go buy you a pair of boots?"

I didn't know if he was being overheard or whether he thought his line might be tapped, but I always appreciate caution. When he suggested Boot World, a factory outlet for all the bootmakers in El Paso and Juarez, I agreed.

There are two ways to avoid surveillance. One is to blend into the woodwork, but Esteban chose the other way. When he came up to me in the parking lot, he made a lot of noise. "I'm telling you this place is great! I tell you, if you can't find it here, you don't want it! Ostrich, elephant, lizard, snake, calf, kangaroo, even eel. If it has a skin on it, they have it. Let's go upstairs where they keep the good stuff."

When we were alone on a balcony where we could oversee the whole store, he thrust a pair of elephant-skin boots into my hands and quieted down. "Cheney, this is an interesting town. I think Darque is the unofficial mayor."

Like most ex-Marines, Esteban habitually understates problems. He'd probably refer to the invasion of a hostile coast as a day at the beach.

"Cheney, you said you wanted to interview Darque. I let it get out that I had some interesting product to peddle, and within half an hour I was talking to his people. They keep an eye on everything in this cabbage patch."

The word in the trade is that seventy percent of all money generated in El Paso comes from drugs. That kind of commerce makes it both easy to get information and hard to take it away in one piece, but Esteban made it sound easy.

"They lean on you?"

"Not really," he said shortly. "They tried, but after I got them out of my face, I hit the bar nearest the International gate. The off-duty Customs people drop in there all the time. I didn't have to buy drinks because they were all talking about it, anyway."

Chitchat in bars supplies more confidential information

than any other source. Most people having an after-work drink will talk shop because they don't have anything else to say to their fellow workers.

"It's simple. The main Customs post gets an anonymous call saying to check the cargo of any truck that has an X marked on the rear license plate. Sometimes it's lipstick, sometimes nail polish, but always an X. When they take the load apart, they don't find contraband. Customs figures it is union trouble or maybe settling grudges among the traders because all the marked trucks belong to Tarahumara Shipping. They know it's a shakedown, but they're in a bind because they have to respond to tips. If they don't, they make the newspapers. Somebody's set up a nice protection racket using the U.S. government as enforcement, and it could work against a lot of companies, one after the other, and at different ports of entry, but nothing like it is happening elsewhere."

Esteban had done a good job and come to the right conclusions, but he didn't stop there. "I still wonder why Darque is doing it. He could make a lot more by not sharing the information with the Customs and stashing drugs in the produce because an incredible tonnage comes across the border here. Anyway, you said you wanted to see Darque, so I checked out his house. It's really something, a *palacio* with a ten-foot wall around it."

I hadn't asked Esteban to conduct a total sweep, but I can't complain when he exceeds orders. If he hadn't done it, I'd have to.

"Good work. There's no contraband in the produce because he wants to ruin the company. When he takes it over, he'll start using it as a vehicle for smuggling. His house, is it easy to get to from here?"

"You could miss it, but you'd have to try," Esteban said. "It's on the ridge overlooking El Paso."

We piled into his car and drove up toward the Organ Mountains. It took ten minutes, and we gained almost a thousand feet of altitude getting there.

"How's that for a dream palace?" Esteban asked. "Total security, and only one entrance."

Darque believed in protection. He lived in a compound at the end of a walled dead-end street. As we drove past, I could see a grillwork gate guarded by a man in a dark suit. Both gate and man looked substantial. Just outside, on either side of the street, two cars were parked, a black sedan with tinted windows and a commercial van with no windows behind the driver's seat. The cars might have been private security, but I made out a federal license plate on the sedan. That gave me an idea.

"Pull up at the first place that has a phone. An opportunity like this doesn't come often. Do you have Darque's number?"

Without taking his eyes off the road, Esteban handed me one of our business cards with a number jotted on the back. "This is his unlisted number. I thought it might be useful. You're not going to give him a warning, are you? He's perfectly capable of sending his people after you."

"I'm going to see him right now. Since the federals are photographing his visitors, he can't touch me. If he's such an enemy of Chess's, we might have a lot to talk about. Anyway, it's time I did something definitive about the Madrid case."

Three blocks down Paisano Drive we found a gas station with an intact phone booth. Darque answered the unlisted number himself.

"Mr. Darque, I'm Cheney Hazzard. Since I'm in town between planes, I thought we could settle everything over the phone."

"I do nothing over the phone. I expected to see you earlier, Mr. Hazzard. I understand you had a little car trouble, but I'll be glad to meet you now."

"Good," I told him. "I'll be arriving at your front gate in five minutes. We can resolve this today."

Darque's voice showed he wasn't used to people giving him this kind of sass, but he agreed immediately. I thanked him for his consideration and turned to Esteban.

"Drive me over and then come back here. The first thing I want you to do is call Olimpia and see if there have been any messages. There probably won't be any, but it will give you a reason to hang around the phone booth. Fifteen minutes after you get back, phone Darque again and ask for me. If they let me talk to you and I call you Esteban, pick me up and we'll catch the late flight back to the Valley. If they don't let me talk, or if at any time I call you Steve, hang up, call the Emergency number and report a fire at Darque's address. Then catch the first flight out of here. I'll call when I can."

Esteban looked doubtful.

"I'll be in no danger," I assured him. "This doesn't even qualify as cheap thrills."

Seven

Darque's guard mutely insisted I submit to a patdown search before he'd pass me through the gate. Esteban was looking worried as he drove off, but gates and guards are part of the cost of big money. As a security specialist, I know crime is a growth industry, but I prefer an earlier world when most people didn't have to lock their front doors. Darque, of course, used walls to keep the law out.

The man on the gate had a metal stock carbine slung over his shoulder, so I followed his directions scrupulously. Behind a courtyard full of parked vehicles of all sorts, there was a private garden of citrus trees and tropical vines that spread over a well-lit half acre.

A second guard led me through the palms to a three-story house built of prestressed concrete. It offered unusual wing-like roof treatments and cantilevered balconies, a very expensive architectural exercise.

My escort silently led me through the open front doors into the foyer of a vast dining room. A tall, solemn man headed up a long table. Two women and a pair of children sat with him. One of the women was a slender blonde. The other was Rita Madrid.

The sight of my lovely rescuer suddenly clarified why Darque was willing to see me in his home. After she rescued me from Teddy and his men, Rita intended to bring me here. What I couldn't understand was why she'd spun the elaborate story about Darque blackmailing the Tarahumara Freight Company. I didn't like the possibilities that came to mind.

Rita got to her feet and moved toward me, looking great in a gunmetal blue dress. "Cheney," she said, as graciously as if we'd been separated momentarily in an after-concert crowd.

"I told you we'd be meeting again soon, and here you are. I don't think you've met Mr. Darque."

From the looks of things, I'd have to play this game without a program. When Darque rose to greet me, he seemed genuinely cordial. "Mario Darque, Mr. Hazzard. My wife Stella, and our children. You have, of course, met Rita. We're having an early meal so the young ones can watch a movie. Would you care to join us in dessert? I hope you were not disturbed by the *federales* posted outside my gate. They should have, I tell them, something better to do than to keep lists of the visitors of a simple attorney."

Darque exhibited the grooming I associate with show business. Every hair on his head was in its assigned place. When he smiled and gestured, he showed teeth and fingernails burnished to a jewel gloss. I couldn't fault the light linen suit that seemed cut from some fabled material not yet available on the general market. His jade-colored shirt was also glorious, unbuttoned and of heavy silk. But instinct told me never to make the mistake of thinking Darque was just an expensive clotheshorse.

Maybe it was his body that jarred the fashion-plate look. He couldn't have been more than six feet, but his arms and legs were incredibly long for his height. He gave an impression of great strength, and there was no wasted movement whenever he did anything. Even such simple acts as rising, bowing, speaking, and indicating a place at the table showed a man who had total control over everything that mattered to him.

Calling himself a simple attorney irritated me. I decided to ruffle his calm surface. "How do complicated attorneys do?"

"As I please," he said serenely, sitting down and exchanging an amused glance with Rita. His wife looked away.

Before the game began, we'd volley for serve a bit. I sat down to scan the sumptuous room. Behind his head, over the dark fireplace, was the original of a Jackson Pollock I'd seen only in reproduction before. This kind of new money could have no legal source. Uniformed servants stepped forward to provide a place setting for me.

"We're having out-of-season pears from our climate-controlled garden, Mr. Hazzard. Please join us."

He attacked his fruit with a knife and fork. The children

sat watching this lesson in impeccable eating, their solemn dark eyes unwinking. Darque set down his fork and turned to his wife.

"My darlings can go now, Stella. Mr. Hazzard and I will talk for a while."

Rita left with the wife and children. Darque offered me a cigar and a liqueur. When I refused both, he lit his cigar and led the way out onto the huge deck opening off the dining room.

The decorative buttresses of the house jutted out, offering us protection from the night wind. Since we were on a shoulder of the mountain range, we had a fine view to the south, east, and west. The high walls in the front marched around the property unbroken except for the gate. No wonder Darque felt like a monarch. He had all the privacy he could want in his little kingdom. Trouble would announce itself a long way off.

He stood beside me, breathing deeply, perfectly at ease. I stared out over the city. Just below us the van and the sedan were still on duty. Down the street, I saw an old Volkswagen parked underneath a saffron-colored riot light that made the many dents in its roof and fenders reflect like gems. Watchers watching watchers.

Darque obviously exercised a lot of power, but with any luck, it would have the half-life of a house of cards. Representing drug interests, he was in a gaudy and violent business in which he could be killed at any moment. He knew it and, instead of being daunted by the prospect, found it exhilarating.

"I'm glad you came," Darque said smoothly. "Call me Mario. I had hoped to encounter you at my ranch in Mexico."

I scanned the brilliant city below. The moon wasn't up yet, and millions of streetlights, headlights, and neon signs defined one half of a metropolis. The darkness began at the Rio Grande, where the lights offered by Juarez, on the other bank, were few and far between.

Darque sketched the river's course with his cigar. "There, Mr. Hazzard, you have all the problems of the world, divided by a shallow river—the post-industrial country and the agricultural one, both strained to the point of bankruptcy by forces beyond human control."

"Some things don't change," I said.

"There and everywhere, drugs have become political. Coca, hemp, and opium have been used as medicine for hunger, weariness, and despair in societies that have nothing else. Now those drugs have become fashionable in the rich world, and people who had nothing now own commodities worth trading."

"Drugs were profitable long before they became political."

"Of course," he agreed equably. "It is a simple economic determinism. And I am a revolutionary."

Politicians have easy consciences and I told him so— indirectly. "The people who grow the stuff are paid in war-surplus small arms. Smugglers and dealers and their lawyers get tax-free payoffs in cash. Buy cheap, sell high. As you say, economic determinism. I can't call it revolutionary."

My anger surprised me. "The farmers use handguns against government soldiers armed with lasers, infrared scopes, automatic weapons—everything except tac nukes. Nobody else in the chain risks skin, only fines or jail time at a country club. It must be a nice living—except when you look at yourself in a mirror."

Darque didn't explode. And he didn't ask me to leave.

"Exactly my view," he said. "I have large plans and I intend to change all that. But that's for later talk. For now, you should know I defend the mules as well as the big dealers, but the mules pay nothing and the big ones pay a lot. The money, I don't touch. It goes across the border. Now, come inside. We'll have coffee and talk this over like men. You came to deal for Tarahumara Shipping. What do they offer?"

I'd never like or respect him, but maybe there was a steel core inside his thousand-dollar suit. I followed him back to the dining room. "You mistook me, Mr. Darque. Tarahumara Shipping offers you nothing. I'm here to shut you down."

I felt no obligation to tell the truth to Darque, so I pressed what advantage I could get from a carefully chosen lie. "Tarahumara uses all the modern technologies. After they played me the tape of your talk, I explained it was a standard extortion scheme, and you were using the Customs people as pawns to enforce your demands. It was a neat scam and Tarahumara was willing to pay any reasonable amount until I explained you didn't want a reasonable amount. What you want is the company."

I might have been talking to a statue. He sat at the table absolutely unmoving.

"After a series of failed and late deliveries, Tarahumara Shipping wouldn't be worth peanuts. Then you intended to buy it with the money you'd extorted from them by pretending to stop the smuggling. Very cheaply, you'd acquire a perfectly respectable front, one you could free from further inspections by getting a stop order for undue harassment."

Darque's face registered nothing. He had a lot of control. I opened up the throttle another notch. "But you made one mistake. Tarahumara is based in Juarez. When your call crossed the international border, you became subject to federal jurisdiction. Tarahumara kept the tape of the conversation."

I'd scored, but he merely smiled and nodded for me to continue.

"When I explained your plan, Tarahumara wanted to demand money damages for the spoiled cargoes as well as lost good will. I explained their greatest need was to learn the names of the spies you'd infiltrated into their business."

Darque's face was inscrutable, but I knew that he'd offer innocent people and leave his own men in place. I disabused him of that idea immediately. "I suggested the infiltrators should be delivered to a place of their choosing, alive and unhurt. If any of the people you name aren't guilty, the tape of your conversations goes to the FBI. It would take them a while to nail you, but think of the publicity, the lawyers' fees, and the prime-time television news. You'd lose a lot of customers for all your enterprises."

"You ought to be working for me, Cheney. How much to forget everything?"

Because people like Darque think anyone can be bought, a bribe is their first idea. I shook my head.

He smiled again, visibly pleased. "All right. I will comply with the terms, but in return, you tell me what Arthur Chess wanted from you."

I thought it over while he stirred his coffee. When he spoke again, he enjoyed what he had to say. "My people have thoroughly infiltrated all of Chess's operations."

He'd given in too easily. Again, I wondered what part of this case was a setup. Since he wanted to play this man-to-man, there was no point in not being frank. "My job is no secret. Arthur Chess wants me to find the Villa head. If I succeed, I imagine he'll have it buried with the rest of Villa in the Monument of the Revolution in Mexico City. Since it's public information, I'll have no difficulty telling you whatever I find out."

"Fine." He nodded. "How do I get in touch with Tarahumara Shipping?"

"They'll call you."

While we'd been talking, I had a clock running in my head. It would be four minutes before my call. Darque threw his half-smoked cigar into the empty fireplace and pressed a buzzer on the sideboard next to the humidor.

Stella and Rita came back. I thought I'd seen everything, but this man rang for his wife.

"Usually, I'm not so reasonable," he told me. Then he looked at the women. "Mr. Hazzard made me an offer I decided not to refuse."

He didn't say anything further till we all sat down. This time, I tried the coffee. It was excellent, tasting subtly of cinnamon. Darque's eyes were on Rita but his words were directed to me. "For a man who is a fugitive on a capital charge, Mr. Hazzard seems very little discommoded by his— awkward—position. Perhaps he thinks his work for Chess puts him above the law."

When he lifted his head to me, his threat was unmistakable. "Put aside all your preconceptions about Chess. He is an old man who presents the face of a benevolent billionaire, but his philanthropy requires huge sums of money. He pays well, but many have died in his service. He has very ambitious plans."

I shrugged.

Darque put down his cup as though he were going to change the subject, but he didn't. "You should visit his ranch in Sonora some time, Mr. Hazzard. Four hundred thousand acres was a large holding even during the time of Porfirio Diaz, seventy years ago. Every now and then a bill comes to the national legislature to dispossess foreign owners, but nothing happens. Such obstructiveness is thought irresponsible."

I could see the whites around his grayish irises. "I think Arthur Chess desperately wants the U.S. to annex the whole northern section of Mexico—everything from Piedras Negras to Los Mochis. Consider the millions of hectares of mineral rights and farming land that would amount to. Consider its impact on your country's economy."

Neither Rita nor Stella appeared startled by his announcement. Could an international lawyer with more than a touch of larceny in his makeup believe this insane scheme? If he did, I decided, he'd make sure he was a part of the operation. I wondered what the average person in Mexico thought.

"Chess is a private citizen, an old man," I said. Darque stepped on my words.

"What does *that* mean? Whenever your country's private citizens wanted to expand, the U.S. expanded. Texas. The War of 1848 when Mexico was robbed of two-thirds of its territory. Why, after years of neglect, did Alaska suddenly achieve statehood? Some private citizens wanted something and your government obligingly got it for them."

"This is your explanation of why Chess wants the head?"

Darque shrugged. "Every Mexican revolution starts in Chihuahua, the warehouse of storms. Villa's head can start a revolution."

I took a sip of the fine coffee. "I think the head is lost beyond finding. Besides, I've about decided looking for it isn't something I care to do."

Darque went on in a more conversational tone, but I could feel his intensity. "It isn't a case of when a skull is needed, a skull becomes available. If Chess sets up a search, the head will be found, and it will be the real thing."

I went over what he had said. If it were simply the government against a united opposition, a token would suffice to spark warfare. If that happened, the head might be symbol enough to breed a revolution which could spread like wildfire among the tinder of South America's shaky governments— and the U.S. would be embroiled in another Nam.

Darque signaled for another cup of coffee. "The other political groups in Mexico are divided into Communists, *Christeros*, PAN, and students of all sorts. Because they hate each other as passionately as they hate the government, any of these groups would give anything for the head. But it would have to be the authentic relic because the opposition would move heaven and earth to prove it false."

Darque watched the servant refill his cup.

"Chess has a good plan, as far as it goes, but we will add

one fine detail. When you find the head, you will give it to me."

That suggestion didn't interest me at all, but for Darque the matter was settled. "You work for me now. I'm sure you don't believe in Chess's fairy tale about his plans to bury the head in the Monument of the Revolution. Just as he would, I'll use the head to take over the country, but my way will be better, bringing wealth beyond belief."

The telephone fluted in a further room. After a moment, a maid came in to announce a call for Mr. Hazzard.

Darque gave me permission. "Go ahead. Your mission is important to many."

That was when Rita broke in with her first words since introducing us. "It's true, Cheney. Chess and Mario are only two of the many contestants. You will have others to meet before you finish."

As she spoke I could almost feel her hands on mine, reading the lines of my palms, the tracery of the future. It was unsettling.

I thought about it as I followed the maid down the hallway to the phone. I didn't like Darque, and I didn't trust him either. On the other hand, I'd liked Chess, but I was beginning to sense he was as slippery as Darque. I didn't speak until the maid was gone.

Esteban was right on time. His message was worth receiving. "Cheney! Olimpia said the bulletin on you has been updated. You're to be considered armed and dangerous. The last sighting is El Paso."

Somebody was turning up the heat. Chess or Darque? Traditionally, in Texas, felons labeled "dangerous" either die or leave Texas before that happens, but a fair number of them fall to the lawmen taking no chances.

"Steve, I really thank you for calling me. It's much appreciated."

Esteban didn't say anything more and I didn't have to.

Darque's and Rita's eyes were on me as I reentered the dining room. Stella busied herself with the silver coffee service. Whatever relationship Darque had with his wife, it didn't involve the important aspects of his life. I had a lot to think about and not much time for the exercise. I hadn't blown the whistle on Rita even though she was sitting in Darque's parlor, and now I was glad I hadn't. Her remark

about other contenders told me she probably counted herself
as one—unless she meant Teddy. I had to get out of Texas. If
I didn't, odds were I'd be dead in twenty-four hours.

"That was a friend of mine. He tells me that in seven
minutes, the Immigration, the DEA, and the FBI, along with
the Texas Rangers, will be descending on this address to
arrest me for aggravated murder. Let's say you convinced me
I was wrong about Chess."

From Darque's expression, I had an idea who had supplied the newest information about my whereabouts. I went
on.

"When and if I trace the head, you're going to get it, but
right now, I need help that I think Rita can supply."

"That sounds like good news. Of course, I have others
who can assist you."

"No one who can help me the way she can. Is that all
right with you, Rita?"

"Of course," Darque said before she could reply.

I ignored him and waited for her answer. Her "yes" was
superbly self-assured. I explained what I wanted. "You drive
a car pretty well. How are you with that three-quarter ton
pickup I saw out in the courtyard?"

"If it has wheels, I can drive it," she said, squaring her
mouth in a way I found charming. I should have stayed with
her from the start. We'd know each other a lot better by now.

Outside, after Rita had changed into a khaki outfit, I
thanked Darque for his cooperation and we explained the
plan to the gatekeeper. When everything was ready and
Darque had gone back into the house, I told Rita the second
part. "I intend to go with the people in that VW to the El
Paso airport. I hardly know you, but I'd like to keep in
touch."

Rita smiled, but then everybody smiles down here. I had
a dozen questions to ask her, but I put them away unasked.
The odds were we'd meet again.

Rita climbed into the three-quarter ton pickup to screech
out onto the boulevard, heading east. She was out of sight
before the sedan got moving. The federals had been on a long
stakeout, which made them slow to respond.

I hadn't expected the camera truck to give chase, and it
didn't. Standing beside the gate, I could just make out the
silhouette of a man inside the van. Still hidden by the wall, I

spoke quietly to the guard, the same one who'd been on duty when we came.

"Do they use cameras at night?"

"All night," he said, "but the camera operator is a cigarette smoker. Terrible discipline."

Distantly, I heard tires scrubbing as the sedan tried to make up the lead to catch sight of Rita.

"I want you to walk to the head of the street. If they don't stop you, stand under the light, looking in the direction the pickup went. When Ms. Madrid returns, make a big thing about slamming the gate behind her. I'll be gone by then. If the man in the camera wagon stops you, give him a hard time, demand to see his ID, the works. Try hard to take his mind off everything else."

"*Mi gusto!*" the guard said. "I have at a distance come not to like him at all."

Then he whispered "*Suerte*" and became a bulky shadow moving against the light at the head of the street.

He was halfway down the block when the van's lights came on, but the guard strode along, not slowing his pace. The van coughed into life and pulled up on the sidewalk, blocking his way. That was when I stepped through the gate and headed out. By the time I was opposite them, Darque's gatekeeper was standing close to the van driver, shouting a stream of curses in his face even though a second man was jamming a pistol into his neck.

I slid around the corner onto the boulevard, hoping the VW was still in place. It was. Of the three men watching the sedan chase Rita, I recognized only Teddy. The sallow, rat-faced fellow was new and there was no fat on the big man. Teddy wore a different outfit, a Western suit featuring stockman's pants and gold stitching on the jacket.

Teddy's friends immediately spread out to make me the apex of a triangle. Their routine was the same as the first time in the Brownsville alley. Mine was different. I strolled over to the battered little bug and climbed in.

"The federals ought to be here in about ninety seconds. So if we're going to go, let's do it now. The lady won't threaten you this time. She's driving that pickup."

Teddy's friends looked to him for instructions. He showed himself a man of initiative.

"*Vamanos!*" he snapped.

*   *   *

I hadn't been planning to visit Mexico, but with an all points out on me for murder, I was willing to leave right now. Teddy's transport might not be first class, but my guess was he'd get me there without too much in the way of border formalities.

Ristra couldn't contain his merriment at my unexpected arrival. He saluted me with what looked like a weighted cane and introduced his companions, one of whom pulled on a pair of brass knuckles while the big one showed me a familiar chromium pistol.

"I am pleased to assist you in your travel projects, Mr. Hazzard. My two *compañeros* are Imo and Jorge. Imo, get in back. Jorge, I hear sirens."

Rita's high-speed truck noises had faded, but distant sirens were winding up, Esteban's contribution to the background noise of my exit from El Paso. It sounded like a vast police dog and pony show was bearing down on Darque's cozy fortress.

Teddy pushed Imo into the back beside me like a mahout hustling an elephant. Jorge looked aggrieved, probably because he hadn't been able to use his brass knuckles, but finally he climbed in the car and fired up the engine. Teddy explained.

"Jorge's brother is in the hospital suffering the unfortunate complications of a nose broken two times. An impetuous fellow was responsible on both occasions. Now, Mr. Hazzard, you have plans and we have plans. What are yours?"

I had no intention of sharing my plans just yet. When the Porsche engine kicked in, I relaxed. If Jorge was a halfway decent driver, we'd be able to outdistance any routine pursuit. He showed his credentials by taking us out onto the freeway without any fuss. Avoiding the high-speed lane, he kept well ahead of the traffic flow by many lane changes and a judicious use of other cars for interference. Like a good ratracer, he spent as much time watching the mirror as he did scanning the road ahead.

At this speed in traffic, all his concentration would be on the road, so I checked out the other dimensions of my transportation problem. Imo, the large man, occupied two-thirds of the cramped backseat with me, and Teddy sat

beside the driver. Every now and then, in a spirit of enterprise, Imo poked me in the ribs with the tiny pistol that was
dwarfed in his big hand. He favored me with a gap-toothed
grin when he did so, which gave me an odd feeling. Imo was
clearly not too bright. Since Teddy had bent down a sun
shield with a vanity mirror on it to keep an eye on me, I
decided the big man was only muscle. Teddy was my problem as well as my solution, so any comments I made would
be addressed to him.

Once through the worst of the traffic, Jorge started
mumbling a line of complaints. I suspected I was the topic. If
I didn't make my pitch soon, his unfriendly attitudes might
coagulate into policy.

I went to work. "Teddy, both the FBI and the DEA want
me. If they set up roadblocks, you won't be able to keep me
long. Why don't we make them think I left the country by
air? I'll buy the ticket if you supply somebody to ride the
plane."

Teddy silently inspected the handle of his heavy cane,
yellow metal worked into the shape of a rattlesnake head. "I
do not have men in infinite supply."

Imo's constant nudges in my ribs with the pistol were
becoming annoying. "How about him?" I suggested. "He
takes up too much room back here anyway. I'll buy the ticket
and he'll fly south—first class. He can drink champagne and
pop macadamia nuts."

"You have that kind of money on you?"

"I have credit cards. A trail showing I left the country
will put all the government people back in their box. Then
we can go wherever you want in peace."

Teddy considered. Almost everything in Texas is negotiable.

"This offer is good for a limited time only. There'll be
roadblocks springing up like toadstools in five minutes."

Teddy gave a professional judgment. "Thirty-five minutes at the best."

There was no point making life easy for my captors, so I
looked dubious. I wanted to lose Imo. Two men are easier to
deal with than three.

Teddy continued to check the deal for holes. I had
decided he was going to turn it down when he announced
definitively, "I like that. Imo will like it too. Won't you,
Magnanimo?"

Imo put away the pistol. *"Champaña,"* he said, his crooked teeth gleaming in the blue-green floodlights as we approached the terminal entrance.

I bought a first class ticket to Mexico City from a stunning brunette and made myself memorable by inquiring about the quality of water in Mexico, the bandits in the interior, and the conversion rates of the Mexican peso. After the usual reassurances, I even filled out a tourist card, an inconsiderable scrap of flimsy paper that clearly had no serious recordkeeping purpose.

Since there was still half an hour to kill, we walked to the all-night cafeteria where Imo went through the line and, after considerable deliberation, chose two entrées and three desserts. Teddy and I had coffee, but Jorge took nothing. He sat and glared at me, the picture of a man thirsting to avenge his brother. He'd clearly cast himself as the hero of this piece.

"Imo always has an appetite," Teddy commented, ignoring Jorge's baleful glare. "I think it's part of being a pleasant person." He stirred his coffee with the wrong end of a plastic teaspoon and regarded me blandly. "Why are you making my job so easy?"

"You've been after me for a long time. Let's say I like to reward persistence. Suppose you tell me what value I have to you?"

He took his time answering, put down his spoon and stared at the palms of his hands. They were callused like alligator hide. I wasn't about to believe anything he said, but lies often tell you more than the liar intends.

"I, Teddy Ristra y Villa, am a minor functionary of a splinter political group. You, on the other hand, are the bosom companion of Arturo Chess and Mario Darque, two persons of great consequence. I will take you to the hacienda of Mario Darque in Mexico, where you will be instructed in how to carry out his wishes."

Minor functionaries never identify themselves as minor, but the reference to instruction on Darque's ranch reminded me that Aristotle said instruction is not unaccompanied by pain. If Teddy hadn't read Aristotle, Darque had.

"And there all my questions will be answered?"

"Probably *you* will answer questions," Teddy said. "When the plane leaves, we will do as you say, drive over the border. Shortly thereafter you will understand many things."

The PA announced the Monterrey–Mexico City flight.

"I want to make a call," I said. "Darque's phone is tapped by the federals. If I phone him from the airport, they'll concentrate the search here."

Teddy heard me out with a half-smile and nodded at Jorge, who escorted Imo to the men's room. When they came back, Jorge had grown a lump under his armpit. Imo gave me an *abrazo*. I handed him five twenties and the tickets and we rehearsed his story. I kept the details skimpy, because he wouldn't remember much. He'd been drinking with a crazy anglo who gave him the tickets out of pure friendship. The alibi would stand up if he did.

Watching Imo waddle off toward the boarding gates, Jorge's expression became even more dyspeptic than before.

As usual, Darque answered without saying hello. "You were right, Mr. Hazzard. We entertained many people tonight who wanted very much to talk to you, both the fire department and others with more serious concerns than a false alarm. The police were most insistent. I assured them that a member of the Better Business Bureau of Brownsville would never be mixed up in such activities. Sadly, they didn't believe me. I suggest you engage me as your lawyer."

"An excellent idea, but I decided to go off with your friends to Mexico City. I'm catching an Aero Mexicano flight in a couple of minutes. I wanted to say goodbye and thank you for your hospitality."

He didn't skip a beat. "I look forward to meeting you again."

"I'll be staying at the Victoriana Hotel in Mexico City if you want to look me up."

There are a million Victoriana Hotels in Mexico. After that, there wasn't anything to say, but I kept talking till a comforting static filled the line. The older equipment used along the border still clicks, coughs, and crackles when eavesdroppers patch in to trace the originating call.

"Well, I've made all sorts of new friends, Mr. Darque. As you said, many people are quite interested in my task. I now find I am too. *Adios*."

When I broke the connection, Jorge was still arguing quietly with Teddy about the phone call. Finally Teddy seized Jorge's shoulder in a grip that stopped all discussion. He turned to me with a bandit smile much like Villa's.

"I was telling Jorge you have played into our hands. With that call, you have ended any effective search for us and for you. Now, if you vanish permanently, it will be thought you did so of your own will."

"That's exactly what I want them to think," I said. His smile broadened.

We left the terminal. Teddy walked casually at my right side. Jorge followed basic procedures and marched three paces to the left behind me.

The Volkswagen was gone when we got to the parking lot. In its place was a black BMW limousine, an older model, but shiny from constant burnishing, a funeral director's processional car. I didn't care for the symbolism, but at least it looked roomier than the VW. Teddy watched me climb in front beside Jorge and fasten my seatbelt before he got in the back to lounge amid the deep cushions like royalty on vacation.

"You have been most cooperative, Mr. Hazzard, so we are using first class accommodations for this little voyage of ours. If you continue as you have begun, there will be only minor inconveniences for everyone."

It was an obvious threat to enforce good behavior, but in the meantime, they were taking me where I wanted to go—south of the border. I made myself comfortable. Jorge, as usual, had nothing to say to me, but Teddy kept up a lively line of talk, his way of keeping me off-balance.

"Jorge thinks I should have you drugged and dumped into the trunk, but I reminded him of the Mexican Border Police."

"Life could be easier if I knew what happened next."

Teddy ignored the hint. "Will this be your first visit to Mexico?"

"I've never been to Juarez before," I told him, trading nothing for nothing. Once across the border, I'd lose them. Then I could clear up this nonsense about my being a dangerous felon in flight from a murder indictment.

We turned off the Interstate at the Juarez exit, didn't slow down at the lights of the U.S. Customs, and rolled across the bridge in seconds to slow for an inspection station where a Mexican official only glanced at the car and waved us on.

"Unhappily, a large car impresses most people in uniform in my country," Teddy commented contentedly as we drove off. "For too many soldiers, civilians with signs of money represent their employers. Poor Mexico."

Lots of people lately had been speaking of their dedication to Mexico, a habit of mind that always makes me nervous. In every country patriots have a knack for getting people killed. Jorge, on the other hand, didn't need patriotism to want to kill me. As we drove through the dark city that was three times the size of El Paso, he picked up his litany of complaint in a wheedling voice.

"How do you expect to get results if you treat him like a bride?"

Teddy caught my eye in the mirror before he answered.

"You treat a bride gently before the ceremony and as you wish afterward," he declared merrily.

That seemed to please Jorge because he shut up and after a poisonous glance at me, watched the road.

I knew there was a federal inspection station on the highway about twenty-five miles south of Juarez. I didn't intend to create a disturbance till that was behind us. Twenty minutes later, the federal inspection station lights bloomed suddenly in the chill desert night.

Jorge turned off the ignition, pulled out the car's registration forms, and led us inside. When I handed over my permit, the sleepy-eyed private took it to an officer who lowered the coffee cup he was holding like a chalice to consult a sheaf of computer printout.

U.S. and Mexican relations are not overly cordial, but there is still information sharing about certain persons who tend to be unpopular with both governments. When the officer, an over-age-in-grade Lieutenant, finished riffling through the papers, he stood up to adjust the drape of his uniform. This required him to suck in his gut. I got ready for trouble, but he merely nodded sourly at the private.

That was when the computer printer began to mutter and extrude folds of printout. The Lieutenant cleared his throat and swung around to look at the machine. Like a magician, Teddy reached into his many-pocketed vest to hand the Lieutenant a cigar. The Lieutenant accepted the gift absently and gave me a suddenly keen look.

"If you had come one second later, I'd have been obliged to check you on tomorrow's list of undesirables. Please enjoy your stay in Mexico."

This time Teddy shadowed me as I followed Jorge back to the car at the edge of the dark parking lot. Suddenly, blindingly, a parked car pulled on bright halogen headlights. Jorge flung one hand over his eyes to shield them, jerked open the back door and brusquely motioned me inside. I looked back at Teddy to see if I was to ride in the backseat this time.

Teddy stood with his arms straight up, partially obscuring whoever was behind him, somebody who'd leaped out of the other car. When I twisted to see what Jorge thought of this, he had Imo's pistol out and pointed at me.

Nobody said a word. I figured it for a standoff until I heard a *phut* and saw blood spurt from the hole in Jorge's face. He wore no expression at all as he collapsed, but I had to give him credit. He didn't let loose of the pistol.

I took this all in while diving out of the deadly glare of the headlights. As I rolled to my feet in the darkness, I heard a second muffled *phut*! Teddy dropped into a crouch and fell gasping at the shooter's feet. Even as I watched, he curled into a fetal ball in the dust and grew still.

"Cheney. Get in the truck. We don't have much time."

This wasn't the time to consider my options. I ran for the truck. Rita had just killed two men, one of whom had been set to puncture me. As an ally, she'd do very nicely.

Eight

I can usually think of something to say to a woman, but right then, I couldn't find the exact words. *Thanks for shooting the brains out of that fellow who was going to kill me* was too understated. On the other hand, *Why did you have to kill Teddy?* sounded downright ungracious. When we were well away from the killing ground and holding a steady seventy on the empty roadway, Rita glanced sideways. "In another second, Jorge was going to shoot you. Those were his orders. He enjoyed his work."

"I gathered that. What about Ristra?"

She took her time answering. "Teddy had another objective, but he was in an unsupportable position. He was ordered to take you to Darque's ranch, but he failed, so he had to be shot. Darque would wonder at a professional of his experience being so inept. It was my only choice."

There's no point in discussing tactics after the fact, but I wondered why she should be worrying about Teddy's good reputation with Darque. Then I remembered her remark about my meeting other contenders for the head.

"So you're after the Villa head too?"

Rita's answer came immediately. "I trade in any commodity except carrion."

Hastily, I changed the subject. "Where are we going?"

"To Chihuahua City by way of Buenaventura if we're lucky, through Hermosillo if not. It's about three hundred miles of bad road. You and I will be honeymooners. You should prefer that to Mario's ranch."

No problem there. Once in Chihuahua City, I'd catch the next flight to the States and dump Chess's case back in his lap. What he had ordered done to Valadez years before told me I didn't want anything more to do with him. Then I was brought up short. Daisy had interviewed Valadez. I couldn't understand how she could be caught up in this game of deceit and death, but she didn't belong here any more than I did. Since I'd be in Chihuahua anyway, I'd talk to the man Valadez had called a Greek god, Anselmo Vigil. Maybe in talking to Vigil I'd discover what Daisy was doing down here. It might be a first step in discovering what went wrong between us.

Rita seemed content not to talk, so I got as comfortable as possible and dozed as we drove along the Mexican side of the Rio Grande Valley. The roadbed of these back roads showed me why the Baja road race is internationally esteemed as a test for both car and driver. I slept about the way I'd expected to, fitfully, waking now and then as the road deteriorated. I roused once when we turned off the river road at Agua Prieta to head south into the foothills of the Sierra Madres. I woke again when Rita pulled off the highway and turned on the cabin light.

She looked tired. "Cheney, I've had to take the longer route because Darque has all sorts of sentries out. We're going over to Hermosillo and cut from there through the mountains to enter Chihuahua from the west."

"If you want, I'll drive, but I'd rather sleep."

"I was hoping you'd say that." She turned off the lights, killed the engine, and cranked down the window before curling up behind the wheel. "Goodnight, Cheney."

Morning found me chilly but not half so stiff as I expected from sleeping sitting up. Rita, maddeningly enough, looked totally refreshed. As evidence of the progress of our relationship, she let me drive.

Once we left the Rio Grande Valley, our route took us through parts of Mexico that haven't changed since the coming of the *conquistadores*. Scanty gatherings of rock and adobe houses, usually topped with corrugated iron, are scattered through the empty desert. The town names show a lot of hope—Cananea, El Oasis, Buenaventura—but reality is introduced by trails scraped in the caliche that lead over the horizon to destinations not shown on any map.

The parched land offers sand and rock strewn sparsely with the finger cactus, saguaro, and salt cedar of the high desert—and nothing else. Here, two hundred miles from the border, the baked landscape seems dull and featureless, but then, as the vast sky presses down implacably, the great emptiness and silence of this desert combine to explode into stark beauty.

Rita said we had thrown off any pursuit. I didn't argue. We drove for hours on what had to be the only road without meeting any sign of life. Behind us stretched the featureless horizon.

Although I relaxed, I had my doubts. No one notices a transient in a city, but in the country, strangers stand out. In an area with a population density of a fraction of one person per square mile, an unknown vehicle could be a subject for conversation for days. About fifty miles north of Hermosillo, I saw we'd had only the illusion of solitude.

The muddy three-quarter ton pickup on the side of the road had a MANIMAL vanity plate from New Mexico. The rifle rack with a carbine I could see through the rear window didn't bother me. I've been in the sunbelt long enough to know the guns displayed in a truck might well be part of the purchase price. Nor was I worried at the sight of the man sitting beside the driver using binoculars on us as we passed. Country people are always curious.

When they started after us, though, I had a question.

"Friends of yours?"

Rita'd been studying them in her mirror.

"They're new to me. What are you going to do?"

"My conscience is clear. I'm going to do a steady sixty and let them pass."

They didn't pass. It took them about three minutes to catch up and move in on us. Rita watched me with a half-smile. Their bumper jolted against ours. They couldn't put us off the road without going off too, but their intention was clearly not friendly. They waved us to a halt.

No chance. I pressed the accelerator all the way to the floor and left them behind. It wouldn't be for long, and I had no hope of outrunning them, but I thought I might have a better chance up ahead.

Rita's pickup had a big engine, but the whole package was built for cargo, not speed. She tightened her seatbelt as she studied our pursuers over her shoulder.

"You think they want to get us up to speed and then shoot out a tire?" she asked in the same tone she would inquire if I wanted cream or lemon in my tea. I wondered what Rita had gone through to make her so calm when people came calling with guns.

"I don't intend to give them a chance," I said. "They may be good old boys who are out of luck hunting and just want some fun. If you're right, be sure to let me know when the copilot breaks out that rifle."

"One of them is talking into a microphone."

"That won't do." I didn't have to tell her hunters wouldn't be using a radio.

We were at the top of a long downslope that turned up at the end for a steeper hill. Here, the road was barely one lane wide with no shoulders. I could keep them from passing us on either side, so I braced my forearms across the wheel and wrung everything out of the engine. I felt a twinge of nostalgia for the Mercedes, but this would have to do.

I was lucky. The other driver lacked nerve. By the time we hit the bottom, we were off the top of the dial and our eight cylinders were growling like a cement mixer. We were probably only doing about eighty-five—the maximum I could expect from a road-tuned vehicle. Our speed fell off a bit as we started up the incline, but not much.

The driver behind me would now be much less interested in bumping me from the rear. At this speed, and with the indifferent road surface, he'd be risking himself if he tried. Another piece of luck was that his seatmate couldn't expect to use a firearm on us because the washboard roadway was jerking us up and down against our seatbelts. A bad hole almost put my head through the ceiling. Nobody could get a sight picture worth shooting with a pistol.

The pickup was jumping all around in my mirrors, but every time the driver attempted to get a pushing angle to send us off the road, I blocked him by using both sides of the road and pulling my lights on and off to make him think I might be braking. It wasn't a great deception, but nobody wants to make a mistake at that speed.

Then Rita gave me the bad news. "His friend is unlimbering the carbine."

This was getting tedious. "Get down below the window level. If they want to stop me, they might shoot you just to get my attention."

She undid her seatbelt and pulled out a big purse from under the bench seat. Only after she jammed it against the seatback and braced her legs against the dash did she slide down below the window line. "Your courtesy will be repaid someday," she said composedly. Given that position, even if we rolled, she'd be in the place of maximum safety.

The way my luck had been running lately, I didn't know why I felt so confident, but I did. And my optimism was rewarded. Just as we topped the hill and came out onto the next plateau, I saw it, a quarter of a mile ahead. It was a narrow cement bridge over a dry arroyo.

Rita felt the loss of acceleration as I hit the brakes.

"Giving up?"

"I will never surrender," I said, quoting a hero of my youth, "though they may think so. Stay down there."

They came over the crest in time to see me screech to a stop. The dust we stirred up enveloped us, and the gravel on the bridge approach was still rattling down the steep banks of the road. By jamming the brakes, I had pulled up just short of the bridge. A curtain of smothering heat immediately settled on us now that we weren't moving.

The bad guys hadn't been making much progress, but now, as far as they could see, I was giving a good imitation of a sitting duck. To help them along, I sat behind the wheel with my hands locked over my head, the picture of a man totally out of ideas. They rolled past me and cut in ahead, just like highway patrolmen.

For a change, everything worked perfectly. They were husky types, rednecks in wide-brimmed silver belly Texas Ranger hats and khaki pants. They both wore gunbelts, so they were full of confidence when they piled out and split up to keep us between them. The copilot was so cocky he left the carbine inside.

I executed phase two. I had the pickup in drive with the brakes on. Keeping my hands locked over my head, I let the truck inch forward. When our bumpers made contact, I floored the accelerator, then hit the brakes.

They could see what was happening, but they couldn't do a thing about it. They watched open-mouthed as I flipped their pickup off the road, over the narrow shoulder, and down into the ravine. It rolled three times and landed in deep sand. Then it caught fire. Little flames skittered across the sand. Yelling curses, they watched us drive off. They were on foot miles from nowhere. More importantly, they couldn't use their radio.

I looked away from the mirror to see that Rita was kneeling on the seat. She had conjured up from her knapsack-sized purse a revolver as big as a monkey wrench. In the professional way, she was using both hands.

I kept up the speed that was too much for the mediocre roadway till another ridge hid us from view. Only then did she make a small sound as she let out her breath.

"I'm glad I didn't have to shoot them."

"I thought you liked shooting people."

Still holding the revolver, she studied my face. "Last night there was no choice. Jorge would have shot you and then me."

As she spoke, I changed my mind about Rita Madrid. Before, with her cheekbones that owed nothing to a dentist and a creamy, flawless skin, I'd thought she was a world class model and not much more. But there was a lot more than fashion magazine polish to her. In the years to come, her looks would, if possible, improve. This woman had a personal force that time could never touch. She knew who she was and it gave her an assurance that added a rare and precious character to that perfect face.

I must have been ready to fall in love again, because when she looked up from under dark lashes with eyes greener than spring grass, every alarm circuit I had went off. The last time I felt like this, Daisy Pruitt had ignited these emotions, but she had gone, leaving no forwarding address. Someday, I was certain, looking into the depths of Rita's beautiful eyes, this woman would ask me to do something crazy. And I'd probably do it.

"Let's not be morbid, Rita," I told her and felt better.

I always melt when a beautiful woman saves my life. This one had done it twice. Since I've spent a lot of time rescuing other people, it makes a nice change.

"If you'd shot that thing off in here, we'd both be deaf. Why didn't you use that silencer you had last night?"

"This piece has greater penetration than a Beretta," she replied. I sighed. She was a gun buff.

I could see tiny diamonds of perspiration at her hair line. Whatever she is, it's all right here. Keep talking and maybe the thrill will ease off, I told myself. It didn't work. You have to feel a little mushy about women who are ready to kill for you.

I compromised in stating my feelings. "I like a woman with domestic accomplishments," I told her. "Please warn me about any others."

We continued south on the unnumbered road that led to Hermosillo. In Texas, it would have been classified as a seasonal highway, but in Sonora, this was the only road from Fronteras, and it desperately needed basic repairs. The road that forked east from it had an advisory sign in English and Spanish promising Dubious Road Conditions at *All* Times.

The sign should have read No Transit. Our speed dropped into the twenties after we chose what started as a country road and gradually degenerated into a cart path. A little later, the path explored such off-road choices as watercourses, animal tracks, and a dry riverbed. When we spent over an hour traversing eighteen miles, I remarked that this route reminded me of a poem about the road not taken.

"Since the destinations are unimportant, the road will not be improved in this century," Rita said. She had stretched her khaki-clad legs straight out and now sat with her arms folded across her chest, gazing serenely at the barren land that was starting to ascend into the craggy peaks of the Sierra Madres. "The only people who live here in great numbers are the Tarahumara Indians and the few anthropologists who want to study their primitive society. Tarahumaras don't vote. For our purposes, that's just fine."

We slept that night at seven thousand feet in separate sleeping bags in the back of the pickup. We hadn't passed a village in hours. About two in the morning I came abruptly awake to discover my sleeping bag was half unzipped. I wasn't just cold. I was freezing.

"Help me," Rita ordered. "Don't just lie there." She was kneeling beside me, outlined against the starlight as she worked at the jammed zipper of my bag. I slid out to make things easier while she unzipped it to re-zip both bags together.

"I gave up waiting for you," she told me crossly.

There was no answer to a statement like that, and I was shivering too hard to make one. When I was warm again, I'd think of a suitable response. I climbed in to clutch her to me, embracing everything available. I was still cold, but this was a distinct improvement.

In a pleasantly short time we were both warm and much better acquainted. When I smothered a laugh, she asked what was so funny. Her breath tickled my neck.

"We don't really know each other but you've killed two men for me, offered to kill two more, and now we're wrestling around in a sleeping bag."

She turned away from me to arrange herself in the classic spoon position.

"This is *much* better," she said.

The time was ripe for an apology. "Much better," I agreed. With that, I'd exhausted the possibilities for conversation. I wasn't cold anymore. I'd been sleeping before, though not very comfortably, but now I was wide awake.

I inspected the stars and thought how infinitesimal we were, two human beings clinging together for warmth in a vast and frigid universe. Considering the dimensions of the cosmos didn't help. Despite the distractions of philosophy and ethics, I could feel myself responding to our intimate situation. In a moment, Rita would know it too. She hadn't said anything for a long while. Maybe she was asleep. Gingerly, I tried to back off from her exquisite form without awakening her. She inched after me, tucking herself up against my increasing embarrassment.

"You feel very much better to me," she said, turning around to face me. "Are you thinking about an escape?"

A complex question, but it had a simple answer, and I gave it. "No."

Of course, then there were all sorts of subjects to pursue, and we discussed them at great length in the only possible way—without saying a word.

We ate breakfast in the pickup, chewing on dry tortillas she'd taken from her knapsack purse. They tasted good. The only thing I missed was coffee.

"Tell me about yourself," I said, thinking that now all the preliminaries were out of the way, she'd explain her complicated relationship to Chess and Darque.

Rita chose to understand my question as a request for autobiography, but in her answer, she seemed to be describing a distant relative. She was born, she said, at Guaymas, in Sonora. Her parents were an anglo mining engineer and the granddaughter of an *hacendado* who'd come through the Revolution with his holdings intact. Her father had insisted on a schooling in the States, but her mother had made sure it was a proper Catholic education. When her father died in a mine accident, her mother brought her back from the convent and immediately married her off to Raul Darque.

"That meant I had a large family for the rest of my life. Even when Raul died, Mario would be my brother-in-law forever. He and I do not agree on any political topic, but he is still my brother. Mario's wife Stella has all sorts of money, but Mario is only the younger brother, and since Raul was the family favorite, Mario will spend the rest of his life trying to outdo him. Even with Raul dead, it's still true."

Such family ties always puzzle me, but then I grew up without a family, so it's a part of life about which I know nothing.

Just then, we came to a deep fissure in the roadway. The winter's rains had cut a gash two feet deep right across the road and one side was sheer cliff, the other, steep hillslope. There was no going around. It took us almost an hour to collect the stones and stumps for the temporary fill. I was bushed and must have looked it because Rita offered to drive. I insisted it was my turn, saying I wanted to hear the rest of her story.

I'll never understand women. Whatever it was I'd said wrong, her look was almost unfriendly. "You heard the story I usually tell. Here's what really happened, which isn't so nice. I grew up in L.A., in the *barrio*. My mother left when I was too young to remember, so I don't know if I'm a U.S. citizen or not. The summer I was sixteen, my father was in jail and Raul Darque picked me up in the parking lot of a Westwood shopping mall. He liked young girls and made me an offer I was glad to take. He was thirty-one, an established lawyer in the state of Sonora. I thought my life had become a movie because this clean, good-smelling man was taking me to Mexico to be a millionaire's mistress."

She gave me a sideways look. I smiled encouragingly and wondered how much truth there was in either story.

"Raul married me. Once in Mexico, I found out Raul was better than a millionaire—he was a man with a large future in politics. He was smart, handsome, rich. He had only one fault. He was an idealist. His talents could have made him a PRI candidate, but Raul made the mistake of taking the wrong side in a labor dispute at Los Mochis, a sugar-refining town on the Gulf of California.

"He was a good lawyer and shouldn't have lost the case. When he did lose, he decided the Institutionalized Revolutionary Party would never bring justice to Mexico. That's when he made a second mistake. He ran for the state legislature against the party. His final mistake was to win. If he'd lost, he would have learned it was futile to go against the party."

A hot, dry wind had sprung up. The western sky, which had been as bright as brass, filled with stinging sand. I was ready to call it a day. I felt filthy and exhausted. Driving on this road, even at ten miles an hour, required at least forty decisions a minute. With the added effort of trying to see through clouds of blowing dust, I soon had a killer headache.

Ten minutes later we came to a town that Rita said was Tecoripa. There was a gas station and a tiny hotel with an attached restaurant. The hotel, a two-story in the territorial style that dated from the last century, didn't look like much.

Nothing was said about air conditioning, but it did advertise showers.

We decided to stop. We could take a nap and then drive on during the night to La Junta when it was cooler and the dust storm had departed. We took showers and ate a meal that made no impression, good or bad, and walked back in silence to our darkened room. Rita pulled the coverlet off the bed and sprinkled the sheets with water from the pitcher in a basin on the vanity.

"It will make the heat more bearable," she explained.

We stripped and lay down. She was right. As long as I didn't move, it was almost cool enough. Her eyes on the ceiling, Rita began to talk. I listened neutrally, as much because there was nothing else to do as from curiosity about this woman who was Mario Darque's enigmatic sister-in-law.

"You see, the PRI isn't a party so much as a machine to win elections. They will welcome a man from the opposition, but only after he has learned his lesson and painfully lost an election to them. But that didn't happen to Raul. He won, took his seat in the legislature, and immediately began to see opportunities for the kind of democracy he'd studied in the National University. Once elected, he rallied dissidents with his white papers about the venality and corruption of the state of Sonora."

She stopped to yawn and stretched out her bare arms to slip off her wristwatch before going on. "Do you mind if we nap now? My sleep was interrupted last night, and my eyes hurt."

I was ready enough, but after I closed my eyes, her small, precise voice continued, telling a story that was anything but tidy.

"Raul worked very hard, and he was successful. He established a group of young politicians called *los colmillos*, the fangs. The name was to call attention to their opposition to the money bribe of the *mordida* which is so central to Mexican life. Their slogan was that they could only be bribed with political freedom. It was a time when all things seemed possible."

The wind started up again. I could hear it slapping at the blinds and lifting the cheesecloth curtains in the open window so they snapped with a popping noise like little whips. It was cooling down. I was half asleep.

"So there I was, sixteen, uneducated, married to a man everyone admired or feared. The only part of my life that was not public was my life at night with Raul. As he got more and more caught up in politics, he had less and less time for me. That was when Mario came around to whisper to me. He wasn't married then, and I think he saw me as some kind of a challenge—a way to hurt his big brother.

"In time, with nothing else in my life, I gave in. It was a situation that couldn't go on indefinitely. Not with Mario. He and I went to bed once and I was no longer interested. But the politics—that couldn't go on either. There were all sorts of warnings, but I was full of myself, bored, and I paid no attention.

"They began with obscene slogans on the walls of our home. Then Raul's car was firebombed. But even that didn't stop him from making public statements to crowds so large the newspapers had to report them. Then he made his last mistake. He announced himself as an independent candidate for governor."

She was suddenly silent and I wondered if she'd dropped off to sleep. I caught a scent of her distinctive perfume, elusive, warmed by her flesh. It set all my predictable responses jingling. When she spoke again, her voice was hard.

"Decisions about who will be a candidate for governor in the states of Mexico are made in Mexico City. The evening of the day Raul announced his candidacy, an oil tanker broadsided his car as he was driving home. They say the explosion was incredible. The police couldn't discover a thing about the missing truck driver or even whose truck it was. But they handled the traffic very well for Raul's funeral. They all wore white gloves and looked very sober."

She choked back a sound that might have been a sob. She turned on the bedside lamp and I saw she was lying there, facing me. Her eyes were tearless but sobs spasmed in her beautiful, naked body.

"Those damned white gloves," she said harshly. "And they were so courteous to the politician's child bride. They wore those ridiculous gloves and came to attention any time my eyes fell on them."

"It's over," I said, putting my arms around her, knowing all too well that nothing is ever over.

"Raul," she said, in a frail voice.
"Call me Cheney," I said softly.

Nine

We started on the last leg of the trip after sunset. I felt great. I'd had some sleep, two meals, another shower, a shave, and a change of clothes into a set of khakis Rita miraculously produced from a bundle.

The fragrant air was cool, with a promise of being cold later. I'd done a lot of thinking about Epifanio's story of his blinding. Even as distant as he felt about this world, he'd suggested I should talk to Anselmo Vigil, the handsome young man who possessed important knowledge. I was going to see Vigil, but after that I intended to charter a plane home. Back in Brownsville, I'd straighten out whoever was framing me for Rasmussen's murder.

Once more aboard the truck, this time with me driving, I started a systematic interrogation, the sort of thing you can't do while the woman you're questioning is in your arms.

"Rita, you said there were other contenders for the head besides Chess and Darque. Who are the others?"

"Whoever represents the *Partido* wants that head at all costs. They may be represented by all sorts of people." She put her hand on my cheek. "I can also reassure you, Cheney, that I am not a participant in this mad race for a scrap of dead flesh. Think of me as an umpire."

That was all I'd learn on that subject. I went back to a topic that interested me more. "When we were interrupted this afternoon, you were a sixteen-year-old widow. How did you graduate from that to a professional bodyguard?"

Till that instant, she'd been vivacious, but she continued her story, again in the tone of a bored student reciting a biography for an uninteresting class assignment.

With Raul's murder, Mario became the head of the Darque family. He moved to El Paso, passed the bar examination, married Stella for her money, and established a successful law practice. Rita took back her birth name, enrolled in the University of Texas, and majored in political science to discover what had gone sour with Mexico's revolution. She earned an honors degree but wasn't satisfied by any of the standard scholarly explanations. It was because Mario expected to establish her as his in-house mistress that she said yes when the CIA recruited her.

"Was that where you learned about weapons and driving?"

"I went through all the orientation and training and did well. When I fully understood the policies I was expected to support in Central America, I resigned."

"That's nice to know," I said. "You have some talents I couldn't explain otherwise."

"Do you feel better about me now?" Her voice was teasing.

"I've always felt very good about you, Rita, ever since the night we met. When you delivered me from Teddy Ristra's thugs in Brownsville, I became a real fan. And in case you're wondering, there was no real need to come on so strong this afternoon."

I sensed rather than saw her smile, both innocent and depraved. "This afternoon was entirely for me, Cheney. I wasn't thinking about you at all. I don't have the standard female attitudes about sex."

She traced a light pattern with her nails up the inside of my thigh. Even through the thick cotton of my khakis, her touch was fire.

"You see?" she said, "a touch is all it takes. Don't worry, we can still be friends, but only friends."

I didn't doubt that. Not then or afterwards.

"You have a lot of valuable and expensive talents. What did you do after cashing out of the CIA?"

"I met Jesuita Contreras. She showed me how inadequate my values were in the real world."

"Is she the godmother you and Daisy share?"

"Yes. You could say she converted me."

Rita offered lots of surprises. I understood she'd slammed the door on any more personal discussion. I asked if her conversion had meant a new career.

"Politics don't interest me. It's the one thing I learned from Raul. Unlike his brother, he truly wanted to serve the people, but people don't need politicians, they need food.

Ever since I've understood that, I haven't enough hours in
the day."

The tone of her voice told me she wasn't talking about
anything as simple as bread. Religions of any sort have always
fascinated me because I can never understand their appeal.
But it always impresses me how any kind of belief can make
people better or worse than they would be without it. Since I
discovered early in life that people don't appreciate objective
discussions of a complex of emotions that holds their world
together, I didn't ask further.

Rita must have felt the same way because she changed
the subject quickly. "The important thing that will happen in
Chihuahua City is your meeting with Vigil."

My doubts about her surged back. How did she know
that I wanted to question Vigil? "Who are you working for,
Rita—Chess or Darque?"

She reached over to pat my knee. "When you know all
that I know, you'll find we're on the same side, Cheney."

Predictably, that made me angry, so I didn't say anything
more. Switching drivers every two hours, we kept going up
most of the night. By moonlight, we climbed an old smuggler's
trail through a pass of exposed rock in the *cordillera* of the
Sierra Madres.

False dawn was lighting the eastern sky when we finally
reached the crest. From there on, we began overtaking farm
wagons and people walking with burdens on their backs. Rita
explained the carts were going to the markets at Cuauhtemoc,
but the walkers would catch a bus at La Junta for Chihuahua
City and we would do the same.

La Junta was a wide spot and a couple of adobe ruins,
but next to some of the villages we'd driven through, it was a
metropolis. As I pulled up to park under some trees, Rita was
ready with her parting advice.

"I'll buy the tickets, but on the bus, we will sit apart.
The city is only three hours away. Mario will have sentries in
Chihuahua looking for you. I'll try to lead them off. Since I
might not be successful, I have something for you. Take them."

She had pulled another surprise out of her purse. In the
overhead light of the cab, I saw a Mexican passport and what
looked to be a U.S. green card, a work permit allowing the
bearer to work in the States.

"I don't need these, Rita."

"You forget that the police are looking for Cheney Hazzard. Luis Montoya is a useful name for you."

"Why Luis Montoya?"

She shrugged and then gave me a quick kiss on the lips as she got out of the pickup. "It's a common name in Mexico. Why not?"

Rita's beautiful face became grave. "You must not underestimate Mario Darque. He's very clever and he doesn't like to be thwarted, which you have done several times already. You can be sure he has a suitable punishment already in mind."

She returned in minutes with my ticket, nodded as if we were strangers, and disappeared into the gray haze of the pre-dawn. When the ancient bus came rattling and groaning down the road from Ciudad Guerrero, she was nowhere to be seen. I left the keys in the ignition and climbed aboard the bus. Only after I was seated and the bus was half full did she get on, leading an elderly woman in a black mantilla to a seat in the rear. She passed me without a glance. For my part, I was fascinated by the elaborate on-loading of a brace of blackface lambs. They were tethered to a post on the roof, ready for the market in Chihuahua City. I hoped that wasn't my fate.

It was broad day when we finally rattled into the outskirts of Chihuahua. To make sure I lost any welcoming committee that might be awaiting me, I joined a christening party that asked to be let off the bus near a tiny church on the edge of town. In a crowd, I'd be safe, but since Mario's men were looking for an anglo on the run, it wouldn't take them long to find me.

I walked with the christening party until I saw Avenue Juarez, a street that in Mexico invariably leads to the center of town, then I wandered off as inconspicuously as I could. I was in luck. I found a dingy haberdashery incongruously called Rodeo Drive, which was just opening.

I bought a lightweight biscuit-colored suit of not too extreme a cut, some pure cotton shirts, and the information that the *zapateria* next door was run by the owner's brother-in-law. There I bought shoes, as well as a suitcase to put the extras in. After the pants were cuffed, I looked respectable enough to go anywhere, but more important, to rent the car I needed to reach Anselmo Vigil.

* * *

Vigil lived in Ciudad Camargo. According to the tourist
pamphlet supplied with the rental car, the city was founded
in 1740 and had remained small, despite being older than
Chihuahua City. I coaxed the rented Pinto up an abrupt hill
and past the stockyards into Camargo.

The old man who served the local Pemex pump looked
like an Aztec chieftain, but he was full of talk, mostly answers
to questions I hadn't asked. The Vigils, he told me, were an
important family. Anselmo and Margarita had come to town
in 1923 and set up the general store. His next bit of news
wasn't good. Anselmo had died five years back.

My eager informant went on to tell me that the widow
Vigil had the double dignity of being a matriarch and the
president of the family business. The Mercado Vigil, he
reported, was just over the hill. Without prompting he added
that Señora Vigil was an educated woman. When I looked
noncommittal, he said she had more knowledge about Pancho
Villa than anyone else in the district. That didn't reassure me,
but I followed his directions to the Mercado Vigil anyway.

Margarita Vigil's son, a dignified, taciturn man in his late
sixties, heard my story and seemed pleased to lead me into
his mother's presence. As he parted the curtains which
separated the store from the Vigil home, I felt like an
ambassador from some barbaric nation visiting the imperial
court. Her overstuffed chair was obviously the center of the
household, a throne only steps away from her bedroom,
where I could see a canopied brass bed dressed with an
elaborate ruffled white chiffon spread.

Margarita Vigil was in her late seventies, still dressed
like a belle, looking both gaudy and frail, like a *piñata,* the
hollow paper construction they stuff with toys for children's
parties. My heart sank. I didn't expect anything much more
substantial than a party favor when I sat down beside her.

Under eyebrows that had been worn down by the ravages of time, her enormous dark eyes were skillfully outlined
with mascara. She regarded me inscrutably from behind a
face that could have been tissue paper stretched over a skull.
While she pondered my greeting, she reached out toward the
small blaze of the piñon hearth fire to collect warmth to heat
her tiny body.

The framed photographs on the table beside her chair, pictures of Margarita when young, convinced me that Villa would have been interested if he'd met her—but then he'd been interested in every woman he ever saw. Margarita wasn't senile—she clearly still made policy for the store below us—but what could she have to say about Villa? Nothing more, I decided, than what could be expected from any young girl growing up in the same area as a national hero.

Her son introduced me with stiff formality and, in Spanish, gave an account of my presence. She dismissed him with a wordless nod and waited until he disappeared before she spoke.

"Everyone is dead," she told me in a voice which was scarcely a whisper. I leaned closer.

"Everyone of my gallants has ridden into the darkness, leaving me alone with memories like smoke."

I was about to thank her for her time and go downstairs to have a beer with her son when a white-hot piece of burning wood popped out of the fireplace onto her long skirt. I flicked it back into the fire. Then I brushed off the soot it had smeared on her skirt.

That was when our conversation really began. Her eyes kindled in timeless merriment. "Many women have said they knew Villa intimately. But my relationship with him was different."

From my readings I knew that every woman who had anything to do with Villa was convinced she was unique in his experience. I knew the role I had to play.

"I'm sure it was a special relationship," I assured her. "The General had superb instincts."

She reached out for the fire as she slowly closed and then opened her eyes wide at me. She inclined her head majestically.

"All Villa's women had a special relationship with him. When Villa was with you, he paid attention to you as an individual, recognizing that every woman is different."

I got comfortable. If there were truth to the idea of reincarnation, I'd like one life as a poet chronicling the legends of fair women.

"If he had married us, we would have had to fit into his life and dwindle into a wife rather than remaining true to our inner selves. His official wife had a terrible time. She raised dozens of stepchildren while she sat waiting for his return. The rest of us are more fortunate. We have brilliant memories."

Most of the important things I know, I've learned from women. And here was one telling me that perhaps Daisy didn't want to fit into my life because she had her own priorities.

"I had a child by him."

I smiled encouragingly, though the story was not unique. After Villa's death, hundreds of women came forward, each dragging a child by the hand.

Her eyes met mine piercingly. The years fell away for both of us. "I had a ghost baby by him."

I remembered my friend Varga's words—Mexico is full of ghosts.

"I was very young when my parents moved to Parral. My father was an officer, a Major. You know, after Villa had made peace and retired to Parral, they always kept a company of *federales* there. You can imagine the stories about him, a man who required a full company of soldiers to watch him when all he did was ride horses on his farm, go to fiestas given by his friends, and drive his large automobile on the highways.

"On my sixteenth birthday, I saw him. He was driving his Dodge car, going very fast, his hat brim bent back over his forehead and his mustache streaming. He waved at me.

"Listen carefully, *Señor* Hazzard, and do not be so smug. I saw Francisco Villa that one time alive and once more in pictures after he was dead, murdered in his car. I could not attend his funeral, but I saw him many times after his death. Would you like coffee?"

When I said yes, she rose to walk slowly out to the kitchen that opened off her parlor. Our talk had taken place against a background of children and adults in the kitchen watching a television drama called *Un Amor Prohibito*. She certainly didn't lack for company, and there was no sign that her mind was out of touch.

Margarita returned, leading a small boy who carried a heavy tray loaded with silver pots and china cups. She waited till he served the coffee and left.

"Villa visited many women after his death, you know. Sometimes he would appear to them as an eagle, sometimes as a serpent. He was surely a witch, don't you think?"

"He was a surprising person alive," I conceded carefully. "Manifestly, he would be surprising dead."

"To me," she went on, her face slowly creasing into a smile that showed me the girl who once had bloomed there, "to me, I say, he appeared as a man. A terrifying figure of a man—large, strong, imposing."

She looked past me at the arrangement of pictures, statues, and religious plaques on the wall. The framed photo of Villa, I noticed, was at the center. I thought of her as a young woman. She'd been close to her sexual initiation, bored by a cloistered life, full of ambivalent feelings about her father. Villa was a symbol of wild freedom, a man around whom her awakening sexual impulses could coalesce. Several times a grandmother, she still kept the Villa altar. She smiled again, her eyes still focused on the wall.

"You must know that my father feared and hated Villa. It had been a happy day for him when Villa was assassinated. With Villa dead, he expected a new assignment in Mexico City and a promotion. For me, it was the saddest time. Villa had been so full of life."

Everyone who knew Villa told the same story. For all of them, he burned with an unrelenting energy like the sun's. It was this energy Chess and Darque hoped to harness to rekindle a revolution.

She went on, leading me into a story that was a secret garden in her memory. "My best friend and I heard the priest at our church announce that Villa was in Hell. But we refused to believe it, and we both began to dedicate all our prayers to get him out of Purgatory. Soon, my friend lost heart, but I did not. I bought a picture of Villa in the car of death and kept it under my pillow. When my mother found it and told my father, he beat me. Then he called the priest, who told me again Villa was in Hell. When I again refused to believe it, he told my parents that I had a vocation as a nun because only a bride of Christ would have such an idea. I had no words to fight with, so I went to the convent to escape my parents. That was when Villa began to visit me—in my cell, after lights were out."

Freud was a real spoilsport. Her interesting story was a textbook example, *The Case of Margarita V.* She kept smiling encouragingly at me, speaking as if the story had happened to someone else. It had, I thought—to a girl in her teens, more than sixty years before.

"He came to me the first night I was in the convent, when I was alone and terribly frightened. He looked horrible. He carried his head under his arm like a helmet and the wounds on his throat pulsed fountains of blood, but his voice reassured me. 'Look, *Chiquita*, Villa is in a bad way too, but I am not down in my heart.' That was the first thing he said to me. He thanked me for my prayers, which were indeed useful to him in Purgatory."

"When did this happen?"

"November the second, All Souls' Day, in 1923. That proved to me he was in Purgatory because that day is for such souls. It proved something else."

The silence ticked on, filled only by the crackling flames and the low sounds of the television in the next room. "It was exactly one hundred days after he was assassinated. That meant he would one day go to Paradise."

Chess had said I'd meet interesting people. She put down her coffee cup and answered my unspoken thought.

"After I let the nuns know I had no vocation, I returned home and told my friend. But she was no longer interested in Villa. Like my parents, she was scandalized by me."

"Is your friend still alive?"

"She died in childbirth some years later, just after I married Anselmo, her brother. He did not wish to continue his family business, so we moved here and founded our store."

"How long did Villa continue to visit you? Did he come after you were married?"

She sat up straight. "Of course not!" she said, pointing in the direction of the picture which I now saw was not Villa but a look-alike. "He would have had none of that. Besides, before Anselmo and I married, I had my ghost baby by Villa."

"Would you tell me about it?"

"It is what I am doing, Señor," she said tartly. "Villa came to me one night at the convent and said his name must not die and I must carry it on. Then he had correspondence with me, even though I was and remained a virgin."

In her wrinkled face, her eyes sparkled with mischief. I'd heard of hysterical pregnancies, but this was outside the usual context. During the Middle Ages, she'd have been burned as a witch who'd had congress with Satan.

"He visited me every night I was at the convent until I began to grow big. That was when the nuns sent me home. The night I returned to the house of my parents, Villa visited me for the last time. He said things had not worked out correctly, that our child would not be born because it would resemble him in Purgatory, not the perfection he would know in Paradise. But he consoled me. He said I would have other children and he would return to me soon, all complete. Then he embraced me once more. I was devastated, but when I awoke, I no longer carried his child."

"But you were still a virgin?"

She gave me a glance that said I was too bold and then forgave me in an instant.

"The next day, I met Anselmo. Then I understood what Villa had told me."

I had the oddest sensation that what she was about to say was important beyond words. "Told you what?"

"As Villa said, to love a ghost would not have been perfect. So he arranged for me to fall in love with Anselmo, a man who resembled Villa as one hand resembles the other. He said I would wed him when he was whole, and I did. If Anselmo had not come wearing Villa's head, I should still be awaiting my first love. But Anselmo made my life a garden."

A loud commercial for *masa harina de los Cuaqueros* terminated the *Amor prohibito* drama on television. Margarita didn't notice. She was sorting through a shoe box crammed with letters and pictures. She handed me a postcard that showed the dead Villa slumped over the wheel of his bullet-riddled Dodge touring car.

I looked at the familiar photo, one of thousands sold after Villa's assassination, then at my hostess, who sat watching me with an expression I could not read. "I no longer need it," she said.

"*Gracias*, Señora Vigil," I said, wondering why I was tempted to say her virtue would be rewarded in Paradise.

"Have you no more questions, Señor?"

My eye fell on the picture of her husband Anselmo. As she said, he was the handsome image of Villa. I remembered Valadez in his monastic garden. I pointed at the picture.

"How do you know your husband was sent by General Villa, Señora Vigil?"

"He told me. He had been working as an apprentice *embalsamador* and when he saw what had to be done to the General before the funeral, he said he wished for another occupation."

"Embalming is a grisly task," I said. "He certainly made a good choice when he decided to become a *mercader*. He was successful in great measure."

Margarita shook her head to show I had missed her meaning. "It was not the work itself, he told me. He said he could never explain to me what he meant because he had sworn a sacred vow. But it was my wedding night and that was when I had my final message from Villa who told me to persist with questions."

I had a pretty good idea of what had disenchanted Anselmo Vigil about mortuary science. Margarita had visualized Villa without his head within days of his burial, yet three years had actually passed before the grave had been violated. I wondered how much of the story she'd created after the fact.

"Señora, all these years you have been keeping an important secret. Now it is time to put down that burden so all Mexico may know what you have borne alone for these many years."

She chirped a little noise that wasn't quite a denial, and I knew I had what I'd come to Mexico to find.

"With respect, permit me. As a child, Señora, you were wise beyond your years. Villa recognized this. I have been sent to bring his name forward once more. And you will be the one responsible."

I'd said all the right words of a familiar incantation. Oddly, I almost believed them. She flashed me the smile that had made Anselmo break a sacred vow.

"Anselmo swore me to secrecy. But there was no point because until you came today no one has ever asked me."

"The time has come," I said, taking what I thought was an appropriate operatic note.

"Alas, I cannot," she demurred.

From the way she examined my face, however, I knew we were close to some kind of an accommodation.

"I would never ask an angel beneath heaven to break a

vow, Señora. Perhaps there is another way. Did your husband perhaps leave a document?"

She stared into the dying piñon embers.

"I did not swear never to reveal the paper he wrote."

I watched my timing. "A paper message exists to be read at some time."

"You are right in that," she said and sighed like a pigeon cooing. "I have kept this knowledge within me for the great General so many years."

Then she clapped her hands.

Her son came into the room as if he'd spent his life on tap for his mother's slightest wish.

"*Chuy*, my casket please. Immediately."

After that, it went rapidly. He brought in a large chest, set it on the table, and unlocked it with a key she took from around her neck. Then she sorted out a packet sealed with bloodwax. She handed it to me with the grace of someone paying a long overdue bill.

"There, Señor. You have what you have come for."

I got to my feet decisively. If this document was false, she certainly produced it in a convincing way.

"I cannot tell you, Señora Vigil, how pleasant this talk with you has been for me. Señor Vigil was a very lucky man."

She smiled her total agreement and told her son to roll in the television set. It was time for her special program, she said. Would I like to watch? I thanked her but declined. I had another appointment.

PART TWO

Ten

Privilege is nice to have, but I never feel comfortable about it. Because I spoke fluent English and was crossing the border in a chartered plane, the U.S. Customs people at Harlingen didn't even examine my Luis Montoya identification papers, much less question them. After a quick glance and a desultory inquiry about any purchases in Mexico, the officer waved me through the gate. There'd have been a different welcome if I'd waded the Rio Grande with all I owned done up in a bedroll.

Even though it was late, the flight out of Chihuahua had drained the tiredness from my bones. The flight attendant had served a good sherry and I decided it was a successful trip. I'd gone into Mexico looking for Villa and I found him.

The papers Margarita gave me turned out to be a sworn statement by Anselmo Vigil as to the disposition of the head of *Gobernador General* Francisco Villa. Vigil described the taking of the head by Dr. Jesuita Contreras, who performed the amputation under the instruction of Señor Arturo Chess, the executor of Villa's will, while the body was being prepared for burial.

I looked out the window to watch the lights blooming in the mist coming in from the Gulf. Out on the water, lighted shrimp boats advanced like skirmishers as they trailed their nets to comb the teeming tropical waters. Inland, on the coastal highway, I saw the revolving lights of two police cars pursuing some errant motorist. The Texas Gulf coast offers constant problems, but coming back I always feel I've found a place to call my own.

I hadn't slept much lately, so I was almost dozing when the landing preparations brought me awake, and I was still yawning when I rented a car. Since the clerk made a point of offering me a cup of coffee, I took him up on it.

The Luis Montoya identification was good enough to rent a car with, so I didn't have to worry about a police pickup. Driving at the speed limit with the windows open, I made it out to the island in plenty of time to give Chess his bad news. The appointment had been set up at a construction site Chess owned on Padre Island. The high rise being built there wasn't completed yet and didn't even have its nameplate up. In the glare and shadow of the work lights, the construction scaffolding resembled the gantry for a space rocket. A uniformed guard under a floodlight attended an open elevator. He shifted his pistol belt meaningfully when I drove up.

"We're not open for business yet, sir. You'll find accommodations down the road. I know for a fact the Bahia Mar isn't full up yet."

I was back in Texas. What was said was polite, but the pistol was close at hand.

"I have an appointment with Mr. Chess. He's expecting me."

I'd said the magic words. The guard motioned me into the gratework lift and signaled to another man who stood obscured in the shadows. Chess's security, as usual, was good. Still, as we rode up the side of the construction, I wondered why Umberto, Chess's little prime minister, had gone to all this work to set up my appointment tonight. I'd have been content to see Chess in the morning.

We stopped at the top floor and were met by another guard. Him, I recognized. I lifted my arms from my sides, inviting him to frisk me, but he shook his head and turned to lead me inside. The inside walls weren't up yet, so I saw Chess from a long way off. He was sitting in what looked to be the mate of that Mexican throne chair he'd occupied when I first met him. Only the table beside him was smaller.

When he stood up, I was startled to see how frail he looked, but after he sat down, he started in with his characteristic energy. "I know," he began. "You're wondering if I'm a villain."

"I know when and how Villa's head was taken, and I know you did it, Mr. Chess. That doesn't concern me, but I'd really like to hear you deny blinding Epifanio Valadez. Since you set me up with that briefcase, you won't be surprised to hear that Mario Darque and I have had a skirmish or two. If you had some idea I'd dust him for you, you should know I don't kill for hire."

Chess nodded, not at all discomposed. "There's no use my denying it, because you wouldn't believe it. But I'll level with you, Mr. Hazzard. Knowing more about me than others do ought to give you a basis for judging what I've done."

This was the frank style he'd used in our first conversation, but I wasn't interested in his showmanship. Chess read my face.

"Would you sit down? I've been feeling poorly lately and I tire easily. If the few things I want to tell you don't change your mind, we'll call it quits."

I sat. I had a strong suspicion he had taken me in royally once, and he was trying it again, but I couldn't help liking him. Everybody needs a father figure once in a while, I guess.

"I'm not here to debate your character, Mr. Chess. That's your affair. I came to resign."

Chess tugged at the blanket covering his legs and gave me his quelling blue-eyed stare. "I want you to listen. Did I have Epifanio Valadez blinded? No, I did not. It took me some time to find out who did, but I wasn't surprised. These days, the man who blinded Valadez works for Mario Darque. He's named Oso because he looks like a bear, but his full name is Fulgencio Encarnación. Valadez offended someone by writing a book praising Villa. Oso also murdered Mario's brother Raul, which just shows you that politicians would soul kiss a crocodile if they saw any profit in it, but that shouldn't surprise you."

Chess sat forward in his chair and opened the humidor at his elbow to take out a panatela. Umberto wasn't along this trip, so Chess bit off the end and lit it himself. If he was smoking against doctor's orders, it meant he felt great or terminal. Or maybe it was another of his subtle gestures to make what he said believable.

"Cheney, I've been an honest man all my life, and I'm not about to start lying now. You may have heard a persistent rumor that I killed Villa."

I hadn't heard that accusation before, and I noticed he

was watching my face carefully. He went on. "It's true, but I want you to have the facts."

I was damned if I was going to let him read me like a book, so I kept my face still and prepared to hear the story. Not believe it, but hear it.

"It began in 1922, when I was visiting Villa at his ranch, Canutillo. One morning, he woke me up early. As always at Canutillo, it was freezing in the morning. Villa came into my room with two cups of chocolate and suggested we go for an early ride because he had a fiesta that afternoon, a name day for one of his many children.

"Villa had a reputation for the girls, and it was deserved. But he liked children almost as much as he liked women. He acknowledged a lot of them who were conceived when he was nowhere near the mother. He told me once that no matter where he went, he always saw a *niño* in the crowd, barefooted and hungry, to remind him where he came from."

Chess stopped, remembering, and I recalled from the briefing book that Chess had once been called Villa's *niño*.

"I pulled on my pants and boots—you didn't take off many clothes to sleep at Canutillo because the only heating was the occasional fireplace. Villa was hotblooded. Cold that froze other people so they could hardly talk was just fine with him. Other people's physical weaknesses were the one thing he never understood.

"I followed him out to the barn and we saddled up. He had a beautiful new bay, one of the dozen or so he'd owned since coming inside the law. My mount was a little mare I'd taken to, *Azucar*, because she was the color of brown sugar and had the sweetest disposition I ever encountered in a four-footed female.

"We walked them a ways, and then we did a good gallop across to the hill overlooking the ranch. I knew he had something on his mind. When he relaxed, Villa talked all the time, making bets, pointing out cloud formations, the color of the hills, whatever. That day he was silent.

"I was down there because Villa had sent me a letter saying we hadn't seen each other for a while and he was lonesome. He was like that. Where it was something he wanted, he'd only hint. If it was for somebody else, a woman or a friend or a child, say, he'd take it. But for himself, he never took a thing. That's why nobody ever found that fortune he was supposed to have hidden. What he had, he spent on his people."

Chess stopped to watch a large vessel being towed past us far out to sea. It was all lit up, so it must have been headed down to the wrecking yards at Andy International on the ship canal.

He looked at it and then back at me. "It had been a dry winter, and the spring rains hadn't begun, though there was a lot of early moisture in the air. The freezing and bleaching by the morning sun left the grass pale as straw. A long way below, someone had a piñon fire going, and you could smell its sweetness in the air, but the only sound was our horses' hooves crunching the frozen grass while we stared at the ranch. Somebody came out of a bunkhouse and started chopping wood. The sound of his chopping reached us when he was at the top of his backswing, so he looked like a toy woodsman.

"That was when Villa asked me how things were going, and I told him I was moving to New York because I'd taken over a company that was likely to make a lot of money. That was Texican Pump. It owned some processes that are still paying off, over half a century later.

"I was talking but I could see he wasn't listening. A big jack, sitting like a statue about thirty yards off, was looking at us. Villa's gun came into his hand like magic and he fired twice, once in the air to get it started and then a second, a neckshot that tumbled the animal into a ball. Villa was after it and off his horse and getting ready to stuff it into his saddlebags by the time I caught up with him. 'That's all I'm doing now,' he told me. 'Shooting rabbits.' His voice was bitter. 'You want to give it a whirl again?' I asked, my heart starting up in my chest. We'd almost done it once, almost put him in the president's chair.

"He did the road-agent spin and reloaded before putting the gun away. He'd spent too long on the owl hoot to short himself on ammo. 'No birds in that nest. The revolution has gone on without me, *niño*. Now I go to fiestas and acknowledge children and have interviews with people who want to make movies. I always knew those *chocoladeros* in the city would win. They had the education.'

"Then he picked a tuft of grass to clean the blood off his

hands. 'I killed many men, Arturo, but Mexico, this old whore, she hasn't changed. What was it for, I ask myself.'

"I told him that he was being too modest, that he could collect people to advise him, but he shook his head like a bull getting ready to charge. Then his arm lashed out. He struck me across the face. It wasn't till later I discovered he'd broken my nose. I stood there with the blood filling my mouth and tears in my eyes and Villa smiled at me. 'I have insulted you, *hombre*.'

"That's when I finally understood. An insult is answered with a blow, a blow with death, the code of Mexico. It was quite an honor. That's why I never had my nose fixed. Villa wanted me to kill him.

"I didn't want to do it, Cheney, but I've never regretted it. That's why I hired you. I thought you were like me, a man who's happy only when he's working for an end larger than his own future."

He shifted in his chair and reached over to the ashtray on the table beside his chair to put the cigar down.

I'd had enough of this posturing about Villa. "Mr. Chess, I'm willing to accept Villa as an exceptional man. But since I took on this task, three people have been killed. Look at it! Rasmussen, a thug named Jorge who tried to murder me—"

"Rasmussen wasn't my man, and no Jorge works for me."

"And the best of the bunch, Teddy Ristra."

That startled him. "Teddy's dead?"

"Shot down while his man was getting ready to kill me."

Chess sat back in his chair, bracing his arm stiffly against the table in a gesture of denial. "He was working for Darque?"

"That was my understanding, but he worked for a lot of people."

"Never for me," Chess swore savagely. "You probably think there's no choosing between Darque and me, but you're wrong."

"You've both tried to get me killed. You set me searching for the head, but I was just a lure to catch Darque."

"And you were successful. Now I know why Darque has suddenly developed such an interest in the Villa head. He intends to use it to start another civil war. Do you like that prospect? Another civil war in Mexico?"

I wasn't impressed. "You and a woman named Jesuita Contreras took Villa's head even before he was embalmed. I have a notarized statement to that effect from a witness. The two of you have had that head for all these years. If you have some idea of putting it in the Monument of the Revolution, why haven't you delivered it to the authorities?"

He shook his head. "Jesuita and I had a falling out sixty years ago. She came down with a religion. I don't know what she did with the head. I figured a handsome young fellow like you could maybe talk her out of it."

I had nothing more to say. When I didn't speak, Chess looked at the cigar that had continued to trail its column of smoke up into the darkness overhead. "Well, you know your own mind, Cheney. You stirred up Mario Darque for me. I guess the least I can do is quash that phony warrant for your arrest."

"You were behind that warrant?"

"Nope, that was Darque's work, but I let it stand because I thought it would send you down to Mexico. Since you're not interested, there's nothing gained by leaving it to harass you."

I saw no reason to disagree with him about that. What did offend me was the idea of two powerful men being able to set up and then quash an indictment.

Chess smiled. "Given your lights, Mr. Hazzard, I see your point. You've suffered some real inconveniences, and I'm sorry for that. The guard will see you to the elevator. I'm going to sit for a while and admire the coast here. I always forget how beautiful it is at night. *Suerte.*"

Once back in my car, I knew I was well out of it. Chess was an old man. With death always by his side, he couldn't understand my refusal to take part in an action just because men would be killed. Still, it was unlike him to accept my turndown so easily. As I loosened my tie, I felt something around my neck. The Villa medallion. I'd send it to him in the mail.

The next day, I slept in. Then I had a big breakfast and went for a stroll, not a run, on the beach. A fog strung out in ropes thicker than cotton candy hung over the sand, but the drum fishermen were out, stolidly standing beside their rigs, watching the water droplets dangling and dropping from the guides of their long casting rods. There was no action, but fishing was the task, not necessarily catching.

I didn't walk long because visibility was down to ten yards and the fog muffled everything into silence. Back indoors, the relentlessly cheery disc jockey announced it would be warm and clear inland in the afternoon. After my shower, I put on a lightweight suit and had my third cup of coffee. Then I shivered in the rental car until the heater warmed up as I drove into Brownsville. I wondered about the fate of my own car, last seen parked in Amigoland with a corpse in the trunk. I hoped Olimpia had taken care of it all. I wanted a quiet and uneventful life for a few days.

The vision of such an idyll vanished when I walked into my office. Olimpia was nowhere to be seen, and a blonde I didn't know was ensconced in her place, typing.

She looked up from her word processor and smiled, showing some great dimples. The name plaque on her desk said Mona Van Detering. "Ms. Suertera has someone with her right now, but she should be free in a moment. Won't you have a chair?"

At least my business hadn't been evicted from the building during my flight from justice. I identified myself to the new receptionist and we were instantly friends. Mona had a great tan and nice eyes of a color between caramel and horehound. More importantly, she looked cheerful, a person who enjoyed her work. That's the quality without which no receptionist is worth anything. I was wondering about the faint scent of fresh paint when the inner door opened and Olimpia came out talking to a man I didn't know.

"Truly, Frank, I'm not sure when he'll be back, but he's never been—Cheney!"

Instantly she was back under control. "Mr. Hazzard, I'd like you to meet Frank Atwood, the gentleman I was telling you about. He's just had an offer from the Dallas PD and I think you'd like to talk to him before he does anything rash, like leaving the Valley."

Atwood was a contained-looking man of middle height. He was wearing a dark suit and could have been anybody, but he was studying me with the same care I'd been giving him. Both of us did our inspecting while pretending to watch Olimpia.

"Mr. Atwood, Olimpia has told me a lot about you, so why don't we go into my office and talk?"

I started toward the door Olimpia had come out of, but she expertly steered me to the left.

"You said to knock out the wall so we could expand, and I did. *This* is your office now."

The corner office wouldn't have been inappropriate for some computer magnate who had a lock on all the important patents, but I could fit in—if I worked at it. Olimpia supervised us till we were sitting down and then disappeared. I got to it. "Why are you interested in private security work?"

He answered convincingly and to the point. Half an hour later, after I'd finished my interrogation, I asked if he had any questions. Atwood had been waiting for that one. He wanted to know how I'd gotten into what sounded like deep police trouble. I gave him a heavily edited version of the official story and we came to agreement about our mutual expectations. He would start Monday.

As soon as Atwood left, Olimpia and Esteban came in. Esteban gave me the *abrazo*, so I figured I'd really been missed by all hands. We got down to a staff meeting and I brought them up to date on what I'd been doing. I'd hired Atwood on Esteban's say-so, and when I said my only question was whether he had starch, Esteban reassured me in depth.

"Frank doesn't smoke or drink, and he's a deacon in his church, but I've seen him in action. About two years ago, I was at the Lone Star Federal talking about a car loan when three guys came in. I knew they were bad news when they shook out sawed-off shotguns from under their coats and ordered us all to get flat. I was a little slow hitting the floor and the leader pumped a blast right past me.

"Just as I went down, I saw a man in a short-sleeved sport shirt walk by the front window. He glanced in but kept on walking. Good, I thought, maybe he'll call the cops.

"But these dudes were *fast*. One guarded us and held a stopwatch while the other two filled trash bags from the money cages. They were going to be gone well inside any kind of response time. They had everything timed, and inside of three minutes, they were in the lobby with two trash bags full of money. I stuck my head over the counter and saw a disposal truck rumble up as they hit the door."

Esteban was enjoying telling this story, and I wasn't about to spoil his fun. Olimpia studied my response.

"Then this same guy in the short-sleeved shirt walked past again. By now, I was on my feet, figuring I'd at least get a license plate number, so I saw it all. The front man was holding one of the bags of money in front of himself, so shirtsleeves punches him through the bag. The bag breaks, money goes flying and it's one down. The second guy drops his bag in time to catch a left to the throat. Two down. The third man brandished his shotgun, but this guy—he's a head shorter than the gunman—takes it away from him and raps the barrel against the side of his head. Three on the sidewalk, quicker than I told you. Then the hero climbs up into the disposal truck to pull out the driver and make him pick up the loose money before the wind scatters it. That's when the patrol car arrived."

Esteban looked at me triumphantly. "That's Frank Atwood. A committed Christian. He especially enforces 'Thou shalt not steal.'"

I decided Frank wouldn't need a long break-in period. Mona buzzed to say a Mr. Washburn was on the line. It took me a second to remember that Washburn was Knocky Polk's real name.

Harrison Tyler Washburn, known in the field as Knocky Polk, is a GS-19 intelligence specialist on loan to the DEA. Knocky and I played liar's poker when he worked undercover, but now he's in the stratosphere and doesn't do field work anymore. We hadn't seen each other for six months, but he started talking as if our conversation had been interrupted five minutes ago.

"Cheney, you're born for trouble. The other day there was an all-points out on you. What the Hell were you doing? Jaywalking? Now the APB's off and all is forgiven. Then I hear that Mario Darque was in on it and I figured we can maybe help each other."

"It was just one of those things. Darque and I are not going steady."

The noise of Knocky's laughter came through the wire like a dumpster tipping over. Knocky's a great guy, a fine father, and a loving husband, but when he wants to break up a target, he commandeers innocent bystanders. He did it to me once, and I spent serious time in the hospital for it. If

Knocky was calling me the first morning I was back in town, it wasn't to discuss old times.

But then I had some questions for him, too. "Are you behind all this? Is Rita Madrid one of yours? Do you have a string on Chess too? You know, when you get right down to it, fundamentally, Knocky, you're a rotten guy."

He sighed. Happy time was over. "No. No. No. OK? You heard of the Cuban Snowman?"

"Sicilia-Falcone? He's doing hard time in Mexico City for exporting without a license."

"And he's going to stay there for a nickel or a dime. All his sticky-fingered chums can't help him now, but his operation is still satisfying the customers up north. So I asked a friend to find out who's minding the store. He offered Falcone a soft drink. Somehow, the idea of carbonated water in his sinuses opened Falcone right up. The operation's being run by a lawyer name of Mario Darque.

"It seems Darque has lots of big ideas. He's Xeroxing drug money in a laundromat called Nepente, Incorporated. Money falls through that machine like a Pachinko game."

At the mention of Nepente, I was startled, but it was only a reflex. I really wasn't interested. "Can't help you, Knocky. You should be able to handle Darque. I met his people in Mexico, and I wasn't impressed."

"Darque had a great education which he's now using to break a lot of laws. He's a smooth item because he breaks Mexican laws in the U.S. and vice versa down there. He's not some street smarty, he's a sophisticated businessman with money. If he goes into politics, he'll have the best help and he'll take over the country. His hired help may not be great, but he has a lot of it."

"You serious about Darque taking over the country?"

"Believe it. Remember, they have a one-party government, and some very straight Mexican cops tell me they're already getting the word from Mexico City to leave him alone. There's a rumble of support for the idea up here—you know, fiscal responsibility, anti-Communist."

"You making this up as you go along?"

"Guess," Knocky said, making it clear we'd be speaking in riddles from here on. "It's only an idea now, but it could be a plan."

When he said "plan," my neck hairs bristled. "What are the numbers?" I asked, wishing I hadn't.

There are units in every government that constantly make contingency plans. Not all the plans come to reality, but even the general public would prefer not to have nasty military surprises opening on television. The U.S. had one such event in Pearl Harbor. Ever since, plans to repel the invasion of Detroit by Canada have been filed somewhere. Some of the schemes are about that weird, but they're maintained. Knocky took his time answering.

"Thirty-seventy was what I was told, but the situation could change any time if a charismatic leader showed up. That translates to me as someone who can speak English."

We're all slaves to statistics today. Politicians examine poll results the way high priests used to check the entrails of birds—and with about an equivalent success rate. But that doesn't stop operational planning in the big agencies from being driven by percentages of probable success. A dumb plan that has a high success number might just be chosen to make something happen. Given the way numbers can be manipulated, a thirty-seventy success number can easily be teased into forty-sixty, which would then be used to justify anything short of charging Hell with a glass of water.

The preliminaries were over. Knocky didn't expect me to do any volunteering, but there was something he did want me to know.

"Reason I called, Cheney, I got it on the roundabout that Cheney Hazzard should be advised to stay inside the limits of the United States till further notice."

I was instantly furious. Some unelected bureaucrat decided to deprive me of my constitutional rights to travel. Then I calmed down. I couldn't see myself playing Paul Revere or Chicken Little about some stupid operation that might or might not come off. Who would I leak it to? One of those supermarket tabloids that constantly report extraterrestrial invaders who got lost in Iowa?

"It's nothing to me, Knocky."

"That's how these things get wheels. Somebody is warned off and backs away instead of blowing the whistle."

"You're warning me. Why don't *you* do something?"

Knocky had his answer ready. "It might be a shill. If it

gets bigger, I'll blow, but I wanted someone I trusted to know about it."

"Good enough," I told him. "I'll keep in touch."

Knocky was no coward, but he was smart to tell me. I made an entry on the log, entering the day, hour, and minute of our conversation.

Then I had a cup of coffee and turned on the weather station. There was a decent wind coming in from the Gulf, and I decided to take the boat out later that afternoon. I had just stuffed a few files in my briefcase and snapped it shut when Olimpia came in.

"Cheney, you shouldn't have. It's so expensive." She tapped the platinum wristwatch with a smile that said volumes.

"I didn't," I said, getting on my feet and stepping over to her, my heart racing. Old habits die hard. "Where did it come from?"

"Federal Express just dropped it off. I thought you'd sent it from El Paso."

By the time she said El Paso, I'd stripped the watch off her wrist and flung it into the corner of the room. I dragged her down onto the floor, putting the desk between us and it.

Silence. Then the wrist alarm went off with a buzz like an angry rattler.

I crawled off Olimpia and helped her to her feet. "Sorry. I have a conditioned response to timepieces that come in the mail."

"You thought that was a bomb!"

"It was a distinct possibility. Do you still have the package this came in?"

She brushed her fingers over the brooch at her throat. "On my desk."

She went to her office to get the wrapping. I examined the shipper's manifest. The sender was named as Mario Darque and the return address was the Doublecheck Company in El Paso.

"You see," Olimpia said. "There's nothing else here except this advertisement for some resort in Mexico."

She handed me a brochure. SUN-FILLED DAYS AND LUSCIOUS NIGHTS AT TOPOLOBAMPO, the caption read. Inside the folder was a snapshot of a beautiful girl and a fatuous-looking beachboy, who was giving the girl what appeared to be a newspaper. The female was Daisy Pruitt.

I picked up a magnifying lens that I'd once received as a joke. The photo was not a casual snap. The boy stood so that the date and place on the newspaper could be read. April 23. The day before yesterday.

Olimpia was still thinking about the watch. "How could they put a bomb inside a watch?"

"Modern technology is wonderful." There was plenty of room in the watchcase to put in enough combination plastic to blow off an arm.

The alarm was the best touch. Darque was a lawyer and he knew all about evidence of culpability. The only thing that had happened was the alarm had been accidentally set. He'd sent it to the right person, Olimpia. He knew I'd consider it far more of a threat than it would have been to send it to me.

"What does it mean, Cheney?"

I looked at the picture of Daisy. It could mean that Daisy, who'd been interviewing Epifanio Valadez for reasons of her own, had been captured by Darque's people. Or it could mean she was on vacation. One thing it certainly meant was that I no longer mattered to Daisy. Still, this picture summoned up every feeling I'd been trying to quench.

Olimpia's face was drawn with concern. I scooped up the watch and handed it to her.

"It's a nice piece of jewelry. You can wear it. I just overreacted."

Olimpia didn't believe a word of it. She looked at the watch and tossed it on my desk. "I don't want it."

"It's worth money. If you don't want it, let's donate it to charity. Call Esteban in. I'm going to be gone again for a while."

Eleven

Getting to Topolobampo was a lot easier to talk about than to do. I caught an early Aeromexico flight to Mexico City. Then it was another jet to La Paz, in Baja California, where I could take a ferry across the Gulf of California or charter a prop plane to get to Los Mochis. Then I'd rent a car and drive to the beach resort where Daisy had spent enough time to get her picture taken.

I'm not the most reflective person I know, but the enforced idleness of the trip made me go over a few questions that I'd put to one side when I was working for Chess. First, if he and Jesuita had taken Villa's head before the funeral, why was Chess making such a production of finding it sixty years later—when it had never been lost? His story that Jesuita had gotten religion wasn't a sufficient answer. If the small army he used to protect his ranch in Texas couldn't take it from her, what made him think I could?

Why had he taken the head in the first place? I could understand that Villa had been depressed enough about the results of his failed Revolution to ask for the death he'd given so many others. But Villa wanted only death. He hadn't asked to be turned into a religious relic. Making his head a totem had been Chess's contribution. Maybe Chess decided to use Villa for his own ends from the start.

I'd posed all the questions by the time I arrived at La Paz, but the answer that pulled everything together didn't occur to me until my chartered prop plane was in the landing pattern at Los Mochis. Like me, Chess was an anglo, and for that reason he couldn't himself lead a revolt in Mexico.

Then, something else that had been troubling me clicked into focus. When I'd told Chess that Teddy was dead, his response was immediate and emotional. Chess wasn't an emotional man. What had Teddy Ristra meant to Chess? Rita had said Chess and Teddy never agreed on any topic, which sounded like something permanent—family differences rather than politics.

The car I rented at the Los Mochis airport was an asthmatic 1978 Chevette with an unlikely five thousand miles on the odometer. I decided to spend the night in town rather than experience car problems at night with a junker car in a foreign country on my way to a village that might not even have a hotel.

I checked into the ever-present Hotel Victoriana and had a good fish, a gray snapper, for supper. Until eleven o'clock, when the processing started, I thought I'd made a sound choice. Then I discovered Los Mochis had a sugarcane factory. The plant uses a steam process that sounds like a catastrophe in a boiler plant.

Since sleep was not on the agenda, I went over the ways in which Daisy could have been caught up in Darque's machinations. It really made no sense. Daisy was a close friend of Rita's, and Rita had made clear that her dislike for Darque and Chess was equal. And Darque was exactly the kind of macho egotist that Daisy would avoid like the plague.

Maybe Daisy really was here on vacation. She liked Mexico, and she loved salt water. Remembering what Daisy liked wasn't getting me anywhere. And so I stopped.

I was more than glad to get up early and drive to Topolobampo, the only place I'd find answers for all my puzzles. Once I caught sight of the empty waters of the arm of the Pacific that is the Gulf of California, I felt a lot better.

Finding Daisy, I decided, shouldn't be too difficult here. Topolobampo is a tiny fishing village on a peninsula without an airstrip, which means only one entrance and exit. There were four bars, three closed for the season, and a sailboard rental—also closed. The tiny general store was open, but a sign on the bank posted only afternoon hours. As I'd guessed, there was no hotel.

The dominant landmark was a white adobe church with an orange clay tile roof. It sat on a small neat square at the highest point in town and had an impressive bell tower the local fishermen probably used as a beacon. I was surprised to find it had no attached cemetery, but given the rock outcroppings, it made sense to bury people further inland.

Most of the houses were very modest, but up on the hills above the town, holiday visitors had built vacation villas. Small as it was, Topolobampo was divided into two worlds, a work world for locals and an idle world for the rich tourists.

My best bet was to find the place where Daisy's photo had been taken. I took out the picture and studied it. The blindingly white wall behind Daisy's naked shoulder held a tile with the number 12 on it. Next to the tile was a shop sign that read *Inversiones*, a money-changing business.

I was only half a block from the Banamex Money Exchange, and according to the picture, Daisy had been at an outdoors table overlooking the beach. In the picture, the sun was directly overhead and I could see a shadow under Daisy's chin, so it had been taken at noon.

It was still early. I parked well away from the beach and went into the bar that seemed only provisionally open. I ordered some mineral water from the little old lady who offered coffee or *agua mineral*. I had a good view of both the beach and the collection of sidewalk tables. Way out, I could see a school of porpoises traveling, every now and again arching out of the silvery water as you've always heard they do. They held my attention for a while. At eleven o'clock, I went outside and things almost immediately began to pick up.

I ordered a Dos Equis beer with lime and salt, sat down under a Pernod umbrella on a wrought-iron chair, and watched the beach fill up with local people, mostly young mothers with preschool children. I was the only customer on the patio and the only anglo.

At eleven-thirty the boy in the photograph showed up, peddling papers. I bought one. I'd briefly considered and then dismissed the idea of asking him about the nice anglo lady. If she came because she wanted to, it wouldn't matter, but I couldn't shake the thought that Darque had brought her. I had to assume he had lots of local helpers. No use in alerting them till I'd figured out how to spring the trap and leave with Daisy.

I practiced my Spanish by reading the few news stories in the gazette and was rereading the *curandera* ads when I saw a gray Bentley sedan, ancient, but meticulously maintained, nose its way down the steep street from the direction of the church.

The sun made the windshield a glaring mirror, so I couldn't make out the front-seat passengers, but as the car turned to enter the promenade, I was able to see inside. Two men, either servants or guards, sat in the front seat. A woman sat stiffly in the back. She was too far away and too deeply in shadow for me to make out her features.

But I recognized the scarf that covered her hair, a green Hermes square I'd bought to match Daisy's eyes. I kept the newspaper high enough to cover my face while the car rolled slowly past on the other side of the parkway. My muscles ached from the effort of keeping still. Because the street dead-ended at the beach, they'd have to come back on this side.

Darque had a knack for presenting illusions. He'd used the Customs service to work a shill on Tarahumara Shipping.

It was possible he'd discovered Daisy in Topolobampo and decided to use her to lure me down here. There were several other possibilities, but I dismissed them when the newsboy stepped out into the street to flag down the limousine.

The car eased to a soundless stop and a man built like a beer keg, a large one, got out to hold the door for Daisy. She reached through the open door to pay the boy for the paper and sat looking out to sea.

The boy said something to the man and pointed up the parkway in my direction. The human beer keg took one look and spun around to slam the car door, shutting Daisy in. Then he jumped into the back and the Bentley started up immediately.

They were a block away, gunning back toward me the way they'd come but on the other side of the parkway. I left my paper, my drink, and my change on the little iron table, but I grabbed my chair and started the intercept. The big machine must have been doing fifty when I released the chair against the windshield. I leaped away to one side, and as I'd hoped, the windshield turned to frost as the chair put one of its legs through the glass on the driver's side. The heavy sedan swung to the left, jumping the curb onto the sidewalk and then scraping to a screeching halt against the foot-thick adobe wall skirting the bank building.

For a split second there was silence, then someone on the beach behind me began to shout, a cry that was picked up by a chorus. I grabbed for the car door handle and pulled, certain I could get her out while the guards were still in shock. But even as I jerked, the door came at me faster, slamming me off balance. The big man boiled out and smashed his ham-sized fist into my chest. It was like being hit by a giant wave. I spun backward, but even before I hit the street, I was trying to catch my breath and get my feet under me.

I did pretty well, but it was too late. My world was still going in and out of focus when the thug climbed back into the car. I watched the driver smash the rest of the windshield glass from the frame with his pistol butt. By the time I was on my feet, he had backed clear and driven off. Those damned Bentleys are built to last. Daisy was no better off than she had been.

The only thing left to do was to go after them, so I sprinted for my ridiculous Chevette, which I'd intelligently parked way out of sight—but not completely out of reach. The newsboy watched, his eyes saucer-wide, as I pelted down the street in the direction opposite the one the Bentley had taken.

He was still staring when I drove by him going the other way. Pressing on the accelerator produced more noise than speed, but when I turned up the corner where I'd seen the Bentley vanish, I knew I had them. They'd turned off the only road out of Topolobampo, so they were stuck in the maze of narrow, climbing streets, all of which led to the church square. It was just a matter of time.

Something had been banged loose by the Bentley's scrape along the wall—maybe a muffler—because I could hear the big engine revving. I worked the gearshift to stir up my valiant little four-banger, but the tiny goat wasn't up to much.

My berserker attack on the Bentley must have made the driver nervous because I heard another loud scrape and a crash and then renewed engine noise. That's when I stopped reacting and started thinking. I'd startled the driver, and when he drove off he wanted only to get away. Now he realized that we were fairly evenly matched inside the town, but if he could get on to an open road, he could leave me in the dust.

I slammed on the brakes and reversed to roar down to the main street. Windows popped open as men who had fished all night angrily tried to find out what madmen were running a Grand Prix in the middle of town.

I drove all the way to the end of the main street and pulled up to fill both lanes. There were no shoulders because the steely gray waters of the bay lapped on both edges of the road.

It didn't take long. The Bentley appeared around a corner headed for distant parts, but when the driver saw I had the road completely blocked, he veered off to take the same road he'd taken before. This time he'd go back where they'd come from, but now their lead was shorter and I had a car. He was still faster than I was, but I'd be able to keep him in sight.

He wasn't the driver for a course this tough, speeding up to no purpose when he'd only have to brake and gear down again a second later, so I was able to use my car's lesser power to better advantage. I still had him in sight when he turned off the Calle de Dominguin into a gate that opened in a house-high wall.

I cut in after him. A stock-car racer once told me, "If you have time to think, you're not going fast enough."

Usually that's good advice. Today, it wasn't. I skidded to a stop and leaped out. The Bentley was stopped at a flight of stairs in the front of the house, its doors gaping open. The driver and the bear were not to be seen, though Daisy got out of the backseat and turned to look at me.

Even before the woman stripped the scarf off her head, I knew it wasn't Daisy.

Then it got worse. Iron clanged behind me. I pivoted to see the driver. He was finishing the job of closing the gates behind me.

I turned to climb back into the Chevette. Maybe those gates might pop open if I hit them straight on. I never found out. The bear came out of nowhere to lift me off my feet with a jab to my gut that did what his first punch hadn't—expelled all the air out of my lungs. I heard him chuckle. Then I was bent over the hood of my gallant little Chevette like a croquet hoop, breathing hoarsely and painfully. We'd tried. But Darque had finally found some professional help.

I expected to meet Mario Darque, but Topolobampo kept up its surprises. The big fellow scooped me up under one arm and effortlessly carried me across the patio into the house. Three strides across a foyer and he dropped me like a sack of potatoes. I got off my hands and knees, still wheezing. When I looked up, Pancho Villa was staring at me across the darkened room.

This time, Villa's eyes and mouth matched, and he was alive. He bit a chunk out of an orange, skin and all, treating it like an apple. It was all there, the puff of dark reddish hair under the campaign Stetson, the massive chest and shoulders filling an embroidered *charro* jacket. The cavalry pistol on the desk completed the picture.

The driver stepped back. In crisp English, he introduced me as an *ingeniero* with a specialization in explosives. The big man behind the desk nodded, but his eyes never moved from my face as he spit out the rind. He understood the eloquence of attention coupled with silence. When he spoke, his voice, low but distinct, had a shrill undertone.

"*Hombre*, I used engineers like you in 1911 to take Juarez, but first it was necessary to override the hesitations of that *hada* Madero. While my men made up the dynamite bombs, I visited the troops and taught them how to insult the *federales*."

He picked up the pistol without looking at it and put it down to demonstrate. "I examined a rifle and it went off. The shot was answered immediately from the federal side. Someone yelled, 'Where did you learn to shoot, *excreción?*'

"Do you know what I said? 'In the barn—your sister taught me!'" He looked through me and took another bite of orange. He chewed for a while. After he spat out a seed, he went on. He was good. He didn't break character for an instant. "The insults and shots kept up all night. In the morning, they were ready, the troops and the bombs. I passed out Havana cigars to light the fuses, and Villa, the *dinamitero*, took Juarez while Madera played with himself. It was the first of my many glorious victories. Can you do as much with macho explosives?"

He turned away, a *torero* who has mastered the bull, to take a cigar from a carved humidor. One of the guards snapped to with a lighter extended. After a puff, Villa stared at me challengingly, waiting for my answer.

"I know all about big bangs," I said. "Your mother and your sister taught me in the barn of your *padrino*. They taught me lots." Varga had been giving me a course in Mexican country talk.

The cigar snapped in his hand. His eyes were threaded with red as he scooped up the pistol to come round the table.

"*Mascota*," I said. "Is this the house of Miguel Raton? Disneyland?"

Despite the enormous shoulders and the big head, Villa was no larger than a ten-year-old, four feet tall at most, but the pistol made that irrelevant. In the instant before he pulled the trigger, he was easily eight feet and growing. I watched him squeeze the trigger. The hammer fell and I braced myself for the blast.

I've never heard a sweeter *click!* in my life.

The overhead lights snapped on and behind me someone

began to clap. It was Mario Darque, sitting at a table behind me, enjoying himself a good deal.

The dwarf looked at Darque. "Papa!" he said in the querulous tone of a child who thinks his parent can do anything. When Darque paid no attention, the dwarf pouted and scuttled out the door.

Away from his mansion and family, Darque no longer seemed to be a clothes-horse. He was dressed impeccably in khaki-colored denims, but they looked well worn. Here, he seemed much more animated, filled with an eager energy quite unlike my first impression of him. The only thing to do was go on the offensive.

"What is this, Mario, amateur theatrical night? Villa ate fruit that way, but he didn't smoke, seldom swore, and never bragged about his deeds. He wouldn't have called Madero a coward or a fairy either." I got to my feet.

"*Very* good," Darque said. "You have mastered the contents of Chess's briefcase. Everyone was convinced there was something important in it, but then Chess is quite clever at misdirection."

"Where's Daisy?"

He shrugged. "Daisy Pruitt? Who knows? She was here, as a tourist, which gave me an idea. Now she's gone."

This was the only crapgame in town, so I had to play. "You must have wanted to see me. What about?"

Darque was pleased to get down to cases so fast. "I want to recruit you, Cheney. You say you won't get the head for Chess, but you *must* get it for me."

"I've seen the head. It was very dead, dried up, useless as last year's onion."

"Where is it?"

I tried some amateur theatricals of my own, doing a man considering all angles. Chess was set up for an invasion, so it wouldn't matter.

"Chess has it at his ranch in Texas. All this playacting wasn't necessary, Mario. You could have asked me. My concern was not to find the head but to authenticate it—which I now have no intention of doing."

Darque put his thumbnail between his upper teeth and raked it back and forth as if sharpening it while he looked through me.

"That is a false head, which is why I haven't taken it.

People who work for me are either friends or family. I think I will make you choose which you will be, Cheney. After you choose, we can come to some understandings."

A smile I hadn't seen before lit his face. "Show him what I mean!"

Things happened fast. Two new guards, large men, muscled and professional-looking, appeared. One held me while the other used a pair of nylon handcuffs to put my hands behind my back. Then we left the place, climbed into the Bentley, and drove inland through Los Mochis. An hour later we pulled up at an old C-47 at one end of an airfield that wasn't the one on the airline map.

Waiting bores me, but we didn't do much of it. They shepherded me into the plane, a black C-47, the twin-engined prop plane used as a workhorse during World War II. Then, it carried cargo and troops and provided transport for parachute drops. This one was still rigged to drop paratroops. The anchor line was in place, along with the metal bucket benches that lined the cabin walls. After a brief run up to warm the engines, we took off.

According to the direction of the sun, we were heading northeast, deeper into Villa country. I started brooding about what being Darque's "friend" involved. Along the Rio Grande, "friend" doesn't mean much, but if you can be trusted with any secret, you're "family." No matter. I was never going to trust Darque. With him, distrust was easier—and safer.

Within fifteen minutes, my heart was pounding and I was really cold. I was glad to attribute it to oxygen lack from the high altitude at which we were flying.

Just then we banked and I had a good look below. It was rocky high desert with a thin pelt of hardship vegetation, gashed by sheer canyons that even this close to noon were still deeply shadowed.

When we started our descent, I saw the pilot was keying on a narrow landing strip that he'd have to know to find. The base was living rock naturally camouflaged with small shrubs. It sloped gently uphill and could stop our plane. The arrangement made sense, but it would never meet FAA standards.

We touched down, bounced once, and the pilot started braking. This strip had all the earmarks of a station on the Colombian pipeline. Maybe Darque had some idea of implicating me in his drug traffic. If so, his recruitment techniques were pretty bizarre. The pilot feathered everything back and we rolled to a stop.

The trip to the middle of nowhere ended when two men in black fatigues pushed a set of metal stairs to the open door. Once in the ship, they made their way past us into the control cabin. My escorts shook themselves out of their blankets. One cut off my handcuffs and shoved me forward down the rickety stairs.

We walked across the strip to a three-quarter ton command and reconnaissance truck which was the inspiration for all subsequent offroad vehicles. My mind sped ahead. Darque had obviously made extensive purchases of U.S. war surplus for his army. The car was built to truck specifications and designed for field work. Given the look of the rock outcroppings and the seemingly bottomless ravines, the heavy truck with its long wheelbase made sense. My only question was how it got up here. I hadn't seen a road yet.

Once we were clear of it, the C-47 took off with a roar. Only when the old plane had jumped out into the void of the canyon and disappeared did my two new guards crank up our vehicle. We drove for no more than ten minutes. Even if I wanted to leave these people, there was no place to go. On one side was the canyon we'd flown over, and on the other a steep hillside that offered no trails or even hand holds. We were chugging up a road that led even higher into the mountains. Wherever we were going, it was high.

The roadbed was merely a track scraped in the mineral dirt and rock. Watercourses had eaten the road away, and the maintenance was on a need-only basis—filling the gaps with large rocks. As we climbed higher, the country opened up. Below, I could see evergreen forests, but at this altitude there were only tufts of alpine grasses and inches-high shrubs that might have taken a century to grow.

We pulled off the road at a point where a footpath slanted upslope and out of sight. The copilot got out and wedged all four wheels before the driver killed the engine and beckoned me out. Up the hill.

The air was freezing. A biting wind sliced through my thin clothes and, after a walk of only two or three minutes, I was out of breath. We stopped at a natural rock platform, about forty by forty, a lookout over the Sierra Madre range. Straight ahead, out in the blue distance of the thin air, a helicopter materialized, the size of a fly. If it was bringing Darque, I was probably going to be treated to scene two in his favorite ongoing melodrama.

As the chopper swooped closer and began the delicate business of settling in, I saw the payload wasn't Darque. It was the dwarf who looked like Villa. He accepted help getting out of the helicopter and then strutted across the barren ledge to stand at the lip of the canyon with a background of mountains leaping behind him. The helicopter slid up and away.

The depraved little image of Villa was wearing a huge sombrero that the wind tugged at, making the gilded embroidery glitter in the sun. He stared at me and then raised his heavy cavalry pistol to point it at my legs. The recoil of the gun jerked the little man's arm straight up. The slug showered rock splinters between my feet. My knees went weak. I'd thought the gun would be empty.

"This time I have bullets," he said, as if reading my mind. "Look out over there."

My two escorts seemed to have no objection, so I walked over to the edge, trying to play the part of an invited guest. The view was impressive, a fantasy of mountains heaped up as tumultuously as waves in a stormy ocean. The hazy gaps across the canyons were smoky blue. While my eyes searched the distance, a biblical quote about a high and stony place flashed at me from my childhood. On the valley floor, so far down I couldn't hear it, a river spread silver threads in a shallows beyond which I could make out a tiny pair of oxen plowing a small field.

The dwarf was knotting one end of a long white scarf around a fist-sized rock.

When he spoke, it was still in that obscenely shrill voice. "It is a drop of two thousand meters. As you will see, it takes a while for things to reach the bottom. But just saying that does not make an impression."

He tossed the weighted scarf past me. Irresistibly, I watched. Over the edge it flew, then straight down, a bird that had taken a heavy load of buckshot. I didn't wait to see it hit the rocks below, but turned back to the dwarf. He frowned petulantly and the two men stepped up to grab my arms. Very gently, as if I weighed no more than a piece of balsa, they lifted me and turned me around.

"Keep looking," the dwarf rasped. "All the way down. You will follow it if you do not give the right answer to a question I will ask."

I don't suffer from vertigo. Like most people, I had dreams of falling as a child, but parachute training ended them. In those childhood nightmares, there was always a reference—a wall, a hole in the ground, the side of a building, something to chronicle motion. But free-fall cancels all those expectations. In a lot of ways, falling to death isn't such a bad exit.

The dwarf giggled. "You see what can be done to you? It is far enough for you to achieve terminal velocity before the rocks in the shallows reach out for you. No one but you and we will ever know what happened."

The rock smashed into a stone outcropping and vanished into the river. A body would have broken to bits. So much for the long death. Like the dwarf's first appearance, this whole drill was just another charade. They weren't going to throw me over the edge, but they were going to extraordinary lengths to frighten me.

"If this is how Darque makes friends, I can see why he doesn't have too many."

For the first time, one of the guards spoke. "Not exactly."

Then the other man released me to snatch up the dwarf by an arm and a leg. He began shrieking and struggling as his feet left the ground, but he had no more chance than a worm going onto a hook. Even as I yelled a protest, he was flung out into the emptiness that began at the cliff's edge.

Falling, the dwarf jerked out the pistol, but his deadly weapon was empty now. I heard the hammer clicking. Even as the screaming began in earnest, I reflected that Darque must have enjoyed planning this demonstration. The dwarf's wail rapidly got faint, but he must have screamed all the way down, because even after he was only a speck, the sound still haunted the frigid air.

I walked up to the edge. Implacably, the chill wind raked over me so I could feel the goosebumps even under my clothes. My teeth were clenched so hard my cheekbones hurt.

When the only sound left was the wind that had chilled me to the bone, the second guard spoke. He wasn't quite as fluent in English as his buddy.

"You seek the True Head?"

I considered my answer carefully. These people had casually murdered a living image of Villa but they half worshiped a lifeless scrap of hair, bone, and skin.

"I do," I said. The echo of my words sounded like a marriage promise.

Twelve

My two escorts walked me back toward the command car, chatting in a dialect that contained a lot of words that weren't Spanish. From their relaxed attitude, I understood that, for them, the job was over. They had done what Darque had ordered them to do. When we reached the car, the driver started up the heavy engine and the one who wasn't driving pulled out a half-liter bottle of Imperial brandy and handed it to me over his shoulder.

Maybe they thought of it as an initiation, but I didn't want to belong to their club. They were talking about what they thought was an interesting topic, a woman named Consuela who had a color television set in her bedroom. I held the brandy bottle and watched the road, which was paved with tar for a hundred yards or so at a time. Now the potholes were small enough to be avoided.

Like most older military vehicles, the C and R has a stick shift on the floor, and, as customary with military vehicles, only rudimentary springing. Still, the driver was making decent speed, putting us through the switchbacks so the car seemed to run on rails.

Half a mile down the road, the next switchback used a substantial one-lane log bridge to cross a watercourse too large to fill. Immediately beyond the bridge was a long straightaway. If the driver took the turn the way he'd handled the other curves—a touch of brakes to snap the adhesion and make the rear come around and then heavy accelerator to blast up through the gears—I could lose these rowdies.

It was a right hander with a good surface and a shallow

exit angle, and the road down to the bridge wasn't too steep. The braking effort was going to be at its maximum at the last moment when we'd still have a fair amount of speed. I was counting on the driver to gun out of the corner to let the steering unwind as the torque came on. That and his not wearing a seatbelt should help a lot.

He was finishing his braking and had the wheel cranked all the way over, ready for gear climbing, when I smashed the brandy bottle against the copilot's skull with all my might as I threw myself headfirst over the seatback. When my shoulder hit the floor, I rotated to jam both my feet as hard as I could against the steering wheel. The driver's startled reaction was to stomp on the accelerator. The front wheels stayed cranked hard left and the rear wheels were accelerating rapidly in our former direction. We were going to jackknife and flip at high speed. I heard the right front tire pop.

As we went over, the centrifugal force crammed me under the dashboard, but the driver flew out from under the wheel and was gone. Not that I could see—my world was gray-red as the blood surged in and out of my head while we went over and over.

The first roll was the noisiest. Metal scraped and crumpled as the roadway simplified the car, swiftly removing fenders and sheet metal. After an eternity, what was left of the car slammed into something so hard that it rammed my forehead painfully against the dash and emptied the breath from my lungs.

The relative quiet came as a shock. The only remaining sound was the engine running. When the nausea passed, I groped up to turn off the ignition. In the sudden silence, I heard a rasping noise I couldn't identify. It was my breathing. Carefully, I eased my deathgrip on the dash stanchions and discovered I was upside down.

The car was resting on its hood and the frame welded on the rear to hold gas cans. Thanking the designer who decided doors on combat cars were unnecessary, I squeezed through the scoop in the side panel with not quite an inch to spare.

The driver had been thrown clear, but not to safety. A bloodstained boulder pillowed his crushed skull. The man who'd handed me the brandy was still in the car. He wasn't moving either.

They were dead because they'd come very close to

frightening me and because I'd responded in a traditional way. The lessons of nonviolence are hard to learn. I'd decided to show them I was no one to trifle with, and now they were dead and I was stranded, with the only vehicle in miles destroyed.

I stood up carefully, feeling boneless and breathing gingerly as I assessed the damage. I hadn't broken any ribs, so I concentrated on the car. Only a vertical bridge support kept it from sliding into the ravine where far below a falls plunged silently into a spray of mist.

"Nicely done," someone observed approvingly. I spun around, ready to attack.

Teddy Ristra was sitting astride one large horse and holding the reins of another one. He smiled and I felt dizzy.

"I thought you were dead. Why aren't you?"

My question pleased him.

"Death, my dear friend, is relative. Especially in Mexico."

My head throbbed and I wasn't in the mood for his games. "A lot of things are relative down here, like your refusing to stay on one side or the other for more than twenty minutes at a time. Let me guess. Not content with betraying Rita and Darque, you now want to sell me off to the highest bidder."

He shrugged. "You think you can walk out of here?"

He had a point. "Let's get this mess off the road. No use leaving a message."

Teddy looked doubtful. "Darque keeps track of his toys. When the truck doesn't show up in Creel, he'll send a squad. It's probably started already."

"I'd like them to think I died in the wreck."

That he could approve of. He dismounted and unscrewed the fuel cap. Only a little gas dribbled out. He easily pried loose one of the split logs that was the bridge floor, a lodgepole pine with the bark still on it.

"We'll lever this *zorra* over the side. The impact will set it afire. Come on, lend a hand."

That was when I remembered that one of the guards had lifted my wallet while my hands were cuffed. I still had a moneybelt lined with gold pieces, but there was no point in being left without the Luis Montoya ID.

"Hold off on the engineering operation for a minute. My wallet's in there."

I dropped to all fours and scrambled under the car. It was one of my grislier jobs. The big fellow was in one piece, but only barely. He'd been caught between the roadway and the seatback. Shutting out the stench of blood and gas, I groped around in the hinder half, but after exploring what I hoped were pockets, I realized I'd guessed wrong. Shifting to the front half, I tried again, finding it in his upper coat pocket, which was great because if I'd had to search further, I'd have been getting into problematic areas where he'd been squashed.

I'd just started to crawl back out when I heard a shot from a heavy pistol, followed by a second one. Peering out, I saw that the driver who'd been thrown free hadn't been killed by bashing his head against a rock. He no longer was propped against the rock but now lay flat on his back, a big automatic lying beside his outstretched hand. Teddy stood looking down at the corpse, then tucked his own little pistol under his belt.

"Great shooting, Teddy."

"Only so-so." Teddy didn't turn. "I shouldn't have let him get a shot off in the first place. Now you're going to have to move that pig of a car off the road without me."

He held his left arm stiffly against his side. Under the fingers of his right hand, a crimson stain bloomed on his sleeve. These damn fools never stopped contending. Even death didn't stop them.

Teddy suggested the driver had to go into the car along with the copilot before we could tip the whole catastrophe over the side. I agreed, but first I tugged the driver's shirt off. It was the size of a tent, but that was all to the good. Ignoring my throbbing body, I dragged his corpse over to the car and shoved it in.

Without Teddy's help, my grisly job was harder. It took two more lodgepoles, which I bound together with one of the dead man's shirtsleeves, but I finally achieved my sufficiently strong lever. When I leaned on it, the car creaked and then slid into the chasm with a scrape that set my teeth on edge. About a hundred feet down, it hit a jutting rock and caught fire, little tongues of flame that didn't amount to anything until it hit bottom, when it exploded like napalm.

"Now I'd like you to take a look at my problem," Teddy said dispassionately, sitting down in the middle of the road.

For the first time, I studied Teddy's sunworn face with-

out the mask provided by the force of his personality. His face
was pitted with what looked like smallpox scars and considerable wrinkles of laughter. Lacking the embellishment of
energy and decision, he was suddenly a man long past his
first youth.

His vulnerability made him seem unexpectedly trustworthy. Wound and all, his deepset brown eyes gleamed with an
intelligence which made an ironic comment on everything he
said.

"This wound isn't much, but I'd like to close it up. The
bullet tore up a muscle or two, maybe a nerve."

He didn't wince when I got him out of his coat, but that
was just part of the show. I raised his left arm and decided
the bullet had passed through both the pectoral and deltoid
muscles of his left chest. A rib had taken the chief shock,
deflecting the bullet through the skin of the armpit before
exiting. There wasn't much blood, just a puckered hole in his
chest that, even as I watched, rimmed itself with the blue
bruising of flesh pierced by a small caliber bullet. Old
soldiers say painful wounds that hammer you like the hinges
of hell are not serious. Of course, you couldn't tell from
Teddy's stoic features whether it hurt or not.

"Do you have any whiskey?" I asked. "We ought to do
something to control sepsis."

He laughed, without concern, and I wondered if he was
in shock. I went on talking while I worked his shirt off. "They
probably have germs out here unknown to medical science. It
would take a specialist to sew this up."

As if coming back from a long way off, he finally spoke.
"I have a specialist out here."

The rocky canyons running off in every direction didn't
offer much promise. "Is your specialist a tree surgeon or a
geologist?"

For the first time, Teddy looked vexed. "Jesuita Contreras
is a sanctified curandera. For this kind of problem, she has
the best cures in the world."

Until he mentioned Jesuita, I'd been of two minds about
what to do with Teddy, but now he and I were going to be
twins for a while because I, too, wanted to see Jesuita. From
Rita's description, she might be the one sane person down
here.

"If you're ready," I told him, "I'm ready to clean this up and rig a bandage."

"With what?" Teddy asked sharply. His wound was smarting.

"The guard's shirt. There's enough material in it to bandage several wounds, but it would be nice if you had a clean handkerchief."

"Good," Teddy said, pulling out a silk square from one of his many pockets. He paused to wipe two bloodstained fingers on it before handing it over. "Make it fast. Then we'll ride out of here."

I'd gotten over being queasy about gunshot wounds long ago. I quickly made pads of his handkerchief and tore the guard's shirt into strips to bind them tightly to the entrance and exit wounds, then used the rest of the strips to make an action sling for his left arm after I put his shirt back on.

I studied his coat and after sticking my little finger through the charred hole of the entrance wound, put it on his good arm and buttoned it, leaving his left arm free for use in an emergency.

When I finished, Teddy thanked me formally and then whistled to his horse, which came up to nose at his bandage. After he put his foot in the stirrup, I handed him the reins and gave him a boost. He slipped into the saddle as smoothly as a key going into a lock.

"There. Much better. Now I can think. You take the other horse and I'll lead us out of here."

"Cheney, I'm a senior agent for the Ministry of Interior of the Republic of Mexico. I tried to kidnap you in Brownsville to penetrate Darque's organization."

I was looking my gift horse in the mouth. "And what story did you tell Darque about Jorge's death?"

"That you overpowered Jorge at the border station while I was inside. It was sufficient. Now, if things go wrong and Darque's people catch up with us, I'll simply say that I was chasing you. That makes me only the first in the pack. Mount up."

I saw an opportunity and used it. "What exactly is this plan of Darque's that these people are willing to kill for to bring it about? All this so he can be the president of Mexico for six years?"

"You must expect more imagination from Mario Darque.

He wants to set up his own country, with his own laws. He intends to separate the northern third of Mexico from the rest. One third of a million square kilometers, from Matamoros to Los Mochis. He will rule a buffer state between poverty-stricken Central and South America and the wealthy United States."

Realpolitik is what it's called. Knocky's words rang in my head. He'd warned me I'd thrust myself into the middle of a nation-sized catastrophe. I stared out into the empty range of mountains, trying to gauge man's puny ambitions on their vast scale.

"Money follows politics, Cheney. If Darque succeeds he will be the Bolívar of *Nueva España*, which is what he intends to call his new country. It will be more wide open than Vegas, with a better climate than Acapulco or Cozumel, and, of course, the drugs will be superfine. It will be the capital of the world's playgrounds. It will be El Dorado."

It was a vision some people would consider worth killing for. "More interesting to you should be why I'm up here on top of the world. I assumed you wouldn't choose a heroic—which is to say a pointless—death, but I thought you might resist. That meant you would need transportation, which this horse provides."

"You're a real sport, Teddy, but in the course of our brief acquaintance you've identified yourself as an agent for everyone. Could you light on one of those explanations and stick with it? I'd even settle for none of these."

Teddy was his old self again. He studied me narrowly before he spoke. "I serve only Mexico."

I sighed. For now, that explanation would have to do. It was time to go. The smoke from the burning truck would soon be a banner in the sky for anyone looking for it.

"Let's get you to your specialist."

Teddy motioned again at the stallion I'd been inspecting. I'd been delaying climbing aboard because it presented a problem. I've seen a lot of Westerns, so I know which side to mount from, but that about exhausts my lore. The animal was quite tall and chocolate-colored. He regarded me steadily. Grasping the saddle horn, I tried to duplicate what Teddy had done. I felt pretty smug when I made it in one.

As I settled onto the horse's back, it let out a hefty sigh.

I had the impression it knew I'd depleted my repertory and was waiting to see what I'd do next. That made two of us.

Teddy turned around in his saddle to make sure I was in place and started off down the road. Luckily, my horse followed Teddy's because I didn't have the slightest idea of how to start the creature, though I guessed that pulling on the reins should stop him. At least riding had to be an improvement over walking.

"What's his name?"

"Who?"

"My horse. What's he called?"

Teddy turned his horse around to watch me as he answered. "She's a mare and her name is Emilia," he said without inflection.

When he lost interest in conversation, I shut up. As a physical shock, being shot is about like being tackled from behind. You're moving along in the current of life and suddenly there is a hideous temporal as well as spatial dislocation that takes a while to get over. Teddy was probably restitching the fabric of his life. Nevertheless, understanding his apparently conflicting loyalties was what my own life was going to depend on—and soon.

We'd come far enough so that my various fierce riding aches had driven every other consideration from my mind when Teddy pulled up to consult his watch, a gold onion he extracted from that incredibly pocketed vest.

"Three-thirty. Where we're going, the sun will be down inside half an hour. You're doing pretty well." His face grew very still when he saw I was standing up in my stirrups. I ignored his effort to keep his laughter inside.

At that moment we both heard a distant drone that had no place in this mountain peace. It was a prop, not a jet, and not, thank goodness, a chopper. With a speed that must have been agonizing, Teddy dismounted, undid the saddle, stripped off the bridle, and softly told his horse to leave. I got off Emilia without much grace but with equal speed and undid every buckle I could find until the saddle fell to the dirt. I fiddled with her bridle till it came off and Teddy snatched it from me with his right hand to lash her away. I was going to miss Emilia.

The rest of the drill I already understood. In a second I

had taken cover beside him under the thin shadow of a dwarf pine.

The noise Darque's C-47 made spooked the horses. Predictably, they galloped down the road, leaving an empty alpine meadow. The plane came over us and flew on toward the ridge we'd left, where a smudge of black smoke from the burning car stained the brilliant blue of the sky.

Teddy's shirt was drenched with sweat. "They'll waste maybe half an hour before they start looking for you on the ground."

"Won't they believe I burned up in the wreck?"

"Darque is thorough. Our only choice is to go down into the *Barranca de cobre*. Undo the lariats from the saddles and let's start walking."

After I tossed the saddles against the trunk of our sheltering pine and slung the looped lariats over my shoulders bandolier-fashion, I followed Teddy toward a place where some natural disaster had revealed a fall of egg-sized shale. It would be hard to track us there, so we stepped into it and began slipping and sliding downhill in knee-deep gravel. Once across the giant slip, we could disappear under the improved tree cover. The trees weren't high, but at least the evergreen foliage was dense.

The C-47 circled back and then flew off in a beeline for the east. They must have seen the car in the ravine and were probably reporting an accident with no apparent survivors. If a search party came back, it would prove Teddy knew what he was talking about.

The track we found in the woods soon petered out into an animal path precisely six inches wide. After we crossed a trickle of water that had accumulated into a pool, the track quickly dwindled into a trace that even a mountain goat would have found tricky going.

The next bit of the way was truly scary. It rimmed the edge of a rockface that ran with a film of icy water. I led the way. Once, moving sideways with both arms stretched out at each side for stability, I wondered fleetingly how Teddy, with one arm in a sling, was enjoying this nightmare tightrope walk. That was when I slipped and suddenly was embracing the cliff face with everything I had. Shale and dirt rained down on me. After a swift review of my past life, I started again, more cautiously. Here the rock was sedimentary and must have spent a lot of time hidden from the sun because the entire rockface was covered with patches of yellow and brown lichens. This time, I stopped while I looked back at Teddy. Because I was going slower, he didn't seem to have too much trouble keeping up with me. After a while, I enjoyed the cool water that was keeping the lichens alive as it splashed on my face. Still, I worried about how Teddy was doing. Each time I stopped, I saw he was right behind me.

Finally, we got beyond the treacherous rockface. The trail down was steep but as we moved lower, the going got easier. The pines, twisted like bonsai, scented the air with the sharp smell of turpentine. They received their water from patches of melting snow thawing slowly in the shadows that were just now being nibbled by the sun. At last we came to a drop-off where the trail lipped over an edge. We stopped to look back and up toward the roadway.

We were surrounded by a silence like cotton batting. Darque's plane had gone long ago. My feet hurt from shoes that weren't made for this kind of use, and I was blinded from the sweat pouring off my eyebrows just often enough to be constantly irritating. That reminded me of the sweat soaking into the matted pads of cloth to salt Teddy's open wounds. He muttered something sharp and we went on.

I was just about to say that at least we hadn't been spotted by the C-47 when my skin prickled at the unmistakable drone of its engines. Unhurriedly, it throttled back and began the slow descent I remembered all too well. A string of jumpers came out—eight, nine, ten of them.

"We have a good two hours' start on them," Teddy said, once more cheery, his teeth dazzling in his pitted face. "They'll start by checking the car. That will take a while. This valley and these slopes belong to the Tarahumara Indians. The Mexican army, the Spanish conquistadores, and even the Aztecs never conquered them—though they all tried. Tarahumaras don't much care for armed men coming into their territory, and these people know it."

The jump plane made a one-eighty turn and came back to drop some equipment bundles. Since they'd jumped from about six hundred feet above the drop zone, the paratroops were on the ground and had their chutes piled when the equipment bundles landed. They had to walk no more than twenty or thirty yards to pick them up. The whole operation had come down in a zone about half the size of a football field. As a veteran of such enterprises, I was impressed. In less than two minutes from start to finish, the troopers would be distributing the contents of the bundles. The plane moved off. The silence of the high sierras closed in again.

"They know what they're doing," I said.

"I'll give them that," Teddy agreed. "But my money's on the Tarahumaras. They don't like green uniforms."

There was no point in waiting for them to catch up with us, so we plodded on. As Teddy said, we had a good head start, and they'd have to figure out which way we'd gone.

The odds changed again when once more the silence was divided by engine noise, this time the muffled *flat! flat! flat!* of a jet transport helicopter. As it passed over us for its landing, the air moved by the giant rotors mashed us flat against the earth. It was an effort to raise my head to see what happened next.

We had a good observation point for the drop zone that the paratroop squad had secured. The chopper touched down to let off three dogs and an old man with white hair and beard. We didn't hear the dogs baying until after the helicopter lifted off. The old man brought out a sheet and showed it to them.

Teddy's eyes were expressionless. "You spent the night in a hotel in Los Mochis. Darque has people everywhere." He got to his feet. "Let's go. Now."

This time, Teddy led. His pace wasn't fast, but it was unflagging. We scrambled down the top of sheer rock ridges as sharp as knife blades and through dense stands of high-altitude firs that got larger as we descended.

The scenery was certainly gorgeous, but going downhill with uncertain footing was a constant sequence of jolts that jarred my spine, which was still sore from the horse riding. I could see dark shadows of perspiration spreading on Teddy's coat, and his neck glistened with sweat. He was making great time for a man with a bullet wound.

I began thinking about my guide. Why did I feel I could trust him, despite all the evidence that he was the smoothest operator of them all? Because my instincts told me to, that was the only answer I came up with.

It was just then, while I was stumbling along mindlessly, putting one foot in front of another, that the attack came.

Something closed around my ankle with the finality of a
bear trap. Looking down, I saw a large mange-colored dog
with a torso like a suitcase. Soundlessly, he had clamped his
jaws on me and settled down as an anchor. The hair on his
neck bristled. Instinctively, I tried to jerk away, but he bit
down and I stopped struggling.

"Teddy," I said in what I hoped was not a carrying voice.
"I have a passenger."

He froze in position, swiftly took in my situation, and
scanned the terrain behind us even as he threw himself down
into a crouch to move toward me.

"Any sign of his handler?" He didn't have to remind me
that at this point Darque probably didn't want either of us
alive.

"I didn't hear anything. Could he have circled ahead?"

Teddy said a Spanish word I'd never heard before. "I
hope you are not a member of the SPCA."

When I saw what he was doing, I understood. While
talking to me, and never engaging the hound's earnest eyes,
he had flicked open a switchblade. The knife gleamed briefly
as it sank into the dog's throat. Teddy thrust his fist into the
wound. The dog died without making a sound.

We exchanged glances, but by the time he'd pried the
dog's jaws open, I'd finished my discourse to myself on the
subject of cruelty to animals and concluded such a topic
would not have bothered the bloodhound. Blood seeped into
my socks. Teddy wiped his blade on the dog's chest. I
grabbed the loose skin of the animal's neck and threw him
away from me as hard as I could.

The dog was an ugly shape in the air, raining gouts and
streams of blood like something in a stockyard before I lost
sight of him in the steep shrubbery on his way down into the
valley below. He'll get there before us, I thought dazedly.

Teddy slipped his switchblade back into a pocket. "The
handler may be ahead of us, but we have to keep going. If he
shoots us, so he shoots us. We have perhaps ten minutes
more of decent light. If we're lucky, it will be no worse than
twilight when we get to the river. We have to get down there
tonight or there will be nothing to eat or drink till tomorrow.
The troops won't keep on in the dark, but we must."

Looking at his pale and sweating face, I knew he was a

lot worse off than I had realized. His rib was probably broken.

When he chuckled, I realized he'd been examining me too. "It's been easy so far, Cheney. From here on, the route will be less certain. I haven't taken this trail for many years. Could you find your way back the way we came?"

"I'm not interested in surrendering, so I'd go on anyway. Why?"

His face told me I'd made the right choice. "Once we get down to the river, we'll be safe from any pursuit. Then all we have to worry about are the Tarahumaras. If we meet them, follow my lead. Despite our national rhetoric, they're not exactly a hundred percent members of our culture. But they are decent, innocent people. Wisely, they don't trust strangers because more than once before, the federales tried a final solution that didn't quite work."

I took a last look up at the pallid strip of sky between the high walls of the canyon before we started down again. As the darkness continued to sop up what light there was, our hike became identical with any other night exercise. At first, I was apprehensive about moving without any idea of where to put my feet, but gradually all my other senses cut in and I began to move in the darkness with an idiotic assurance that became justified as I followed the quiet rustling Teddy made through the increasing undergrowth.

Skills I hadn't used in a long time returned. The deeper we went in the darkness, the higher the surrounding temperature and humidity became. I began to pick up smells and sounds, the almost imperceptible echoes of our silent progress. I could have been back in Nam on a long-range patrol, and for whole minutes of time, I behaved that way.

It never got much worse, but it didn't improve either. Once off the rockface, the trail was overgrown by vines tipped with fiery briars. At unexpected times came the whiplash of a springy branch, arriving unannounced and always at stinging face height. The descent seemed to go on forever.

Thorns had made my shirt a tattered rag, wet from the exertion of climbing down an almost vertical cliff face in total darkness. When I commented on the heat, Teddy told me the Tarahumaras moved from the valley top to the bottom following the seasons. Down here it was perpetual summer.

My thrusting hand suddenly encountered a vine that didn't feel vegetable. It filled my hand with a kind of electric energy. Instinctively, I whipped it away. It fell through the matted vegetation, hissing all the way.

I was thinking that adventure through when Teddy stopped. I walked into him.

"It's not much farther." His voice betrayed his exhaustion. "We're just above the river, but first, we have to get down to it. Negotiating this rock will be a bit tricky because it's hands and feet all the way down."

As soon as he mentioned the river, I realized I was dying of thirst, even though I was both parched and wringing with sweat. I shook out the lariats that had been chafing my shoulders for hours. "A little rappelling ought to give us an appetite. You go first."

We might have been team climbers. I tested a tree and decided that it could hold either of us. I made a slip loop in the rope and Teddy stepped into it before waving as he slid off down the wall. Even before I'd paid out all the rope, it went slack.

"Teddy?" I said, but there was no answer.

I waited for sixty seconds and then flung the rest of the line over the side. I went down the cliff face without any idea of what I'd find at the bottom.

It was boring, creeping like an inchworm down an invisible and interminable wall. My hands blistered and the rope rasped at all the friction points of my uncallused skin. Still no sound from Teddy.

After an eternity, I heard the sound of running water, then I put my foot down on a spill of gravel, stumbled, and sat down, heavily. I was at the bottom.

I looked up at the faint pinpoints of the first stars high above. Then I saw the white of Teddy's shirt-sling. Behind him, I saw a strange shape, like a large X. It was lighter than the darkness of the underbrush that began at the edge of the sandy beach.

We'd made it to the *Barranca de cobre*. The smell of invisible water was maddening, and I pushed past Teddy to throw myself down on the bank for a long drink of Urique River water.

I stood up to find out what Teddy'd been inspecting. I

hoped I wasn't seeing what I thought it was. Teddy stood silently.

The light-colored X I'd glimpsed was a naked man, strung up off the ground by his arms and legs. He'd been hanged and drawn by the trees he was strung up against.

"The dog handler we were afraid would get ahead of us," Teddy said, turning away from the sight. "Apparently, he did. The Tarahumaras never forget. He shouldn't have been wearing green fatigues."

Thirteen

I'll never know how many times we crossed the Urique River. At first, the water seemed icy in contrast to the warm, perfumed air. After a while, I looked forward to the involuntary dowsings to rinse away the salty sweat which burned like acid in the scratches on my face and chest. We stumbled along, up sandbanks and down into marshes, into the water, along gravelly beaches the size of apartment patios, and over fallen tree trunks. Finally, I saw a light ahead.

"That's a Tarahumara camp," Teddy gasped. "They are very shy, and this may take a while. Stay behind me and don't talk. Don't smile. Don't frown. Coming out of the dark, we may be sorcerers as far as they're concerned, so wear your best poker face."

I followed Teddy into the ring of dim light cast by the smoky fire. He sat down to stare off at an angle, careful not to catch anyone's eye. I did the same. After a decent interval he began to talk, or rather, sing. It wasn't Spanish. Since it couldn't be mere entertainment, I guessed what I was hearing was Tarahumara.

Trying not to stare, I watched the three tiny people who reminded me of children playing at being grownups. They wore loincloths and nothing else. In the darkness it was impossible to determine their sex. They paid no attention to me or to Teddy's song. One was combing long hair with a pine cone. Another pulled branches out of the fire to inspect

them now and then. The third and smallest lay on the
ground, unblinkingly watching the reddish embers.

Teddy finished his song. Nothing happened. We waited.
I decided the smallest Indian must be a child because it wore
no clothes, not even the loincloth, and seemed entranced by
the fire.

Finally, the man who had been combing his hair—I saw
his mustache in the kindled fire—stepped into the shadows
and came back with a cigarbox violin. He put it against his
shoulder instead of his chin and began to extract noise from
it. When he sang, in a voice like a boy soprano with a
stopped-up nose, his version sounded a great deal like Teddy's song, but I didn't like it either. At last he finished, put
the instrument away, and nodded. We'd been invited to the
family fire.

Close up, I could see the firetender was a tiny woman
wearing a short leather apron. She was checking pieces of
meat on the sticks to see if they were done. Teddy began
again. Mercifully, this time he only talked. The woman pulled
one of the sticks out of the fire and handed it to the child,
who took it eagerly and gnawed the meat off the wood as if
this were some kind of campout where anything tastes great.
Probably rabbit, I guessed, or a small bird. Whatever it was,
it smelled wonderful.

The man answered Teddy's questions at length, pointing
downriver several times. When Teddy turned to me, the man
said something to the woman, who handed him a stick with a
scrap of meat on it.

"He says we're in luck. The *hechicera* we seek is only
three camps down the river. He has no place for us to sleep
here, but he offers food if we have anything to trade."

I had only the damp clothes I sat in, but Teddy took a
cloth packet out of a vest pocket and extended it to the man.
The woman crowded close and peered inside.

For the first time, she looked animated. *"Hikuli!"* she
said. *"Hikuli!"* She showed us her teeth and rewarded us
each with a stick to seal the bargain.

Teddy popped the bit of meat into his mouth without a
glance. I inspected mine. Impaled on the green branch,
charred to a crisp, but still recognizable, was a mouse.

I ate it and two more. I tamped them down with three
gritty, earth-tasting corn tortillas and a piece of rotten fruit

that, to judge from the way the child ate his, was a great delicacy. When he'd finished and licked his fingers carefully, he said something to the man.

Teddy looked grave, but his voice reflected no concern. "He wanted to know if you were my *demonio* because you are not a member of the people and you have a light skin. His logic says you must therefore be a devil. It's making the father nervous."

The father had an old man's face on the body of a stunted twelve-year-old. He kept stealing glances at us.

Teddy sighed and shifted his sling. "We've worn out our welcome. He fed us, but they don't offer strangers a bed for the night because nightwalkers are often the ghosts of their enemies. He says some way down the river there's an unoccupied sandbank underneath a fig tree. He suggests we spend the night there if we do not wish to see the *hechicera* tonight."

Stiff from sitting, I got to my feet and made a point of helping Teddy up. The Tarahumaras watched our movements with mounting suspicion. We slowly made our way to the river. By the time we reached the water, the fiddle had started again.

"He's playing a tune to keep us away from the camp all night. The child convinced him we're either ghosts or devils, so he decided we're witches."

"Why don't we press on to see your specialist tonight? The moon is getting higher and it ought to make traveling a lot easier."

"I think we must," he agreed, but his voice was not as strong as I'd like. "Now listen carefully. The man said we must keep along the river banks and whenever you hear a rattler, cross the river."

I wondered if his wound had made him a little crazy. With a soft chuckle, he went on to explain. "They have rattlers tied up to signal the route."

That didn't help much, and when I said so, he coughed a while. Teddy had excellent manners. "These rattles are no longer attached to the snakes. It's a witch-protection device. All that singing is to warn camps down the river we are coming. The rattles will warn us to avoid the other camps. Let's start now," he said abruptly.

I led the way into the gradually lifting darkness. Over

twelve hours had passed since I'd escaped Darque's guards.
As time went on, the walking got easier. After we crossed the
river several times, the moon had climbed high enough to
pour light straight down into the canyon. But the light wasn't
of much use because it made the shadows darker and leached
out the texture of shapes, turning them into pale abstractions,
visions of houses and mountains, puzzling forms.

Several times I heard the lethal buzz of snake rattles and
followed the instructions to cross the river. The last time that
happened, Teddy lost his footing and fell into a deep pool. I
managed to catch hold of him and drag him ashore.

So far, he'd been able to keep up with me, but I could
see he was played out and half-drowned. He needed help.
This was no place to stop, even to rest, so I got him on my
shoulder in a fireman's carry and set off again, a lot slower. It
was uncomfortable for both of us, but he didn't complain.

It felt like hours before the river and the valley widened,
and I could smell a heavy perfume in the air. I hoped it
meant we were nearing the end of the day's journey, since
surely, this couldn't be a natural perfume. I propped Teddy
against a tree while I rested.

"We're here," he said. "That's Jesuita's plant, datura. It
grows here and blooms at night. They call the blossoms
trumpets of the moon. All parts of it are magical. When it is
burned, the smoke can make you see the future. I think I can
walk unassisted now. I'm sorry I fell apart that way."

He took hold of my shirt and pointed across the river.
"You are looking at the *palacio* of Jesuita Contreras, *curandera*
extraordinary."

At first all I saw was the exposed rock of the cliff face that
was blanched by the moonlight. It reminded me of the
baroque facade of the Hotel Rex in Rio de Janeiro, an
architectural wedding cake designed by an Argentine archi-
tect inspired by Gaudi. Then the shadows shifted and I
picked out the maze of walls and patios carved and built of
the same rock that guarded what seemed to be the entrance
of an enormous cave.

A light appeared in the cave mouth, and a tiny voice
began to sing another Tarahumara song. Calling on what must
be his last reserves of strength, Teddy managed to walk alone
as we splashed across the shallow river into the softly blooming amber light of a kerosene lantern.

*   *   *

As soon as I saw her, I knew the lamp bearer was Jesuita Contreras. In an earlier age, she could have been a queen or a saint. Either way, she would have been burned at the stake. Teddy stepped to her side and dropped to one knee to raise her hand to his lips. It was a strange sight, the cynical soldier of fortune at the feet of the tiny medicine woman, but then everything about this trip had been strange.

She put the lantern on a waist-high wall to pat Teddy's head. Not a Tarahumara—she was considerably taller than the woman who had served me the mice. She was not an Indian, but she had the serene expression which the Tarahumara habitually wear.

I fell in love. Jesuita had been extraordinarily beautiful when young. She still was, though her face had sunk onto her bones like an apple too long unpicked from the tree. Her shining eyes, bright as a child's, gazed at the world from an ancient face. I had the feeling she wanted me to know we shared some common knowledge. She looked at Teddy—with the same intensity.

"I smell blood," she said, in English. Her speaking voice had an almost operatic resonance. "When Teddy comes, there is always blood. Come in."

Even though Anselmo Vigil had identified her as a doctor, I was ready for folk remedies—spiderwebs for Teddy's wounds, a broth made from reptiles and root herbs, maybe a little ghost dancing by an open fire. Instead, Jesuita picked up the lantern and led us into the cave. Once inside, she touched a switch to start a gas generator. An overhead light came on to reveal the whitewashed walls of what was clearly a hospital emergency room.

Teddy sagged against me, feverish and exhausted. When Jesuita pointed to a padded table, I shouldered him onto it and stepped away. She swiftly undid the makeshift arrangement of bandages I'd created for him, now stained with dirt and blood. She made a few chutting noises and spoke briefly to the nursing team, three little Tarahumara women in long white T-shirts that came below their knees.

They looked like nurses, clean and competent, but it was startling to see a barefoot emergency crew in operation. One of the nurses ran for the intravenous rig while another began swabbing Teddy's chest and back with hydrogen peroxide. After Jesuita scrubbed, the third aide helped her into a pair of surgical gloves. After the I.V. solution bottle was in its rack and flowing to her satisfaction, Jesuita picked up a probe and began to explore the wound.

"You did a good job of bandaging," she commented without looking up. "The wound has not picked up any foreign bodies. The bullet passed through. I wish all my tasks were this simple."

In seconds she had dusted the site with sulfa and inserted a small suction catheter to assist the drainage. When she was ready, one of the little nurses held out a suture needle and another stood on tiptoe to put a pair of glasses on Jesuita's nose. She looked like a granny at her mending.

Teddy hadn't stirred. I was about to commend her on her light touch when she spoke.

"There are very few nerves on the surface in this area, so it is no use wasting drugs. The muscles were parted by the path of the bullet, but it was a small caliber, so the healing needs no surgical intervention. Until the dura mater on the rib regrows, Teddy will know whenever it threatens rain. He should be recovered enough to travel by tomorrow morning."

She left the final work of bandaging and taping to the little nurses, though she watched them carefully. When they finished, they slid Teddy onto a wheeled stretcher and rolled him out of the operating room into the shadows.

Jesuita stripped off her surgical gloves and picked up the kerosene lantern before she shut down the electrical system. Immediately, we were back in the wilderness. She put a hand on my forehead. Her bones were as delicate as a wren's.

"You're generating a fever, young man. Come. I have something in the dispensary for you. You drank water from the river, didn't you?"

"Yes, but it's more likely the roast mice I had for supper."

She smiled her disagreement but didn't correct me as I trailed her into the dispensary, another room in the cave with whitewashed walls. She didn't turn on the electricity but held the lantern up while she opened a cabinet to take out a pair of bottles. She shook capsules out of two different bottles and beckoned me to follow her through another passage.

The echoes of my shoes on the cave floor made it sound

like a large place, but since Jesuita's lantern made little impression on the surrounding darkness, I couldn't be sure. We walked toward the only other illumination, the ruby embers of a fire that sent up blue-green flames in a column of sweet smoke. This room, I decided, must be deep in the earth because the cylinder of smoke was solid as metal in its ascent through the still air into the darkness overhead.

Jesuita stirred up the fire and sat down on a cushioned bench, her movements graceful as a young girl's. Absurdly, it made me wonder if she had a cure for the ravages of time. I thought of all the men who must have loved her and went to the end of the line. She motioned me to sit.

She was studying me carefully as she talked. "Out here where the human density isn't too high, field mice live very clean lives, so they're wholesome. The Urique River drains all these mountains with predictable results. Take these," she ordered, handing over two capsules and a saucer holding a cup she poured full of an anonymous liquid. "They will reduce your fever and quench other problems as well."

I chased the medicine with what had to be Earl Grey tea.

"I have few vices left," she said, smiling faintly. "Thankfully, tea is a virtue out here because all the water has to be boiled. Now, give me your account of what brought you here."

This was no time to lie, but a little drama might be forgiven. I answered her question precisely. "Two men, a live one and a dead one. Arthur Chess and Pancho Villa."

I might have been discussing the possibilities for rain. She took a sip of the tea. "Once I knew them both, but now I am the priestess of Quetzlcoatl, whose ghost walks forever, reborn over and over to prove that death ends only life, not existence. Simple people believe he is reborn when sufficient wrongs have gone unredressed. You wear his amulet around your neck."

I'd forgotten about the tiny farthing-sized medallion. I fingered it now.

"It shows Francisco Villa on horseback," she said, putting a hand to her throat to lift out a mate to the tiny emblem I wore. "Give it me. I will show you a wonder."

Mesmerized, I lifted off the fine silver chain and handed it to her. It must be, I thought, some talisman that Chess had supplied to Jesuita as payment for keeping the head. She took the tiny coin and snapped it between her fingers. Then she did the same with the one she'd worn, switched the pieces and put them both in her palm and extended it for me to inspect.

She had broken the two coins along a yin-yang pattern and put them back to back. Now the medallion made what had been a figure on a rearing horse into a feathered snake, rampant. The odd hieroglyphics that had spelled Francisco now read Quetzlcoatl.

"Many still believe Francisco Villa was Quetzelcoatl's *retornero*. The signs were displayed in his life—years of war, many campaigns, and a charmed life, never a wound. Strangely, nothing yet has resulted from those glorious beginnings."

She looked at me enigmatically. I was willing to listen as long as she wanted to talk.

"As with most articles of faith, reincarnation cannot be proved wrong. Nor can you believe. Nevertheless, Cheney, you are here."

Her knowing my name startled me, and I did what I always do in doubt. I went on the offensive.

"I'm here because sometime yesterday Teddy Ristra turned a pistol on himself after he'd shot an already dead man. You saw the powder burn on his coat as well as I did. If you have that kind of control over your believers, why don't you use your power for good?"

"Teddy shot himself so he could be with you when you came here. He wants to know what you will discover."

"I was just trying to get away from Darque's thugs. What does Teddy think I'll discover here?"

"Villa's head, of course."

"You know," I told her, letting her hear irritation in my voice, "I must be the last agnostic in the western hemisphere, but I don't believe in the miraculous values of heads that aren't attached to living people. If Teddy wants this relic so badly, why didn't he come here and take it?"

Jesuita smiled. "Why ask me questions to which you already have the answer? If Teddy took Villa's head and anyone tried to make political use of it, Chess would simply bring forward his imitation. He certainly has it done up more convincingly than the real thing."

The worst mistake to make in any argument is to assume

you're brighter than your opponent. I'd been doing that, so I stopped immediately. "Do you have the head?"

"Of course. Why do you think Chess gave you the amulet if not to identify you as his agent? Later, I will show it to you. I knew Villa in life, so it is difficult for me to think of him as a religious relic, though many do. He was a handsome, appealing man who came into the hospital I was heading and asked what he could do to help. After I told him he could stop killing so many people, we got on famously. Neither of us ever tried to change the other. I do think he'd be amused about all the fuss over his head."

It was an odd experience. I began by quarreling with her and now I realized we shared the same views. Or maybe I'd changed my mind while she was talking.

"All right, Teddy wanted to bring me here and you knew I was coming. For what?"

"That's up to you, Cheney."

Her patience with my questions seemed endless, as was her ability to give me ambiguous answers. I wondered if it was a skill she'd taught Rita. I wondered what Daisy thought of her. *We share a godmother,* she had said.

At that moment, in the lantern light, Jesuita looked like the Queen of Heaven I had seen in São Paulo. The life-sized doll had worn a tiara of seed pearls and many layers of rich fabric in a court dress that spread yards wide, but Jesuita's simple dress of plain material seemed endowed with the same unearthly richness of texture and color. Her bare feet were a sign of dignity. When my eyes reached her face, a glory burst around her head.

She noticed my reaction and smiled. "The medicine was a simple antibiotic, but the herbal tea will give depth to feelings you already entertain. By the morning, it will be metabolized."

She began to chant, gesturing at the column of smoke from the fire, which, stirred by her motions, had begun to move in whorls and elaborate designs. It wasn't exactly hypnotism, nor was it entirely the effect of the drug, but as she spoke, her appearance began to alter. Luis Montoya had taken her place.

Weirdly, I felt no apprehension looking at the man I'd killed. He didn't seem to hold a grudge. Not surprisingly, he wore the uniform I'd last seen him in, outsized jungle dunga-

rees that looked two sizes too large. As he always said, Luis
was a born civilian.

In life, he'd been a philosophy student, which meant he
had a full deck of outrageous ideas on any subject, and he
could talk endlessly. Tonight, he sat on the bench, his legs
crossed, waving his arms as he always did when he thought
the parade of his arguments was going well. He told me that
reincarnation was not necessary to this belief, though it
served as a decent metaphor since it sees historical deeds as
indigestible bits of reality that crop up eternally for each
generation's use. As always, Luis persuaded by offering his
views as paradoxes. I'm dead, as you know, he told me, but
here I am and you're listening to me, so I'm once more in the
flesh. I'm as alive as Socrates or Marx or Villa, which is good
enough for our purposes.

When I didn't object to this idea, he began to speak in
words instead of ideas, gesturing with the stub of the ever-
present, smoldering cigarette he used as a wand to make his
points. Persuasion was something he didn't expect to happen,
but he was always hopeful.

Finally he said what he had returned to tell me. He
explained the irony of his going to a war zone to be killed in
order to teach the ultimate power of peace. "I was a lesson for
you, Cheney. Don't forget it."

As Jesuita returned, Luis stopped talking and shrank into
himself until he was only a convolution in a column of smoke.
I was under the influence of a drug and in the hands of a
priestess, but I didn't have any feeling of unreality because
Luis was only repeating what I had told myself a million
times.

Jesuita and I began to talk. Whatever her religion, it had
served her well. She was old, certainly, but she had her own
teeth, her white hair was luxuriant, and her fine skin was
smooth. Under her simple clothes, she was strong and active.
What impressed me most was not her contentment, but her
tangible happiness.

"Cheney, I am sure you feel satisfied with yourself for
doing the best you can, but everyone else does their best too,
so it isn't much of a claim to make. Only witches in a fable say
they intend to pursue evil for the sake of evil."

Even if she'd been saying things I didn't want to hear, I'd
have been captivated by her voice.

"Do you understand what that means? No one commits a sin, they merely act on partial knowledge."

"In your religion there is no sin?"

"If a student makes an error in working out a mathematical problem, and you identify it as a sin, I doubt anyone would ever learn any arithmetic. Error is the price of the future. Do not make it more than it is."

I didn't want to deny what she was saying, but I've had too much experience of life to accept convenient views just because I wanted them to be true.

"But some acts really are evil. What about what was done to Epifanio? Does his suffering mean nothing?"

"You wish to give him back his sight? Do it if you can, but nothing less will help."

"He thinks God blinded him. Is that your view?"

"My view, Cheney, is that believing God did it to him gives Epifanio peace as no other explanation would."

It was true. But I couldn't stop. I argued because I'd always wanted to be persuaded, and I thought now it might happen.

"If you believe that, no wonder you live like a hermit, here, where no violence will ever touch you."

"Here is where I met Villa many times. You are here, and you make your living from violence. *Barranca de cobre* is not my retreat from brutality but only from earlier stages of life. Now I contemplate the world because I have lost the illusion of changing it."

If I hadn't been drugged by the datura, I'd have found the chink in the armor of her beliefs by now. "You must have become a doctor because you hoped to cure the world's evils."

"True," she answered serenely. "And the person who came here before me was a botanist who expected to improve the world. The one who will follow me is sure commerce will bridge any canyon."

At last, I thought, something tangible. "And Rita Madrid is the one who comes after you?"

She nodded.

"Is she your daughter? Granddaughter?"

"Biology is so unreliable. We choose our successors rather than bearing them. I have an obligation to fill my position before I can leave it. That means I must be sure of

Rita before I can depart. And she cannot take my position until she finds her own successor for the distribution of food. Many are starving, many need our help."

"Are you the godmother Rita refers to?"

"It is really Daisy you ask about. She is a good example of one who chooses to defend the helpless who are always in her sight. Perhaps that is the reason she is thinking of having a child."

Her reference to a child gave me a jolt. Daisy and I had never discussed having a child. And maybe that was an explanation itself.

One thing I had to ask. Before I could formulate my question, Jesuita answered it.

"Daisy does not work for me, and she never has."

"Then she didn't interview Valadez in El Paso?"

Jesuita shook her head. "That was Rita."

Of course. Rita was short for Margarita. The sister had called the visitor anglo, but Rita could appear to be anglo, Spanish, whatever she wished. I'd been so sure Daisy was involved, wanted so badly to see her again, I'd worked out the translation just to make myself feel better.

Jesuita went on. "After Daisy left you, she spent some time in Topolobampo at a house we have there. Now, I believe she's in Hawaii."

"So she's not a part of this?"

"Only as a wish on your part. Cheney, you must learn that the only reality is the present. Your love for Daisy was in the past, as is hers for you. Accept that you had it once and now you have nothing to complain of. Think of the untold millions who never experience what you shared. I tell you finally, Daisy is safe from any harm."

Jesuita had given me a lot to consider. Then I remembered that Socrates had learned all he knew about love from an old woman.

"You're saying Daisy is safe because she's a communicant in your faith?"

"Faith is too strong a word. It is more an acceptance of ideas about appropriate conduct. I would give you the example of Luis. He seemed to have discovered it."

Just when I thought I'd found an opening, it closed. She had mentioned Luis. Could I have said his name when he'd appeared in the column of smoke? My mind fumbled in the fragrant darkness. There had to be an explanation for all the things she knew.

"Do you spend all your time here in the wilderness? If you have a religion, why aren't you living out in the world where more people can hear your message?"

"For many years I did, but now each year I spend more time here, where the equation of life and death is marked most clearly. Rita has taken over most of my responsibilities in our enterprises. Soon she will have them all. I think I have finally reached the point your friend Luis spoke of. This is life enough for me."

I had the feeling she might evaporate before my eyes. I hurried a final question.

"Did Rasmussen work for you?"

"Probably for Rita. She is very good at recruiting unlikely types for her purposes. You, Cheney, are the important one, at this moment. I want you to dispose of Villa's head." She was present again in all her force.

It was an effort to contradict her. "I'm not involved."

"You are involved. You are here."

When I reviewed the effort required to bring me to the cave, I had to grant her point. But I wasn't giving up.

Before I could speak again, she put her cool hand across my lips. "You wonder on what authority I assign you this task? None. In the moments left until you see poor Villa's head, there are some last things you must learn."

She contemplated the column of smoke ascending slowly into darkness.

"At the time I took Villa's head, I thought Arturo had a sound idea—put a tangible object at the center of Villa's legend, and it will never die. But very soon I understood that a relic can mean what anyone wants it to mean. I had thought it would instill hope, but Arturo, tempted by politics as he would never be tempted by money, chose to make the head a counter in his game of power. His punishment is to be no better than those he hates. It has driven him mad."

It was a history lesson delivered by a sybil. She sat facing me, one hand holding the elbow of the arm that rose to put a finger across her lips as she spoke, telling me secrets I didn't wish to hear.

"Arturo always loved Villa, but he was also jealous. He was never convinced that Teddy was indeed his son and not

Villa's. These men!" she said, her mood changing. "Do you
know how his son responds to this foolishness? By insisting
that he is Villa's child, and not Arturo's! I loved Villa, but we
never were lovers. That way was to join a multitude, and I
have always walked alone. Now, it is time for you to see poor
Villa's head."

In the darkness behind her, an altar. Atop the rough-
hewn stone something glistened like a jewel.

"Villa knew the only future that may be controlled is
one's own. Since I agree with Villa on this, I told Arturo I
would yield the head only to a messenger, never to him, and
that messenger alone would have the disposition of the head.
That is why I've waited for you all these years. It took him
that long to choose. Since I no longer decide such things, it
will be a choice for you to make—no one else."

Jesuita's words were arresting, but the sphere on the top
of the altar was burning in the center of my awareness. It
floated in the darkness, tantalizing, ambiguous. It could be an
olla. Was it sculpture?

"What you must do, only you can do."

The sphere might be a stylized head. It was almost the
size of a bushel basket. I wondered if Jesuita used it as part of
her cult but then dismissed the idea. She was concerned with
practicalities, not rituals.

She proved it again. "Any further questions, you may
address to Rita. She will be seeing you for some years to
come. I will go now."

"That piece on the altar. Is it a sarcophagus?"

She gave me her last smile. "See for yourself. In this
place it has been safe from evil chances for half a century.
Don't take it elsewhere lightly, for its revelation will cheapen
it, but it is yours to dispose of."

For someone who declared herself outside history, Jesuita
knew how history worked. I tried a last question. "Why does
Villa excite this fanatic devotion?"

"Never ask a woman why she loves."

"But you said you were comrades."

"Isn't that love? I have had him with me for half a
century, years longer than any of his wives. But I have grown
tired of the task, so I leave it with you. From this moment
on, you are trapped. You must decide what to do with his
head. Shortly, all the contenders will know you have it."

Curiosity drew me across the room like a magnet. I put my hand on the coarse-textured rock that was the plinth for a large *olla* painted in carnival gold and red and violet. The *olla* was a giant head, with the forehead exactly as wide as the jaw—the symmetry symbolizing godhood the world over. Nowhere on the deep glaze could I see a line marking a lid. When I lifted the jar to inspect it, the whole object came up in my hands.

There on the raw stone, looking like the head of a man immersed to the neck in concrete, stood a relic I had no trouble recognizing. Unmistakably, it resembled every picture I'd ever seen of Villa. The only difference, an authenticating one, was that time had turned the skin to leather. The jawline was like the prow of a boat, the teeth pushed the heavy lips into a pout below cheekbones as pronounced as kneecaps. The thick hair that had once shadowed the brow was now only a memory of bronze stubble.

I studied the face and tied into it all the stories I'd read and heard about Villa—his courage, his unpredictability, his seductive mixture of naivete and insight, his explosive emotions, his river-like generosity. All passions could find a home on this face. That was why everybody wanted it, would kill for it. When I saw how sunken the eye sockets were, I knew this head had not been embalmed, though the lips had been sewn together, as had the wounds that matched those in the picture of Villa dead in his car.

When I picked up the head, I found it much lighter than it should be. The bottom of the neck, where a rough gather of skin could be expected, was perfectly smooth. The skin had been sewn together in a tiny pattern of baseball stitches, the same precise needlework I'd seen Jesuita demonstrate on Teddy's wounds.

As Anselmo Vigil's deposition stated, Jesuita had surgically amputated Villa's head within hours of his death. Then she had used the Egyptian method of preservation, surgical excision of the cranial contents and a slow dessication in a desert atmosphere. I stared at the object in my hands, wondering how many had died to protect it, how many more would die.

But when I turned around to ask her, Jesuita was gone. I hadn't heard her leave, not even the feathery scuff of her bare foot across the stone floor. I sat down on the edge of the platform with the head between my knees.

It was just a skull, the empty envelope that had once contained a person. I remembered what Valadez had said about Villa being charged with high-voltage electricity. Teddy was outside somewhere, willing to do almost anything to possess what I held against my knee.

Teddy, Chess, Darque—they were all fools, but I understood how Jesuita had trapped me. She'd played on my memories to make me see just how empty are the political talismans of this world. Knowing I had no interest in Mexican politics, she foresaw what my relationship with Villa would have to be.

Fourteen

I was awake. Stiff and hungry, but most of all, thirsty. Then I looked down at Villa's head, on the floor at my feet, glaring up at me. I'd fallen asleep while puzzling over the problem of disposing of Villa's head—without playing into the hands of people who would kill me to get it and thousands of others once they had it.

Letting the head go could be as strenuous as finding it had been, so it was urgent that I make a few arrangements. The sun shafting down from the opening directly overhead reminded me I didn't have forever to work up a solution. Still, it was another quarter of an hour before I got up from my seat before the altar.

There were lanterns on a rack inside the mouth of the cave, so I lit one and set out to find my own cache for the head, one that didn't have to last for half a century. It took a while, but I found the place, a shadowy, dry ledge on the far side of a shaft that led to an underground river. Only then did I make my way to the cave's mouth to stand again in the searing light of day.

Teddy was waiting for me, sitting on a low wall at the

entrance, whittling with his switchblade on a long willow wand. He seemed quite recovered from his injuries.

"Why didn't you wake me?" I asked.

He pointed with the switch at the entrance to the cave over my head. Crudely painted in a reddish ochre clay that resembled dried blood was a large Y. One arm of the figure ended in an arrowhead but the other had an X. It had a power of infinite suggestion, like a skull and crossbones.

"That's Jesuita's sign," Teddy said. "It means bad things will happen to anyone who chooses to enter that cave without her permission. No native will go in there, and I'm just primitive enough so I'd think twice about it myself."

"Where's Jesuita?"

He shrugged and threw the switch away. "I woke up at first light and I've been waiting for you here all morning. She never came out. Have some coffee," he said, picking up a large stainless-steel thermos. "Guaranteed, one hundred percent pure coffee, no additives."

Without waiting for an answer, he filled a heavy glazed mug obviously made out of clay from the riverbank below us.

"Start with the sign," I said. "A Y with an arrow and an X on its arms is one I've never seen."

I took a sip of the coffee. After the potions I'd been drinking lately, it tasted insiped, sanitized.

Teddy smiled at my suspicions. "I've been drinking it all morning. The Y was a pre-Christian symbol of a moral crossroads, a time of choosing between heaven and perdition. As she uses it, the arrowhead indicates a continuing direction, but the X marks destruction. She put the X over the cave mouth to keep people out."

The sun's flare would burn off the high overcast shortly. I was once more in the world and I had things to do, but I luxuriated in the silence. Across the river, the grass was a wan gray, and despite the rising heat, the scene wore the desiccated look of winter. Last night this place had been a tropical paradise. Now the dry leaves and the stand of corn on the opposite riverbank rustled like paper. I felt the edge of a cool breeze lifting from the river and shivered.

"Teddy, I know you shot yourself yesterday to bring me here. What side are you really on?"

A dust devil rose across the river. It picked up loose stubble and leaves and was now two or three hundred feet tall as it worked its way up the rising ground on the other bank of the river.

"There's only one side, Cheney. Mexico. You have in your hands the future of my country. What you do will influence our history for all time to come."

The dust devil dissipated, broken up by the rocky cliff. Teddy is a patriot, I thought, and felt tired. He's much more dangerous than self-seeking scoundrels. There's no limit to his goals or what he'll do to achieve them.

Looking more than ever like a skilled workman in some heavy trade, Teddy intently studied his fingers as he began to unwind a raveled thread from his shirt cuff. "You have looked on Villa face to face, Cheney. I know it. You have seen the relic of the true Revolution."

I was a poker player who had little to bet with. He sat forward to put his hands on his knees, a seated monarch from some ancient past.

May as well tell him. "Yes, I saw Villa's head last night. It was withered skin on bone so old it was as light as balsa. His wounds had been stitched up. It didn't inspire me at all, but then I don't have your perspective."

That seemed to be what he'd been waiting to hear. His face glowed. "I knew it. Villa was a great man. In his life, he was the flag of Mexico—as noble and undaunted as the eagle, as sudden and violent as the snake. That is needed again. There are many wrongs to be righted."

When he looked past me, his expression changed. "Did you know that Villa thought the rattlesnake was his totem animal? It is an honorable serpent. Only under the direst circumstances does it strike without warning. Now I must tell you, having introduced the subject, that this is the time of day—"

Moving only my eyes, I glanced down in the direction of his gaze. Sure enough, a diamondback rattler about a yard long was unleashing in the shade of the rock bench we sat on, inches beyond my bare foot. The austere metallic architecture of his head glinted and his tongue flickered like a match flame.

"Don't bother to tell me not to move," I said quietly. "What's the Spanish for rattler?"

"*Culebra de cascabel*—or *cascabel* in a hurry. He's only

seeking a cooler place to wait for the night. I'll tell you when it's safe to shift your feet."

After the longest ten seconds I could remember, Teddy's shoulders relaxed. The rattler was vanishing into a crevice in the wall. I was surprised to find I'd been holding my breath. The beauty of any wild animal affects me like strong drink. Danger is everywhere, but why did the rattler put me in awe, while I had nothing but contempt for the man who had blinded Epifanio? After all, both of them were animals, and Epifanio had felt about the man who maimed him as I did about the snake.

I turned back to Teddy. "Thanks for the warning. I'm going back to Chihuahua. If you and I are on the one side, you can come with me as either a guide or a companion. Interested?"

He grinned. "*Comprendo, compañero.* The Tarahumaras will be coming back here to see what Jesuita has left them on this visit, so it is wise for us to leave."

He pointed to a neat pile of clean clothes and a pair of field shoes. "It's a long walk from here, so put those on. They've been washed in the water of the Urique River and mended by Jesuita's people. They're very clean, but they look tired. I think it is the beating on the rocks that has taken away their texture, but they're an improvement on your present clothes."

No argument there. The khakis looked flimsy, but the leather shoes were a welcome change from the loafers that had disintegrated on my feet during yesterday's march. So, cleaned up, informed, but still not totally enlightened, I was ready to start the long climb out of the barranca. Teddy changed my mind.

"The head. If it's still there, I'd like to see it."

"Let's go look." I had nothing to hide. "It's inside a big painted jar on an altar."

Teddy let me lead the way into the cave, and after a couple of false starts, I brought him into the cool big room that tapered down to the monolith at the far end. The fire was out and the furniture was gone, but the aperture high overhead gave us light enough to see the olla.

I started to point to it, but Teddy brushed past me to lift it off the altar.

As Villa would say, No birds in that nest.

*   *   *

As soon as we left the cave, Teddy began talking non-stop. He obviously thought we'd been through enough together to become, as he said, companions. As he talked, he slipped into Spanish.

He began by telling me his life story from the time he discovered at the age of seven that Villa was his father. I wondered why Teddy was confessing to me, and then I understood. I was a totem object. Since I had seen Villa's head, I shared Villa's power.

No point in having an advantage and not using it.

"Teddy, Jesuita told me she was your mother. She also said Arthur Chess, not Villa, was your father."

I'd probably gone too far, but taking risks was the only way I'd get through the troubled times ahead. I was tired of their illusions. Teddy stood like a statue. When he turned to face me, he had his face in order.

"When my father denied his parentage and disgraced my mother, I did as Villa did. I chose my own father. Villa came to me many times when I was young and taught me many lessons."

I thought of Señora Vigil, sitting in the room behind the store, safeguarding memories of Villa. Make enough noise in your life and you won't be forgotten. Teddy drew himself up to stare balefully at me. "Poor Mexico is the country of my birth, but its rightful position is to be the capital of both Americas. I have spent my life working for the elimination of all borders. That is an ambition worthy of the son of Francisco Villa."

There was no comment to make about that. It didn't matter, because a dam had broken. Teddy went on at great length about what he called the "migration of peoples" that could swamp every political border that ever existed. I wondered if this was some form of the ideas I'd heard Rita and Jesuita voice, that an international border is only an opinion. I decided I preferred the pragmatic approach of the women because Teddy, as he had identified himself when I first met him, was a long-term troublemaker.

There were lots of ways to take his views, but I saved my breath for the climb. Teddy was guiding me through rough country. We were either climbing a steep slope or skidding

through a fall of shale. Going into the barranca, I hadn't been
aware of the scenery because I was concentrating on Teddy.
Now he told me the history of a part of Mexico still largely
unknown even to many Mexicans.

"It was only in 1961 that they managed to complete the
Chihuahua al Pacifico railway. Dozens of engineers from all
the countries of the world had tried to do it, but our people
succeeded. It is the first and only link between the plains of
northern Mexico and the Gulf of California.

"I love this area. From the beginning of time, it has been
Mexico's frontier. That makes it the destination for all sorts of
people who wish not to be followed. Some call it the Texas of
Mexico, full of Mennonites, Mormons, and people who don't
like police. Villa spent a lot of his life here."

Climbing back up to ten thousand feet required a lot
more oxygen than I'd needed going down. By the time we
crossed the ridge into the next valley, the *Barranca de San
Miguel*, our routines had become rituals. When we found a
Tarahumara camp, Teddy bartered *hikuli*, peyote buttons, for
food. After the lengthy civilities, we would sleep under a tree
in humid darkness as warm as a watch pocket.

We'd traveled for three days when it happened. It was
just before sunset and I'd made out the firefly lights of a pair
of guttering campfires in the purple gloom of the valley's
bottom. I'd grown accustomed to Tarahumara hospitality and
I was looking forward to meeting our hosts for supper. Then I
heard the heavy *flat! flat! flat!* sound of a transport helicopter.

It took a long time to reach us, its heavy engines
straining, but when it arrived, it blotted out the bright sky
over our heads like a gigantic locust. In the thin air of the
Sierra Madres, the engines were at maximum power and the
echoes off the valley walls redoubled the eery keening of
the turbos.

For days, we hadn't heard a sound louder than an
occasional rapids, and I'd grown accustomed to the lesser
sounds of the wild—the calls and howls and cries of the birds,
wolves, and cougars, the occasional whisper of wind, and the
odd music the Tarahumaras teased from their homemade
musical instruments. If the unmuffled sound of an assault ship
affected me like that, I wondered what the Tarahumaras made
of it.

When I turned to ask Teddy, I saw a mask of anger on his

face. He looked at me accusingly. "That isn't the *federales* on a drug sweep," he said.

"Are you sure? The way you've been distributing peyote could lead them right to us."

He shook his head stubbornly, in no mood for jokes. "There are no markings on that plane. They are not federals but people looking for us. It's a good thing we haven't visited the village yet. Now. No matter what happens, we stay here."

We took cover behind the trunk of a house-sized fig tree about half a mile uphill from the Tarahumara camp, so we saw it all.

Black against the orchid sky overhead, the big helicopter settled toward the cleared area beside the river. The infantry used to call rigs like this gunships because they carried enough armament for a navy vessel. Now I'm sure they call them Deathstars. As it crossed the sun's shadow line at the tip of the valley, I could just make out the installation of a remote gun turret on the jutting chin of the craft.

The craft's landing lights came on, brutally illuminating the area below like a stage set. Frozen into stone but ready to flee, the tiny Tarahumaras stood gaping at this visitation from the twentieth century. One of them fitted an arrow into his little bow.

With a sick feeling, I knew this scene had been enacted hundreds of thousands of times, all over the world. Among the black camouflage uniforms stood a small man wearing a dirty T-shirt and nothing else. Under white hair, his face was wrinkled into a prune. Using the bottle in his hand, he pointed at the bowman. Men leaped from the dark maw of the cargo door to fan out into an arc, automatic weapons at high port.

Within seconds, the archer was surrounded, the bow was yanked out of his hands, and he was lifted off his feet and dragged to the door of the chopper. The engines were idling, but the rotor blades hadn't stopped cycling.

The little Indian took the bottle out of his mouth to translate the questions asked by a soldier who wore a black sweatband around his platinum blond hair. The bowman looked from the other Indian to his interrogator, but said nothing.

The questioning didn't go on long. With an impatient gesture, the questioner barked an order. The bowman was handcuffed, lifted off his feet, and tossed into the cargo door like a not very valuable trophy. The scouts, their weapons outthrust to cover each other from possible attack by the bowman's family, backed into the helicopter.

Beside me, Teddy had half risen to his feet, fumbling under his shirttail for something in the small of his back. Then, with a detonating blast that settled into a roar, the heavy ship lifted off under maximum accumulation. Thunderously, the chopper ascended. The downdraft was a hurricane and the Tarahumaras on the ground scattered.

After a moment, the little Indian was dangled outside the door, then jerked back in. This was repeated three more times.

Even in the horrendous din of all that horsepower holding the helicopter overhead, I heard Teddy's sudden curse. I turned. His pistol was aimed at the ship.

"*Chivatos! Pinchi batos!*" The shout seemed torn from his guts.

I jumped him, desperately trying for the gun with both hands.

Teddy managed to get one shot off, and then we were rolling over and down the steep hill, each of us with a contrary idea—he to shoot that hellish plane out of the sky with a toy-caliber handgun and me to stop him from shooting. We both got quite a thumping and scraping from boulders, decayed tree stumps, and gravel slides. What finally stopped us was the bole of another fig tree.

Fortunately, it knocked the breath out of Teddy. I reached to jerk the gun out of his slackened grasp and throw it uphill.

I glanced at the helicopter. Even as I looked, the little Tarahumara flew out the door. I tackled Teddy, who was scrambling uphill to get at his weapon.

The Indian fell straight down, his arms doubled behind his back and his legs flailing at strange angles. He landed at the water's edge, a crumpled heap. Beneath me, I felt Teddy's body sag.

Most of the camp, perhaps a dozen people, ran toward the dead man. Even before they had a chance to lament, I saw a mist rising from the ground in a large arc. I didn't have to hear the familiar static crackle of what I recognized as electric powered gun cannons raining death down from above.

The Indians melted into the ground like candles subjected to intolerable heat.

Teddy wrenched free of me, wrinkles I'd never seen before carved into his grim face. A sob choked in his throat, but he made no further movement. "*Pesadilla*. A nightmare of our century."

"It's been going on forever," I told him. "Only the weapons have changed."

The helicopter had finished its lethal mission and listed into its flight angle to disappear behind the jagged mountain-tops. We were alone in a profound silence.

"Somebody has to be alive down there," Teddy said hoarsely as he started down the hill. I knew better, but I followed him anyway.

The cyclic rate of an electrically driven set of gun cannons is faster and noisier than a Pachinko game. The mist we'd seen rising was churned-up dirt, rock, trees, and human flesh chopped into bits no bigger than hamburger. In less than a minute, an area the size of a football field had been carpeted with high velocity metal.

Inside that hellish circle nothing was left intact. The air was corrupted by the smell of blood-soaked earth, smashed vegetation, and the gamey scent of human tissue that has been seared by white heat. Nothing lived there anymore.

But Teddy proved me wrong. Someone was alive. She must have been full grown because her swollen body betrayed that she was pregnant, though at first I thought she was a child who'd taken a slug in the middle because she was curled in a tight fetal position around the butt of a madrone stump. Teddy dropped to his knees to lift her gently away from the tree.

The woman's face was a dusty mask smeared by the pale trails of her tears. Otherwise, she didn't seem to be marked. When Teddy began talking to her quietly, she listened intently, studying his face for answers. He was not a member of the tribe and she had every reason to associate him with the disaster that had rained on her world from the sky.

Finally she blurted out a halting flow of consonants and choked sounds that could have been incoherent sobs. Teddy started to lift her onto her feet and then changed his mind in mid-effort when he looked down.

"Get my pistol. I'll wait for you here."

I considered a protest, but Teddy knew things I didn't, so I crawled up the hill to find his gun. Something told me the woman was badly hurt, even though she'd given no sign of being in pain. She was able to sit up in Teddy's arms, so her back wasn't broken.

As I came back down the slope, I saw Teddy was on his knees before her, strewing dust on her face in an elaborate pattern. When he stood, I saw what had happened. Her legs had been cut off just above the knees. The severed femoral arteries had emptied life from her body in seconds.

"Her husband was the man with the bow and arrow. He had been to the mission school in Creel. He told her to run because he had heard of these gunships and how they are used. She almost got far enough. They did not even pretend to be *federales*, no talk about marijuana fields or gun smugglers. They had sketches of two men, a fat one and a tall one."

He saw my puzzlement. "A big Tarahumara weighs maybe one hundred and ten pounds and stands five feet. That makes me fat and you tall."

I wanted to talk, but I had nothing to say. Teddy looked at me. Tears coursed down his face. "You are hard, Cheney. Let us bury her here with her people."

It didn't take long. The chopped-up earth was soft as humus, so we dug with our hands. When we had put her out of sight, we climbed back up the hill and lay down wordlessly in the cool darkness under the fig tree.

I listened to the bats eating the figs in the tree overhead for a long time. Teddy wasn't sleeping either. Finally, he sighed.

"I know where that gunship has to be hangared. I'm going to find it, work out a way to put its crew on board, and then I'm going to blow the bastard up. Want to come along?"

"No," I said, listening to my voice as if it belonged to someone else. Killing begets killing, just as Luis had said. There had to be a better way. The people who gave the orders had a heavier guilt than the men who carried them out.

"I'm going to find Darque. He's had things his own way too long. But I'm not going to kill him."

"Do what you wish, Cheney, but I'm going to kill everyone who was a part of what we saw."

Numbly, I worked out the logic bridge. Chinook helicopters have been around for years, time enough to sell them to a variety of nations. But they're expensive to buy, to operate, and to maintain. With just that gun turret they could expend thousands of dollars worth of ammunition in seconds. Only Darque and Chess had that sort of money.

Teddy was sure Darque was behind a plan to carve a buffer state out of northern Mexico. Knocky's informants thought Darque intended to take over the entire government of Mexico. Either way, somebody had managed to convince some committee of fools in Washington that Darque was someone they could use for political purposes of their own in Central America.

When I factored in the way Chess had gotten the All Points Bulletin on me quashed in minutes, it seemed likely that he, as well as Darque, was playing on all the primitive fears of my government's policymakers—the illegal immigrants, the drug trade, the possibility of Communist infiltration in this hemisphere—to convince Washington that just one more intervention in Central America would solve all our problems forever.

Lying in the sweet-scented darkness of the Sierra Madres, I knew I must stop this madness. That was the real mission that Jesuita had bequeathed to me. My first step was to meet with Mario Darque on my terms, in public, in Juarez, the unofficial capital of Chihuahua.

PART THREE

Fifteen

Old timers say Juarez is just a spit and a streetcar ride across the Rio Grande from El Paso, Texas. The local news in Juarez is covered by the El Paso newspapers, so that was my insurance that Darque wouldn't be able to kidnap me—as long as I stayed in the public eye. The most public place I could find was the year's first *corrida*. I decided it was a prudent use of assets to spend the rest of my available money to rent three of the boxes they call *barreras*. A ringside seat for the bullfight should keep Darque's bully boys at a decent distance.

As with every public event in Mexico, whether an important funeral or an election, a *fiesta mercado* had been set up to take advantage of the throngs of customers flooding the streets as they headed for the *Plaza de toros*. All of the *aficionados* of bullfighting and half the population of the state of Chihuahua were pricing, buying, or peddling cheese, meat, fruit, electronic gadgets, used furniture, lottery tickets, minor surgery and major dentistry while waiting for the spectacle to begin.

PRI candidates gave impassioned speeches while derelicts gargled gasoline and then set it afire for a tip of ten pesos. The smells were free: something septic—aged horse meat, I thought—was modified by baking bread, which was instantly replaced by the acrid bite of soldering that conjured elaborate ornaments out of five-gallon tins, but that in turn was damped down by the fermenting odor of wet reeds used to weave vases, animal shapes, and even waterproof *ollas*.

When the trumpet sounded at two o'clock, a black Lincoln with darkened windows nosed through the crowds to the front entrance. I'd left tickets for Darque at the front

197

gate, but I wasn't going to enter the center box until I assessed his protection.

As I'd instructed, he brought only one person. I'd expected his massive bodyguard, the man named Oso. When Rita got out of the car, I felt a stab, whether of surprise or disappointment it was hard to tell.

This afternoon, Rita wore the khaki pants and shirt of our drive through the mountains, adding an indigo silk scarf tied around her dark hair as protection against the blowing dust. It made her face severe and beautiful and impossible to read. She was carrying her outsized purse. I couldn't believe she'd kill me, but my confidence went no further than that.

She and Darque walked through the entrance, and the crowd melted to give them passage, commoners before royalty. That wasn't reassuring, but then I spotted an ace I hadn't realized I had in reserve. Teddy Ristra was sitting in the topmost row in the roofed section of the stadium.

He and I had separated casually at dawn on the city's outskirts, but I had expected to meet him again. He wouldn't keep Darque from taking direct action, but I might use him as running interference. I spent the time before the march of the *toreros* looking for Darque's people. When the ceremonial parade before the event began, I strolled down to the box and eased into the seat beside Darque.

"You took your time getting here," he said, eyes on the surging crowd below us. The seats were the New World's version of an imperial box. We had the best view of the stage below, and we were easily seen by the rest of the audience. Darque was used to this treatment. He spoke as confidently as he had in his living room.

"In Topolobampo I learned to be cautious." I looked at Rita. "And not to be taken in by appearances."

"It was all wasted effort. My men are everywhere."

We were still volleying to loosen up, so I broke a personal rule and topped him. "Yes, but you're here. And I have one man who's watching you with great care. I'd advise you not to make any sudden gestures while I'm with you."

Slowly, Darque turned to gaze at me, his head revolving on his neck like an owl's. "What do you want?"

"To tell you how my search is going. I found Villa's head."

He turned back to the doings in the bullring. It was a

brilliant, noisy parade of everybody who took part in the proceedings—the splendidly arrayed matadors, the picadors, the banderilleros, and even a couple of men leading a team of draft horses whose function wasn't clear to me.

"You are an *aficionado*?" he said, not really interested. Like me, he was still warming up.

"No. I just prefer to transact private business in public places."

"Where is the head?"

"Arthur Chess has what's left of Villa in a vault on his ranch—in Texas."

"You're certain?"

"I've studied Villa's head quite carefully," I said, telling the truth briefly enough to mislead.

"Bring it to me."

A roar erupted from the crowd when the bull came out. They subsided as the animal charged first one and then another of the bullfighters. I didn't think the chap had his heart in what he was doing, but he was determined to give good value. It was enough. The crowd roared again.

"I'm a businessman, Darque, not a commando. Chess has security at military levels. I didn't engage with anyone to steal the head, merely to find out if it was authentic."

Darque stared at the goings-on below in the bullring. The bull had almost a dozen targets, but they vanished whenever he attacked one. Losing patience with this routine, he finally chose a spot across the ring to stand and survey his tormentors, his flanks heaving.

The crowd had quieted down, but now it began to complain at the bull's lack of enterprise. When the matador came out with a cape and the other contestants retired, the bull obligingly charged and missed. This went on for a while. The matador seemed to be ahead on points because the crowd shut up.

The picadors on horseback entered from behind the barrier entrances of the ring. Still not looking at me, Darque patted Rita's knee, giving me a minor conniption, though I had no grounds for it.

"We have had some misunderstandings, Cheney, but I do not believe in wasting resources, and you are a resource. I offer you an accommodation. Despite your independent ways, I'm willing to continue on the same terms, even though you have made my men look foolish and you killed many of them when you blew up my helicopter."

Teddy had kept his promise. The Deathstar had been destroyed. I still had my promises to keep.

Darque took a minute to savor his irritation at the wasted assets. "Before going further I need assurance you're not working for Chess."

That was easy to answer. "I don't work for anyone who sets me up to be killed. If you want Villa's head, go get it. I've told you where to go for what you want. The important material I have in a safe place—proof that this is indeed Villa's head."

Two different picadors had plagued the bull. From my reading I understood they were making him mad and tiring him out by sticking him with the tips of lances and letting him try to gore the padded horses. It seemed to be working. I hoped the same thing was happening to Darque, but when he spoke, his voice was calm.

"I have some large and important operations in final planning, and I want someone with your talents."

The crowd set up a roaring as the *banderilleros* spread out to place the ribboned sticks with a hook on the end into the bull's neck. What I was doing with Darque was probably a lot more dangerous.

"You need somebody with talent. Most of your hired hands are not very impressive—except at gunning down unarmed civilians."

He explained his personnel practices. "I pay for assistance in getting what I want. It doesn't matter how it happens. For example, you're here, in Mexico, as I wished."

His attitude reminded me of Mercedes, the spoiled darling I'd let get away with murder. I took a page from her book. "It must be boring, having to hire everything done. Don't you ever wonder how you'd do without all the bought help?"

I hadn't laid a glove on him. He shrugged and sat forward in his seat to watch the cape work.

Rita spoke up. "We're not alone, Mario."

"She's right," I told him with some satisfaction. "My backup is sitting behind us. The show was so exciting I didn't bother to introduce him, but he makes friends wherever he goes with his pistol tricks."

The crowd emitted a roar. The matador was engaging the bull close up and they loved it. Darque's cheek twitched. He was wondering if this was a bluff. After all, he'd caught me bluffing him before.

It was just luck. Teddy was supposed to be a distant spectator of this meeting, but he had entered our box as silently as snow falling. He'd picked up enough of my scam to play a part. Gently, he put his folded program against Darque's back. There might be a pistol hidden there, but all a casual observer could see was a fan calling a friend's attention to a fine point of *tauromachia*.

I had to admit I enjoyed putting Darque under pressure. A lot of violence had been done in this man's name while he stayed snug at home.

But Darque wasn't sweating, not even at the prospect of a Walther pressed against his spine. He leaned forward as the matador ended a series of maneuvers with the cape that left the bull standing stolidly in the middle of the ring. Darque began to clap. So did everyone in the crowded arena except for Teddy, Rita, and me.

Darque sat back, looking pleased. He wasn't going to melt in the sun. "So, you say Chess has the head. It is of no use unless you can trace its trail from the cemetery to the present day. You say you have done that?"

"I've done it," I said and then lost interest in badgering Darque when another idea struck. "Arthur Chess is an old man. He's not interested in seeing trees blossom after he's dead. Money in hand has always been his interest. He says it's the only way to keep score. So we're going to hold an auction—for Villa's head and its absolute, authenticating proof."

Darque started to make a gesture with his program, but I cut him off. "Let me tell you the proof is in the United States in a place known only to me. Chess holds the head in great security. Both items will be brought together and put up for bid at a time and place I will determine later. If anything happens to me in the meantime, the auction is off. I have arranged this meeting to invite you to join the bidding. If you're interested, bring money."

"Who are the other bidders?" he asked, showing a rim of white around his pebble-gray eyes. I had him going at last.

"I'm not at liberty to disclose that, but Mr. Chess has alerted a number of organizations he feels have both the interest and the assets to make substantial bids. I qualify for the facilitator's percentage, so it's no use trying to bribe me."

That last made it irresistible to Darque, but Rita's face had turned to stone. If she was Jesuita's successor, she knew that I, not Chess, had both Villa's head and the authentication. What she wasn't so certain of was whether I intended to run an auction. She'd kept me in the dark for quite a while. It was a fair return.

Now, having lit the fuse, I had to work out a getaway. "I know neither of us trusts the other. With good reason on both sides. So, let's exchange hostages."

In the arena, things got very quiet. The matador signaled for his sword. Darque's head came round as if he had a well lubricated ball bearing somewhere in his neck.

"Here is my brother's widow. I trust her and she can protect you, if necessary."

I looked at Rita, but she'd stopped paying attention and was watching the ring. The sword went in. Suddenly, the bull was on his knees, coughing his life out into the sand.

Either I'd done it or Darque had—run a successful con. I stood up. "And my bodyguard, Señor Ristra here, will stay with you. Enjoy the rest of the show."

The air crackled with the bloodthirsty howls of the crowd. I didn't know how Rita was going to respond and I wasn't certain how Teddy would negotiate this situation. Teddy gave me one of his enigmatic looks and unfolded his program to reveal it was empty. Then he sat down casually beside Darque, a couple of old friends.

Rita stood waiting, purse in hand. She and I wove through the crowd that was already eagerly discussing the main event coming up. The bull's death had been forgotten except by the men who had brought up the rear of the opening parade. They hitched a team of horses to the dead bull and began dragging him out. All that remained was the dark stain of blood on the sandy floor of the arena.

Once outside, Rita turned into a drill sergeant. "Take off your coat," she said, instructing a dull recruit in something either difficult or important. "Sling it over your shoulder as though you were too warm. In a minute, we're going to buy you a *vaquero* sombrero, very gaudy, with a large brim. It's in terrible taste, but put it on. After that, we'll be stopping to look at various booths. Stay close to me," she said with a smile that didn't say anything except that she assumed people were watching. Still, the smile stirred up all sorts of contrary feelings. I didn't know if I was glad or sorry, but I did what she said. We both knew too well that hostages count for very little when the stakes are high.

We hadn't walked more than a minute when Rita pointed, still smiling, at a dark shop in an adobe building across the square from the cathedral, where stacks of straw hats hung on hooks from the ceiling. The gnarled little man who sat napping in a bentwood kitchen chair jumped up when we walked in. Before I could say anything, he reached overhead and broke open a stack of hats to hand me one. It fit perfectly. He nodded but sat back down when I reached for my wallet. Rita took my arm to pull me out of the shop.

All this prearrangement showed me that Rita was working to a plan of her own. That wasn't a surprise. My problem was whether she and I interpreted the rules of this game the same way.

Out in the hot sun again, we strolled along the line of canvas-walled sheds set up against the cathedral wall. We inspected leather goods, hammered silver jewelry, and cotton stuffs from Tabasco. If Rita was nervous, she didn't show it.

We came to an intersection. A late model American car with two men in it pulled up to block the other end of the street. They could have been Darque's people because Rita suddenly pointed at a palm reader's sign sandwiched between a taco stand and a booth full of women's shoes. The *zapateria's* customers were women of all ages standing like storks trying on footgear of an astonishing variety. The taco stand was jammed by a crowd of children who had noisily erupted from a battered yellow bus pulled up across the narrow street. The bus was named *La Luz*. It was decorated with Christmas tree lights as running gear. Schoolchildren on an outing. I couldn't tell how much of this action was Rita's plan and how much was daily life in a market town.

"Let's have your fortune told," Rita said abruptly.

But there was no one in the little roofless booth made by cloth walls. Rita pointed to the painted cloth that hung from the poles at the back of the booth. On the ancient canvas there were crude but elaborately detailed pictures of two women. Once the colors had been vivid, but now the sun had faded them into pastels. I worked out the lettering. *La*

Santisima Virgin de Guadalupe was the label above a dark-skinned representation of the Virgin Mary. *Nuestra Señora de San Juan de los Lagos* was incorporated into the stiff gown and mitred crown worn by the other. Both figures had bare feet.

The school bus outside sounded a *rat-a-tat* horn signal, and the children who had been milling in front of the taco stand flocked away, giggling. At the same moment, the painted tapestry I'd been studying was lifted at one corner. A man held it aside so a woman wearing khaki pants and a shirt could come through.

The man was in his early twenties and about my size. He took my sombrero and jacket while the woman swiftly wound Rita's silk scarf around her head. He hooked my coat over his shoulder and whispered *Suerte* as they sauntered out of the booth. He was looking down at his palm and talking to the girl in a low tone.

We'd escaped surveillance for the moment, but the bluff wouldn't last long and we both knew it. The people following us were professionals. Rita took my arm to lead me through the curtain to face the wall of the cathedral. Inches behind the billowing cloth, a small door stood ajar.

The doorway couldn't have been much more than five feet high and eighteen inches wide, but the door itself was three inches thick and the bars across it were bridge timbers. I bumped my head when I straightened up, but Rita strode ahead in a grayish gloom that seemed to have no source.

"Phosphorescent paint," she said, opening an even lower door that I had to get through on my knees.

We were in the sanctuary of the cathedral. I looked up at the blue dome above the altar where golden stars bordered a picture of gates opening into heaven. I listened to the sound of our shoes echoing on the stone walls and remembered the cathedral had been begun in the sixteenth century when most worshipers couldn't read. Artists solved the problem by covering the walls and ceiling of the sanctuary with pictures of the faith. You didn't have to be literate to understand that there was a world of beauty beyond this one.

Off to one side, contemplating a bank of votive candles, a man in a cassock turned and stepped toward us. Rita walked faster, keeping to the lectern side of the chancel. The priest, I saw out of the corner of my eye, was locking the door we had

just come through. When Rita stopped again, we faced
another paneled wall against which a plaster statue of the
Lady of Saint John of the Lake stood. Rita genuflected
gracefully and then glanced over her shoulder. No one was in
sight, so she touched one of the panels and a part of the wall
slid sideways with a soft scrape.

I squeezed after her. In the darkness, her perfumed hair
brushed my face. "We have escaped from them all. From now
on, everything we wish is ours."

Her hand closed around mine. We were not standing in
a room, but in a corridor. I could feel a cool breeze moving.

"The Franciscan Brothers dug this tunnel to connect the
cathedral with the Church of Saint Francis when the Indian
attacks were a problem. It was used for precisely the same
purposes we are now using it. Come!"

With a confidence based on nothing, I let her lead me,
brushing aside the cobwebs that laced the roof of the tunnel.
It was a flaw, I knew, but I always take direction well from a
woman, especially one as beautiful as Rita. Finally, we came
to a door rimmed with light. She opened it and I followed her
out to stand blinking in the blinding sunlight.

We were on an anonymous back street. All of the
surrounding houses seemed abandoned. The only sign of life
was a windowless dry-cleaning van parked with its engine
running and the cargo door open. Rita led me inside and
closed the door. The truck started, jolting us back into racks
of naphtha-smelling clothes. The truck had been standing a
long time in the blazing afternoon sun. Already my shirt was
glued to me by sweat, and the heat that had built up inside
the van could have baked pizzas. About the time I was very
well done, the truck lurched to a stop.

Rita pushed open the door. We were inside a big garage.
There were two long, black La Salle limousines and a Reo
hearse parked against a backdrop of caskets of all sorts
stacked ten feet high. It was the reception/warehouse area of
a successful undertaker.

"We will now become two other people," Rita said, "and
this is an ideal place for us to die and be reborn with new
identities."

In half an hour we had our costumes. Rita and I both put
on blond wigs, mine considerably more conservative than
hers. Then we changed into designer sport clothes, artfully

stressed denims and khakis, natural fiber lightweight sweaters, and the like, to make it very clear we were from the priviledged bank of the Rio Grande.

I was astonished at how dramatically Rita's appearance was changed by the disguise. With her dark hair, she was the embodiment of a Spanish *doña*, but the blonde wig made her into a sunny California beach beauty. I inspected myself in the mirror and decided I just looked silly. When I complained, she had an answer ready. "We are twins now."

I rather liked the idea of being her twin since she had once said siblings were more meaningful to her than mere lovers.

Our destination, she explained, was Cuauhtemoc, a town about forty miles outside Chihuahua City, populated almost exclusively by Mennonite farmers from Germany who raise fruit, don't speak Spanish, and marry only among themselves. With our blond disguises, we wouldn't attract much attention. Once past Chihuahua City, we could drop these identities and be safe. Even if the rural police stopped us, they were not usually interested in anyone who seemed peaceful.

When a buzzer sounded, we left the roomful of caskets and climbed the stairs to join a group of mourners for a caravan ride to a cemetery outside the city. After the brief graveside service, we stood in the crowd waiting for a chartered bus, then rode with some of the mourners as far as Delicias and got off with half a dozen others in a village noted for its great-tasting water and not much else.

The priest who had officiated at the grave silently led us to a mustard-colored Pinto. Rita handed me the car keys, which was proof enough that she was running a large clandestine operation with a great many helpers.

The priest warned me in English to keep an eye on the Pinto's temperature gauge. Then he turned to Rita and spoke in Spanish: "You will be met at the house by a Captain Ruiz. If you are polite to him, there will be no difficulty because he only awaits his pension. It is nice that our tyrants are corrupt and inefficient in equal measure. The combination makes life bearable." With a nod, he left us.

We drove south at a steady fifty, passing *barrios* of incredible poverty—houses made from pieces of corrugated iron, cardboard cartons, and scraps of canvas, all congregated around a single village pump. Strangely, the people living in them were all busy and seemed cheery—working, talking, some of them even singing.

"They're from Ecuador—refugees," Rita said. "They're being trained so they can move further north."

"Good for them. What happens to our doubles when Darque's people catch up with them?"

She gave me a hit with those electric eyes. The heart-breaking lines of her face were even more startling under the curly mop of pale yellow dynel.

"They will evaporate at the border. The initial difficulty was finding a man your size and shape who could drive across the U.S. border, so I found two couples. One man doesn't look like you, but he's driving a U.S. car. The woman will stay with him till they reach the border. That's why I'm keeping this wig on till we meet the district captain. Sooner or later, they'll work out what happened. This way, there will be false clues all along the way."

Rita did good work. We turned off the paved road onto a scraped one that meandered through low dunes. Once out of sight of the national highway the road went to hell in a hurry. We bumped along painfully until we came to a herd of steers. They were in no hurry to accommodate the traffic of strangers, so I pulled to a stop.

We sat with the afternoon sun in our faces. Off to the west, I could see the shimmering blue curve of the Sierra Madres. In the distance I could hear the *vaquero* urging the straggling animals on with whistles and stones, without much success. A breeze had sprung up and I could feel the perspiration on my shirt beginning to evaporate.

Rita turned to me. "You intend to auction off Villa's head to the highest bidder?" The question set off all my alarm circuits.

A cow broke free of the herd and came over to stare through the windshield at me with a melancholy intensity. Even after the barefoot *vaquero* lashed it with a rope end, it stood waiting for my answer.

"As long as they're squabbling over possession of the head, people will continue to be killed in greater numbers. I want the deaths to stop."

I honked the horn. The cow didn't budge.

Neither did Rita. "How does an auction end anything?"

"Isn't it a toss-up between Chess and Darque?"

"An auction will change only who gets killed."

The cow lowered its head in disgust. Rita continued to stare into the slanting sun without blinking.

Our argument was generated by the heat and the dust, the noisy cattle, and our uncertain future. "Rita, you always want answers, but you never give me any. What have you done to make Darque trust you?"

Why do you ask such a stupid question? I've taken you to bed. I've saved you from him. What more do you want?"

"Some truth."

Rita's profile was beautiful and serene. "If you have questions, ask."

"Who was Rasmussen working for? And don't say CIA."

"He worked for Jesuita and me. Since Chess's judgment is not always the best, Jesuita needed to know if you were the right person to be his messenger. Your responses convinced all of us. One of the men with Teddy killed Rasmussen."

"Teddy doesn't seem to work for Darque, though Darque apparently thinks he does. Whose side is he on?"

"Hasn't he told you?"

"He's given me about four different accounts."

"They're all true. Most recently, Teddy has been with *Gobernación*. At this moment, he is probably making a deal with Mario. If Mario gets the head, Teddy will undertake to get the authentication from you. After that, he'll have no further interest in keeping you alive."

The cow apparently thought that was a sufficient answer because it finally turned and lumbered off after the herd.

I put the car in gear. "Answer my next question and I'll tell you something you don't know. Jesuita cut off Villa's head and kept it for fifty years. Why did she give Chess a medallion to identify me if she no longer wanted him to have any control over it?"

Rita put her arm along the back of the seat to run a fingernail from my earlobe down the side of my neck to the inside of my collar. "She came to regret her promise when she discovered Arturo's plan." Her fingers slipped the top button of my shirt open. "Jesuita wouldn't break her word, so she adjusted the bargain by arranging to have me choose the messenger. Your interview with Rasmussen was our final proof that you were personally honorable, as you understand the term, and that you aren't taken in by political slogans."

"What's Darque going to do when he finds out the head I'm going to auction is false?"

Rita sat forward to turn and face me. "Cheney! Did you think I didn't know that Jesuita put the head in your keeping?"

That was the item I'd been waiting for. I'd arranged things so not even Teddy knew that. Rita knew because Jesuita had told her.

Despite the heat, Rita slid closer to adjust herself to me. "We can go now, Cheney."

Half an hour later we came to a scatter of low adobe buildings that could have been the headquarters of a sizable *hacienda*.

"Las Varas," Rita announced. "The Stakes. It was originally a fort against Indians. Mario is annoyed with you, but we will be safe here. Villa often used it when things got too complicated elsewhere. Many of his followers still live around here. Villa's friends are ours. If we're not safe here, then Mexico is no longer safe for us."

"Who are we, by the way? Officially, that is."

She smiled the way she had the day we first met as she gave me the details she would later be laying out for the PRI representative

It was as well she did, because, as the priest had said, Captain Ruiz was waiting for us in the front room of the small adobe cottage. Ruiz was a lively old dandy, a well fed fellow with an elaborate white mustache and sideburns that contrasted sublimely with his olive skin. Here, in a part of Mexico where men's dress suits are usually a funereal black, he wore a white Palm Beach suit. He held a coconut straw hat under his arm like a trophy as he bowed over Rita's hand and clicked his heels. Much taken by Rita's blonde wig, he studied her with the dedicated gaze of a lifelong street-corner connoisseur.

"Ahhh!" he pronounced, showing teeth as even as piano keys when he kissed her fingers. "*Rubia!*"

Then he looked at me. "*Rubio y rubia,*" he corrected himself, taking the sheaf of papers Rita had handed to him. "A blonde lady and a blond man, twin *norteamericanoes*. Do not disturb yourself about the paperwork. I trust you. My curiosity alone is hungry. Why do you come to Las Varas? Surely, it is not our world class tourist delights?"

I gave him a big, uncomprehending smile and began

offloading the bags and boxes with which the back of the
Pinto was stacked. Our story was that Rita alone spoke
Spanish. She was my wife and secretary. Patting her Dolly
Parton wig, she smoothly laid out our story. I had been hired
by a demographic institute in the United States to conduct
some highly sophisticated marketing surveys among the people of the state of Chihuahua.

Then Rita mentioned the study was sponsored by the
Interior Department. In Mexico, the Interior Department
has in its keeping both interior and offshore responsibilities
for harmony and security. It is answerable to no one. Captain
Ruiz lost interest in our activities. Rita picked up an IBM
printout of the Juarez street directory reduced to number
codes she had thought would be useful window dressing. The
plump little captain was as impressed as he was supposed to
be, though he was a politician all the way. He hefted the
booklet.

"And for what purpose is this?"

With a great show of pedagogical enthusiasm, Rita launched
into the advantages of a stratified as opposed to a random
sample. Ruiz began glancing nervously at me for a hope of
escape as she enthusiastically explained that we had achieved
cloture on the urban populace and were now looking at the
rural stratum. I smiled vacuously.

"*Mi casa es su casa*," I said ponderously like a person
who spoke only English and was a fool besides. "A drink
perhaps?"

He accepted a lemon Coke and that ended our official
scrutiny. When his jeep drove off, I heard the shower in a
further room cut in. I finished unpacking our props. When
the shower quit and I heard Rita singing wordlessly to herself
in that way women do, my resolution to let her make the first
overture collapsed. I walked into the bedroom. Rita had both
arms up, drying her hair. Whether she was using her body or
my heart to ally me with her suddenly seemed unimportant.

"I expected company in the shower," she said, turning.
The curls of her damp hair spilled over her naked shoulders.
"I wondered why you seemed so distant."

Her tongue slid between her teeth as she tugged my belt
buckle loose. "But you're not distant now, are you?"

Sixteen

I was feeling irascible when I should have been calm, settled, and philosophical. Had it been any of a dozen different women, I'd have said nothing. For Rita I made an exception.

"Why does Darque trust you?"

Rita's head rested against my chest. Listening to the primitive songs of my heart, she called it. She'd been working on some interesting novelties to adjust my rhythms, but now she sat back on her heels without releasing her hold.

"What business is it of yours?"

She had a point. Rita had killed for me, but her life when we weren't together was a mystery to me. Maybe I was annoyed by Darque's calm assumption that whatever he asked of her, she would deliver. I'd learned enough in my relationship with Daisy to know that wasn't the question to ask, so I tried another.

"You say we're friends as well as lovers. I need to know how far I can count on you."

Rita got up and began to dress. "This sounds like the beginning of a lovers' quarrel. Maybe we should leave it at that."

She was both right and wrong. I got out of bed to make my point. "Lovers' quarrels involve the past. I'm talking about our future."

She stopped, standing on one leg to slip on a sandal. "Cheney, can't you ever let the present be enough?"

"The present doesn't last."

As if proving my point, the country quiet was broken by the sound of a distant car. Cars are a rarity in rural Mexico, and most of them belong to the government. Rita turned swiftly and tossed my shirt to me. By the time the car drove into the courtyard, we were in the kitchen drinking coffee.

We watched through the window as Captain Ruiz climbed

out of his ancient jeep, straightened his cap, and resettled his gunbelt on his plump hips. His face was set in stern lines. With an unpleasant duty to carry out, Ruiz no longer looked quite so dapper. Since he was alone and hadn't undone the flap of his pistol holster, I felt fairly optimistic he was here for a bribe.

Rita gave me one of her sidelong glances. "No matter what happens, Cheney, let's do what he says."

Ruiz didn't represent much of a threat, but we'd probably have to leave this place—and soon. I'd expected to wait till dark and then have Rita use her talents to put me across the Rio Grande. Now all that was up for grabs.

His rap on the door didn't sound like much, but Rita opened it to him as if he were a long-lost uncle.

"Captain Ruiz! Please come in. Some coffee?" she asked, taking him by the hand and leading him into the living room where I stood holding a cup and saucer.

He was still the old rake, but now he was a worried old rake. "Señora, please forgive this interruption of your marital bliss, but a formality requires your presence at the cuartelillo. I forgot the signature on the registry for extraños, because you are foreigners. One signature will be sufficient for the household, so your handsome husband can come with me to accomplish this, though I would prefer your company. A thousand pardons for my miserable mistake. One of you must come."

He stopped to watch this go down. "Ahhh," he said with a sigh, "These miserable and unintelligible government regulations."

I didn't believe a word, and I doubted that Rita did either, but her response was magnificent. "How gallant you are, Captain. In the United States, it would not be a minor matter, but that is one of the many things I love about Mexico. Since I speak Spanish, I will go and let my husband study our strategy for tomorrow's interviews. Shall we take our car?"

Ruiz was startled by Rita's easy acquiescence. He fumbled to hide his surprise. "Oh, no, señora. Though it will be but a few moments, you must ride in the official car."

Rita turned to me and spoke slowly, making sure Ruiz caught every word. "My dear, there is nothing to worry about. You have the Pinto here if the need arises. In the meantime, remember, we want to get an early start in the morning."

We had intended no such thing. She gave me a quick, wifely peck on the cheek and left before I could say a word.

Ruiz handed her into his gravel-pocked jeep with gestures appropriate to a limousine entry. I seem to spend a lot of time watching beautiful ladies walk away.

The sun was still a couple of hours before setting, plenty of time to get moving. Her mention of the Pinto told me to vacate the area, but only when the jeep bounced out of sight did I give it serious thought.

Since it didn't matter which of us accompanied Ruiz, the object of this exercise clearly was to separate us. When Ruiz and Rita passed their lookout, the first team would know I was here alone. I wasn't going to wait. I'd gassed up the Pinto in Delicias, so even with poor speed on the road, I ought to be in Presidio, Texas, by ten o'clock.

To check my theory, I went to stand in the doorway, looking woebegone as I gazed into the slanting rays of the sun in the direction Rita and the Captain had taken.

Sure enough, a *thwack!* was followed by an instantaneous echo. I dodged back inside. He'd had a standing target, outlined by the darkness of the doorway and fully lit by the horizontal rays of the sun. And he'd missed. I hadn't caught the muzzle flash, but I saw a rustle of movement only seventy-five yards away.

I'd found out what I wanted to know. He'd been told to keep me here, but the near misses said he didn't have orders to kill me. Otherwise, I'd be dead now.

I went through the door. A second shot clipped a chink out of the adobe wall above my head, but I kept on walking. Shooting that bad had to be on purpose. The sun was still putting out heat as I made my way across the courtyard, but I was no longer sweating.

I climbed into the Pinto and drove off. By now, my keeper would be on the radio asking for instructions. I knew things they had to know, so they wanted me alive. That was the edge that would keep me alive.

I estimated it would take the shooter five minutes to come after me, and I was right. His pursuit vehicle was a motorcycle with a radio antenna. A rifle stuck out of the saddle scabbard. He hung back about a quarter of a mile. He wore motorcycle skins and a visored helmet. With that helmet, he didn't need a windscreen over his handlebars, a good sign he was an all-terrain cowboy.

After I got through Camargo, I turned onto the lesser

route marked "Other Roads" on the map. It led through one
hundred and twenty miles of desert to the U.S. border, but I
figured it couldn't be worse than the mountain roads I'd
explored already.

In half an hour we were out in the middle of the desert
and we might have been alone in the world. The motorcyclist
was willing to let me have all the room I wanted. He wasn't
interested in witnesses either.

Up till now, I'd followed the priest's directions about not
overtaxing the engine, but since he'd loaned it to people on
the run, I assumed he didn't expect it back. I bore down on
the gas. The engine began to make laboring noises and the
cyclist speeded up. I guessed he figured he had me now.

The sun slanted splinters of light into my eyes. What was
lit by the glaring rays was clear, but the shadows were
lengthening and getting blacker by the second. The road
wasn't too bad, but it was uneven enough to make my
pursuer not try to hang on my rear bumper. Very slowly, my
odds were improving, except that the Pinto's temperature
gauge had started its inexorable march toward a blown head.

After I'd put almost half a mile between us, I hit the
brakes and let the car slow. Then I geared down into first and
pounded the accelerator. Raw gas overfilled the carb to give
me the backfire I wanted. I rolled to a stop, undid the
seatbelt, and bailed out, leaving the Pinto in the middle of
the road.

I'm no longer the world's fastest runner, but I had
enough of a head start to get out of sight of the road and into
the low dunes which rolled to the horizon. My company
made the choice I wanted. He wheeled his machine off the
road and started after me into the scanty chaparral of the
central desert. I made sure he saw me now and again and did
my best lope on a beeline he ought to be able to predict. I
wanted the man on the motorcycle to be very confident.

Actually, he had a lot to be confident about. As I loped
along in the alternate deep sand and exposed adobe clay that
was riverbed when the rains came, I kept looking for the
right place—a patch of smooth adobe where my pursuer
would be able to get up to speed. I hadn't practiced this
particular sequence lately, and the last time I'd done it, I was
in much better shape. My worst problem was that I seemed
to be running low on lope. If I intended to work this, it

would have to be pretty soon or I'd be too worn down to get my coordination right.

I stopped to take in a ravine where surface waters congregated during rainstorms. It led to wherever rain goes in the landlocked plain of central Mexico. The ravine floor was about twelve feet below the rest of the plateau. Going into it would cut down my options for escape pretty drastically, but at least our encounter would be out of sight of any chance observers, and the lower surface offered the mix of good and bad traction I wanted.

I slid down the steep bank into deep sand and kept on running. About the time my second wind cut in, I heard the drone of the cycle's engine again as it crept up on me. I found the spot I needed not a moment too soon. The roar of the closing machine was getting loud enough to irritate.

When the engine noise slacked off suddenly, I looked up. The shooter had stopped at the edge of the tableland above the ravine and was pulling out his rifle. Fortunately for me, the ravine turned north in a steep curve. I made it out of sight before he could take my picture.

He had a choice. He could drive his fancy machine down into the dry riverbed after me, or he could go an additional half mile on the outside curve and take a chance I might be able to hide. I heard the roar of his big cycle. He was coming down.

Sometimes almost everything works out. Around the curve, I found the best spot for my stand I'd seen yet. I slowed to a walk and shook my shoulders to get loose. From now on, it was a matter of timing and body memory.

It was a large open patch of adobe, fairly smooth, with only the ribs of wind and current to mark it, great traction for a motorbike. Where I'd be safe was the deep sand that commenced at the farther end and nourished the creosote bushes growing luxuriantly head-high in the dry sump of the seasonal river.

Once out in the middle, I listened hard for the sound of his heavy cycle. I kept walking, a prey to leg cramps and heat exhaustion. I trudged on until I was only forty yards from the cover of the chaparral.

He came around the bend with a roar of engine noise. I knew that he might stop and reach for his rifle, but I was too close to the wall of creosote and mesquite where I could lose myself. In the interests of speed and efficiency, he chose to run me down.

As he accelerated, I broke into a running limp. About ten yards from the end of the good surface, I fell, clutching my leg. His response was to crank up his speed another notch while I scrambled to get my feet under me. Looking back, I saw the oval black visor of his helmet glinting in the sun as he came at me. I put out a beseeching hand, trying to hold off a nightmare. He let the throttle out another notch.

When he was ten feet off, I crouched to jump awkwardly to one side and face him. He'd already adjusted to keep me centered, and I caught a glimpse of white teeth through the black visor. I started right, felt gravel scatter under my feet, and halted. He turned back at me and I dodged away. He compensated, and I went over his handlebars into his face in a leaping body block.

The bike's handlebar gave me a terrible crack on the shin that left me nauseous, but the biker was sprawled, boneless on the adobe, all his circuits cut.

He looked like I felt—as if my body had done a mile inside a cement mixer. The bike kept on going, momentum carrying it along to smash into the mesquite, where it subsided and stalled out.

I pulled the biker's helmet off. It was the big fat man, whom I'd kicked in the stomach in Brownsville. No wonder he wanted to pay me back by running me down.

He was breathing, though he'd feel like death warmed over till his chest and neck recovered from the whiplash of my body block. But there wasn't any time for pity, because behind me I heard a familiar menacing buzz growing louder.

The helicopter was moving fast. Of course they'd have a radio fix on his cycle. Dropping the helmet beside the cyclist, I dived into the chaparral to take cover. I felt the sudden cool in the dry air as the helicopter's shadow slid over me.

It was a reconnaissance craft, fast, a ship that can stick close to the terrain and avoid radar. When it was overhead, it did a large circle and then settled down within yards of the cyclist. A man in a gleaming white suit jumped out and immediately waved the chopper off with his broad-brimmed panama. The machine left as fast as it had come.

With my chin on the abrasive rocks where I had taken cover, I strained to recognize the newcomer through the stinging cloud of sand and pebbles thrown by the chopper's departure.

I recognized Teddy. Calm, as usual, he stood there surveying my handiwork. Then, without turning, he spoke, his voice eerily magnified by the sudden silence left in the copter's wake.

"Cheney. Come out. It has been a long day. I don't want to spoil this suit by going after you."

Keep talking, Teddy, I said silently. It would take a lot to convince me he wished me well.

"I'm a policeman. This man tried to kill you. I'm going to arrest him for attempted murder. He exceeded his authority."

I didn't move. More than one innocent man in Mexican history had found himself dead of a policeman's bullet.

"Rita got away from us. She kept a gun on Captain Ruiz and the old fool drove right through the roadblock."

Rita was safe. If Teddy wasn't lying. As usual, everybody seemed to know all about everything everybody did. Everybody except me.

"I have information you need, Cheney. The United States border is closed against you. You must have offended someone very powerful."

I remembered Knocky's warning about not leaving the States. By now Teddy had worked it out that I had Villa's head hidden somewhere. If he could get it from me, he'd be a hero with the present government, because the grisly relic would no longer be a rallying point for dissidents. But he knew as well as I did that Chess had no intention of giving up Villa's head.

"Cheney, it is important that we talk. But if you don't come out, I will leave you here. I'll invoke the *ley de fuga*. You'll be shot on sight."

The sun dropped below the first ridge, and I felt an instant chill. Very soon, this stand of chaparral would come alive with creatures that had spent the day holed up against the heat. I got to my feet.

"All right, Teddy, let's hear what you have to say."

He spun around as I picked my way through the clumps of cholla cactus and the briary whips of the ocotillo bushes. "You must know I won't allow you to take the Villa head from Mexican soil."

For the first time, I noticed that he was breathing

rapidly and his face was bejeweled by beads of sweat. Then I understood. Believing Villa was his father constituted the keystone of Teddy's personality. He was afraid of losing his emotional patrimony.

"It's still in Mexico, Teddy."

"And the authentication?"

'It's safe in the United States. I think of it as my passport out of this mess."

"You intend to sell it all to Mario Darque?"

"I'll sell to the highest bidder."

He took his time thinking that over. His suit was an unearthly white in the gathering shadows. "You understand I meant it when I said the United States will arrest you at the border."

"If they recognize me."

"Do you need any help?"

"I'm being met by friends. If you'll give me a number, I'll get word to you about when and where the auction is to take place."

His fingers dipped into one of his many vest pockets to emerge with a card with just his name and a Juarez exchange phone number on it. He stood looking at the motorcycle cowboy who was showing the first signs of coming around, a muscle spasm that generated a low groan.

"This man exceeded his orders. I wanted only to talk to you because I knew you must come back."

I took the card and walked over to right the motorcycle. When I had hauled it upright and climbed aboard, I turned on the ignition. When it worked, I let it die and was ready to be magnanimous. "He was moody about my running over him, so he decided to return the compliment. It was understandable."

Teddy still had a problem. I could see he was toying with the idea of trying to force me to tell him where Villa's head was, but his logic said the head was no good without the authentication. "I cannot convince my superiors to let me bid. Villa belongs in the Monument of the Revolution."

"Teddy, I wouldn't be surprised if your people won out at the auction—even without money. Good enough?"

Teddy and I had gone through a lot together, but we had different priorities. He gave me a sideways look and then slapped at the saddle of the bike, a horse trader swatting a horse's rump.

"*Suerte*, Cheney. Your next visit to Mexico, you must stay longer."

I didn't like the sound of that, but I told him I'd give the invitation a lot of thought. He watched me as again I brought the cycle to life. While it sputtered and settled into patterned noise, I readjusted the cyclist's helmet so it fit me. He was on his feet now, groggily pressing his hands against his chest and staring at the ground between his legs. Teddy fired a rocket pistol to summon the chopper. They'd have an easy trip, and I had some tough miles to go, but I preferred my destination.

Seventeen

I planned to cross the Rio Grande at Presidio, Texas, a toy town in the empty Big Bend country with only two destinations, Marfa and Terlingua, and both of them are a good two hundred miles of empty prairie from a town with more than one McDonald's.

Across the river from Presidio, in Mexico, Ojinaga offers the usual small border town attractions: godawful gewgaws, revenue-free liquor, and a flourishing Boystown for people interested in economical sex. Since the place is on a branch of the Mexican National Highway that leads to Chihuahua and Mexico City, Teddy probably expected me to catch a bus south to Mexico City and cross the border at thirty thousand feet, courtesy of Aeronaves Mexicano.

That would be pretty fancy footwork, but I wasn't interested in going deeper into Mexico while Darque had thugs looking for me with guns. I've been a consultant for immigration about transient identification, so I was not going to cross the border at an air terminal where the electronic gadgetry can establish everything except your preference in the next presidential primary. That meant it had to be Presidio, population 1723.

In Ojinaga, I rode the cycle into the Pemex station.

While the attendant yawned and sorted bills for the gas, I requested directions to the nearest *casa de juegos*. Without looking up, he suggested the Star Bar Mercado and Posada where, he said, all sorts of things were for sale. I thanked him, glad I didn't scratch out a living pumping gas in a border town.

The Star Bar had a five-pointed star picked out in twenty-five-watt bulbs on a red, yellow, and green sign. The lights flickered on and off uncertainly in the gathering dusk. Inside, the illumination was fed by direct current, the better to check out the incredible bargains—pot metal statues of Elvis Presley, rattan furniture, leprosy-stricken leather goods, pottery with a lead glaze, and theater-sized posters of movie stars not much younger than Douglas Fairbanks Senior.

The bar, a nearly deserted alcove opposite the dining room, was my destination. I was looking for an unattached female. Several were scattered around the room, but I forgot them when a man sitting by himself scratched a match and held it to his face to show me he was Eliseo Varga.

Briefly, I wondered if he'd been pressed into service as someone who could recognize me under any circumstances, but Varga and I have gone to the well together more than once and he was out of his jurisdiction. With those odds, I strode through the crowd of empty tables.

"*Hombre*! Is this seat taken?"

He blew out the match. "It is now. Cheney, you must have a really serious problem. They've activated me and every other lawman who knows you by sight to cover all the border crossings into Texas."

"How'd you happen to choose this one?"

"This afternoon I had a phone call from a Mexican lawman I met at a convention a few years back. His name is Teddy Ristra and he said a mutual acquaintance might come through here this evening and if I was so inclined, I might be able to help him."

"Is Daisy out looking too?"

Varga gave me an odd look before shaking his head.

Since he was working on a half-dead Carta Blanca, I ordered two more. When the barman brought two new chilled glasses and opened the bottles at the table, I was impressed by the hospitality.

So was Varga. "This is a good place. If it weren't out in

the middle of empty real estate, they'd do a lot better," he told me.

I took a long cold drink. I hadn't ridden a motorcycle in years and, among other problems, I was dehydrated. "All this surveillance for what? The Rasmussen matter was taken care of."

Varga's face was impassive. "Rasmussen's old business. This is a new shill. The federals no sooner removed the lookout for you than another was put on. This one is from the DEA. Top priority. You're to be picked up on sight."

"On what basis?"

"It seems a bale of marijuana was sent to your business address, very smelly and spoiled by seawater. Even I knew it was Florida cargo. Your friends have a strange sense of humor."

"Knocky Polk."

"That's what I thought. When I phoned, he told me these things happen. He probably needs to talk. What do you want?"

I didn't say anything. Varga picked up his glass. "I came down here so we can talk informally. Then I'll decide whether to take you across or not."

"The first part of that sounds good, but I'm not interested in being arrested. I have a lot on my mind."

He nodded to indicate he registered my point, not to show agreement. When he didn't say anything else, I understood he'd wait all evening for an answer.

It took most of an hour to tell it, starting with Chip Stackler and working through Arthur Chess's fortress in the desert and ending with Teddy's man working first with a rifle and then with his motorcycle. When I finished, Varga had one question

"If I hadn't been here, what were you going to do?"

There was no need to be devious now. I explained I'd intended to go to ground by having one of the unattached women in the bar take the motorcycle in exchange for twenty-four hours in her apartment while she was somewhere else. Then I was going to find somebody too drunk to drive who needed a friend in order to get home.

"It might have worked if I hadn't chosen this crossing," Varga told me affably. "I think you have a good idea, but let me improve it. In about ten minutes, I'm going to finish up

here and hike back over the bridge. Why don't you find
somebody to take that hot bike off your hands and come on
across?"

Getting rid of an expensive Japanese motorcycle cheaper
than free in a border town is not difficult. I mentioned my
problem to the bartender, who wasn't especially interested
until I mentioned I had a legal Mexican registration.

He made one phone call and the same sleepy man who'd
steered me to the Star Bar arrived within two minutes. He
was the bartender's brother, which either shows there's pattern in the universe or people in a marginal economy help
each other—if they're related.

He gave me a doubtful look before firing up the engine.
"You sure this *cicleta* isn't *radiactivo?*"

I told him it was colder than his girlfriend's mother's
heart, which seemed to reassure him. I had only one request,
that he follow me partway across the bridge, where I would
give him the registration.

He sorted me into the category of rich eccentrics and
asked one more question. Was I from Guatemala? I had the
strangest accent he'd ever heard. It was my turn to give him
a long look before I started over the bridge.

He did a figure eight or two at low speed and then
started after me slowly, keeping about ten yards back as he
gazed down the sluggish length of the Rio Grande, a man
with all the time in the world and the bike to do it with.

Things didn't get exciting till I stepped up to the Customs
window and the man on the bike reached the head of the car
Customs lane. As it turned out, it was just as well there was
no other traffic.

Varga came out of the witness port and started yelling.
"There he is! That man's Cheney Hazzard! Don't let him get
away!"

I jumped back from the door I was about to go through
and ran at the motorcyclist. He hadn't been expecting this.
He'd been expecting to have me give him the registration slip
at the midpoint in the bridge. He killed the engine and then
we both had a few seconds of frenzy as he restarted it just as I
grabbed him and locked an arm around his neck.

"The title is in the *bizaza*. Get out of here right now!" I
hissed. *"Rapido!"*

He responded by doing a wheelie that left me flat on the

oily cement of the roadway. By the time I got to my feet, he was across the bridge, past the guards on the other side, and into the night.

When I turned around, a guard with a paunch that made him eleven months pregnant put a sweaty grip on my arm. The other stood six feet off to show me his pistol. I became very still as Varga sauntered up. He was full of the importance of a visiting policeman on special perilous assignment.

He looked at me an eloquent minute and then shook his head. "You really blew it this time." He turned to the guard. "Timing. This guy does not have it."

I broke in, sounding edgy. "You called his name! Dammit! Another two seconds and he'd have been in the chute."

Varga shook his head sadly. "He was already starting his turn. He smelled a rat. I yelled to warn you. You weren't even watching him."

He turned back to the guards. "Hazzard's not coming through here. Now the action'll be at El Paso for sure."

"Just a minute here," protested the guard with the pistol. "I thought this guy was Cheney Hazzard. He looks enough like the Identikit."

Varga studied my face skeptically. "Hell, everybody looks like those kit pictures. I see what you mean, but this is Harrison Tyler Polk—for better or worse, my deputy. Show your badge, Harry."

I brought out the Deputy badge he'd given me, and that was that.

The guntoter shuffled back to his station, but the paunchy guard was wired up from what had almost happened. Genially, he accompanied us back to Varga's cruiser.

"A hundred years ago, Presidio was pretty high on the charts, an important fort. But now, this is the most excitement I've ever seen here. This is just an entrance for tourists in a hurry to spend money in Mexico City. They may be having a drug storm at every other gate, but not ours. That's not to say we didn't catch a fellow with a full packet of NoDoz once, but that was a while back."

He turned around to point out the spotlights focused on the American flag. "Look at us, lit up like a whorehouse on Saturday night. Why would any illegal go through that when he's got three hundred miles west and a hundred east of dark, unfenced, uninhabited territory separated by a river I could piss across if my kidneys were in good order."

"Maybe Hazzard's a city boy," I said.

Varga gave me a dark look. "No more smart remarks out of you, Harry. You did enough tonight. You drive. I'm tired of standing around. You didn't have Hazzard hooked very tight if he took off like that."

"Win some, lose some," I shrugged, watching the paunchy guard shake his head as he plodded back to his duty station.

"That's tedious duty. I'm glad I'm not in the border patrol," Varga said when the guard shuffled out of sight.

I agreed, but not for Varga's reason.

"What do you do now?"

"I'm going to give Arthur Chess a chance to be a real philanthropist."

"How are you going to get around? That APB is serious."

"Since everybody else is playing fast and loose with the law, I've decided to fit in. I have a full authentic set of alternative ID that makes me a genuine citizen of Mexico."

Varga's laugh was a single bark.

This trip into Chess's ranch was different from my first. This time the driver had a backup. The second man sat behind us with a machine pistol across his knees. They'd been waiting for me at the ranch gate, but there were no dogs. When I asked, the driver said curtly, "They died. L. O. D."

I thought about a line-of-duty death as we rode through the elaborate plantings while the tires whispered on macadam already softening in the morning sun. Something was very wrong. By the time we came over the lip of the hill where the house grew out of the ground, I saw what it was.

The front of the massive house was blackened by fire, and one of the steel doors had a hole in it only a rocket could have made. The military attack the house had been built to withstand had finally arrived.

Umberto met me at the outer door, did his bow, and led me into the entry hall. The atmosphere was that of a command post after a successful operation. Down a corridor to one side I could hear field phones rattling peremptorily. The air was acrid with cordite fumes. Opposite the front door, the

adobe barrier wall was gouged to a depth of a foot where the
rocket had lost its final velocity. On either side of the front
doors, expended shell casings glittered in brass dunes where
the defense had met the attackers. The two men who were
cleaning up the mess looked both tired and exhilarated.

There was blood on Umberto's formal vest, and as I
followed him I saw the cartridge belt he still wore disturbed
the fit of his tailcoat. All the impressive artwork had been
carted away. Across the wide foyer the sound of our heels
clattered like rocks tossed down a well.

Umberto's voice was monochromatic. "We were ade-
quately prepared. As a result, Darque no longer has an army.
That fool was willing to sacrifice everything to get the head,
but the sacrifice was for nothing."

The big double doors swung open so promptly that I half
expected to find Chess waiting for me inside. But the acre-
sized desk and the throne behind it were empty. Umberto sat
down with a sigh and gestured at an alcove where the fake of
Villa's head sat openly on a plush cushion. "Arturo said when
you came back, you would know everything."

All of Umberto's body language told me Chess was dead.
Given his frail appearance on our last visit, I was not too
surprised, but Umberto would tell me all in good time. I
glanced over my shoulder and saw the guards had left us
alone. "I found Villa's head exactly where Chess hid it years
ago."

He nodded impassively. "Arturo said you would have no
difficulty."

I thought that over as I inventoried all the aches and
twinges resulting from my recent experiences. Most of them
were mental, but I was in one piece. "Did Chess die in the
fighting? Was it a paratroop operation?"

Umberto took a long time opening a cigar and getting it
lit before he answered.

"Five attack helicopters came up from Mexico, escorting
two transports. It is interesting that none of the national
border defenses were alerted, though we had the planes on
our radar screens from the time they left Cerralvo. No
matter. They've been disassembled and buried. After that,
the infantry attack had no chance to succeed. Arturo waited
to have his heart attack until it was clearly over."

The old man's dark eyes regarded me steadily. "Darque

was never an honest man, but once he started defending major drug smugglers, he was supping with the devil. This time, he went too far and we burnt his lips. It's up to you to make him drop the spoon."

I stood up to examine the false head. "My assignment was to validate Villa's head, not to eliminate Darque."

Through a wreath of blue smoke, Umberto looked offended. "Arturo is dead. I am the executor of his estate. Darque must pay for killing my friend."

I wanted Umberto's cooperation, but it had to be on my own terms. "I'd like to punish Darque because he wants Villa's head for the same political purpose Chess did, but I won't be a party to killing."

The cigar jutted out of his stony little face like a length of iron pipe. When he shifted the cigar, the better to speak, he sighed as he had upon sitting down. Then he undid his cartridge belt and dropped the heavy cavalry pistol on the table.

"Señor Arturo was my *compañero de armas* since the *Revolucion*. Together we won and lost many times—with bullets and money. We did not always agree, but we were always together. We did not agree about the head of Villa. But we remained brothers, even in disagreement."

He sat like a little Mayan statue behind the massive desk, gazing at me with eyes hard as pebbles. Finally, he put the cigar into the large pottery tray.

"It was an old man's whimsy, an attempt to deny the passage of time. I knew it was foolish and dangerous. But he was living always on that day in Mexico City in 1914 when Villa sat in the Presidential chair. It was his way of remaking history."

I felt a little better. Chess had been caught up in a de lusional system, and for billionaires, there aren't many reality checks.

"I would never equate Arthur Chess with Mario Darque, Umberto."

The dark eyes flickered away from mine. "Of course. But antique folly can do many things that are out of character. I did not agree with his plans to use you to destroy Darque."

"Darque deserves anything I could do to him."

Whatever it was Umberto wanted to tell me, he was

having difficulty voicing it. "Arturo was a good man. Our only quarrel was about what we did with you."

Before I could protest that I had taken on the assignment with no illusions, Umberto continued. "The head had been safe for half a century in Jesuita's care. But this past year, Arturo often did things that were not usual for him. I think when he learned he was running out of time, he began to worry about those things in his life that had not worked out. They were few, which made them most important."

"Arthur Chess was a fine man. We all make mistakes," I told him.

Umberto nodded but kept doggedly on with what had to be said. "Some mistakes are worse than others. Mario Darque did not send you Ms. Pruitt's picture. We did. Arturo was determined to make you continue the search. To underscore the importance of the task, he suggested the message come with an expensive watch for your secretary. He knew your lively mind would respond very predictably. Ms. Pruitt knew nothing about the picture that had been taken of her. The wristwatch, of course, was harmless, but we thought even the hint of Darque harming either your lawyer or your secretary would send you back to Mexico as nothing would."

These old timers had been jerking me around Mexico like a Chihuahua dog on a short leash.

Umberto looked grim. "For Arturo, the disposition of the head was neither a matter of money nor of politics, but of vanity. As he lay dying this morning, he understood it at last. He told me he owed you an apology."

Arthur Chess had been manipulating people like me for a long time. It shouldn't be surprising that the old master had taught me a thing or two. In this business, you're always learning.

Umberto's grim little face lightened as he watched me work through their planning. "I have a great deal of latitude to help you until the official reading of Arturo's will. Then I become the steward of his heir, whoever that may be."

"Good. I'll need help." I felt good—in charge for the first time in a long while. "I want a commercial artist, someone who doesn't mind working with unconventional materials."

That settled, I picked up the phone and called Fred Werkshul's emergency number.

"Cheney! You're not in over your head, are you, son?"

"Everything's working fine, Fred, but I need a little research backup. No, I take that back. I need a lot of information that only you can give me. Is there any chance National Security is monitoring this call?"

Fred's chuckle was a reflex. "Only about ten-tenths. They monitor all international radio talk. Also, every call I get is recorded, but don't let it worry you. They do so much eavesdropping on voice traffic that keyword analysis is all they can do. As long as you don't use a name on their list, we're safe enough."

Working with Fred is a mixed blessing. He has access to all the major data files and owns every state-of-the-art software trick going or even thought about. That means he could find out everything I needed to know in nanoseconds and tell me as fast as he could read. But the keyword scan meant our talk would set off alarms if I mentioned Chess or Darque by name. Given the way things go in intelligence operations these days, all the wrong people would be alerted—especially if, as I had begun to suspect, Darque had serious U.S. backing.

I got started on the name-substitution game, in which Chess became "the checkerplayer" and Darque turned into "an international shyster I know." When Fred finished listening, the eerie echoes on the radio phone transmission left me thinking I'd mailed a letter down a tree stump. Then he came back.

"I've looked them all up in my weekly reader. The second fellow is high voltage, well attached to all-weather, three-prong fixtures to ground him during any storm because many of his friends on both sides of the river are in public office."

Fred's voice shifted casually to a different register. "Another thing. I checked you out, and some very odd people are asking pointed questions about a certain former shake-and-bake noncom."

While I thought that over, Fred kept up the chatter. "You could probably get some kind of charter flight out of there. Or if you want, I'll be glad to send one of mine to pick you up. Either way, I think you ought to drop by and see me. No jurisdictional problems out here."

He must have thought I was in deep if he was offering

sanctuary on his island. He's gone to a lot of trouble to keep bother and business far away from his paradise in the Caribbean.

"You're misreading the signals, Fred. Everything is working out just fine. I could use two pilots, though. Trustworthy, not afraid of a little noise. One should be qualified in choppers. Would that interest Ramon?"

"I'll have him call you on a ground line," Fred said and hung up.

After Ramon got back to me, I tried Knocky's official number. When I identified myself as Eliseo Varga and my business was a Hazzard spotting, Knocky came on immediately.

"Shee-it, Cheney, Varga would never drop a dime on you. He might arrest you, but he would never inform on you. Sorry about the border closing, but I used it to find the fellow who was telling everybody about my good intentions. He's washed up, but that's the end of the good news."

Knocky is great at communications, clear, quick, and he keeps your attention. I didn't have to wait long to hear the bad news.

"My office has been ordered to bring to a screeching, skidding, goddamn halt any and all activities that target one Mario Darque, whether in this country or any other. My office will do exactly as ordered. Personally, I'm taking a week's leave, starting tonight. If anybody carrying contraband lands at any of those airfields along the TexMex border, I'll only be doing my duty if I arrest him to the full extent of the law. In the right situation, I figure I can pump spitting-on-the-sidewalk up to a charge worth ten years to life. Is that any kind of possibility for you?"

I hadn't been counting on that much help. "Thanks. Why not stick around El Paso? If things work out, I could pay you back with a rib dinner at a little place I found in Mesilla. They make their horseradish daily."

It was nice to know I had some place to dump Darque. Now I had to create what Knocky called a "situation," a set of incriminating circumstances no politician on either side of the border would risk getting smeared with. It wasn't ethical. It wasn't legal. But it should work.

Eighteen

On the *Cinco de Mayo*, Mexico celebrates with firecrackers and brass music the date in 1867 when three centuries of European rule ended. One hundred and twenty years afterwards, I'd flown back to the rocky outlook over the *Barranca de cobre* to bring another period of Mexican history to an end.

Umberto supplied the picnic lunch and the panniers with the stage properties, but the air support came from Fred Werkshul. Fred's pilot had made a low-speed pass over the spot and said he'd used worse commercial fields to deliver nitro. His only question was how I'd get out of here. I told him I expected transportation to be provided by the people I was going to entertain.

After I watched him out of sight, it was a brisk hike up the road to the rocky platform where the dwarf had died ten days before. Burdened down with all my gear, I used the time to go over everything that could go wrong. Usually, I'm not so nervous, but lately I'd been having to rely more on luck than I like.

While I waited for customers, I sampled the picnic fixings and considered my collection of Villa heads. I stood some on rocks, wedged others into crevices, and propped the rest in forks of the stunted trees that marked the corners of my stage. The heads were brooding mood pieces. The brutal cheekbones, the heavy jaw, and the forehead arching above nightmare eyes all worked to create a Halloween atmosphere. Umberto's artist had added a genius touch, black surgical stitching to hold the meaty lips together but not quite hide the feral teeth.

My contribution was to wire each head on top of a mousetrap baited with a blasting cap. If people kept their distance, the explosions would be only moderately dangerous. Since my customers were all high energy types, I didn't want to leave anything to chance.

Like the set dressing, my plan was elaborate. What worried me was my need for offstage help, but it was the only way I could convince the audience I had fifty-two aces up my sleeve. Given their past performances, it would be fatal to seem vulnerable even for a moment. I wouldn't get a second chance. The extra heads were a distraction to make sure no blood of mine was shed on this famous date. Of course, there'd be split lips, bloody noses, and hurt feelings, but any sufferers in my scenario would bring it on themselves.

The time allotted for the auction was from eleven-thirty till noon. The timing was crucial. To keep from checking my watch, I went over the worst case situation offered by Mario Darque.

For the first time, Darque would be at a disadvantage. By having Chess destroy Darque's army, I'd fixed it so he wouldn't have his usual manpower backup. Maybe this time I'd be able to wipe that sneer of superiority off his face. Of course, I still expected him to offer threats and bribes in equal measure, and he might have a personal desire to see me thrown over the precipice, but while I controlled Villa's head, I'd be out of his reach.

Carefully, I worked over all the possibilities. Teddy and I had gone through a lot together, but he sometimes claimed to be an official of the Mexican government, and he certainly was a fan of Villa's, which made him unpredictable. The PRI was doing well without Villa, and they wanted nothing changed. As a matter of duty, Teddy might do his best for the PRI, though I didn't think he'd defend Darque. Teddy, when you came down to it, was anybody's occasional ally.

That left Rita. Since I'd seen her use a gun, I couldn't deceive myself that she was wholeheartedly a believer in Jesuita's nonviolent religion. When I thought about it objectively, I decided Rita might well be a smart woman who'd been planted in Jesuita's religion a long time ago. Of course, she might have been converted anyway. Jesuita's religion offered a lot to energetic people who wanted to improve the world. That's how spies become double agents. Guardedly, I'd trust Rita in a crunch. Guardedly.

The sound of muffled rotors brought a reconnaissance helicopter over the lip of the canyon. It was an older Bell Kiowa model and like all of Darque's equipment, it bore no markings. In the moment while the downdraft from the blades was still flattening the sparse grass and shrubs, Darque,

Rita, and his bearlike bodyguard, the man called Oso, climbed out. Oso slid the port shut and the ship swooped away over the edge, no sooner arrived than gone. Oso carried a black satchel. I wondered if it was bribe money. But from the way Oso's flat eyes followed my every move, I didn't think so.

Rita gave me a small smile and I noticed she was carrying her big purse. It was sad to see my doubts about her activated so immediately. Darque was well supplied with bodyguards. Maybe it would make him easier to deal with if he felt secure.

As usual, he was impeccably dressed. Today he wore a khaki safari outfit with all sorts of buttoning flaps and a campaign hat that shadowed his face. His glossy caramel-colored iguana boots made him even taller. After a brief, appraising look, he began as though we'd been doing business for years.

"Hazzard, I feared you might be a political idealist. Now I see you are, like any sensible person, a realist. With Chess dead, an auction is obviously the only answer."

He stopped to consider the stage dressing. "I can always use clever men. Excellent."

The word might have been a signal. Both Oso and Rita stepped clear. They'd have an open shot if I had any idea of disagreeing. He glanced at them as if settling armor on his shoulders. "I don't care who else is invited today—I'll be heard first. This morning I received my final assurances. You are looking at the Bolivar of New Spain. Our new country makes geopolitical sense. It polices the U.S. border, creates enormous profits, and holds at bay the Godless Hordes of International Communism and so on and so forth."

It doesn't take a genius to create a new country these days. The job is half done by balancing political apprehension on one side against economic possibilities on the other. Unless I could stop him, Darque would have his way and thousands would die.

He took my silence at his own valuation. "I buy those who can help me, Hazzard."

Mario was on a razor-edged high, one that came from politics and economics, not cocaine. I didn't have time to respond to him because Teddy Ristra came driving up the road from the airstrip in a camouflage painted all-terrain vehicle. I'd expected him to arrive by helicopter, but perhaps he'd decided there should be no official witnesses to this meeting.

Teddy's forest camouflage fatigue uniform, elephant-sized binocular case and pistol belt hung with canteen, snake-bite kit, and a forty-five in a canvas holster, made him look like a white hunter ready for a long safari. He took his time locking the jeep before he strolled over to us. He nodded to Rita and Oso but greeted Mario Darque with an *abrazo*.

"My orders have come through, sir," he said. "I am at your disposal, Señor Darque."

I'd been warned that Darque had influential friends in Mexico City, but I had hoped that Teddy would be an alternate bidder rather than an ally. Now that I saw I couldn't count on him, my strategy was clear.

"Since the formalities are over, I want all of the armament tossed over there, where I have the refreshments laid out. I don't conduct auctions while I worry about guns going off."

For an instant, no one moved. Then Rita unslung her big purse and tossed it over to the pile of insulated picnic bags. Teddy undid his heavy pistol belt to put it down beside Rita's purse. Then he helped himself to a bottle of mineral water and came over to line up beside Darque's other allies.

As I'd expected, Oso regarded me unblinkingly. He wasn't going to make a move of any sort. Since he wore only denim pants and a shirt, and the suitcase at his feet was not a weapon easy to access, I passed him by. Mario prided himself on not needing to carry a weapon, so I'd done what I could to keep things calm.

Mario clearly relished my stage dressing. He kept studying the many heads of Villa. "When Villa hanged men in trees, they were called Villa's Christmas gifts. It is poetic that you have exhibited him this way. Oso! Bring me one to inspect more closely."

Oso really did look like a bear. With stolid obedience, he shambled across the clearing toward the nearest head. I saw now what the dirty gray T-shirt didn't quite obscure—the descending dove tattooed on his chest. Here was the man who, years before, had blinded Valadez.

He deserved something a lot worse than accidental death, so I interrupted. "All the heads sit on top of spring fuses, including the authentic one. If they're moved, they'll explode. You wouldn't want to destroy the thing that brought you here."

Oso glanced back at Mario for instructions. The first

explosion came right on schedule. The head he had been
reaching for vanished in a flash of angry red-orange followed
by a slamming impact that flattened my shirt against my chest
and startled everyone else.

A burnt metallic smell made it momentarily difficult to
breathe. As the echoes diminished, I explained things. "We
have about ten minutes to settle this."

Darque glanced at Teddy and Teddy snapped to attention. "Colonel Teddy Ristra y Villa, Supervisor General of the
Northern Area for *Gobernación* at your service, sir." Then
Teddy turned to me briskly. "Mr. Hazzard, where is the true
head of Pancho Villa?"

"Right now, Colonel, it's a long way off, in a holding
pattern. In seven minutes, a plane will arrive. If I don't give
the correct signal, the pilot will dump Villa's head in the
Pacific. Now. What am I bid?"

Silence greeted me. Overhead, way up, I could see the
Mexican eagle, the *aguila*, soaring in slow circles, looking for
lunch. I let everyone think things over. From here on, the
action would take care of itself.

A second head exploded, tearing a branch off the tree it
sat in. Darque looked thoughtful, Rita stared at me as if, for
the first time, she thought I knew something she didn't.
Teddy popped the cap of the bottle of mineral water. He
exhibited no response to my words or the explosion. Oso
looked at Darque and leered, showing uneven yellow teeth
stuck in his gums like kernels of corn.

When Darque nodded, Oso bent to open the satchel. I
wondered if this was the money bribe, but I was wrong. Still
showing his teeth, Oso extracted a live snake. Then with an
agility amazing in a man so massive, he lunged at me.

The snake *was* scary, a fat, hissing, twisting, many-
buttoned diamondback rattler. The hot sun gleamed on the
dry, iridescent scales. Since Oso hadn't managed to catch it
behind the skull, it coiled around his forearm and struck at
me with the enraged energy of a cracking whip.

Rita's scream set my teeth on edge, but I didn't budge.

"People always overestimate Oso," I said, more to myself
than to Darque. "If he roots through a bag with a rattler in it,
you can bet the snake's fangs are drawn. A screwdriver is
more his style."

I ignored the snake slashing out inches from my arm.

"Kill me and you can grow old here waiting for something that won't happen."

If Darque heard, he didn't listen. His handsome profile was serene. He spat out another one word command. Oso dropped the reptile and reached for his screwdriver.

I thought I was prepared for anything, but as the tool rose in a deadly arc, the memory of Epifanio's ruined eyes chilled me to the core. My body was suddenly drenched with sweat.

Teddy shouted, *"Hola! Guapitta!"*

His right hand held the flare pistol he'd pulled from his binocular case. Teddy had a bead on Oso's middle, but Oso wasn't impressed. He had only one thought now: to answer the insult of being called a little girl. I was forgotten. Oso took the first step toward Teddy. Teddy fired. The rocket drew a straight line to the giant's solar plexus. The magnesium slug pushed him back a step, but Oso kept walking toward Teddy, the screwdriver raised above his head. Then the flare buried in his waist ignited with a muffled *pop!* The big bear looked down at his vast middle with the first grimace of pain that had ever crossed his ugly face.

The sound he made as he tried to pull the burning projectile out of his stomach was terrible. It didn't budge because the flare was burning fiercely. In the sudden blinding fury of light, I could see the skin crisping around the edges of the entry wound. Then phosphorescent smoke spurted from the beak of his tattooed dove. The air stank of phosphorus and frying bacon.

Maddened with pain, Oso stamped his feet, bracing to yank out the inferno burning inside him, whirling in drunken circles. At last he fell to one knee at the edge of the cliff, screaming horribly. Eyelids sewn shut in agony, he lurched to his knees. As he crawled forward, a nightmarish wail came from his mouth. When only his will was left, he struggled upright. The flare was still burning deep inside when he stepped over the edge into the *Barranca de cobre.*

In his fall, he made no sound at all.

Teddy looked at Darque. "If he had killed Mr. Hazzard, it would have been a shame."

The third explosion went off, fragmenting another head. When the echoes stopped, I could hear Darque, his voice quiet, reasonable. "Poor Oso. How will I ever replace him?"

I glanced at my watch. Eleven-thirty. In the distance I heard the drone of the prop plane that had brought me.

"I'm still waiting for bids."

A fourth head shattered, raining bits of skull.

Darque sighed. "I will pay whatever you ask. Give me the head."

That was for effect. I looked at him. Smiling slightly, he raised his bid. "I will give you the killer of Rasmussen."

Fascinated to discover what he thought was important to me, I said nothing.

I was waiting for a better bid when the plane with Chess's logo appeared on its ranging run. I waved as it thundered over. When it returned, the pilot tossed out a bundle with a ribbony drop chute on it. Placed nicely, it came down well back from the precipice, raising a tiny cyclone of dust.

I walked over to it. It was a canvas roll that I unbuckled to reveal a heavily taped Styrofoam package. I took out my penknife and slit the strapping tape. I noticed that none of my audience was interested in coming too close.

When the package was open, I lifted out the head I had used as a model for my Halloween effects. Taped to it was a flat paper pack to which was attached a small black plastic box the size of a deck of playing cards. I arranged everything carefully on the ground and stepped back so everyone could see it.

Darque smiled. "You have given up your only safety."

I smiled too and took a device out of my shirt pocket. "I am very cautious when my personal safety is at stake. This is not a television remote. The head, of course, has a bomb wired to it."

Just then, another head exploded, sending a geyser of dirt and gravel ten feet into the air.

Darque's eyes were on the bundle at my feet. "I'm the only bidder. That package is mine."

"What's your bid?" I asked.

Now Darque was happy. Negotiation was how he assembled his world. "I don't think you care for uniforms, but how about being the civilian Chief of Security for the new nation of *Nueva España*?"

Teddy and Rita seemed to have stopped breathing.

I told Darque what he wanted to hear. "I have no

interest in politics, but a new nation will need a chief of
security. I assume we are talking about salary payments to
offshore banks in currency of my designation?"

Darque sighed. At last we were on the right frequency.
"Hazzard, you are a man after my own heart."

"I'd agree with that," I told him with a straight face. "We
have a deal.'" That settled it.

Darque walked over to the picnic hamper and helped
himself to a bottle of water. He stood looking puzzled at the
top. It must have been the first time he'd encountered twist-
off tops. His servants kept him insulated from the world. I
hurried to detach the wires that secured the bomb to the
base of the head and pulled loose the primer. Then I handed
over the head and the package sealed with red notary wafers.

"You might want to have witnesses present when you
open the envelope to read the authenticating documents."

Darque nodded curtly to Teddy. "Signal the helicopter,
Ristra."

Teddy pulled a handy talky unit off his belt. He looked at
me and shrugged.

"We policemen are never paid enough for the risks we
must run, Cheney." Then he recited some numbers and we
all stood around waiting for Darque's helicopter to come back.

When it did, the pilot got out and helped Darque into
the plane with the care usually reserved for royalty. Darque
paused in the doorway.

"I see no reason for either of them to walk away from
here, Colonel Ristra."

When the chopper lifted out of sight, Teddy turned back
to me, his eyes narrowed against the stinging cloud of dust
that hung in the air like a veil. His voice was casual. "Quite
by accident, Mario Darque will be flown over the border to
the Biggs military airbase outside El Paso. There he will be
met by a friend of yours, a Mr. Harrison Washburn. I
presume the packet contains a substance Mr. Washburn can
use to make Mario Darque a dead letter in Pan American
affairs. I should tell you that this turn of events is my own
idea."

Things were working out, but Teddy's stern face signaled
me it was nothing to build my own future on. He went on.
"Cheney, you did not send him off with the real head. You
did not include any authentication in that package. We have

both remarked that Darque's weakness is to let underlings take care of matters best settled by the principals."

Teddy broke open the flare gun to insert another cartridge. "Now it is time for my bid. Your life. In exchange for the true head and the authenticating papers."

Overhead, the *aguila* was circling lower. I decided disbelief was the best ploy. "Teddy, you're going to kill me for the PRI?"

He frowned. His finger caressed the trigger of the gun. "Not for the PRI. For myself."

That was when a couple of things I still hadn't worked out finally slammed together.

"You've been manipulating Darque right along. You made him think it was his idea that I would go to Topolobampo looking for Daisy. But Chess had been in touch with you all the time."

Teddy gave me credit and added a fillip. "Chess served me well for many years. As you have."

"Forget it," I said. "You're ready to kill me because I'm one of the few alive who knows Villa wasn't really your father. You're worse than those bastards in the Deathstar who gunned down the Tarahumaras. Go ahead, Teddy. Shoot me, but you're not getting Villa's head. I'm sorry to have known you."

There wasn't anything left to bargain with but his own vision of personal honor.

It didn't work. "Sadly, I must shoot you if you do not give me the true head. As you saw, it is quite a painful way to die."

He cocked the flare gun. This was his final bid. Unlike Darque, he knew what he was doing.

He wore an expression I'd never seen before. "I do not expect you to understand, Cheney, but I have come into my legitimate inheritance from both my fathers. Arthur Chess has made it possible for the Mexican Revolution as symbolized by the Villa head to continue. All the wealth he has assembled is mine for the political purposes we have always shared. It has taken many years for this to come to pass. You have removed Mario Darque. I am trusted by the *Partido*, and now I have the money to pay off the opposition. Villa will live!'"

I hate politicians. They announce your death sentence and expect you to applaud their noble reasons. I'd thought

Teddy was a patriot, but he was only a politician. "Now, *Compañero*," he said, raising the pistol. "The true head of Franciso Villa."

Recollecting that, as Chess had said, things might get beyond my control in Mexico, I pointed out the head at the top of the tallest pine, the one I'd wired to go off last.

"There it is, the piñon over by the insulated bags. You can take it yourself, Teddy. It's not wired."

"And the authenticating documentation?"

Teddy intended to cross the *t*'s and dot the *i*'s before he put my lights out.

I sighed. "Reliant Security's vault in Brownsville."

"Good," Teddy said and made his first and last mistake.

The flare pistol exploded. A whoosh of fire zipped past me, singeing the air, straight down into the empty air between our feet. I dived at Teddy, but he was already flat on his back, his arms thrusting out in agony.

Rita stood over him, holding her big pistol in both hands. She kept it pointed at him till he no longer moved.

This time she had killed him for real. She stood looking down at his body, her shoulders shaking and her face wrenched by sobs.

"CIA?" I asked.

"I told you I resigned," she said flatly. "What matters is that I won't be doing this sort of thing any longer. Jesuita has died and named me as her replacement."

Rita picked up the rocket gun and reloaded it. At this distance, she was too far for me to attack and too close for her to miss.

The muzzle of the flare gun came up. I could see the deadly gray nose of the flare inside the barrel.

She fired.

"You do good work, Cheney," she said. "Tarahumara Shipping will be in touch with you. But I have an urgent appointment elsewhere."

"I liked Teddy," I told her, watching the flare create a circus in the bright air high above us. Why had I thought she was going to shoot me, when she'd just saved me from Teddy? I'll never understand women.

"Teddy was easy to like. He was the first person I had to kill that I cared for. For years he stood against all sorts of corruption, but clever Arturo found his soft spot. Like all of us, Teddy was an idealist."

"Was Teddy your uncle?"

"In a sense." She sought the right words. "He was Jesuita's son, but he didn't follow her."

"Do you? I wouldn't have thought there was a place for a killer in Jesuita's religion."

She smiled wistfully. "Think of me as a shepherd who protected you from the wolves. Would you rather I hadn't?"

I didn't like being compared to a lamb. Now she wore Jesuita's expression. She reached across a thousand miles to pat my cheek. "The places you go and the things you do, you need a bodyguard. Goodbye, Cheney."

That seemed to be the end of that, but I couldn't let her go so easily. "Don't you care about Villa's head?"

"Of course not. I know you, Cheney. You wouldn't turn that kind of totem over to any politician. Also, you'd never trust anything important to a safety deposit box. Governments can always find reasons to rifle them."

I wouldn't believe she was going to fly out of my life. Before I could say I was in the book, the chopper landed and took her away. The noise and dust settled like a prayer. I was alone with Villa's head at last.

Oso's rattler had coiled itself in the shade of the last of the insulated bags. I reached across for a bottle of now warm Carta Blanca and he took a shot at my arm. His jaws closed around my flesh in a gummy kiss, no worse than getting smacked with a ruler by a Sunday school teacher.

I sat in the dust and waited. At exactly noon the last head exploded. I listened to the frail detritus from the head rain down around me. I didn't bother to look. I'd told Teddy the truth when I said it was really Villa's head. My lie had been in saying it wasn't wired.

It had been some time since I'd had a beer and a chance to rest. I spent the afternoon thinking. As the air cooled, the rattler moved over to coil against my side. Companionably, we lay sprawled in the slanting rays of the sun.

He gave a sleepy buzz when I stood up. As I turned away, I heard a commotion behind me. The *aguila* was bearing the rattler away in its talons.

I pondered the symbolism as I watched them go. Some would say Villa was showing his satisfaction with my decision. Even a *retornero* gets tired of being reborn to spend a futile life raising hell to no purpose. This had been quite a merry-go-round.

I had one more beer. Then I walked down to jump-start Teddy's car and begin the long trip out of Mexico.

Nineteen

As always, Olimpia looked freshly picked from a mountain meadow, but this morning the dew was still on her. Ever since I'd returned the week before, she had been in a wonderful mood. I assumed she was in love. I didn't ask. If I heard about how wonderful it was now, I'd be obliged to listen to how awful it was later on.

I poured myself a cup of coffee and looked at my reflection in the chromium decanter. After the way things had worked out in the *Barranca de cobre*, I'd lost all interest in what struck me as minor problems.

I took my cup and stalked into my office to feel irritable. I've spent most of my life falling in or out of love. Right now, I was not in either situation and I intended to stay that way. I decided I meant it, at least until I met another woman who would rearrange my world.

The coffee was excellent, but the business news had an ironic edge. The Stackler Trust had decided to make a major investment in Mexican land futures and were inviting the public to join them. All Chip had wanted was to have a chunk of a playground south of the border. He should have consulted his trustees. If he had, he'd still be alive.

The quarterly report from our accountants was calculated to improve my jaundiced mood. Our franchise had surpassed every activity goal I'd set. Esteban and Olimpia had run the place superbly all the time I'd been gone, and Frank Atwood was working out.

I attacked my accumulated mail, which Olimpia divides

into three stacks. The "A" pile includes stuff that has to be
read and responded to the day of arrival. The "B" pile
consists of routine matters I ought to know about. They don't
necessarily demand action. The "C" pile bears my name but
it's mostly occupant junk I can dump without opening. Any
personal mail gets opened and sorted according to these
rules. I don't have any secrets from Olimpia, but she probably keeps a few from me.

After I'd worked through the "A" stack, I got myself a
second cup of coffee and felt better about tackling the rest of
it. On top of the "B" stack was an envelope postmarked from
Hermosillo, in Sonora. The address made me think briefly
about Rita, but I quit that pretty quick. Our parting had been
just as definitive as the one with Daisy. Inside the envelope
were clippings from the local Mexican paper giving the
biographies of the young people who had won Chess Foundation scholarships.

Umberto had phoned to explain that the board adminis-
tering Chess's estate had decided to sell off most of Chess's
assets in the States in return for hard currency, now that
Teddy was dead. It made sense, but it ended the possibility
of a major assignment of security contracts for Reliant. To
make it up, Umberto had named me a member of the board
of directors for the Chess companies in Mexico doing business with the United States.

I could thank him sincerely. I'd been dreading the
busywork of administration that went with a nationwide
contract—spending most of my time in committee meetings
or on the phone. This way, I'd have access to the business I
was interested in, jobs that generated excitement, not ulcers.

There were other clippings from the El Paso papers.
First was a long article about the death of Mario Darque.
After his helicopter landed by mistake at Biggs Field, he'd
been arrested in a routine Customs search for carrying a
fortune in cocaine. He was given a one-million-dollar bail and
made it immediately. The next day he'd been killed in a
terrible traffic smash on Interstate 10. A gas tanker had
changed lanes abruptly, jackknifed, and caught fire. Darque's
limo had rammed into the flaming wreck at high speed. The
same people who had killed his brother had apparently
decided Mario was no longer useful. Then I remembered
Umberto's stony face.

That seemed to clean my desk of all the vexing problems left from my time in Mexico except for the priest whose Pinto I still felt bad about abandoning with all the gauges redlined. I made a note to buy him a car.

That got me to thinking about the kind of life I'd been leading for the last few weeks. It seemed that more should come of it than my simply being glad it was over.

I buzzed Olimpia. Even over the intercom, she sounded bubbling with good spirits.

"I want you to make a donation to the scholarship fund of Southmost College. Double the usual amount. Anonymous."

I hung up and felt only marginally better. In Mexico, I ran for my life, wore tattered clothes, and ate the bitter food of poverty. Unlike the Mexicans, I could escape all that by coming back to the States. Donating to charities would be one of my priorities from now on. If Chess could do it, so could I.

That left the last item in the "B" stack—an envelope containing a second envelope, heavy paper, linen finish. I wondered which member of the Valley legal and business community was getting married. Since Olimpia had put it in this pile, she thought I should remember to offer congratulations, but I wasn't expected to send a wedding present.

When I got it open, I read the announcement of the wedding of Daisy Margaret Pruitt and Judson Mills Weatherly, in Houston, Texas, on the fifth of May.

I went through all the insights about the ebb and flow of human relations I'd been receiving from Rita and Jesuita and Señora Vigil.

I studied the announcement a long time.

In the end, it wasn't a choice. My only question was what to send.

ABOUT THE AUTHOR

R. D. BROWN is a college administrator. He spends the academic year in Bellingham, Washington and the remainder in Albuquerque, New Mexico. *Hazzard*, the first Cheney Hazzard mystery, was nominated by the Mystery Writers of America for Best Paperback Original in 1986. He is currently at work on the third of the Hazzard series, *A Foreign Sun*.

THE WORD IS OUT ... BANTAM HAS THE BEST IN BOOKS ON TAPE ENTERTAINMENT

INTERNATIONAL INTRIGUE ...

☐ **THE BOURNE IDENTITY by Robert Ludlum**
45053/$14.95

He is a man with an unknown past and an uncertain future. A man dragged from the sea riddled with bullets, his face altered by plastic surgery—a man bearing the dubious identity of Jason Bourne.

Now the story of Jason Bourne comes to life in this exciting audio adaptation. With a special dramatic reading by Darren McGavin this double cassette abridgement (125 minutes) gives you the unique opportunity to enter the world of the master of modern espionage.

MYSTERY ON THE STREETS ...

☐ **SUSPECTS by William Caunitz**
45066/$14.95

Searingly authentic, William J. Caunitz's SUSPECTS takes you inside the world of cops. With a special dramatic reading by Edward Asner this double cassette abridgement combines non-stop excitement and gritty realism in a compelling police thriller that will keep you rivetted until the stunning and unexpected end. (120 minutes)

MURDER IN THE OLD WEST ...

☐ **SHOWDOWN TRAIL by Louis L'Amour**
45083/$14.95

Louis L'Amour introduces his fans to one of his favorites—and lesser known—characters from his vintage "magazine novels." Now the story of Rock Bannon comes to life again in this exciting audio program. With a special dramatic reading by Richard Crenna this double cassette adaptation brings you L'Amour at his story-telling best—in three full hours of authentic frontier adventure! (180 minutes)

Look for them at your bookstore or use the coupon below:

Now, the complete stories and novels about the master of detectives, Sherlock Holmes, by Sir Arthur Conan Doyle are available in paperback for the first time:

SHERLOCK HOLMES:
The Complete Novels and Stories
Volumes I & II
from Bantam Classics